The perfect wedding can be murder...

PRAISE FOR KATE WHITE'S BAILEY WEGGINS NOVELS

'TIL DEATH DO US PART

"White's slick tale is as fun as nabbing a couture gown at a sample sale."
—*Entertainment Weekly*

"Ever-present suspense, amid the drama of Bailey's life, creates a fascinating plot...a captivating white-knuckled ride...Four stars."
—*Romantic Times Bookclub Magazine*

"A lot of fun...brisk and breezy, perfect for those who like their mystery spiked with a bit of chick-lit sensibility."
—RomanceReadersConnection.com

"Kate White wows us with this third novel...As always, she hooks us from the first chapter and keeps us guessing up to the very last page."
—BookReporter.com

"Thrilling...Bailey Weggins is great fun to be with."
—BookLoons.com

"Exciting...a great crime thriller."
—Harriet Klausner, TheBestReviews.com

"An entertaining, well-written story...engages the reader from the first sentence."
—ReviewingtheEvidence.com

more...

Also by Kate White

A Body to Die For
If Looks Could Kill
Why Good Girls Don't Get Ahead But Gutsy Girls
Do: 9 Secrets Every Working Woman Must Know

'Til Death Do Us Part

KATE WHITE

WARNER
VISION BOOKS

NEW YORK   BOSTON

Copyright © 2004 by Kate White
Excerpt from *Over Her Dead Body* copyright © 2004 by Kate White
All rights reserved.

Cover design by Diane Luger
Cover photograph by Herman Estevez

Warner Vision is a registered trademark of Warner Books.

Warner Books

Time Warner Book Group
1271 Avenue of the Americas, New York, NY 10020
Visit our Web site at www.twbookmark.com.

Printed in the United States of America

Originally published in hardcover by Warner Books
First Paperback Printing: June 2005
10   9   8   7   6   5   4   3   2   1

To Peg Schmidt, fabulous friend for life

ACKNOWLEDGMENTS

Thank you to those who so generously helped me with my research: Paul Paganelli, M.D., chief of emergency medicine, Milton Hospital, Milton, PA; Barbara A. Butcher, director of investigations for the office of the chief medical examiner, New York City; Matthew J. Friedman, M.D., Ph.D., professor of psychiatry & pharmacology, Dartmouth Medical School; Mindy Hermann, registered dietician; former FBI profiler Candace deLong.

And special thanks to my editor Caryn Karmatz Rudy for her great guidance.

'Til
Death
Do Us
Part

CHAPTER 1

THE FIRST TIME she said her name on the phone that January night, I couldn't place her—though there was something vaguely familiar about the voice. It had a snooty, trust fundy tone, as if she were announcing, "I own a Marc Jacobs bag and you don't."

"Ashley Hanes," she said once more, this time with exaggerated emphasis and irritation, the way American tourists sometimes speak to foreigners who don't understand them. "We met at Peyton Cross's wedding. I was a bridesmaid, remember?"

Ohh, right. We had been introduced late last April in Greenwich, Connecticut, during the infamous Cross-Slavin wedding weekend. Ashley had graduated from the same exclusive private high school as the bride and was now working, if my memory was correct, as an interior decorator in Greenwich—though working was apparently something she chose rather than had to do. An image of her began to loosen from my memory: long, chestnut-colored hair, slim as a French baguette, and haughty as hell, just like the voice. She was the kind of woman who would meet you at a party and look right through you, as if you were a potted palm.

"Oh, right, I'm so sorry," I said. "I'm in a little bit of a fog at the moment. How are you, anyway?"

I was pretty sure what was coming next. Since I'm a contributing writer for *Gloss* magazine, I often get phone calls from people I've met asking for fashion- or publishing-related favors. But I write gritty, true crime and human-interest stories for the magazine, and I'm not connected to the glittery, glossy stuff. My name is Bailey Weggins, by the way, and just for the record, I am categorically unable to help someone become a Ford model, gain admittance to a Chanel sample sale, or publish a confessional article on how a liposuction procedure left ugly scars along her buttocks.

"I need your help," she said.

"Okay," I said. "Though if it's—"

"There's a very serious situation, and I have to talk to you about it."

"Serious" to someone like Ashley could mean her hair stylist was out of town for the week, but the alarm in her voice sounded real enough that I was concerned.

"Is it about Peyton?" I asked. Though I had spoken to Peyton on the phone once last summer, I had not laid eyes on her in nine months—not since she had dazzled a room of five hundred guests in a satin Vera Wang wedding dress with a low-cut, crumb-catcher bodice. From there she had headed off for a cruise of the Greek islands with her new, older husband, David, who'd made a fortune in the world of finance—whatever *that* means.

"No. Well, *indirectly*, yes. Look, it's not something I want to get into on the phone. Can you meet me to talk about this?"

"All right. Tell me when—and where. Are you still living up in Greenwich?"

"Yes, but I'm in New York tonight. At the Four Seasons Hotel. Could you come by here for a drink?"

"Tonight?" I exclaimed. It had started to snow a few hours earlier, and as I glanced across the room toward the terrace of my fourteenth-story apartment, I could see it was coming down harder now—in big, crazy swirls. I live at the very eastern end of Greenwich Village, on the corner of 9th Street and Broadway, and it would be a bitch getting a cab up to 57th Street in this weather—and an even bigger bitch getting one back.

"It's urgent," she said. "When you hear what I have to say, you'll understand why I need to see you immediately."

It didn't seem that I had much choice but to acquiesce. She sounded about as eager to hear me say no as she would be to travel by Greyhound, and besides, if the situation really did involve Peyton Cross, even indirectly, I was curious to know what it was. I explained to Ashley that it might take me forty-five minutes to get there. We agreed that I would ring her on the hotel house phone when I arrived and she'd come down to the bar in the lobby.

I'd been reading a book when she called, dressed in bagged-out sweatpants and drinking a cup of instant hot cocoa in honor of the snowstorm, and now I was going to have to head out into the mess. Several months ago I'd moved into a steady relationship with a guy named Jack Herlihy, but because he taught psychology at Georgetown University in Washington, D.C., we saw each other on weekends. Some nights I'd see a movie or have dinner out with friends, but more weeknights than not, I was holed up in my apartment, either alone or chatting with my seventy-year-old next-door neighbor, Landon. Though I looked forward to my weekends with Jack, the rest of my nights had become about as scintillating as C-SPAN. Landon had told me lately that he was worried that I might start adopting stray cats.

I changed into a pair of tight dark jeans, a black turtleneck sweater, silver hoop earrings (in an attempt to look a little dressier), and my snow boots, which I found after foraging through my closet for five minutes. It was actually the first time this winter that we'd had more than flurries in Manhattan.

I was surprised when I stepped outside to see that about two inches of snow had already stuck to the ground, and you could tell by the swollen look of the sky that more was on the way. I opted for the subway, the number 6 train at Astor Place. It would be faster than hunting for a cab—and it would take me to within a few blocks of the hotel.

As the train hurtled through the tunnel, its floor sopping wet with melted snow, I had time to consider what trouble might be brewing for the captivating Peyton Cross. From all reports, her life couldn't have been going better. In her early thirties like me, she'd recently been dubbed the next Martha Stewart—or "Martha Stewart wannabe"—in the eyes of the people who envied her so much they couldn't stand it. She ran a combination cooking school, successful catering business, and gourmet kitchen and food shop out of an old farmhouse and barn—known as Ivy Hill Farm—on the outskirts of Greenwich. Her first cookbook was due out sometime this year, and she was a frequent guest on the Food Network. The last I'd heard, her new husband was funding the construction of a TV studio on her farm so she could produce her own show.

As they say, I knew her when—she was my roommate freshman year at Brown. She was extremely vivacious, pretty in that kind of scrubbed-face, not overly sophisticated preppy way, and, from what I could tell, afraid of absolutely nothing. Though some guys were totally intimidated by her, more than her share were mesmerized, and she generally had several in a lather at any given time. Her taste ran toward hunky, bad-boy types, the kind of men who often left women emotionally bruised, but for the most part Peyton outsmarted them.

Life as her roommate was entertaining but also exasperating. That's because she could be selfish and rude. She'd ask me to meet her at dinner and then make me wait for an hour in the cafeteria, or she'd borrow my best shirt and then leave it balled up with the dust bunnies under her bed. Over time I figured out how to avoid situations with her that could end in me cursing under my breath. The trick for surviving, I learned, was to keep my expectations low and enjoy the show.

We both got singles sophomore year, and though we were friendly and occasionally grabbed a beer together, we didn't see a huge amount of each other. I bonded with several women who, unlike Peyton, seemed to carry the good-girlfriend gene. After college Peyton and I stayed in touch by e-mail, though infrequently. After gigs as a reporter for the *Albany Times Union* and the Bergen County *Record* I headed for Manhattan, hoping to break into magazines. I called her for some insight. At the time she was working for *Food & Wine*, developing recipes. She promised to introduce me to a few people in the business, and to my surprise she actually came through. She also invited me to Greenwich several times for parties she was throwing as part of her burgeoning catering and event-planning business. That was the thing about Peyton—just when you were ready to strangle her, she could charm the pants off you.

Her wedding had been one of the more lavish I'd ever attended. It was held in a historic house on the outskirts of Greenwich, and Peyton arranged for her own company to do the catering. That was partly because she didn't trust anyone else to do the job with her degree of genius, but also for the PR value for her business. Friends of mine had sworn I'd bag some rich guest that day, but David Slavin was fifteen years older than Peyton, and his business associates and friends were paunchy and pathetically boorish. I'd spent a good chunk of the day flirting with one of the bartenders.

The snow was coming down even harder when I emerged from the underground at 59th and Lexington. I felt relieved when I finally stomped into the marble, two-story-high lobby of the Four Seasons. I rang Ashley's room to tell her I'd arrived and then headed over to the lobby bar, requesting the most private table they could manage. Like the lobby, the entire area—the marble walls, the Roman shades, and the furniture—was done in shimmering beige. A little too mausoleumlike for my taste.

Though I hadn't recalled Ashley's name when she'd first said it on the phone, I had no trouble recognizing her as soon as she strode purposefully in my direction. Several heads turned to watch her. She had a rich girl's air of self-importance and entitlement, the kind that many A-list actresses try for years to acquire but never do.

As she got closer, I realized that the dark plum thing she was wearing was actually a fur coat. Either she was planning on going out afterward or she'd been reluctant to leave it in the room. It was, I suspected, sheared beaver or mink, lush and plush and worth at least twenty thousand dollars. I wondered if her car sported a bumper sticker that read I *DON'T* BRAKE FOR SMALL ANIMALS.

She slid into the chair to my left without bothering with a perfunctory air kiss or even a hello. I guess she figured we'd gotten our pleasantries out of the way on the house phone. She wore her chestnut hair pinned back tonight, accentuating the slenderness of her tanned face. Her cheekbones were so high and sharp, you'd risk a paper cut if you got too close to them.

"Did you order yet?" she asked briskly, shaking off her coat to reveal a sleeveless lavender wool dress and thin buff arms. She glanced at my turtleneck and jeans with a soupçon of disapproval, as if I were wearing one of those plastic lobster bibs that says I'M A PIGGY.

"No, I was waiting for you," I told her.

She jerked her head around toward the center of the room and signaled for the waitress. She appeared on edge, and I assumed it had to do with the news she was about to divulge. There didn't seem to be any reason to spend five minutes on small talk, so as soon as she had ordered a dirty martini and I'd asked for a glass of Cabernet, I jumped in.

"So tell me, what's going on?" I asked.

"When was the last time you spoke to Peyton?"

"It's been a while. Last summer, I guess."

"Do you remember the bridesmaid with the short black hair? Jamie Howe?"

Jamie. She was the bridesmaid I'd spent the most time talking to, mainly because she was also in the magazine business. She'd met Peyton during her tenure at *Food & Wine* and had since become an editor at another food magazine. I hadn't particularly liked her. She was sullen and, I suspected, jealous of Peyton's success. She kept talking about how lucky Peyton was to have David to foot the bill for all of her ventures.

"Sure. She lives here in New York, right?"

"Lived," she said almost defiantly. "She's dead now."

"You're kidding," I exclaimed. The news took me totally by surprise. *"How?"*

"She was electrocuted in her apartment—down on the Lower East Side. It happened in September."

I sat there momentarily speechless while Ashley took a fortifying sip of her martini. As she swallowed, she laid her French-manicured hand flat against the front of her dress, as if it helped the vodka to go down more easily. When she set the glass on the table again, I caught the cloying scent of olives.

"Gosh, I vaguely remember hearing that someone in the business died like that," I said finally. "But I had no idea it was her. What happened, exactly?"

"She was taking a bath and a CD player slipped into the tub," Ashley said.

"That's horrible."

"I know. And hard to believe someone wouldn't know better than to set it so close to the tub."

She had an odd way of punctuating her comments with a sniff. "What do you mean?" I asked. "Are you thinking—"

"Until last week I didn't think much about it at all," she said, suddenly sounding frantic. "I'd never even met Jamie before the wedding. But—you're not going to believe this. Two weeks ago another of the bridesmaids died. My roommate—Robin Lolly."

I let out a gasp so loud that a media mogul type at the next table turned his head in our direction. She was right. I could barely believe what I was hearing.

"How?" I asked.

"She was taking antidepressants, and she had some kind of fatal reaction. It was from mixing them with the wrong kind of food." Her eyes filled with tears as she spoke, but they seemed to come as much from nervous tension as from sadness.

"Robin?" I said. "She's the one who managed the shop at Peyton's farm?"

"Yes, yes," Ashley said impatiently. "She was the pretty one—with the long blond hair. She may have still been using her married name when you met her— Atkins."

"That's terrible," I said. "Were you two very close?"

"We weren't what you'd call best friends," she said, shaking her head quickly, "but we'd known each other since high school. Robin, Peyton, Prudence—she was the maid of honor, remember?—and I all went to Greenwich Academy together. Robin and I started sharing a town house last March. My roommate had moved out, and Robin needed a place to live after her divorce."

"Was she at home when she died?"

"No, she was up in Vermont—all alone—at a ski house her parents left her. She'd driven up on Friday, and the coroner said she must have died shortly after she arrived—though her body wasn't discovered until a cleaning person came in Monday morning." Her voice choked as she spoke the last sentence.

"I'm so sorry," I said. "This must be awful for you—and for Peyton, too."

"Look," she said, suddenly, grasping my arm so hard that it would have taken the Jaws of Life to remove it. "Don't you find it odd that two perfectly healthy young women who were in a wedding together would die within a few months of each other in such bizarre circumstances?"

"Are you saying you think someone *killed* the two of them?" I asked. "Because they were *bridesmaids*?"

"All I know is that something's not right about it—and I'm going out of my mind. Robin and Jamie hadn't even met until the wedding. But they became friends after that. And now suddenly they're both dead—as a result of these strange accidents. I'm terrified something could happen to *me*."

"I know how upsetting this must be, but it really sounds like nothing more than an awful coincidence."

She shook her head agitatedly. "That's what *everyone* says—Peyton and everyone else."

"Well, do you have anything else to go on?" I asked.

"To begin with, I find this whole food-and-drug-mixing thing preposterous. Robin was very clear about the foods she wasn't supposed to eat. She told me what they were so that if I ever cooked for us, I wouldn't include any of them."

It was hard to imagine Ashley doing anything with food other than calling the Zone Gourmet delivery line.

"But sometimes people cheat with food, no matter how religious they say they're going to be about their diets," I told her.

She glanced nervously around the room, as if she were afraid of eavesdroppers, then leaned closer to me.

"No, she knew how dangerous even a tiny slip in her diet could be. I just don't think she would have cheated. And that's not all. After Jamie's death, Robin got really weird. She seemed nervous and tense."

"But that was probably just normal grieving," I suggested.

She let out a ragged sigh. "I can't believe this," she said. "I thought you of all people would take it more seriously. I guess if my life is in danger, I'm going to have to take care of myself."

There was a manic edge to her voice, and the media mogul glanced over again. It probably appeared as if I were trying to talk her down from a coke high.

"Ashley, look, you need to chill on this. Even if the worst happened and someone killed both of them, it may have to do with their being *friends*, not being in the wedding together."

"No, no," she said, shaking her head. "I thought that too for about forty seconds, but then I remembered something. Right after Jamie died, Robin started asking me about the wedding. She wanted to know if anything had seemed strange to me that day."

I felt the hairs on the back of my neck shoot up, as if they'd been lollygagging around, half listening, and now something had finally caught their attention.

"What do you mean, *strange*?" I asked.

"I don't know. Nothing occurred to me when she asked other than the fact that the damn bridesmaid dresses made us look like giant balls of butter—and when I asked her to be more specific, she told me to never mind. At the time I didn't associate her question with Jamie's death, but now I see it has to be connected."

I asked if she'd pointed any of this out to the police, and she said she'd told the officer in charge of the investigation of Robin's death about Jamie, but he had dismissed it. The out-of-state factor had clearly deterred the police from seeing any connection.

"So what exactly is it that you want from me?" I asked finally.

"Come to Greenwich. Just look into this. Isn't that what you *do*?"

A woman like Ashley wouldn't care that it wasn't *really* what I did. Yes, I'd gotten involved in a couple of murder cases, yet basically I'm just a reporter. But trust fund chicks like her were only interested in locating the spot where their needs intersected with what you had to give.

I thought for a moment, sipping my wine. It sounded on the surface as if the situation really *were* nothing more than a dreadful coincidence. But the question Robin had asked about the wedding disturbed me. At the very least I wanted to talk to Peyton. She must be reeling from it all.

I told Ashley okay, that I would visit Greenwich—to talk to Peyton and possibly make some other inquiries. The next day, Wednesday, would actually be the best day for me to make the one-hour drive, because I needed to be at *Gloss* on Thursday afternoon for a meeting with the deputy editor. Ashley seemed instantly relieved. I took down her number and told her that I would be in contact with her tomorrow, after I figured out what time I'd be leaving.

We asked for the check and she paid it, though there was a moment when I thought she was going to ask me to split it. Typical. After walking her to the elevator, I slipped out the rear entrance of the hotel on 58th Street. The snow was still coming down hard and cars crawled along the street, their wheels sometimes spinning and whining. Miraculously, a taxi appeared and no one tried to bulldoze me for it. As I nestled into the warmth of the cab, I realized that a knot had formed in my stomach. The conversation with Ashley had rattled me.

Back in my apartment, I pulled off my coat and boots and, without turning on the lights, flopped down on the couch. I don't exactly live in Hilton-sister style, but for a single girl in Manhattan I've got a pretty nice place—a one-bedroom with a living room big enough for a dining table and a terrace off it. The view is to the west, to nothing in particular, but it's charming. I see dozens of gray- and red- and sand-colored buildings with old shingled water towers scattered over the rooftops.

Lit by the blanket of snow on the terrace, my living room was practically aglow. I sank back into the cushions and tried to conjure up Peyton's wedding day. Much of it was a blur by now, though I could recall the big details.

The ceremony, in a Protestant church in Greenwich, had taken all of fifteen minutes. The reception, on the other hand, had gone on for hours, starting with a cocktail hour that had featured a vodka-and-caviar station among other extravagances. Dinner was five courses long, including a cheese course before dessert.

The phone rang suddenly, startling me. I picked it up from the side table next to the couch. It was Jack, just calling to say good night.

"I tried earlier," he said. "I didn't think you were going out tonight." Not accusatory, just curious. I blurted out the whole story.

"That's definitely weird," he said. "But I wouldn't let it worry you. In all likelihood, it's just a coincidence."

"Doesn't it defy some natural law of probability?" I asked, knowing that because of his training as a shrink, he might be up on such things.

"Not really. It's known as a cluster. It's a set of random events that seem significant because there is more than an average amount of them. But they're just that—random. They really don't mean anything."

He told me again not to be alarmed, and then we moved on to a discussion about the upcoming weekend. It was momentarily distracting, but no sooner was I off the phone than I felt a new wave of disquietude. The two deaths could be random, sure, but then there was that odd question Robin had asked of Ashley: Did anything about the wedding seem strange? I couldn't imagine, though, what occurrence that April day could possibly have led someone to murder two women who had just met.

I finally turned on the lights, and after traipsing down the hall to my tiny office—which had once been a walk-in closet—I rummaged through my desk drawer until I found a photo of the wedding party that Peyton had sent me last summer as a souvenir. There were Peyton and David in the center and, off to David's left, the best man, Trip, one of his business partners, and several older groomsmen I'd barely spoken to that weekend. Off to Peyton's right were the maid of honor and the five bridesmaids. And there I was among them, my short, blondish brown hair shellacked into a Doris Day style and all five feet six inches of me entombed in yards and yards of yellow taffeta.

You see, that's why Ashley's story troubled me so much. I'd been a bridesmaid in Peyton Cross's wedding, too.

CHAPTER 2

I KNOW WHAT you're wondering right now. If Peyton Cross considered me such a good friend that she'd asked me to be part of her bridal party, then why hadn't I seen her since her wedding day?

Well, have you ever heard the term *Bridezilla*? It refers to a bride who acts so monstrously that by the time the wedding is over, everyone who was intimately involved in it feels terrorized and nearly trampled to death. That phrase fit Peyton to a T. As I mentioned, she's always had a flair for self-absorption, but during the weeks before her wedding it became clear to me that she had begun to morph into some kind of maniac, a true überbitch.

It wasn't just that she'd picked out those heinous dresses for her wedding party and insisted that everything else we wore be identical, right down to the Donna Karan nude hose (frankly, I was surprised that she didn't inspect our panties to see if they matched). She also made insane demands about our physical appearance. We were forbidden to tan in the two months before the wedding because she didn't want to appear paler than any of us. And we couldn't highlight our hair without her permission. She was constantly haranguing us via e-mail with new details about the event and our role in it. The night before the wedding, the two carloads of bridesmaids were delayed on our way from the church to the rehearsal dinner because of a traffic accident. We ended up being about twenty-five minutes late. Rather than show any concern about our well-being, Peyton had thrown a shit fit when we appeared. She dressed us down right in front of the guests, claiming we'd disrupted the rhythm of the evening.

I'd actually been surprised that Peyton had even asked me to be in the damn wedding. Or, rather, basically informed me that I would be accepting this honor. Her strategy had been to call me out of the blue the previous autumn and inquire what I was doing the third weekend in April. When I'd answered, "Off the top of my head, nothing," she'd made her request, leaving me without an out. She'd reminded me then that she had promised me back in college that no matter *when* she got married, I'd be in the wedding. I'd clearly been smashed at the time because I had no memory of such a pact.

When the wedding weekend was winding down, the other bridesmaids seemed willing to let bygones be bygones. They blamed Peyton's behavior on a kind of "perfect storm" stress situation: getting married, marrying one of the richest men in town, and catering your own reception. Several of the bridesmaids worked for Peyton, so I guess they had to forgive her or forgo their paychecks. But I had no such conflict, and all the bluepoint oysters, Beluga caviar, and Veuve Clicquot champagne in the world couldn't make up for her bad behavior. So I decided just to avoid Peyton for a while. When she called in August to ask me to a special event at her cooking school, I politely declined. I think she could tell I was ticked— or maybe not. By then I'd become convinced the only mood Peyton Cross had any interest in monitoring was her own.

None of this, however, prevented me from phoning Peyton's home as soon as I fixed myself coffee Wednesday morning. Someone sounding like a housekeeper answered the phone and said Peyton had already left for the farm. The switchboard there put me through to her.

"Oh, Bailey, it's so nice of you to call," she said after I told her that I'd heard about the tragedies. "As you can imagine, it's been perfectly dreadful here."

I told her that I was thinking of driving up to Greenwich around lunchtime and was hoping I could stop by the farm and speak with her. I explained I was concerned about the deaths and would like the chance to talk to her about them. She hesitated for a few seconds, perhaps either caught off guard by my request or not keen on a visit from me—I couldn't tell. But then she announced that by all means I should come.

Next I phoned Ashley, who answered on the first ring. We agreed that I would first stop by the town house that she and Robin had shared, and then we would head over to the farm together. She provided some sketchy directions to her place; people who live in swanky neighborhoods always seem to assume others will know how to get there. So I augmented my scribbles by checking out a couple of Internet map sites.

I ordered my Jeep from the garage for an eleven o'clock departure and then made a few phone calls, hoping to flesh out the little bit of information Ashley had provided about Robin's and Jamie's deaths. My first call was to Paul Petrocelli, an ER doctor I use occasionally as a resource. I'd interviewed him once for a story, and since then he's always been happy to field basic medical questions from me. As luck would have it, he wasn't in the middle of suturing a gash or pumping someone's stomach and said he had time to talk. I asked if he was familiar with any antidepressants that interacted badly with food.

"Must be an MAO inhibitor," he said matter-of-factly.

"Explain, please."

"Monoamine oxidase inhibitors are a type of antidepressant. They're used as a last resort for people who don't respond to the new drugs like Prozac. They were pretty popular at one point, but then it turned out there's a big downside. If you mix them with certain foods, they can spike your blood pressure—in some cases fatally."

"What kinds of food?"

"It's a fairly long list. Any fermented or aged foods. Preserved or smoked meats—you know, salami, sausage, that sort of thing. Soy sauce, caviar, chicken livers, I think. Beer. And cheese. You gotta stay away from the cheese. In fact, the hypertensive crisis that can occur is sometimes called a cheese reaction."

"What happens exactly?"

"Okay, stop me if I get too technical. All the foods I mentioned contain tyramine, a molecule that affects blood pressure. MAO enzymes in your brain get rid of any excess tyramine. But if you're taking an MAO inhibitor, it eases depression but can't stop tyramine from building up. You can end up with a brain hemorrhage.

"So you'd be really stupid to eat any of that stuff intentionally."

"Yeah, but some people can't resist cheating—just like on any diet. They sample a little bit and discover nothing bad happens. That's because foods don't always contain the same amount of tyramine. You may get away with cheating once or twice, but then it's the third or fourth time when you have a reaction."

"How long would it take for the reaction to occur?"

"A few hours, I'd say. It wouldn't be instant."

"One more question: Could you murder someone on a MAO inhibitor by making certain they ate these foods?"

"It's always murder with you, isn't it, Bailey," he said, chuckling. "Well, I suppose you could sneak it into a person's meal somehow. But what happens in most cases when there's a problem is that people just go off their diets. They just give in to the temptation of a nice, runny Brie, and it proves to be a fatal mistake."

I thanked him for the info and signed off. Next I called *Gloss*'s food editor, who I figured might have crossed paths with Jamie and would have heard details about her death. No one picked up in her office. I left a message but knew from past experience calling her for recipes that it might be several days before she checked her voice mail.

When I left my apartment building just after eleven, the streets had been thoroughly plowed, but the city still looked like a wonderland. The snow was the kind that twinkles in the sun, and it was still in pristine condition.

There wasn't enough traffic to have turned the piles of it along the road into giant black cinder blocks.

The first half of the trip to Greenwich was easier than I'd expected. The highways were mostly clear, and traffic was light. But Greenwich itself was another story. Greenwich Avenue, a main street lined with impeccably maintained little shops, was clogged with cars. Obviously people had decided not to let the snow prevent them from shopping for expensive wines and cashmere sweater sets.

My ex-husband had once suggested we look at the suburbs, and I'd nearly had a panic attack at the thought. I'd fallen in love with New York and couldn't imagine leaving. Of course, this was before I'd figured out he had a hopeless gambling addiction. It would soon become apparent we wouldn't be living *anywhere* together for the rest of our lives.

When I finally reached Ashley's town house, not far from the center of Greenwich, she answered the door as quickly as she had the phone. She was dressed in pale peach today and was holding a lit cigarette, one of those superlong ones that made it appear as if she were smoking part of the Alaska pipeline.

"Nice place," I said as I stepped inside. The living room was decorated within an inch of its life in reds and golds, and there seemed to be a monkey theme happening—monkeys dancing on fabric, monkey lamps, a monkey on its back holding up a bowl of potpourri. "Did you do it yourself?"

"*Of course,*" she said in an impressive mix of exasperation and condescension. "I'm a *decorator*. Would you like something to drink?"

"I'd kill for some coffee," I said. She seemed to wince at my poor choice of words.

"I only have those teabaglike things," she informed me. I was desperate enough that I accepted the offer.

She led me back to a small kitchen with a black-and-green granite countertop and shiny new appliances. There wasn't a speck of dirt or grease anywhere, and nothing was out of place. It appeared that the only food that had been consumed there recently might have been a single Carr's Table Water cracker.

Ashley stubbed out her cigarette and filled a teakettle with water. Her movements as she lit the stove were jerky, and she seemed as wired today as she had been last night.

"Ashley, you've got to try to calm down," I said.

"Last night, before I got together with you, I actually thought that if I talked to someone about my fears, they might suddenly seem silly to me. But that didn't happen. I feel even more scared now than I did before."

"But this really could just be a coincidence."

"But what about that question Robin asked me—about whether anything had seemed strange at the wedding?"

"She might not have even been thinking of Jamie's death when she said it. Maybe something else was on her mind. Tell me, how is it that the two of them struck up a friendship?"

"From what she told me, they just started talking," she said. "You know, at the rehearsal dinner or the wedding. Jamie had recently broken up with someone, I guess, and Robin had just split with her husband. Robin indicated that they talked a lot about their situations. I guess you could say they bonded over bad men."

The teakettle whistled shrilly, making Ashley jump. She poured hot water into a bright red mug and then dipped the coffee bag into it several times with a squeamish expression on her face—you would have thought she was dunking a mouse.

"Milk?" she asked.

"Yes, please. Was that why Robin was taking MAO inhibitors? Because of her divorce?"

"Excuse me?"

"MAO inhibitors. They're the type of antidepressant I believe she was taking."

"Robin had a depression problem since high school. She'd tried stuff like Prozac and Paxil, but nothing ever seemed to work for her—there were always these awful side effects. Last summer the doctor put her on this other drug—whatever you called it—and she really started to feel great."

"Was it hard for her to stay on the diet? I did a little research yesterday, and apparently an awful lot of foods are off-limits when you take this type of drug."

"I'm sure it *was* hard. Robin loved food. In fact, Peyton got furious with her because she gained a few pounds before the wedding. But none of that means she cheated. Like I told you yesterday, she was extremely careful about the foods she needed to avoid."

"Do you know who her psychiatrist was?"

"No, but . . ." She strode jerkily across the kitchen and yanked open a drawer. From inside she took a wrinkled yellow Post-it note and handed it to me. The initials *C.B.*

were written on it in pen, along with a phone number with an area code I didn't recognize.

"Robin had this on the refrigerator. When I asked her what it was, she said it was her *lifeline*."

"Is any of her other stuff still here?" I asked, copying down the phone number on a pad in my purse.

"Very little. Her parents are both dead, but she's got a brother in town. A few days after the funeral, he and his wife just dropped by out of the blue and took the clothes and jewelry and any papers that seemed important. They were borderline rude about it—I almost had the feeling they thought I was going to *take* some of her things."

I asked if I could see what was left, and she led me upstairs to the second floor. The bedroom was shockingly bare. Cream-colored walls, simple white Roman shades, and, except for a double bed, dresser, and desk, no furniture or decoration.

"Pretty picked over," I said.

"It didn't look much different when Robin lived here—she never got around to fixing the place up. I think she was taking a while to get used to the fact that she was now single."

"Why'd they split up?"

"Brace is a Wall Street trader and a real maniac about his job. When they were married he was out practically every night with clients, and he was always getting calls from places like Japan in the middle of the night. He never had any time for Robin, and it was making her depression worse. Of course, the minute she splits, he's all sorry and keeps calling, saying he'll be different. She talked to him a few times about getting back together, but eventually she realized he wasn't going to change. He finally got the message and backed off."

I walked over to the small desk and let my eyes roam over the top of it. Nothing seemed significant: empty file folders, envelopes, a stack of catalogs filled with kitchen supplies.

"What did Robin's job with Peyton entail, exactly?"

"She was the manager of the shop and also the buyer. She ordered all the kitchenware and the gourmet food they sell. Peyton had this idea for a line of her own products, and Robin was looking into that, too."

"She and Peyton were pretty close?"

"Relatively so. I mean, they met in *grade* school. But I think their relationship had more to do with how far back they went than any special thing they had in common. The work arrangement served both their purposes. Robin never felt she could handle some big office job, and running the shop was perfect for her. And Peyton has always preferred to be surrounded by a posse of people she knows. To be honest, I'd been encouraging Robin to start thinking about moving on—especially since she was feeling so much better. Peyton—well, you've seen her in action. She's gotten very demanding in the last year, and working for her is no picnic."

"What about you? You work for her, don't you?"

"Yes," she said, followed by a sniff. "But only sporadically. Peyton developed a taste for decorating when she did her house, and she likes supervising most of the big projects herself now. If something small or unappealing comes up, she'll include me. In fact, I'm involved in a project there now—turning the silo into a gallery. Peyton couldn't be bothered with it."

"Was it a problem for you—when Peyton started using you less?"

"No. My business has really taken off—in part because of the work I did initially for Peyton." It was said without gratitude but also unbegrudgingly, as if she had come to accept the fact that Peyton giveth and Peyton taketh away.

I turned back to the desk and pulled open the single drawer. Inside were some art postcards, a bunch of pens in a rubber band, an emery board, and sheets of stationery. I lifted the paper to see what was underneath. There was an envelope from a photo development lab. I flicked the flap up with my thumb and slid out the stack of photos. There were about two dozen shots from Peyton's wedding. I started to glance at them, one by one.

"I gave a box of Robin's photographs to her brother, but I didn't notice these," Ashley said. "Maybe she took them with one of those disposable cameras they had on the tables that night. You were supposed to turn those in at the end of the reception, but I guess Robin decided she wanted the pictures for herself."

"Yeah, except . . ."

"Except *what*?" she asked anxiously. She sounded ready to freak at the slightest provocation.

"I don't think Robin took these pictures," I said. "See, she's *in* so many of them. And they're not posed pictures, so it doesn't appear as if she asked someone to take some shots of her."

I thumbed through the stack again. There were two photos of Peyton alone, looking spectacular in her gown, and one of David and Peyton outside, kissing passionately under a trellis. There were also quite a few shots of guests mingling and talking and dancing and a few more of all the bridesmaids. All the bridesmaids, that is, except for one.

"I think *Jamie* took these photos, not Robin," I said. "She's the only bridesmaid not in any of the shots. And I remember she had her own camera that day. It was one of those baby Nikons—I asked to take a look at it."

"But what—? Omigod, Jamie asked Robin to keep these pictures for her, didn't she. You see, there *was* something strange about the wedding. Maybe Jamie discovered it and told Robin."

She went all nervous Nellie on me, whipping her head from side to side like a dog with a shoe in its mouth. But I had to admit there was something weird about the fact that Jamie's photos were tucked away in Robin's drawer.

I turned over the envelope and saw by the name and address stamped on the back that the photo shop was in lower Manhattan—where Jamie had lived. That meant Jamie probably had the photos developed, then brought them out to Greenwich for some reason.

"Maybe Jamie didn't want the pictures in the end and passed them along to Robin," I volunteered.

Ashley shook her head again, as if my words had done nothing to mollify her. "No, there's definitely more to it than that. Jamie saw something that day, and she gave Robin these pictures for safekeeping."

"Please try to stay calm, Ashley," I said, slipping the photos into my purse. "I'm going to look into this, okay? Now tell me. Do you know how to get in touch with Peyton's other two attendants?"

"Prudence is living in London—her husband took a job there. Of course, she was the maid of honor, and I have no idea whether that *excludes* her from all of this. And Maverick's in New York. She's the one who handles Peyton's PR. I have no clue where she lives, but we could get her number from Peyton—or it would be in the book under Maverick PR."

I suggested we go back downstairs and then head over to Ivy Hill Farm. Though I'd tried to reassure Ashley, finding the photos disturbed me. Maybe Jamie *had* seen something odd at the wedding, something she'd captured in one of the pictures. Then she'd hinted at it to Robin. But I still had a hard time imagining someone killing her—and later Robin. The question I kept coming back to was *why*? Plus, there was apparently absolutely no evidence of foul play.

We agreed that I would follow Ashley in her car, which was parked not far from mine behind the town house. I slipped into my Jeep and waited as she set several shopping bags of fabric samples into the backseat of her red Mercedes coupé. Seemingly out of nowhere, a tall blond guy in his early to mid-thirties strode over to her car and spoke to her. In his navy blue wool coat and plaid scarf, he was clearly some sort of business type. Ashley listened to him with a haughty gaze and then shook her head vehemently. Maybe it was a neighbor, claiming she'd hijacked his parking spot. She brushed past him to get into the front seat of her car. He turned, trudged across the parking lot, his feet clad in a pair of those floppy black totable snow boots, and climbed into a car of his own.

The farm was north, in an area known as the "backcountry"—where there were numerous multimillion-dollar estates and horse farms. Owing to a combination of poor road conditions and heavy suburban traffic, the trip took longer than it should have—about twenty minutes. I'd been to the farm before, but I'd forgotten how truly lovely it was. Covered in snow, it looked like a Christmas card. Though the original farm had been huge, most of the land had been sold off years ago and was now spotted with mammoth houses. Peyton's property amounted to about five acres. The main buildings were an old white clapboard farmhouse, used for offices, a big red barn where the catering was done and the cooking classes were taught, a smaller gray barn that housed the gourmet shop, and a wooden-shingled silo. Past the farmhouse I saw a new building under construction—the TV studio perhaps.

The parking lot was only a quarter full, and I ended up pulling into a spot right alongside Ashley's. After she'd extracted her shopping bags from the back of her Mercedes, she pointed in the direction of the silo.

"I'm going over there," she said, her face still furrowed with stress. "It doesn't call for much decorating, but I want the walls to look nice—plus I've pulled some great fabrics for the bench cushions."

"Would you like me to meet you over there when I'm finished?"

"No," she said, "it's really messy. The workers are almost done but there's junk all over. I'm just going to double-check some fabrics against the wall colors and then I'll come to the kitchen. Being in the silo alone gives me the creeps."

As she turned to go, I asked who the guy was who had stopped her by the car.

"That was Robin's ex, Brace Atkins," she said. "He

had the nerve to ask me where her things were. He was irritated when I told him that her brother had taken them."

She hurried down the path, not seeming to care that her thousand-dollar brown leather boots were plunging into the snow. I headed up the shorter path to the barns. I felt something wet touch my nose and realized that snow had started falling lightly.

The smaller of the two barns, the gray one, was the shop, and through the window I could see a young female salesclerk ringing up a customer. Just beyond was the large barn, freshly painted red, and inside I found half a dozen people bustling around. It was a big, gorgeous space with pine cupboards, a brick fireplace, massive stainless-steel stoves, and several huge stainless-steel refrigerators—kind of Colonial Williamsburg meets *The Jetsons*. Peyton was working at a large butcher block island with several women, but she raised her hand in greeting as soon as she saw me. I crossed the room toward her.

"Hi there," she said, putting down a utensil I didn't recognize and giving me a hug. Her long, lank, strawberry-blond hair was pinned up in a French twist, a signature look she'd adopted in the past few years on her way to being a media star. She was wearing a green Diane von Furstenberg–style wrap dress—not exactly cutting-edge, but fashion had been one of the few things Peyton had never quite mastered. To my surprise, she looked as if she had gained about ten to fifteen pounds since the wedding. I wondered suddenly if she might be pregnant.

"Do you remember Bailey Weggins?" she asked the two women closest to her. "This is my cousin Phillipa—

you probably met at the wedding. And Mary, my executive director. We've got a party tomorrow night, and we're doing the prep work."

I shook hands with both women. Mary was probably around forty, one of those preppy types you see around Greenwich who seem vaguely asexual—blondish brown hair cut in a bob, no makeup, skin lined from the sun. I *did* remember Peyton's cousin from the wedding, in large part because she had seemed so self-conscious and sour that day. She was green-eyed like Peyton and had blond hair, too, but hers was almost platinum and very shiny. She was no more than five feet four, and my guess was that she weighed close to two hundred pounds.

"I talked to Ashley this morning and she said she was coming with you," Peyton said, looking around.

"She went over to the silo with some fabric swatches," I explained. "She's going to meet me here later."

"It's going to be fabulous over there when we finish. How about a piece of lemon tart?" she asked.

"Sounds good. I'm famished."

As Mary and Phillipa returned to their work, Peyton turned and swung open the door of one of the Sub-Zeros. It looked morgue sized, big enough to hold four or five cadavers. She emerged, instead, with a tart covered with plastic wrap, and she cut a wedge for each of us. Then she led me to a wooden farm table at the far side of the room, away from the kitchen staff and near the fireplace, where a stack of logs burned and crackled. There was a coffeepot already on the table, and after we sat down, she poured us both a mugful, adding a smidgen of milk to mine. That was Peyton. As self-absorbed as she seemed, she always remembered little details about you, like how you took your coffee and the nicknames of your siblings.

"So how are you doing?" I asked once I'd slipped off my coat and taken a sip of coffee. Despite the extra pounds she was as pretty as ever—the pale, flawless skin lightly dusted with freckles, the pink cheeks, the perfect small nose.

"Like I said on the phone, it's been a big mess," she said, digging into her tart. "I threw my back out, which always happens when I'm stressed. We thought about closing the shop for a few days, but that seemed fairly pointless."

"Ashley thinks the two deaths could be connected somehow. What do *you* think?"

"Not simply connected. She thinks someone *killed* Robin and Jamie. That's why you're here, isn't it? She wanted you to investigate things."

"She's pretty upset, so I said I would make a few inquiries."

"Well, I know Jamie and Robin had become friends, but it all seems like an awful coincidence to me. Robin apparently ate food she wasn't supposed to. She was on some kind of medication that required a restricted diet, and she ignored the rules. Jamie had some senseless accident. I don't know as much about her situation, though—we'd had a bit of a falling-out in the summer. I hadn't spoken to her for weeks before she died."

Had Jamie reached her limit with Peyton, just as I had? I also wondered if a falling-out might explain why Jamie had decided to give the wedding photos to Robin.

"Why?" I asked.

"She was hoping to open her own gourmet food store

in New York—in the East Village. She was having trouble finding investors and getting things off the ground, so I offered her some advice. And she acted indignant, as if I were totally out of line. To be perfectly honest, I think she was jealous of me. I hate to say it, but that's becoming a bigger and bigger problem for me these days."

She glanced toward the kitchen work area.

"Could you excuse me for a couple of minutes, Bailey? I need to make sure they're not destroying anything over there."

After she walked away, I took a black-and-white composition notebook out of my tote bag and opened it. Whenever I write an article, I make notes in a composition book—tidbits of information, observations and impressions, questions to myself. I do the actual writing on my computer, of course, but I find that jotting down notes with a number 2 pencil gets my brain working in a new way, helps me see the facts from a different angle. And sometimes when I'm rereading my notes I'll see a connection or something significant that wasn't apparent when I first put pencil to paper. I'd used this tactic with the murder investigations I'd been involved in, and I was going to do the same thing with my research now. It all might amount to nothing, but I liked the ritual of tracking my findings and impressions in a clean, no-frills notebook, and I harbored the vague hope that it would impose clarity and order on a puzzling situation. As I worked, I kept one ear partially cocked toward the kitchen. Watching Peyton's staff interact with her—asking questions about ingredients and cooking times and garnishes—I realized that they moved around her as if they were walking on eggshells.

Suddenly I heard Peyton's voice rise in anger. "You never use *aged* goat cheese with this, you idiot," she shouted, at the same decibel level someone might utilize to announce that the barn was in flames. "It crumbles too much."

I glanced over to see Phillipa storm off through the swinging door at the end of the room, followed a moment later by Mary. The others, who had frozen in position momentarily, resumed their work with lowered heads, somber as restroom attendants.

I returned to my lemon tart and my notebook, jotting down what I'd learned earlier from Ashley as well as from my brief conversation with Peyton. The more I thought about Ashley's theory, the more preposterous it seemed. As I worked I glanced up every once in a while, observing the action in the kitchen. It seemed that one minute Peyton would play helpful instructor and the next she'd turn into a shrew. After about twenty minutes I caught her eye as she was whipping something with a giant whisk, and when she spotted me, she gave me the five-minute sign. Ten minutes later, she finally strolled over, wiping her hands on an apron.

"Sorry," she said, "but it couldn't be helped. Listen, why don't you come by the house for dinner tonight? I'd love for you to see my place."

"I've got a meeting at *Gloss* tomorrow, but I'll take a rain check," I said. "Just a couple more questions if you don't mind. Did Robin eat lunch here every day?"

"Yes. The employees generally help themselves to food left over from parties."

"Well, did you ever see her eat foods she wasn't supposed?"

"I have *enough* to keep track of without checking up on someone's diet. But I know that she was *always* grazing. And she had terrible willpower, especially when she was in one of her slumps—I'm sure Ashley could tell you about that."

I wondered suddenly what was keeping Ashley. I glanced out the window, and to my surprise I saw that it was snowing hard. I cursed myself for not having checked the weather report before I left New York. I told Peyton that I probably should get going and asked if it was possible to phone the silo.

"No, the phone lines haven't been put in," she said. "I'd be glad to walk you over, though."

After we'd both buttoned up our coats, we headed outside. It was a different kind of storm from yesterday's—the snow wasn't nearly as dense, but it was gusting hard and the flakes felt like pinpricks as they made contact with my face. There were only a few cars in the parking lot and not a soul in sight. High in the trees the wind made a sound like pounding surf.

As we approached the silo, I realized that the windows cut out of the sides were all dark. If Ashley was still working inside, a light should be visible. My heart began to beat harder.

"Could she have gone to a different building?" I shouted over the wind. "I don't see any lights on."

"I know—that's odd," Peyton shouted back, a look of concern forming on her face.

She reached the door first, a wooden door without windows, and turned the handle. The door seemed to stick, and she leaned her body against it, giving it a big shove. With a groan, it finally opened. With the little bit of daylight that flooded inside, I could make out an open space with a circular staircase.

"Ashley," Peyton called, reaching for a light switch. "Are you here?"

It took Peyton a few seconds to find the switch, and as her hand fumbled along the wall just inside the door, I could hear my heart pounding in my ears. Suddenly light filled the space—and Peyton screamed.

Ashley was lying face-up at the base of the circular staircase. Her eyes were totally vacant and her mouth was twisted, caught forever in some state between surprise and terror. She still had her coat on, but she'd unbuttoned it and each side had flapped open, revealing her pretty peach pantsuit. Her right leg was tucked at an unnatural angle behind her, like a branch partially snapped on a tree. And beneath her, on the pale stone floor, was a pool of blood, forming a bright red halo around her head.

CHAPTER 3

I STARED AT Ashley's body in horror and then slowly trained my eyes upward. From what I could see, the staircase rose the entire height of the silo, past several landings where I assumed art was going to be displayed. Because of Ashley's position and her oddly angled leg, it seemed likely that she had tumbled down the stairs—or over the railing of one of the landings.

"Is she dead?" Peyton wailed beside me. Her voice echoed upward through the silo.

"Yes," I said softly.

But I wanted to be absolutely sure, so I knelt by the body, picked up Ashley's right hand, and pressed down my fingers in search of a pulse. Nothing.

I stood up and glanced around the space. There were some boxes and paint cans by the wall and two gallery-style benches, one with a swatch of fabric draped over it. The bags Ashley had carried into the silo with her were nowhere in sight, and I guessed that she had taken them to one of the higher levels—from where she'd fallen. Or been *pushed*. Had someone done this to her? I wondered, my legs feeling limp with fear.

Once more I looked upward, this time listening for any sign of movement. It was totally silent on the floors above.

Behind me, though, I suddenly heard a gagging sound. I spun around to see Peyton hurl the lemon tart she'd eaten earlier against the cream-colored wall of the silo.

"Don't look anymore," I said, trying to steady her. "We need to go—and call for help."

She moaned and grabbed her mouth with her right hand. I led her toward the door, and as Peyton reached for the handle, I turned and looked at the room and the body once more, capturing it in my mind.

No sooner had we stepped outside than Peyton launched the rest of her lemon tart into a snowbank. While she wiped ineffectively at a ribbon of vomit on her mouth, I found a napkin in my coat pocket. I thrust it into her hand, where it flapped in the wind.

Taking Peyton's arm, I guided her along the path. Through gusts of snow I searched the property with my eyes, but the only sign of life was the smoke curling from the chimney on top of the larger of the two barns. If someone *had* pushed Ashley, he or she either worked at the farm or had followed Ashley here earlier. But it all seemed so improbable. Why would someone want to pick off a bunch of bridesmaids? And even if someone *had* murdered Jamie and Robin because of a secret they shared about the wedding, why kill Ashley? She didn't know anything. Yet I couldn't get past the fact that one day after she came to me, fearing for her life, she was dead—from the same sort of freak accident that claimed the lives of Robin and Jamie.

There were four girls in the kitchen when we stepped inside, including Phillipa, who had obviously licked her wounds and returned. Peyton yelled for one of them to bring her a phone. A girl with a tartan skirt beneath her apron rushed over with a cordless phone. Peyton glanced at me momentarily, her eyes asking for clear directions.

"Call 911," I told her.

The four workers all froze in their places, their kitchen utensils poised, like orchestra members waiting for their cue. When they heard Peyton say that a woman was lying dead in the silo, they all gasped in shock and then let go with a torrent of questions. Half listening to Peyton's discussion with the operator, I hurried over to the group, urging them to be quiet for now. I told them all I knew: that Ashley was dead.

"Do you know where Mary is?" I asked urgently. Since she was the executive director, Peyton was going to have to rely on her for help today.

"I'm right here," she said, suddenly appearing in a doorway on the far side of the room. "What's going on?"

I met her halfway across the room and quickly explained that we had found Ashley's body on the floor of the silo.

"And she's *dead*?" she asked.

"Yes," I said, though I had just told her that.

"Ginger, come here," Peyton yelled to the girl in the tartan skirt. "They want someone to stay on the line until the police get here." She thrust the phone at Ginger and then joined Mary and me.

"Is there anyone else on the property?" I asked the two of them.

"Peyton's assistant is over in the office—in the farmhouse—along with a few administrative workers," Mary said. "And we have a clerk in the shop."

I suggested that she call the entire staff and have them come over right away; it would be smart to have all staff immediately accounted for. Within a few minutes they all had arrived, their coats thrown hastily over their shoulders. While Mary, Peyton, and Peyton's assistant, a small, dark-haired girl, conferred in a corner and the rest of the staff put food away, I sat alone at the table, a hard knot forming in my stomach. I hadn't particularly liked Ashley, but I'd felt a bond of some kind with her, and it was horrible to think of her lying dead on the floor of the silo. As I looked around the room at the group of WASPy young women, all employees of the burgeoning Peyton Cross empire, I wondered if one of them could possibly be a murderer. I also wondered if I should have done something to secure the silo. But I figured that the police might be annoyed by any attempt at interference, so it was probably best I hadn't.

It was a good fifteen minutes more before help arrived—an ambulance, quickly followed by a black-and-white police car with a red stripe from the town of Greenwich. Peyton and Mary rushed outside and spoke animatedly to the two patrol cops. In unison they all turned toward the silo. After a minute more of dialogue, the two women scurried back in from the cold. "Detectives are already on the way," Peyton proclaimed.

We all stood bunched together by the door, waiting for things to unfold. About two minutes later an unmarked car pulled up. Two regularly dressed men, obviously the detectives, jumped out into the swirling snow and were greeted by one of the uniformed cops, who had emerged from the silo. He pointed in that direction and then back to the barn. The detectives nodded and then strode toward the silo, while the uniformed cop headed in our direction. He rapped once on the door and entered without waiting for us to answer.

"Is everyone who works here accounted for?" he asked Peyton. He was short and baby-faced, like a little kid playing a cop in a school play.

"Yes, yes," she said impatiently.

"And what about customers? Was there—"

"There's been no one here for an hour at least," she said. "Because of the snow."

"Why doesn't everyone have a seat for now," he announced, turning his attention to the rest of us. "There are two detectives here already and they'll be over after they've taken a look at the situation. I'd appreciate it if you didn't speak among yourselves."

Most of the women withdrew reluctantly from the knot by the door and perched on the edges of chairs and stools around the room. For the next fifteen minutes— which seemed like an eternity—we waited. Peyton paced, stretching her neck as if she couldn't bear having her head attached to her body. One worker sniffled from time to time, clearly distressed, and the others just sat there looking stunned. Finally the detectives arrived, their hair and shoulders dusted with snow.

Because it was Greenwich and not any old town in Connecticut, I figured the detectives might be fairly spiffy, and it turned out they were. The older of the two, a burly guy with an affable face and a brown mustache streaked with gray, walked directly to Peyton, clearly recognizing her, and introduced himself as Detective Pichowski. The younger, Detective Michaels, was about thirty, a collegiate-looking guy with a corduroy sports jacket peeking out from under his long winter coat, as if he were headed to someone's house for brunch and Bloodys.

"What happened to her—do you know?" Peyton asked almost desperately.

"That really can't be determined until our people have studied the scene and an autopsy has been performed," said Pichowski in the kind of gravelly voice that made you want him to clear his throat.

"Who was it that discovered the body?" he asked.

"We did," Peyton said, gesturing toward me. "She'd been gone too long and we went to check on her."

"And you are . . . ?" he asked, turning to me.

"Bailey Weggins. I drove over to the farm with Ashley today."

He shut down any more talk about Ashley right then and asked Peyton about the layout of the barn. When he learned there were rooms in the back, he asked the officer to accompany everyone back there—except me. He told Peyton he would speak to her next and asked that she provide a phone number for Ashley's next of kin to the officer.

As soon as the three of us sat down at the wooden table, I felt my stomach start to churn. I'd become infatuated with the last cop who had questioned me at a murder scene, and now I was experiencing a discomforting flashback. I told myself to stay calm and focus on sharing every single detail I could recall.

After asking for the spelling of my name and my address, they got right to the point. What could I tell them about what happened today? I started instead with yesterday, with Ashley's call to me, her concerns about the two dead bridesmaids, my decision to come to Greenwich, and how I'd waited for Ashley in the kitchen. Their eyes seemed to widen as I unfurled the whole story, though I couldn't tell if it was from concerned interest or skepticism.

"What was Miss Hanes hoping *you* could do?" Pichowski asked when I finished.

"I'm a reporter," I revealed. "I write true crime articles, and I think Ashley thought I might be able to offer some insight. She told me she'd shared her fears with the police here, but they hadn't seen any evidence of foul play."

I saw Michaels shoot a glance at Pichowski. I figured they had to be familiar with Robin's death, but they didn't give any verbal confirmation of that. They asked me then for anything I knew about Jamie's situation, which of course wasn't much.

"Let's get back to today," Pichowski said. "Did you see anybody around when Miss Hanes headed over to the silo—or when you went back there looking for her?"

"No, it looked deserted over there. But I find it hard to believe that this could be a *third* fatal accident. Don't you?"

"What about the people who work here?" he asked, ignoring my question. "Did you see anybody leave the kitchen when you were sitting here waiting?"

I thought carefully about how to answer because I didn't want to get anyone in trouble needlessly. I stated that Phillipa and Mary had gone off at some point but I wasn't sure if they'd left the building entirely.

Suddenly I remembered the incident with Robin's ex-husband, and I told the detectives about that as well. Michaels stopped his note taking to shoot Pichowski another fast look.

Pichowski went through a few more basic questions—had Ms. Cross and I touched anything, had the lights been on, had we noticed anything odd or heard any sounds? As he was finishing up, he took his wallet from his jacket pocket and, with a hand the size of a bear paw, withdrew one of his business cards.

"If you think of anything else over the next few days, I want you to call me. I'd also appreciate it if you hung around for just a bit today. Once I hear what the others have to say, I might want to ask you another question or two."

By all appearances he was a decent guy, a straight shooter, yet I couldn't tell how he was viewing the situation.

"Doesn't it all seem odd to you?" I asked, trying to feel him out again. "I mean, the first two deaths could be considered a horrible coincidence, but three—that seems to defy the laws of probability."

"Well, we're certainly going to look into it, Miss Weggins," he said pleasantly but the tiniest bit patronizingly. "Until we know more, I'd ask you to please be careful."

Oh sure, I thought. Let me just give Britney Spears a call and see if she'd loan me one of those four-hundred-pound bodyguards I'd seen in paparazzi shots of her.

Michaels rose from the table and directed me out of the main kitchen along a narrow corridor to a small room in the back. Mary and the rest of the staff were sitting around a table, with a uniformed cop holding up the far wall. Peyton was nowhere in sight.

"Where's Ms. Cross?" Michaels asked after a quick glance around the room.

"I think she went to the ladies' room," Phillipa said sullenly. "It's down the hall."

Michaels strode off, looking slightly annoyed.

For the next hour I waited in that small room, ready to jump out of my skin. I felt a strong urge to be on the move and find things out, but I didn't know *what*. Every ten minutes or so Michaels would pop in and collect someone for her interview with the police, while the others waited behind silently. All the women seemed stunned. The one who had sniffled earlier continued to do so off and on, and periodically several others followed suit. I wasn't sure whether it was because they were close to Ashley or were just completely distressed by their proximity to her death. Mary, her expression impenetrable, turned her attention to a pile of paperwork she'd brought in with her. With her reading glasses perched on the end of her nose, she went through the stack methodically, sometimes scribbling notes in the margin. And Phillipa chose the most interesting pastime of all: She gave herself a mani. Filling the air with the overpowering scent of nail polish remover, she stripped off her color with cotton balls and painted the nails on her surprisingly slim hands with three coats of dark pink polish. Though she was careful with each stroke, there was a manic quality to her work, as if she had chosen to concentrate intensely on this one task so she wouldn't have to focus on the tragedy at the farm.

As for me, I sat there sullenly, sickened by the thought of Ashley's death and also feeling guilty as hell. Just three hours earlier I had stood in Ashley's kitchen and advised her not to worry. Now she was dead. I was desperate to know what had actually happened to her. I was also nervous about my own safety. Three of Peyton's bridesmaids were dead, which left me, Maverick, and the maid of honor, Prudence.

Periodically I glanced out the window. From this end of the barn I couldn't see any of the police activity, but I could watch the storm. It had turned into a real nightmare, and driving back to the city would be hairy. I decided that the smartest thing would be to ask Peyton if I could spend the night at her place. That would also give me a chance to talk to her and discuss everything that had transpired.

Gradually the space emptied. Since no one came back into the room after being summoned, I assumed the cops let them go home before the storm worsened. Peyton never returned to the sitting area, either, but at one point I spotted her in a small kitchen across the hall, about a quarter the size of the main one. A couple of minutes after the last employee had been summoned, the uniformed cop left, too.

"Am I allowed to leave now?" I called out to him as he headed down the corridor.

"You need to check with Detective Pichowski."

I stuffed my belongings into my bags and hurried down the corridor to the big kitchen. The two detectives, both of them now bundled up in their coats, were standing by the door, talking to Peyton. She looked weary and frazzled. Strands of strawberry blond hair had come loose from her updo, as if she'd just played several rounds of Twister.

"I have a reputation to protect," she nearly shrieked as I strode across the room. "You have to figure out what happened."

"I understand," Pichowski said. "We have our best people on it."

The two detectives said good-bye to Peyton and nodded in my direction. Obviously they didn't have any additional questions for me.

"Have you found anything out?" I asked before they could leave.

"We aren't at liberty to say right now. As I said to you before, please be careful until we know further."

"Did they tell you *anything*?" I asked Peyton after the two detectives had stepped out into the storm.

"All I know is that they're going to be over at the silo for the rest of the afternoon and maybe tomorrow. I tried to explain to them that this could be very damaging for business, but they don't seem to care."

"How much later are you planning on staying?"

"I'm getting out of here *now*. Mary's staying on in the office, and she's going to make sure things get locked up after the police leave. They asked that we not open up until tomorrow afternoon. I can't imagine how we're going to pull off the party."

I hit her with my request to spend the night at her place.

"Of course," she said. "I'm sorry you even had to

ask—but you were so adamant earlier about getting back."

"What about David? Have you called him?"

"I've left a million messages for him, but he's apparently en route from New Haven and his cell phone isn't picking up. I tried his partner, Trip, too, but he's gone off somewhere and no one knows where he is."

I stepped closer and touched her shoulder. "And what about *you*? How are you doing, anyway?"

"Not good. Look, we had better get out of here."

A few minutes later I was in my Jeep, headed past several police vehicles in the parking lot. My windshield wipers groaned as they worked, shoving more than an inch of snow to each side. I glanced at the silo one last time. It turned my stomach to imagine Ashley's body inside, being photographed and pored over by crime scene experts.

I'd never been to Peyton's house before—it had been under renovation at the time of the wedding—but I knew it was just a few miles from the farm. I followed carefully behind her green Range Rover, fearful that even with my four-wheel drive on, I'd end up skidding or getting stuck in a snowdrift.

My jaw dropped when we finally pulled through the stone-and-wrought-iron gate and I caught a glimpse of the house through the snow. It was colossal, a mansion, really—white-painted brick, black shutters, and endless rows of shining windows. I knew David was loaded, so I should have realized Peyton was living like a princess. But I was still stuck in the single-girl, one-bedroom-apartment mind-set, and my brain hadn't stretched far enough to imagine this for her.

She pulled up directly in front of the house, and I jumped out of my car right behind her. "Just leave your car here," she yelled as she unlocked the door. "Someone will get it later."

Inside, the house looked like an English manor, the kind I'd seen while writing a travel article about the English Cotswolds. There was an enormous hall with a six-foot-high fireplace hosting the proverbial roaring fire. I wouldn't have been surprised if a couple of corgis had come bounding in our direction. Instead, a middle-aged housekeeper appeared, dressed in a simple black dress.

"Is David here, Clara?" Peyton asked impatiently.

"No, Mrs. Slavin. I haven't heard from him today."

"All right, then, I need you to show Miss Weggins to the guest room and then bring some chilled white wine to the library.

"Can you make do without me for a while?" Peyton asked, turning to me. "There are calls I'm going to have to make. But I'll join you later in the library. Clara will tell you where it is."

As Peyton flounced off toward the back of the house, I was led up a huge staircase. The house appeared to be decorated fairly classically, but with some quirky touches that kept it from being stodgy. The guest room, or at least the guest room I'd been assigned to, was at the end of a long hallway on the second floor and was about three times the size of my living room. It had a huge four-poster bed with a little step stool beside it and was decorated in florals and yellow and white stripes. Peyton, I realized, must have believed that yellow was a color that flattered and soothed everyone. Unfortunately, nothing was going to soothe me tonight.

Seeing I was without bags, Clara asked if I needed anything and promised to find me a toothbrush. After she was gone I dug my cell phone out of my purse and called Jack. There was no answer at his college office, his apartment, or his cell phone. I left messages for him to call me as soon as he could.

After splashing some water on my face in the adjoining bathroom, I found my way to the library using the directions Clara had provided. It was painted a deep, mossy green, not only the walls, but the bookshelves, though they had been treated some way that made them look like leather. There were several nubby green sofas, and the floors were covered in a soft green-and-beige-checked wall-to-wall carpeting. Accenting the room were antique Chinese pieces, including a red-lacquer chest used as a coffee table and a red desk painted with willows and pagodas.

I helped myself to the French white wine being chilled in a bucket on the coffee table. The phone on the end table by the couch rang often but was immediately intercepted by someone in another room.

I took a large swig of wine, though I could tell that alcohol wasn't going to be able to take the edge off. Just as I was about to flop down on one of the sofas, I caught sight of a row of photos lining the mantel and walked over to inspect them. Though there were some shots of family members, most were of Peyton and David leading the good life—on sailboats and terraces and in the kinds of outdoor cafés they had only in France and Italy. One especially large photo was of them on their wedding day. It was a formal pose from the waist up—Peyton in that fantastic crumb-catcher bodice, David in his tux with a simple white rose boutonniere. They looked triumphant.

Sinking into the couch, I opened the composition book that I had brought down with me. What I was anxious to do right now, before things got any crazier, was to make a time line of Peyton's wedding. Robin had asked Ashley if she had noticed anything strange at the wedding, and it was time for me to dredge the recesses of my memory.

The weekend had kicked off with a bridesmaids' luncheon, held on Friday afternoon—and it was actually the first time that several of us had met one another. Robin, Ashley, and Prudence were all childhood friends of Peyton's. I hadn't met any of them before, nor had Jamie. Maverick, Peyton's PR person, had seemed familiar with Robin, but I wasn't sure if she'd known the others. Bridesmaids who were strangers was a fairly typical situation, but in other weddings I'd been in, you at least got to know the rest of the wedding party in the weeks before the big day—either while planning a shower or hosting a bachelorette party.

But Peyton had wanted neither. As for the girls' night on the town, she'd declared that she was now a public figure and didn't want anyone snapping a picture of her coming out of a place where men—in her words—"stripped to G-straps and let women stuff ten-dollar bills next to their cocks." She didn't bother explaining her veto of the shower, but it was easy enough to interpret. Peyton had very particular taste and was marrying a ton of money. The last thing she needed was a backflow of blenders and a bunch of ugly place mats.

I couldn't recall anything out of the ordinary about the bridesmaids' luncheon—other than how subdued it was.

And it wasn't simply because some of us were strangers. By then Peyton's Bridezilla side was full-blown, and each one of us was trying to keep her meltdowns to a minimum.

The rehearsal dinner, on the other hand, wasn't so calm. There had been that ugly scene when the six of us had arrived late—Peyton dressing us down while her very dignified mother tried fruitlessly to get her to chill.

Though there would be limos for us the day of the wedding, that night we'd been expected to drive ourselves. Prudence took Robin and Ashley, and I followed with Jamie and Maverick in my Jeep. As we approached an intersection not far from the church, two cars collided right in front of us. Though no one was injured, both cars had taken a nasty beating and the driver in one insisted that we wait for police. I actually hadn't seen the accident, though a couple of the girls in the front car had, and they gave accounts to the police when they pulled up a few minutes later. Someone called the restaurant to explain our plight, but apparently the message had never been relayed.

A fairly minor traffic accident. No one injured. But it would be worth following up on since it was an event that we'd all been involved in.

Then there had been the wedding and reception. Both had seemed to go off without a hitch. For me, the reception was mostly a blur of eating, drinking, escaping the advances of boorish male guests, and flirting with the bartender-slash-actor I'd promised to call but never had. If something strange had happened that day, I hadn't witnessed it.

"What are you writing?"

I glanced up, startled, to find Peyton standing in the doorway, holding two plates and silverware.

"Just some notes about today. I'm trying to make sense of things, but I can't."

"I made us some dinner. I thought it might be easier just to have it in here."

"Sure, that's fine. But you shouldn't have gone to the trouble. I know how awful you must feel."

"To be honest, the distraction did me good. Cooking always takes my mind off anything horrible that's going on around me."

"Have you reached David yet?"

"Yes, he's home. He sends his apologies—he's gone upstairs to his office to make some calls about all of this. I know this sounds perfectly dreadful, but we could be sued by Ashley's parents."

Three bridesmaids dead and she was considering how to protect her hide. Well, that was Peyton. But then, more charitably, I admitted to myself that she was right to guard her flank. Many people *did* want a piece of what Peyton had.

She set the plates and silverware on the red-lacquer chest. The meal was breaded chicken cutlets covered with a chopped-arugula-and-tomato salad. She pulled the bottle of Pouilly-Fuissé from the bucket on the coffee table, refreshed my glass, and poured herself one. Did this mean she wasn't pregnant?

"This is great," I said after taking my first bite of chicken. "You made it yourself?"

"Yes, it's simple, really. Chicken Positano. The chicken's breaded and sautéed and then topped with the salad. It's better if you marinate the cutlets first in lime juice, but needless to say, I didn't have time."

"It's just what I needed. So I've heard the phone ringing off the hook. Any developments?"

"Not from the police yet, no. But the press is now on to this. The first two deaths were under the radar. Maybe because Robin and Jamie lived in different states, no one connected them—to each other or to me. But they've put it all together now. The press are all fucking hyenas."

"Well, at least if there's press interest, it puts pressure on the police to take it seriously," I said. "Did anyone on your staff hear or see anything?"

"Not from what I can tell. They put that cop in the room with us so we wouldn't talk to each other, but I eavesdropped on as many of the interviews as I could, and no one offered up anything. Do you think Ashley was actually *pushed*?"

"Three fatal accidents in six months. As of right now, we don't have any reason to believe they were more than freakish accidents. And yet it does seem to totally defy probability. And Ashley, as you know, was certain that something sinister was going on—she believed Robin and Jamie were murdered."

"Well, what do *you* think? I mean, this is your specialty, right?"

"Well, two things come to mind if we're going to go down that road. Jamie and Robin had gotten very tight. Maybe they were involved in something that led to their deaths—and someone thought Ashley knew about it. She lived with Robin, after all, and had started telling people that she thought the two women had been murdered. The other thing to consider, of course, is that all three women were bridesmaids in your wedding. Tell me, do you remember anything strange happening that day?"

"Strange?" she said almost contentiously. "What do you mean by *that*? As far as I'm concerned, it was as close to a perfect day as anyone could imagine."

"Peyton, I'm not trying to suggest anything disparaging about your wedding or reception. But Ashley wondered if Jamie—and perhaps Robin as well—may have witnessed something that day or overheard something she shouldn't have."

"Like what?"

"I don't have any details."

"Well, there's nothing *I'm* aware of," she declared.

"Okay, then, how about this? Is there someone who resents you and your marriage to David? Who might be doing this as some symbolic act?"

She stared into the fire, not saying anything for a minute. Then she turned back to me, her face set in a look of conviction.

"David's ex-wife, Mandy," she announced. "I know this sounds horrible, but she could have done this. She hated the fact that he was divorcing her—and she despises me."

"She lives around here?"

"Yes. She's one of those women who live off their divorce settlements and spend their entire lives being gym bunnies. She still even uses the name Slavin, for God's sake. And she and David have that kid, Lilly, who Mandy is always thrusting on us."

"It's something to consider. But for now we need to wait to hear what the police turned up in their investigation. If Ashley was pushed, there might be scuff marks on the landing."

We talked for a few more minutes—mostly about her work, just to take our minds off everything else. She also managed to ask a few questions about *my* life. Eventually I felt fatigue grab hold of me and announced that I needed to turn in. Leaving our dishes for the housekeeper, Peyton gave me a quick tour of the ground floor. The living room was a mammoth space, with three or four seating arrangements, all done in creams and brocades, the walls boasting breathtaking landscape paintings. I was also given a peek at a large formal dining room, with walls covered in a bird-covered chinoiserie, a billiards room, a media room with a huge plasma screen in the wall, and a sunroom or conservatory filled with bamboo. The last time I'd seen this many different rooms in one house, I'd been playing Clue. If I hadn't been wrestling with so many other emotions, I might have felt engulfed with envy.

Once I was tucked in bed, I tried to put off going to sleep for a while longer. Ever since my divorce a couple of years ago I'd been dogged by insomnia, and I had a nasty feeling that it was going to rear its head tonight. I leafed through the latest issue of *Gloss*, which I'd crammed in my tote bag. There was a story on readers' most embarrassing beauty questions, including "I Have Dark Patches on my Inner Thighs—Help" and "How Do I Prevent Hump Hair?" Hump hair turned out to be that thick matt of hair that develops after you've shagged someone for seven hours straight. God, if only that was all I was contending with tonight, instead of worrying about whether someone was killing off Peyton's bridesmaids—with me possibly next. Just as I felt my eyes growing heavy, I heard someone yell from another part of the house.

My heart leapt like an antelope, but I lay as still as I could, trying to hear. Someone was definitely shouting, a man, and it seemed to be in anger rather than any kind of distress.

I crawled out of bed, and since I'd been forced to sleep in only my lime green panties, I wrapped myself in a cashmere throw blanket from the end of the bed. As quietly as possible, I turned the handle and opened the door. The only light in the hallway was from two dim wall sconces.

Now a woman was yelling, too. I was pretty sure it was Peyton. I crept down the hall toward the door of what I thought must be the master bedroom. That was where the angry words were emanating from.

"You're not even thinking about me in all of this, are you?" Peyton shouted.

"Why should I?" It was David's voice now. "You do enough of that for all of us. God forbid there's ever a moment in the day when you're thinking of someone other than your fucking self."

CHAPTER 4

As curious as I was to know more, I felt guilty listening to their marital scrape. On tiptoes I began to make my way back to my bedroom, fearful that at any moment one of them would fling open the door in retreat and I'd be caught standing there in my makeshift toga.

I climbed back into bed, blisteringly fatigued but at the same time totally wired. What the hell was going on with Peyton's marriage? David's voice had sounded positively ragged with frustration. Was the flare-up I'd overheard simply a result of all the tension lately—from Robin's death and now Ashley's—or was it an indication of deep, serious trouble? As I lay there pondering and fretting, my cell phone went off on the bedside table, scaring the bejesus out of me. It was Jack.

I poured out the whole awful story to him. He listened in that nice Jack way of his, periodically asking for more details.

"I hate the idea of you being there alone," he said finally. "If I were in New York tonight, I'd drive out to Greenwich and pick you up."

"Thanks," I said. "But I feel safe enough here. The house is practically a castle, and I'm sure they've got every type of security short of a moat."

"What do the police make of this?" Jack asked.

"The guys who interviewed me weren't giving anything away. Listen, Jack, when you and I spoke yesterday about clusters, we were talking about only two deaths. Could *three* accidental deaths like this still be just a cluster?"

"Believe it or not, yes. It could still all be random. Though if you ran a probability study on it, you'd most likely find that the chances of it happening are astronomically low, so Bailey, you have to be careful. You need to stay out of this and let the police investigate it."

I knew I should appreciate his concern, yet I found it irritating and patronizing. Not only was I a crime reporter, but in the last year I also had played a key role in *solving* two crimes. I didn't say anything, just let his remark hang there.

"And I want you to call me as soon as you get back to New York," he added. "You're coming home tomorrow, right?"

"Yes, I have to be back for a meeting at *Gloss*. Look, you've got classes in the morning. I better let you go."

He hesitated for a second, then simply told me again to call him tomorrow. I wondered what he'd been about to say. Some kind of endearment? That was still a bit of a tricky area for us. We had done the L-word limbo in the past month or two, saying things to each other like "I love when you do that" and "I love that shirt on you." But neither one of us had ventured further than that. Which was okay with me because my feelings were still evolving. I was definitely in lust and very deeply in like, but I couldn't yet say whether I was in love with him.

I turned off the bedside light and lay in the dark, totally wide-eyed. Whatever fatigue I'd felt earlier had been chased away by the altercation down the hall. At one point I thought I heard raised voices again, then realized it was only the wind, which had begun to howl. I finally fell asleep at about one and thanks to sheer exhaustion slept straight through till seven—when the roar of a snowblower jarred me awake. From my window I could see a man in a green parka riding it, working along the edges of the large circular driveway in front of the house. I took a hot shower and used the time to plot out my morning.

Despite what Jack had suggested, I wasn't going to leave things entirely to the Greenwich police. Maybe they'd rule Ashley's death a murder, maybe they'd even reopen Robin's case. But that might take weeks, and I would have a hard time sleeping unless I proved to myself that there really *wasn't* a killer at large, a killer with an apparently exorbitant interest in Peyton Cross's bridesmaids. So I needed to turn over a few rocks and see if anything nasty crawled out. At the very least, I owed it to Ashley. And it was certainly better than waiting around for an ax to fall—on me.

As soon as I got back to New York, I would find out all I could about Jamie's death and learn more about Robin's dietary restrictions—I planned to call the number I'd copied from the Post-it note Ashley had shown me. And last but not least, I wanted to hook up with the other bridesmaid, Maverick, who handled PR for Peyton.

Before I left Greenwich, however, there were a few things I needed to take care of. I was going to drive back out to Ivy Hill Farm and talk to the staff at the kitchenware shop—to learn whatever I could about Robin. I also wanted to talk to the wedding planner Peyton had used. I happened to remember her last name because it had amused me when I'd first heard it last spring. It was Bliss, and her company was called Bliss Weddings. Using my cell, I got the number from directory assistance and scribbled it down on a piece of paper. If anything strange had happened at the wedding, she might know about it firsthand.

I expected there would be some early morning hustle and bustle in Peyton's house, but as I stepped out of my bedroom, wearing my bagged-out pants and sweater from yesterday, I was greeted by total silence. Walking down the big staircase, I felt a little like Joan Fontaine in *Rebecca*—a girl totally out of her element at Manderley.

I took a peek into some of the main rooms on the ground floor—living room, sunroom, library—and finding them empty, I headed toward what I thought must be the door to the kitchen. It swung open suddenly and Clara emerged, a small tray in her hand covered with a cloth and hosting a white porcelain teapot. She greeted me and explained that breakfast was laid out in the kitchen and Mr. Slavin was having his morning meal in there now. As for Peyton, she was under the weather and had requested breakfast in her room. I couldn't help wondering how much of Peyton's condition had to do with Ashley's death and how much was related to the family feud that had transpired last night.

I pushed open the door to the kitchen. The room was as big as the kitchen at the farm, but sparkling white and ultramodern. There was a contemporary-style fireplace, with the hearth at waist level and a gas fire giving off a faint hum. David was at the far end of the room, sitting at a sleek black table and reading *The Wall Street Journal*.

"Good morning," I said, for lack of anything better to say.

"Oh, Bailey," he replied, rising from his chair to greet me. "I didn't hear you come in. Here, please join me."

He was a little over six feet, barrel-chested, and handsome for a guy almost fifty—hazel eyes, soft, full lips, and gleaming brown hair that had begun to thin slightly on top. Personalitywise he was pleasant enough, but he had this supermature quality that I found totally offputting. I'd always figured that going to bed with him would be like shagging the U.S. secretary of state or the loan officer at your bank. I mean, it was tough to imagine being buck naked with him and asking him to lick chocolate sauce off your nipples. Over the years Peyton and I had known each other, she'd definitely bragged about her fair share of adventurous sexual exploits. In fact, in the months before David, Peyton had mentioned that she'd been dating a stunning young stud who, she crowed, was unbelievable in bed. Still, maybe David was up for more than he let on. And there was all that money, of course.

"Dreadful situation, isn't it," he said, pulling out a chair for me at the table. He was dressed in a dark blue pin-striped suit, a white shirt, and a dazzling silk tie that illustrated why Marco Polo had been so eager to find a road to the Orient.

"Yes," I said, "it's just awful. Will there be a funeral here in Greenwich, do you know?"

He drew a deep breath. "From what I've heard, the parents are coming east for the body, but they want the service to be held back in Arizona, where they've been living. Ashley apparently spent a fair amount of time there—they've had the place for years."

I poured myself a cup of coffee and picked a croissant out of a basket lined with a white linen napkin that had been starched to within an inch of its life.

"Any word from the police yet?" I asked.

"Not officially," he said, scowling. "But I have connections in the department, and apparently they've more or less concluded it was an accident. It looks as if Ashley climbed a stepladder on one of the landings—perhaps to adjust a light—and lost her balance. It's not very wide there, so when she fell, she hit the railing and toppled over the side. They're going to keep the silo closed for a few days while they make some inquiries, but they've said that the farm can open first thing this morning."

So they'd decided: The third accidental death in six months. I found it hard to believe.

"Of course, someone could have pushed her without leaving any trace of having done so," I asserted.

He nearly choked on his coffee when he heard my words. "But for heaven's sake, *why*?" he asked. "Peyton told me that Ashley thought the other two had been murdered, but it's totally implausible."

"Robin apparently asked Ashley if she remembered something strange happening at the wedding—or perhaps during the wedding weekend. Does that ring any bells for you?"

He snorted, as if the idea were absurd. "I find everything about big weddings strange," he said. "I have no idea why people insist on doing them."

Odd answer, I thought, from a guy who had married nine months ago in front of five hundred people.

"Is there someone who might be *angry* about the wedding?" I asked. "Who might have done this as some kind of revenge?"

He stared at me, his hazel eyes holding my gaze. "Do you mean Mandy—my ex? We've been separated for two years, so I think if she were going to take her revenge, she would have done it by now. Besides, I can't imagine her doing anything like *this*."

"Anyone else? A disgruntled client of yours, for instance. Issues with your business?"

"A *client*? Of course not," he said dismissively. "This is all just some horrible chain of events."

"How's Peyton holding up?" I asked, watching him closely. I was intensely curious about how he'd be when he discussed her.

"As you can imagine, she's very distressed. She doesn't even want to get out of bed today."

His tone was sympathetic, but for the first time since we'd been talking, his pale eyes pulled away from me. He used the moment to slide his chair back and toss the napkin from his lap onto the table. Clearly, talking about Peyton had made him uncomfortable. Was it because of the tiff last night? Or because of what he'd *said* last night—that Peyton was concerned only for herself?

"If you'll excuse me, Bailey," he announced, "I'd better push off. My partner is picking me up in a few minutes. Despite the weather, we have to drive to Stamford today."

"Do you mean Trip—the one who was your best man?"

"Yes. In fact, Peyton had this idea that the two of you might connect. He's still available, by the way."

Trip had laid it on thick the day of the wedding, at least until he realized I was registering no interest. He was by some standards an attractive guy, but so intense that it was unpleasant to talk to him.

"Thanks, but I'm seeing someone right now."

David leaned toward me and did that ridiculously affected thing of kissing me on not just one cheek but both. His cologne smelled citrusy, an odd choice for a winter day.

"Terrific," he said distractedly, clearly anxious to be gone. "Good to see you, Bailey, despite the circumstances."

"You, too."

When he reached the door of the kitchen, he stopped and turned back to me.

"I know this has been very stressful for you, but try to put it behind you now. As I said, it's just an awful chain of events."

"Maybe. But I'm not entirely convinced. I'm going to check out a few things on my own and try to determine once and for all what's going on."

He stared at me, his expression pensive. "Be careful. This is not a town that appreciates people asking lots of questions."

Was that just an observation he wanted to share, or did

he mean it as some kind of warning? Well, I certainly wasn't going to be intimidated by the country club set.

"Three women are dead," I said. "And I need to know what happened."

He shrugged his shoulders and left. After the door had swung behind him, I quickly finished my croissant and gulped down half a cup of coffee. It was time to be on my way.

I found my coat in the hall closet and did another search of the ground floor, looking for Clara so I could tell her I was leaving. I finally stumbled on her in the sunroom, talking to a maid who was in the process of washing windows with a squeegee.

"I'd like to go up to say good-bye to Peyton," I told her.

Her expression turned fretful, as if I'd just announced that I'd tracked tar on the front hall carpet.

"Oh, Mrs. Slavin is sleeping," she said. "I don't think we should disturb her. Maybe you could call her later?"

I nodded and tore a page from my composition book, scribbling a farewell note to Peyton. Clara accepted it and led me to the door. I had the feeling she suspected that I'd sneak upstairs to Peyton's room if she turned her back on me for even a second.

David must have stepped outside just moments before I did, because when I emerged from the house into the frosty morning air, I found him tossing his leather briefcase into the trunk of a silver Mercedes. Trip was at the wheel, his dark hair slicked back along the sides as if he hadn't bothered drying it after his shower. He was ten years younger than David, though his craggy features made him appear over forty. As I stepped off the stoop of the house, David slipped into the passenger seat on the far side of the car and Trip lowered his car window.

"Well, if it isn't Bailey Weggins," he said, training his dark blue eyes on me. There was a nick on the left side of his chin where he'd obviously cut himself shaving. "It's Trip, by the way. Trip Furland."

"Of course. How's it going?"

"Not bad. That's terrible news about Ashley. Were you two friends?"

"I just knew her from the wedding."

"Well, I'd better not keep the boss waiting."

A memory came to me then, unbidden. The night before the wedding, when we were preparing to rehearse in the church, the maid of honor and bridesmaids had been ushered into a room along the side of the church to wait for our cue. As we entered, we heard voices on the other side of an old wooden folding screen that had been used to divide the room. It was David and Trip. They had obviously been sent into the room from another entrance. At first they spoke in hushed tones, and then their voices rose in anger. A few of us glanced at one another with questioning looks, wondering if we should alert them to our presence, but before we could do anything, the voices halted and David stuck his head around the screen. He looked extremely uncomfortable when he discovered us all there. But clearly whatever he and Trip had quarreled about that day had not gotten in the way of their business partnership.

My Jeep was parked farther along the entrance drive to the house, near the garage, and as I approached it I saw that a man in a dark green parka with the hood up was wiping off the window.

"Good morning," he said in what I thought might be an Australian accent. "She's all ready for you."

"Thanks," I said, realizing he must be some kind of caretaker type.

"I kept her warm. It's brutal out today."

He was right. He'd kept the Jeep perfectly toasty. God, I thought, I could get used to the good life if only someone would give me half a chance.

There were already about eight cars in the parking lot of Ivy Hill Farm when I arrived—mostly workers, I assumed. The silo rose forlornly in the background, and my stomach turned over just seeing it. I trudged toward the buildings along a hastily shoveled path. Through the window of the big barn I could see a cluster of workers by the counter, chopping and stirring away. Phillipa was among them, and so was Mary.

I turned instead toward the smaller, gray barn where the shop was located. As I stepped inside, I found the same girl behind the register whom I'd spotted yesterday. There was one customer at the moment, paying for a set of Asian-inspired place mats and napkins. While the salesclerk folded the place mats into a bag, I waited by a table stacked with kitchenware, feigning a fascination with a set of ramekins.

"May I help you?" the clerk asked as the door slammed. She was young, no more than twenty, with her blond hair pulled back prudishly in a tight bun. I wondered if Peyton made her wear it like that.

"Actually I'm Peyton's friend Bailey Weggins. I was here yesterday when this whole awful thing happened. I'm trying to help Peyton in any way I can."

At the mention of yesterday, her lower lip, glistening with pale pink lip gloss, began to tremble.

"It's just terrible, isn't it?" she said. "And did you see what that awful New York paper wrote?"

"No, I didn't. Do you have it here?"

After glancing toward the door, she reached below the counter and pulled out an already opened copy of the *New York Post*, pointing to a small item titled "Is There a Peyton Cross Curse?" The article recapped all three deaths, suggesting that there was a bizarre curse—like something out of *The Hound of the Baskervilles*—on everyone in Peyton's wedding. Then it listed the names of the three remaining attendants, including mine. Peyton had said the press had started calling practically immediately yesterday, and I was curious how a New York paper had gotten word so quickly. Had someone at the farm tipped them off?

"Do you think there *is* a curse?" the clerk asked mournfully.

"We don't really know *what's* happening," I said. "Did you happen to see anything odd yesterday?"

"No, nothing. Like I told the police, I ate lunch in the big barn with some of the other girls at around twelve, and then I never went out of the shop again."

"Did you have any customers in the afternoon?"

"It was sort of busy right after lunch—we had about ten or twelve people in here. But as soon as the snow started coming down, business totally fell off."

"You'd worked with Robin for a while, right? I mean, she oversaw the shop."

"That's right. Ms. Cross is doing it now—until we replace Robin."

There was no joy in her voice as she said it. In fact, she sounded like someone who'd just learned all her wisdom teeth were impacted and had to be extracted.

"In the weeks before she died, how did Robin seem to you? Was she different in any way?"

"How do you mean?" she asked anxiously, as if she were afraid the wrong answer might earn her a penalty.

"Her roommate said she seemed worried about something."

She thought for a moment, her brow wrinkling again.

"She did seem sort of worried—or maybe it was just that her mind seemed to be on something else. She took meds for depression, you know? I mean, that's what ended up causing her death. I just thought maybe she was in kind of a down period."

"You don't recall her saying anything that would explain her mood?"

"No—but my mind is in such a jumble right now. Can I think about it?"

"Sure, that would be great," I said. I handed her a business card and told her to contact me if she thought of anything.

I thanked her for her help, and after reviewing with her the directions to downtown Greenwich, I took off. Once in town I had to stop twice for directions in order to locate the street I was looking for. I spent another ten minutes trying to find a parking space.

The Bliss Weddings office was on the second floor of a well-kept two-story building. I tried the door, only to find it locked. But after rapping several times, I picked up the sounds of someone moving across the floor in my direction. The door swung open and I was surprised to discover Megan Bliss standing there herself. She was in her late thirties, I guessed, and no more than five feet two, though with her thick raven hair, high heels, and nubby white wool suit, she seemed to take up more than her share of space. I caught an annoyed, "this morning is starting to work my last nerve" expression on her face that quickly turned into a beaming smile. It was clear that she had just mistaken me for a bride-to-be.

"Oh, you're early," she said as chirpy as a chickadee. "I was just preparing for our meeting this morning. Please come in."

I stepped first into a small reception area, and then she led me through to a large office, which looked more like a living room. There was a couch and coffee table, an armchair, and a round conference table with chairs. The entire room was done in what the *Gloss* decorating editor might describe as champagne color. It was a sort of blushed beige that gleamed.

"It was lovely of the Hubbels to recommend me," she said, gesturing for me to take a seat. "Is your mother not going to join us after all?"

"Actually I'm not planning a wedding. My name's Bailey Weggins, and I was a bridesmaid in Peyton Cross's wedding. I was hoping to talk to you for a few minutes."

The annoyed look returned with a vengeance.

"I have a new client coming in just a few minutes. That's who I thought you were." As she stared at me, I could tell she was mentally clicking through the Rolodex in her mind, trying to recall me from the wedding.

"This will only take a minute," I said, smiling. "And

it's important. Did you hear about Ashley Hanes's death?"

She nodded, still wary, and I went on to explain what had happened to both Robin and Jamie. Her blue eyes widened with each detail I revealed, and it was clear that the other deaths were all news to her.

"How perfectly awful," she said finally. "But I don't see how you think *I* could help. The wedding was last April."

"You were very involved in everything that happened that weekend. I was wondering if you saw anything out of the ordinary. Perhaps it's something that didn't seem strange then, but now, with hindsight . . ."

"There was *nothing* ordinary about that wedding."

"I realize it was all very special, but what I'm wondering is whether—"

"I'm not talking about how special it was. I'm talking about all the—how shall I say this? We faced enormous *challenges* working with a bride like Peyton Cross."

"I imagine she wanted it all to be perfect."

She sank into the couch, and I took the armchair across from her.

"Perfect? She wanted *beyond* perfection."

"That *must* have been tough."

"It's not that I'm unfamiliar with difficult brides," she said, folding her arms across her ample breasts. "They all suffer from various degrees of what I call PMS—pre-*marital* syndrome. And that makes them absolutely crazy at times. They take it out on me, their mothers, their bridesmaids, even their fiancés. Sometimes the craziness doesn't stop even when the wedding is over. You may find this hard to believe, but an associate of mine who runs a bridal dress boutique was actually sued in small claims court by a woman who claimed that her dress restricted her ability to dance at her wedding reception—and that the trauma from it lasted a year. But in all the years I've been doing this, I've never witnessed anyone like Peyton Cross. Nothing, absolutely nothing, pleased her. I shouldn't be talking out of school like this—I never do, you know—but I really don't care in this case. I had this idea when I took Peyton as my client that it would be a feather in my cap, but it was hardly worth it."

"Since she catered the wedding reception herself, what exactly was your role?"

"The catering involves just the food. I took care of everything else—the invitations, the setting, the flowers, the decor. Peyton had pretty clear ideas about what she wanted—my job was to supervise and make certain it all came off flawlessly. Unfortunately, Peyton Cross's idea of flawless is something no human can achieve. The day of the wedding she threw this enormous hissy fit when she decided the roses were the wrong shade of yellow. I half expected her to ask me to *paint* them."

"Think back on the day of the wedding, will you? Was there anything that didn't seem right to you?"

"There was a terrible problem in the kitchen. The crust on the sea bass was soggy, and you would've thought there was a tsunami wave on the Long Island Sound by the way people were running around in hysterics, thinking that Peyton would have their heads. That poor executive director of hers was supposed to be a guest at the wedding, but she spent half the night in the kitchen with a tea towel tucked into the waistband of her party suit."

"But I mean with people. Any friction? Any quarrels? Anyone acting really secretive?"

"Well, I probably shouldn't be saying this. But I've worked with much happier couples."

Oh boy. I flashed back on Peyton and David's altercation the night before. "How do you mean? Did they fight a lot?"

"Not *fighting* so much. But at times you could cut the tension between them with a knife. When I first met them, I could tell he thought he was winning the trophy wife to end all trophy wives. But as time went on, I think he started to . . . to know the real her, if you get my drift."

"Were there any problems on the day of the wedding?"

"He was annoyed at her."

"*Really?* They seemed really lovey-dovey to me."

"In the beginning of the reception, yes. But later in the day he was clearly miffed. Everyone was looking for her to cut the cake, and it turned out she'd gone back upstairs to the dressing room to nurse a headache. Can you imagine someone feeling entitled to a nap in the middle of her wedding?"

I vaguely recalled the moment. Peyton's mother had come up to me, twittering like a bird and wondering whether I'd seen the bride.

"And nothing else? Nothing that seemed odd or unexplained?" It was hard to pursue this line of questioning when I had no idea what I was looking for.

"Not that I can think of. Look, I really need to get ready for my appointment."

I told her I understood and gave her my card, asking her to let me know if she thought of anything.

"That wedding couldn't have been much fun for you, either," she said, walking me to the door.

"I survived."

"She kept sending all of you those awful e-mails and cc'ing me. I remember she was terrified that her maid of honor was going to get pregnant again and it would spoil the pictures. And then that poor cousin of hers."

I froze in my steps. "You mean Phillipa?"

"I'm not sure of her name. The one who works with her. She was dying to be a bridesmaid, but Peyton wouldn't let her."

"You're kidding?" I said. "She wouldn't *let* her?"

"That's right. I mean, the girl is seriously overweight, so I could understand on one level. I still remember the exact phrase Peyton used. She said if we put one of the yellow bridesmaid dresses on her cousin, half the school-children in Greenwich would attempt to board her."

CHAPTER 5

FIVE MINUTES LATER I was dashing down the steps of the building on my way to the street. I'd wanted to probe more about Phillipa, but just as I'd started, there was a tapping on the door. It was the bride-to-be and her mother, tall brunettes dressed in nearly matching brown mink coats, looking like a pair of selkies who'd once lived in the Long Island Sound but had decided to try their luck on land.

As I unlocked the Jeep, I looked up and down the street a couple of times. Should I be nervous? Was there a chance my life really *could* be in danger? If someone wanted to murder me and make it look like an accident, what would they try?

After I'd navigated my way out of Greenwich and onto I-95 back to New York, I called Maverick PR in New York, the only agency I'd ever heard of using the owner's first name. Maverick turned out to be as anxious to talk to me as I was to her, and we arranged to meet at her home office at six.

Once I was off the phone, I had time to focus on what I'd learned this morning from Megan Bliss. Peyton's cousin had wanted to be in the wedding, but Peyton had cruelly denied her. I knew that my boss at *Gloss*, Cat Jones, sometimes took actresses off the list of potential cover subjects because they'd packed on the pounds and had failed to pass what she called "the chubby check," but this was real life we were talking about. It must have been humiliating and painful for Phillipa. Was she so angry about her rejection that she was killing off all the girls who *had* been bridesmaids? It didn't seem to make any sense. If Phillipa had acted out of rage and revenge, why wait several months between killing Jamie and Robin? And then why kill Ashley only a few weeks after Robin's death? It was also hard to imagine how Phillipa, who did not appear to have set any land records as a runner, could have gotten to the silo, climbed the stairs, and pushed Ashley to her death, then turned out all the lights and escaped before Peyton and I arrived.

Despite a bottleneck near New Rochelle, I was back in my apartment by noon. I took a quick look around. My terrace was locked tight, just as I had left it, and nothing seemed amiss. I told myself I was being silly. But it made me wonder again about Jamie's death. If she actually was murdered, how did the killer gain access to her apartment while she was taking a bath? Since there was apparently no sign of a break-in, he must have been either given a key by Jamie or let in by her. If she'd opened the door for him, why climb back into the tub? Could he have been her lover?

I hurriedly changed my underwear and threw on a pair of black pants, a white-collared shirt, and my black leather jacket. My first stop was going to be *Gloss*. I not only had my appointment with the deputy editor, but I hoped to find the food editor, Babette. Later I'd head to the Upper East Side for my meeting with Maverick.

As I was trying to tame my flyaway hair, which I'd recently grown out to chin length, the phone rang. It was Jack again.

"I thought you were going to call me as soon as you got back," he said.

"Sorry," I said. "I actually did just get back—I ended up making a few stops in Greenwich."

"Bailey, you've got to let the police handle this."

I appreciated Jack's concern, but he was starting to sound a little like my mother.

"It doesn't look like they're going to," I told him. "They apparently believe Ashley just fell off a stepladder. But it all feels too weird to me, and I can't sit around on my butt not knowing the truth about what happened."

"Well, we can talk about it when I get to the city," he said. "Unfortunately, I've got a meeting late tomorrow and I'm probably not going to be able to get on a shuttle until seven. That gets me into New York about nine."

"That's okay. I'll just wait for you here, then."

Before I left my building I slipped a note under Landon's door, asking if by any chance he could come for dinner that night. I was anxious to fill him in on everything that had happened and get his insight. He was always a wonderful sounding board when I was in the middle of some mayhem.

I took the N train to 57th Street and Seventh Avenue

and walked the couple of blocks west and south to *Gloss*. Though there were snowbanks along the curb, they'd clearly shrunk over the last day or so and were now pock-marked and plastered with litter. It was cold as hell out, and it seemed that every woman who wasn't wearing a fur coat had a colored pashmina scarf double-wrapped around her neck.

As a freelancer and contributing writer, I'm not really entitled to an office at *Gloss*, but because I produce so many pieces for the magazine each year—and because Cat and I go way back—I've been allowed to set up shop in a tiny office in the back of the floor. In the days before the Internet, it had been a storage space for research books.

Though there's a back way to my office off the elevator, I usually go the long route through the "pit," the large newsroom-style area that holds the cubicles for the art, photo, and production departments and a few of the junior articles editors. The newsroom setup is a little pretentious for a monthly magazine like *Gloss*—I mean, the only breaking news that people out in the pit ever deal with is whether they're ordering Thai or Italian takeout for lunch—but the layout does generate a lot of energy and buzz. I like to swing through there to get a sense of what's happening—and discover what kind of mood Cat has cast over the place on a given day.

As I walked into the pit that Thursday afternoon, the photo editor was on his way out, and when he spotted me he stopped in his tracks.

"Hey, I saw your name in the *Post* today," he said, beaming. "In that story about Peyton Cross. That's amazing."

He was making it sound like something I should be proud of, as if they'd run an item saying I was a shoo-in for a Golden Globe nomination.

"Oh yeah, just great, isn't it?" I said, though I wasn't sure he detected the sarcasm in my voice.

"You know, the *Post* called here yesterday looking for a picture of you, but because they wouldn't tell us what it was for, Cat said not to give them anything."

"Thanks," I told him. "I appreciate it." Again, I wondered how the papers got on to the story so quickly.

I hurried across the pit and down two different corridors to my office. Out of the corner of my eye, I saw several people glance curiously in my direction. Obviously, word about the *Post* story had spread.

As I said, my office is toward the back of the floor—directly across from the fashion department space, a large room set up with a bunch of cubicles, almost like a mini version of the pit. Today the hallway outside was lined with two large racks of juicy-colored bathing suits. I knew, from having overheard last week's chatter, that those suits were just back from four sunny days in Cozumel. Inside the room, two twenty-something editors were standing in front of a mannequin dressed in a satiny skirt and shirt, staring at it with the kind of reverence someone else would reserve for Michelangelo's *Pietà*.

"Cat was looking for you," one of them called out as I dumped my bags onto the extra chair in my office. They probably thought I'd literally start shaking in my boots at this news, but I was one of the few people on staff who was tremble-proof when it came to Cat.

I peeled off my layers of outerwear and checked my voice mail. The most recent message was from Landon, saying he'd love to have dinner—and that he'd be by at eight. There were several calls from friends who'd seen the *Post* item and wanted to be sure I was alive. To my dismay, the other six messages were from reporters: two from a woman at the *Daily News* who simply asked me to call her and four from a guy at the *New York Post*, who announced in a grave voice that he *urgently* needed to speak to me. He sounded as if he thought I might have critical information on the Kennedy assassination. I had zero interest in returning either call.

After grabbing a cup of coffee at the food station, I hurried over to see Cat. Her office is at the far end of the pit, and through the glass wall I could see her standing in front of her desk, talking on the phone. She motioned for me to come in.

Cat was in her late thirties but easily could have passed for ten years younger. Her shoulder-length blond hair was stick straight today, framing her gorgeous face. She was dressed in a sleeveless white wool minidress and thigh-high red patent-leather boots—a kind of *Mod Squad/Avengers* look that I assumed was totally au courant.

She signaled with one finger that she'd be just a minute longer. I took a seat on the brown Ultrasuede love seat and sipped my coffee. There was no denying that ours was an odd relationship. She was my employer, but she was also my friend—though we weren't the kind of friends who got together over white wine once a week and bitched about the fact that the men in our lives drank orange juice straight from the carton. We'd met about seven years ago at a now defunct downtown magazine called *Get*, where I'd landed after I left the newspaper business to make my fortune (I'm joking) in magazines. Four years older than me, she was higher up on the totem pole, but I soon became her confidante. Not long after she'd scored the job of remaking *Gloss* magazine, she offered me a gig as a contributing writer. Her goal had been to turn *Gloss* from a tired women's service magazine featuring frumpy clothes, make-your-own-deck instructions, and recipes that routinely called for a can of cream of mushroom soup into a sexy, exciting read for married women. From what I could tell, she'd succeeded.

Cat certainly had her fun, charming side, but she was also fiercely ambitious, demanding, and frequently brusque. Those words also could have been used to describe Peyton, yet the two women were very different. Cat could be tough as hell, but she rarely lost her cool or acted crudely the way Peyton did. I'd seen her be a bitch, but never a banshee. Plus, Cat wasn't unrelentingly selfish like Peyton. She was there for her friends when they needed her.

After a minute of eavesdropping on the phone conversation, I realized she must be on the line with the new beauty editor. The previous one had bailed shortly after returning from maternity leave, and this one, from the scuttlebutt I'd heard around the office, was having a hard time acclimating to *Gloss*.

"Forget the homemade beauty routines," Cat said curtly. "Our average reader is married with two little kids and a job. She barely has time to pee, let alone make a pumice of oatmeal and honey."

Pause.

"Fine. I'm leaving at five, so I need the copy by then. And please don't use the word *skinpert*. It's doctor or dermatologist or skin expert. Skinpert sounds like some kind of sexual predator."

She tossed the phone on the cradle and spun around in my direction.

"My God, I saw the *Post* story," she said. "What the hell is going on?"

"I haven't a *clue*," I said as she took a seat across from me in a small armchair. "The story was basically accurate. Three bridesmaids dead. I was up in Greenwich yesterday when the third death happened—at Peyton's farm. You know her, right? Peyton, I mean. I think I asked you that around the time of her wedding."

"I've met her socially . . . ," she said, letting the uncharacteristically noncommittal remark hang there.

"And?"

"I hope you don't mind my saying this, but I wouldn't call her one of my favorite people. She's got this enormous sense of self-importance, and every conversation is all about *her*. I wouldn't mind that if she were totally brilliant or if she were doing something to change the world. But despite what Peyton Cross thinks, knowing how to pipe Roquefort cheese into a snow pea pod doesn't qualify you as the most fascinating person in Manhattan."

It was amusing to hear her put down Peyton's self-absorption, because Cat had been accused of having more than her fair share of it, too.

"I'm not offended," I said. "I don't have any blinders on when it comes to Peyton."

Cat then pumped me for details about the situation. She wanted to know about all three deaths and what I thought of them.

"The police have concluded that they're all accidents,"

I revealed. "And yet it seems so far-fetched that all three women could have died in such a short time."

"Are you wigged-out by this?" she asked.

"It's unsettling, yes. And it bugs me that no one seems inclined to at least consider the possibility of foul play. The next thing you know, the *Post* will be doing a piece on the Bridesmaid *Suicides*. What do *you* think?"

She paused, gathering her thoughts.

"I don't know enough to offer any real insight, but I admit, it does seem awfully strange. Years ago I read an article about intuition that said it's really all about the ability to connect the dots. I can't help but want to connect the dots with these three deaths. It seems as if they have to mean *something*."

"Mean something. In what way?"

"I don't know."

"Well, I'm not going to sit around wondering about it. I'm going to look into all of it and see what I can find out."

"Just be careful, please. This all sounds really spooky. And you've had enough excitement in the last year."

As I started to leave, Cat touched my arm gently.

"Remember, if there's a story in this, I want it."

I should have known. Cat cared, she really did, but she never allowed it to interfere with her need to titillate her readers.

Rather than return to my office, I went in search of Babette. Her office and the test kitchen she worked out of were on another floor, along with test kitchens for several other magazines in the company. As I pushed open the door to the kitchen, I was relieved to see that Babette was there, sliding a pan into the oven.

"Mmm, what's cookin'?" I asked as she turned around at the sound of my entrance.

"Well, what a surprise," she said when she looked over and saw me. "Pork roast with a balsamic-and-Madeira sauce. What are you doing up here?"

Without bothering to go into too much detail, I explained my connection to Jamie and how I'd just learned what happened. I asked if she knew anything about the situation.

"It's awful, isn't it?" she said, stepping over to the sink and pumping liquid soap on her hands. "My mother always told me to be careful about appliances and water, but I've never actually heard of anyone dying that way."

"Did you know her very well?"

"No, just to say hi to—you know, from seeing each other at industry stuff. This is awful to say, but she got on my nerves a little. She always seemed to be complaining about something."

"I was hoping to get some information. Do you know anyone who might have known her fairly well?"

As she lathered her hands, she raised her eyes upward, thinking.

"You know who you should talk to?" she said. "Did you ever meet Alicia Johnson, the food stylist we use sometimes? About thirty, African American? She knew her. In fact, I think she actually lives in the building where Jamie died."

It sounded like a promising lead, though as I told Babette, I didn't recall ever meeting Alicia.

"Actually I just booked some dates with her yesterday. Why don't I call her for you? Here, follow me."

I trailed Babette to her small office across the corridor,

which had cookbooks stacked on every surface. After thumbing through a giant Rolodex for the number, Babette got Alicia on her cell phone and briefly explained the situation. Then she handed the phone to me. Sounding rushed, Alicia explained that she was in the middle of a shoot but would be happy to meet with me. We agreed to get together the next morning at her place down-town—at ten o'clock.

It was finally time for my meeting with the deputy ed-itor. I needed to discuss my latest story with her to make sure she was happy with the direction I'd decided to take the piece. The story centered on a twenty-three-year-old pregnant woman who had disappeared without a trace from her home in New Jersey—and her husband was be-having extremely suspiciously. The girl's family was sure he'd killed her and dumped the body in a reclusive spot, à la Scott Peterson. I'd already driven out to Jersey to in-terview cops, family, and friends, but that wasn't going to be enough. The story had received national media cover-age, so for a monthly like *Gloss*, which couldn't keep up with breaking news, I needed a special angle or sub-theme. I loved what I'd come up with. According to sev-eral studies I'd seen, the number one cause of death among young pregnant women was murder by the father of the baby, and I was going to weave information about this into the piece. The phrase *I'm pregnant* has always been bad news for certain men, but it seemed that these days more than a few were taking action to unload them-selves of the perceived albatross.

I sat down with the editor and ran my idea by her. She thought it was fascinating and told me to go ahead with it. I could have just cleared it with Cat personally, but I'd always tried to follow proper channels at *Gloss*. That way nobody thought I was abusing my relationship with Cat, and in the end things just ran more smoothly for me.

I grabbed another cup of coffee on my way back to my office, and once I was at my desk, I got busy. I had time to kill before I met up with Maverick, and I wanted to do as much background research about the bridesmaid deaths as possible.

First, I tried the number from the Post-it note that Ashley had pulled from the kitchen drawer. Robin had called it her lifeline, and I had a hunch it was the psychiatrist who had prescribed the MAO inhibitors or possibly a therapist Robin had been working with. To my surprise, there was a recorded message from someone named Carol Blender announcing in a light, breezy voice that I had reached her cell phone and please leave a name and number. She sounded a little too perky for a shrink. I left word saying that I was both a reporter and an acquaintance of Robin's and I wanted to talk to her about Robin's death.

Next I went on-line to find out what I could about electrocution by small appliance. According to the Consumer Product Safety Commission, the electrocution rate had been declining since 1994, yet on average a few hundred people died that way each year. Extension cords, microwaves, and battery chargers were the big offenders, with CD players very low on the list. Interestingly, hair dryers *used* to be a major culprit, but since 1991 they have all been manufactured with shock interceptors that switch them off instantly if they fall in water. CD players have no such device.

I also did a search on MAO inhibitors. Several sites

carried information on them, though what I came away with was mostly an expansion of what Dr. Petrocelli had shared with me. They were mood lifters, held in regard by many doctors but dangerous when taken with certain foods. I learned that in addition to the foods Paul had mentioned, overripe fruit was a no-no and so were yeast extracts. And a whole list of other items—like coffee and chocolate—could be eaten only in moderation.

I became so immersed in my research that I was running late by the time I left for Maverick's. Her apartment turned out to be on the thirty-ninth floor of a building on the corner of Third Avenue and 70th Street, and my ears popped as I went up in the elevator. Even though the doorman had announced me, Maverick kept the chain on when she opened the door and replaced it as soon as she let me into the apartment. She was at least five feet eleven, mid-thirties, more handsome than pretty. She'd cut her hennaed hair since the wedding. It was short now and brushed back today under a two-inch-thick stretchy brown band.

"Come in," she said. "As you can probably guess, I haven't been out of my apartment today." She was referring to the fact that she was wearing a fairly low-key outfit—slim navy pants, a navy shirt with three-quarter sleeves, and a pair of brown leather slides.

"Are you worried something might happen?" I asked.

"Worried? Try *terrified*." Her speaking pace was clipped and rapid-fire. "My husband's in Dallas on business, and I demanded that he come home. Do you want sparkling water? Or a glass of white wine?"

"Actually, wine would be great," I said.

She led me down the hall to a large open living space

that included kitchen, living, and dining areas, all decorated with bold, modern pieces. But the best part was the view. The floor-to-ceiling black-framed windows were slightly curved, and I could see not only south but to the west and east. A million city lights twinkled below. It was like being in the cockpit of a plane.

While I parked myself on the low black couch, Maverick pulled a bottle of white wine from the refrigerator, opened it, and poured us each such a large glassful that if I'd come by car, I would have had to ask for a designated driver.

"You've been in touch with Peyton, I take it?" I said as she set the wineglass in front of me on the coffee table.

"No, I haven't gotten through to her," she said. "I've tried her house four or five times and gotten either voice mail or the housekeeper, who said she was unable to come to the phone."

"But the press is already onto this. Shouldn't she be strategizing with you?"

Maverick had taken a seat across from me, and she paused before answering. Nestled in the lower lashes of one eye was a tiny beauty mark that made it look as if that eye were tearing up.

"I don't do Peyton's press anymore. I haven't since late October."

"Really," I said. Was this yet another falling-out? "How come?"

"Nothing negative," she said, clearly reading my mind. "I run a small, boutique business, and Peyton and I both felt she'd outgrown me. We've been together for three years, and we've had a great run. But I don't have the manpower to handle an account as big and important as hers is now—and I'm not interested in growing. I suggested a few bigger companies, and she went with one of them. Of course, I'm a friend and I'm available for private consultation if she needs me."

She had slowed her pace a bit as she spoke and chosen her last words carefully. I suspected I wasn't getting the full story.

"I'm surprised she hasn't returned your calls, though," I said. "I would have thought she'd want your input right now."

"But what about *us*?" she demanded. "Aren't you worried we could be in some kind of danger?"

"I'm trying not to jump to any conclusions," I said. "Instead, I've been gathering information. That's why I thought it might help if you and I talked. Something significant might jump out as we compare notes."

"I don't think I can contribute very much. The police sent someone here today and—"

"They sent someone *here*? Maybe they're taking it more seriously than I thought."

"I wouldn't bank on that. I got the feeling it was just a routine visit. Them crossing their Ts. And like I said, I didn't have much to offer. I've been out of the loop since October."

"How well did you know each of the girls who died?"

"Jamie I didn't know at all. I met her the day before the wedding, and I doubt we said more than two words to each other the whole weekend. I'd seen Ashley at the farm a few times, of course. We'd chatted briefly, but that was about it. But Robin—well, I *did* know her fairly well. We worked together on some of Peyton's television gigs and big cooking demonstrations. She used to help pull in props for us. I was very upset when she died."

"Did any alarms go off in your head when you heard about the *way* she died?"

"I have to say no. Like everyone else, I assumed that Jamie's and Robin's deaths were just—"

"I know, a bizarre coincidence."

I took her then through my side of things—the visit from Ashley, her fears that Robin and Jamie had been murdered, our trip to the farm yesterday.

"My God, we really *could* be next," she said, her voice cracking.

"Think back on the wedding, will you?" I urged. "You were working with Peyton then. Can you imagine any reason someone would want to harm one of the bridesmaids? Did anyone have an issue about the wedding or a complaint or a grudge?"

"The *wedding*?" she exclaimed. "Can't you see? This has nothing whatsoever to do with the *wedding*."

CHAPTER 6

"WHAT ARE YOU saying? Do you know of some other connection they had with each other?" I asked Maverick, caught off guard by her remark.

"Not some other connection. I absolutely think they died because they were Peyton's bridesmaids. But it's not because someone has a grudge about the wedding."

"Then what?"

"Don't you see?" Maverick asked. "It's because someone has a grudge against *Peyton*. They're out to get her, bring her business down."

I took a sip of my wine, staring out at the twinkling city.

"I've considered that," I said. "But if someone wanted to get Peyton, why go about it in such an indirect way? Why not sabotage her business instead? They could burn down her catering barn, for instance."

"Because if you did a direct hit to her business—

burned down her barn, as you say—people would be out-raged on her behalf. They'd probably rally around her. And Peyton would also be able to confront the situation, deal with it directly. There's practically nothing she can do with *this*. There's no proof even that anyone did any-thing. It's what in my business I call an 'ether attack.' You can't see it or touch it—but it can kill you."

"But how can the deaths possibly hurt her business? They're a tragedy, and tragedies usually produce sympathy."

"Not if the tragedy is that people around you are drop-ping like flies," she said. "Peyton's business is successful in huge part because of her image, the aura she has as a supersuccessful domestic diva. This situation is going to create a stain of some kind on her. The food she makes in her catering business, the recipes she demonstrates on TV—those won't change. But there'll be this free-floating sense that there's a negative force around her. And people don't want to be connected to that."

I took another sip of wine, rolling her words over in my mind. Considering the way the media had reacted so far, she could very well be right.

"I take it you saw the article in the *New York Post*."

"That's exactly what I'm talking about," she said. "They've even got a name for it—the Peyton Cross Curse. The irony is that I gave Peyton a big lecture on this kind of thing last summer."

"Why? Did something happen?"

"Nothing major, but it had the potential to be a prob-lem. Peyton burned her arm while testing recipes in the barn. I happened to be there that day and I saw her do it. It was bad enough that it had to be bandaged. Well, she was being interviewed that week, and when the reporter commented on it, she refused to talk about it. Maybe she wanted to look invulnerable in the kitchen. But in the article her evasiveness came across as odd—suspicious, even—and I'm sure people wondered about it. I mean, she'd just gotten married, and now she had a mystery bruise—how fast can you say 'Nicole Simpson'?"

"Was there any fallout?" I asked.

"We were lucky. It was only a local paper, and nothing came of it. But I warned her and Mary about ether damage and how they had to be careful now that Peyton was on her way to becoming a household name."

"Okay, so let's say someone *is* out to get her. Got any ideas?"

"No, I mean, there's a long, long list of people who don't like her. People who feel she's cheated them or stolen their recipes or not given them credit. But I can't think of anyone capable of going to this kind of extreme—I mean, killing innocent women."

Though Maverick's theory made sense, I spent the next few minutes asking her about the wedding weekend just to cover my bases. Had she noticed anything strange or disturbing? She thought, her brow wrinkled, then shook her head slowly. I also inquired carefully about Peyton's cousin, not wanting to throw unnecessary suspicion on Phillipa but eager to learn just how upset she'd been about being passed over as a bridesmaid. Maverick appeared to be out of the loop on the subject. And she remembered little about the car accident—she'd been riding in the second car with me and hadn't seen the crash.

"You still think the deaths have something to do with the wedding, don't you," she said.

"I'm not dismissing your theory. I think it makes a lot of sense. But last fall Robin asked Ashley if she'd seen anything strange at the wedding, and I keep coming back to that."

"There *is* one thing," she said suddenly.

I froze, my wineglass at my lips. "What?" I asked.

"That fight between David and his best man. Remember how they started practically shouting at each other during the rehearsal in the church—not knowing we were right on the other side of the screen?"

"I was thinking about that last night," I admitted. "I don't remember much about it—other than that it seemed work related. Do you recall what they said?"

"No, just that David seemed to be chewing Trip out—which pleased me at the time since that Trip seems way too big for his britches. Do you think it's significant?"

"Well, it couldn't have been that major of a disagreement considering that they're still working together. Maybe the flare-up was due simply to prewedding tension."

I glanced at my watch. It was nearly seven o'clock. Landon was going to be at my place at eight. I needed to get rolling.

"I better split," I said. "But let's stay in touch, okay? I promise to let you know if I hear anything relevant if you'll do the same with me."

"Absolutely. Safety in numbers."

"Speaking of that, what about Prudence? I hear she's in London, but someone should get in touch with her."

"I can do that. We have some mutual friends there, so I happen to have her number."

She walked me to the door, rubbing her arms as if she

were suddenly cold. She had relaxed as we'd spoken, but now she looked wigged-out again.

"One more question," I said as we reached the door. "What advice would you give Peyton now? I mean, if she called you tonight and asked for your opinion on how to handle this from a PR perspective, what would you say?"

She let out a soft sigh. "Well, the first thing I'd tell her to do is get out of her house. Famous people tend to panic when this sort of thing happens, and they make the mistake of holing up and obsessing. But you've got to get out in full makeup, have lunch, and look as if you aren't damaged in any way. And then . . ."

Her eyes glanced up to the right as she spun a plan.

"And then I'd announce something big—for instance, that Peyton was talking to a large network about a syndicated television show of her own."

"What if she doesn't have anything like that in the hopper?" I asked.

"Doesn't matter," she said, shaking her head. "It's called a phantom project. It doesn't have to exist."

God, I thought, I was clearly hopelessly naive when it came to this PR stuff. Perhaps I should have gotten some advice from a spin doctor after my divorce. I might have been told to charge around Manhattan in full makeup, looking as though I didn't give a damn, instead of limping off like a deer that had taken a glancing blow from an SUV.

I said good-bye and stepped outside. She closed the door quickly behind me, not even bothering to wait for me to board the elevator. I stood in the hushed hallway for several minutes, my anxiety growing, until the elevator finally arrived with the sound of rushing wind.

Running late, I opted for a cab rather than the subway. I had the driver let me off by the deli across from my apartment building, where I picked up some salad greens and a carton of cream. I'd decided to make Landon a salad and fettuccine Alfredo. Peyton had pointed out last night that whipping up dinner for us had eased her stress, and I was hoping standing over a hot stove would do the same for me. Besides, over the past year, I'd been doing my best to learn how to cook.

During my marriage we ate out more nights than we ate in. At first I'd enjoyed it. My husband, a lawyer, seemed to have money to burn, and I liked sampling restaurants all over the Village, SoHo, and TriBeCa. But eventually our restaurant hopping took on a manic quality. I offered on many occasions to try to wrestle a chicken breast to the ground at home, but my suggestions were always rebuffed. Only later did I learn that by then my husband was knee-deep in gambling debts. Sitting in a dark booth in a restaurant on Prince Street or North Moore probably seemed a million times better to him than hanging out at our apartment, wondering if someone was about to show up at the door with a tire iron.

In the first months after we'd split, I felt incapable of eating solid foods, let alone *cooking* them. But eventually, as I started to get my bearings back, I decided to try my hand in the kitchen. Not only, I reasoned, would cooking enable me to repay Landon, who was constantly inviting me over for cassoulet or coq au vin, but I'd also be able to have the occasional dinner party.

My first attempts in the kitchen were nothing short of pathetic. One night I made a shrimp dish with a roux sauce, and because of some misstep on my part, the flour and water turned into plaster of paris. I served the shrimp in what appeared to be—and tasted like—tiny body casts. But over the next year I managed to teach myself a dozen fail-safe recipes: chicken with two vinegars, barbecue spareribs, bluefish baked with potatoes, and a few pasta dishes. Nothing fancy. Nothing that involved blanching or braising or wrapping a bundle of herbs in cheesecloth—but tasty enough to serve friends. I was going for something particularly simple tonight because I needed to discuss my situation with Landon.

He arrived with a bottle of wine just as I was setting the salad on the table. Landon's about five ten, compact, with close-cropped silver hair and a perpetual tan. For seventy he looks fantastic. He must have come directly from a meeting because he was wearing a navy sports jacket and a pin-striped oxford-cloth shirt, open at the collar. He designs hotel lobbies for a living, though lately he has started to work less and travel more.

"Wow, this is an expensive wine," I exclaimed as I glanced at the label. "I don't know if I deserve it tonight. I'm serving you a main course that's ninety percent butterfat."

"Actually, I'm hoping a good wine will help purge the memory of my date last night."

"Oh no," I exclaimed. "Bad?"

"Let's just say things fell a little *short* of my expectations. Do you remember how I told you I met him?"

"You sat next to him at that dinner party, right?"

"Correct. And remember how I told you that I hadn't noticed him during cocktails? Well, the reason is the man is *five feet four*."

"You're kidding! And you couldn't tell that when he was sitting down?"

"No, he's extremely low waisted." He had taken a corkscrew from the cabinet in my living room where I store my meager liquor supply and opened the wine with a soft pop.

"Oh God. I know you're not wild about shorter men."

"Dearest, at this point in my life, I'd settle for short, but this wasn't short. You've heard of that condition called Munchausen by proxy? This was *Munchkin* by proxy."

I burst out laughing, but there must have been something in my expression because he paused, wine bottle in one hand, corkscrew in the other.

"What is it?" he asked. "Something's up with you."

"Yeah, something awful. Remember that wedding I was in last spring? The one where you said my dress had enough fabric to have decorated half of Versailles? Well, three of the bridesmaids are dead now."

"What?" he exclaimed.

"It's a whole terrible saga, and I'm desperate to tell you about it. But sit, why don't you. I'll put on the pasta and then we'll talk."

Over salad, I shared the whole story.

"My goodness, how dreadful," Landon said as I stepped inside my tiny kitchen to drain the pasta into a colander. "And you're thinking someone *killed* the three of them?"

"I don't know what to make of it yet," I called out. "Ashley certainly thought her life was in danger, and she turned out to be right. All I know for sure is that I'm having a hard time dismissing it as a bizarre coincidence—

especially after seeing Ashley's body lying there. I'm afraid that if I'm not careful, I'll end up in a story called 'Four Funerals and a Wedding.' "

"And what do the police have to say?"

"I've only talked to the ones in Greenwich. They appear competent, and yet they've apparently concluded that both deaths under their jurisdiction were accidents. And that's the problem. On the surface they *do* seem accidental. There's not a shred of evidence of foul play."

"I wonder what the motive for murder could be. Do you think someone is out to sabotage Peyton Cross?"

"That's exactly what Maverick, the PR person, suggested. But I keep coming back to the remark Robin made about the wedding—about the possibility that something strange went on there that we might have witnessed. Or maybe that Jamie witnessed and said something to Robin about. Jamie apparently gave Robin photos she took of the wedding, and there's a chance they hold a clue—but I can't see anything of significance when I look at them."

"What does Peyton have to say? This must all be pretty disturbing to her." He took a sip of his wine and stared at me over the top of his glass, waiting for my answer.

"To be perfectly honest, she seems more concerned with how all of this is affecting *her*."

"I hate to sound like a player hater, but she doesn't appear to be a very nice person."

"I'm trying to see it from her side. She's got a lot at stake these days."

Over dessert—baked apples, which I served with mounds of whipped cream—I changed the subject. Just like Ashley, I found that talking about the situation had made me feel *more* anxious rather than less. So instead we discussed the trip Landon was planning in May to Provence and a lobby project he was considering on the Upper West Side.

I slept fitfully that night. From my bedroom I could hear the wind rattling the door to my terrace, and I crawled out of bed once to check it. Several times I thought how good it would be to have Jack lying next to me, then chided myself for being such a baby.

Despite my exhaustion, I bounded out of bed in the morning, anxious for my meeting with Alicia. But as I stepped out of the shower, she called to say that she needed to fill in for someone at a shoot today and would have to postpone our appointment until Monday. I just couldn't wait that long. I went into pester mode and she finally agreed to meet me at seven that night after the shoot was over. Jack wasn't due in until late anyway.

After hanging up, I tried to reach Peyton—both at home and at the farm—and I was informed by someone at each end that she was out and wasn't expected back anytime soon. Maybe she was charging around in full makeup, getting ready to announce a special TV project.

Next, I called the Post-it number again. Still voice mail. I left another message. I also tried my contact in the medical examiner's office. She had five minutes to spare, she said, and I asked her to talk to me about death by falling. If it was a homicide, what kind of evidence might there be? She let out a long sigh and explained that these were often tough cases to prove. If there was a struggle, you might see scuff marks, even a shoe left behind, but if the person had been caught off guard, there'd be little ev-

idence. "It's actually a pretty decent way to kill someone," she concluded ruefully. I assured her I wouldn't
take this as advice and hung up.

With the rest of the afternoon free, I set to work on my
article about the missing wife in New Jersey. I was now
running a few days behind, and I needed to hustle. I
reread some of the transcripts and started the first draft. It
was a gripping story, yet my mind was constantly yanked
back to my own situation.

At six, I threw on a long jeans skirt, black boots, and
my black turtleneck sweater, eager to finally meet up
with Alicia. Just as I was reaching for my coat, the phone
rang. The elusive Carol Blender was on the line.

"Thanks so much for calling back," I said. "It's a
pretty urgent matter."

"When you left a message saying you wanted to talk
about Robin's death, I was completely shocked. I'd had
no idea she'd died. I made some inquiries yesterday and
learned more about it. I'm very, very upset." Her voice
held a trace of a Long Island accent.

"Can I ask what your relationship to her was? She told
her roommate you were her lifeline."

"I—look, I don't know how appropriate it is for me to
be talking to you. I don't even know who you are."

"Like I said in my original message, I was an acquaintance of hers, but I'm also a journalist. There's a possibility that her death wasn't an accident, and I'd really like
to talk to you. I promise to keep everything confidential."

"You're in New York?"

"Yes, though I'd be happy to meet you anywhere you
say."

"Okay," she said finally. "I'm going to be out of town tomorrow, but I could meet you on Sunday at noon."

She suggested a place, a small restaurant called the Mansion in the East 80s, and said she'd be wearing a red coat. I gave her a brief description of myself. I wished the meeting could have been sooner, but I clearly didn't have a choice. I realized as I hung up that I still didn't know what she did.

At six-thirty I split for Alicia's. Usually it's a cinch to find a cab on the corner of Broadway and 9th Street, but tonight cab after cab sailed by, all with their roof lights off. Finally, just when I was about to change location, several empty ones came down the street, and the first one screeched to a halt when the driver spotted my raised arm. I gave him Alicia's address on Ludlow Street.

The Lower East Side, an area south of Houston Street, north of Canal, and bordered to the east by SoHo, had grown into one of the hippest neighborhoods in New York. Back in the late 1800s and early twentieth century, it had been home mainly to Europeans and Russian Jewish immigrants, but they were long gone and today it was populated mostly by Chinese, Hispanics, urban artists, and trendy twenty-somethings looking for semiaffordable apartments. There were still some traces of the old days. Wine bars and hip boutiques coexisted with hundred-year-old fabric stores and a matzo factory, as well as graffiti-covered Spanish delis. Still, it was getting harder and harder to imagine the streets once teeming with people and pushcarts.

Alicia's apartment was in a five-story redbrick tenement building typical of the neighborhood. I rang the bell twice without getting an answer, and just as I cursed under my breath, her voice came through the intercom, sounding breathless.

"Hi, sorry. Who is it?"

"It's me, Bailey Weggins."

"I'm on three," she said, and buzzed me in.

There was no elevator, and I had to trudge up three dingy, poorly lit floors. I thought I heard the buzzer go off again in the vestibule, but when I glanced down the stairwell no one was there.

I knocked on the door and Alicia opened it almost instantly, dressed in a bright orange sweater and brown corduroy skirt. She was stunning, tall, with skin the color of light coffee and long, straightened hair. Her coat was draped over a table, and her boots, dripping with water, were lying on their sides by the door. It was apparent she had just beaten me here.

"Thanks for seeing me," I said. "I'm sure you've got better things to do on a Friday night."

"It's not a problem. My boyfriend had to work tonight. He's at *Newsweek*, and Fridays are super late nights for them. Here, come on in."

I followed her into the living room. She had decorated her place 1960s style, in pinks and greens and reds with lots of Marimekko-style fabrics. It should have been jarring, but the effect was fun—and it was in total contrast with the building's grungy hallways. I perched on the edge of a daybed strewn with throw pillows. Alicia chose a seat across from me in a small white bucket chair.

"So you and Jamie were friends?" I asked.

"That's a stretch," she said. "I mainly knew her professionally—we worked together on a few shoots. I bumped into her late last winter and she said she'd broken up with her boyfriend and was looking for a place to live. I knew the apartment across the hall was about to become available, so I arranged for her to meet the owner of the building."

"Did you get to know her at all?"

She made a face.

"Was there a problem?" I asked.

"After she moved in, I got to know her a little better, and to be honest, I really wasn't crazy about her. She seemed to have a big chip on her shoulder."

"What about? Did she ever say?"

"Well, her boyfriend had dumped her, and that seriously bummed her out—though right before she died I think she'd started seeing someone new. But her main complaint was not being able to get this store of hers off the ground. She wanted to open a gourmet shop down here, and she was having trouble finding investors. She didn't think it was fair that people like Peyton Cross had rich husbands who could fund their businesses and she didn't have *anyone*."

It was the same bitterness that *I'd* picked up on.

"Were you here the night Jamie died?" It was time to zero in on what I'd come for.

"For part of the evening. I was leaving on a junket to California the next day, and I stayed at my boyfriend's on the Upper East Side that night. I left here about ten, I guess."

"Did she seem klutzy enough to knock a CD player into her tub?"

"I can't imagine *anyone* doing that," she said, rolling her brown eyes. "But I know she liked to listen to music in the tub. She told me once that her nightly ritual was to soak in there with a glass of wine, listening to Norah Jones. Maybe the CD player was just too close to the edge and when she went to reach for something, it fell in. I even wondered if she might have had too much to drink that night—and didn't see what she was doing."

"Did she drink a lot?"

"I'd seen her looking fairly tipsy from time to time. Where are you going with this, anyway?"

"A couple of other women she knew have died since then. I'm wondering if Jamie's death might not have been an accident."

"Whoa—you're kidding me." She put her thumb in her mouth and gnawed on the edge of it.

"What?" I asked. "You're thinking something."

"Someone was there that night," she said. "I could hear her talking to someone when I was locking my door—before I left for my boyfriend's."

I felt the hair on the back of my neck shoot up.

"Was it a man or a woman?"

"I couldn't tell—because mostly I heard Jamie. At first I thought she was on the phone, but then I heard her say something with the phrase *look surprised* in it—like 'You look surprised,' or it might even have been 'You don't look surprised.' I don't recall exactly, but the way she phrased it made me realize that someone was sitting in there with her."

"Did you tell the police this?"

"There didn't seem to be any reason to. By the time I got back from L.A., they'd said the death was an accident, so I figured it had just been a friend stopping by long before she took her bath. I mean, if it had been an argument, I might have spoken up, but it just sounded like normal conversation. Nothing significant."

Was it significant, though? I wondered. Could this person have dropped the CD player in the tub as Jamie lay there relaxing? But it was hard to imagine her taking a bath with someone still in her apartment—unless it was a new boyfriend spending the night.

"And there was no sign of forced entry, right?" I inquired.

"No—I wouldn't still be living here if there was."

"She lived *directly* across the hall?"

"Yeah. And it gives me the creeps every time I look at her door. It would be so much better if someone moved in there."

"It's vacant? Have they had a hard time renting it because of what happened?"

"Please, this is New York City. It could be *haunted* and they'd rent it. No, what happened is that after Jamie died the landlord decided to hold it for his nephew, who was supposed to graduate from college in December. But now the kid isn't getting out until spring."

I leaned forward in my chair, wondering what other ground to cover.

"Is her place set up just like yours?" I asked, looking up and down the apartment.

"Yeah. But flipped. Do you want to see?"

"What do you mean?"

"I've still got a set of her keys. She asked me to hold them in case she ever lost hers. I don't think the landlord's changed the locks yet."

"Sure," I said. I didn't know what I'd be looking for, but since I'd come all the way down here, it seemed silly to pass up the chance. I followed Alicia out to the kitchen, where she rummaged around in a drawer until she found two keys held together with a rubber band and a piece of paper that said "Jamie."

"You don't mind if I don't go with you, do you?" she asked, opening her door. "I couldn't stand it."

She waited while I fumbled with the keys, figuring out which one worked the lower lock and which the upper. I pushed open the door, found a light switch to the left, and flicked it. Nothing happened.

"Oh, the power's probably off," Alicia said. "Wait, I'll get you a candle."

She returned in a minute with a chunky candle, already lit and smelling like coconut. I took it from her with a wan smile and slipped into Jamie's apartment. I turned the bolt on the lock so the door wouldn't close all the way behind me and a little light from the hall could work its way in.

I was standing in an entrance hall just like Alicia's, though it was hard to see anything. To my right was a kitchen, a surprisingly decent-sized one for the apartment's square footage; this had probably been high on her priority list as a foodie. I peered inside. The only remnant from Jamie's life was a swag of cloth across the window.

To the left was the living room, and it was even darker in there—the two windows faced the side of another building. Not a lick of furniture remained. I could see that the wall nearest me was pocked with picture hook holes, signs of a life once lived here. There were two doors at the far end of the room. I could see the bedroom through one, so that meant the other must be the bathroom. As I took a step forward in that direction, the light seemed to dim. Glancing down at my candle, I saw that the melted wax had begun to engulf the wick. I didn't have much time before it went out. I stepped carefully across the room and swung open the door to the bathroom. The tub was modern, probably a replacement for an old claw-footed one. Next to it was a toilet and next to that a sink. There was enough space between the tub and toilet to have put a small table or stool—and with the faint glow of the candle I could see a socket on the wall to the right of the sink. It was possible that Jamie had set the CD player there or possibly on top of the toilet. I tried to imagine how she might have knocked it in the water. Maybe, as Alicia had said, she'd been reaching for something—bath oil or soap, for instance—and accidentally dragged the player into the tub when she sat back down again.

Suddenly there was a faint hiss as the wax smothered the flame, and the candle went out, leaving me in nearly total darkness. Shit, I thought. I eased my way out of the bathroom and, using my hands, crept along the walls in the direction of the living room.

When I was halfway down the room, I heard the front door open and close.

"Alicia, is that you?" I called out.

There was no answer, just the sound of someone's quiet footsteps coming in my direction.

CHAPTER 7

MY HEART STARTED to race as fast as a greyhound. Could it be the super? Maybe he'd heard noises and come up to see who the hell was prowling around a supposedly empty apartment. I could easily make up some song and dance for him, or even tell him the truth. But I didn't dare call out again, in case it *wasn't* him. I inched my way along the wall as quietly as possible. My eyes were beginning to adjust to the darkness, but I still couldn't see much. I heard more footsteps and froze in place. A form appeared in the doorway from the living room. I didn't know what the super looked like, but the figure was too tall to be Alicia. The head was rounded, as if there were a cap over the hair. I held my breath, willing myself to shrink into the walls. For a few seconds he just stood there, his head looking left and right. Then the movement ceased as he picked me out in the darkness. In one swift move he bolted toward me. He reached clumsily for my arm and yanked, trying to pull me to the ground.

"Alicia, help!" I screamed as I struck him in the chest with the candle. I felt the soft wool of his coat against my bare hand. He shoved me hard, so hard that I lost my balance and stumbled backward, falling onto my butt. I screamed again, louder this time. As I struggled to stand up, the figure turned and staggered through the darkness, out of the room. I heard the creak of the door opening, followed by the pounding sound of footsteps on the stairs.

I could finally see, because the front door had been left wide open and light was flooding in from the hall. I struggled to my feet, my heart still racing. Hurrying to the front of the apartment, I glanced cautiously out the door and down the stairs. No one was there, but two flights below I heard the heavy slam of the front door to the building.

From Alicia's apartment I could hear hip-hop playing, and I pounded hard on her door.

"You done?" she asked after opening the door a crack.

"Yes, let me in," I pleaded.

She closed the door for a split second to remove the chain and then opened it quickly.

"What's the matter?" she asked anxiously as she let me into the apartment.

"Someone came in there after me," I said. "A guy."

"You're kidding. Are you *okay*?"

"Yeah, just shaken. He knocked me down, but as soon as I screamed, he took off."

"Did you see what he looked like? There's a very creepy guy living on the fifth floor."

"It was too dark to see his face. But I don't think it was

someone who lives here. I heard him run down the stairs and go out the front door."

"Should we call the police?"

"Not a good idea. They wouldn't be too happy to hear that I was trespassing like that. Look, I better split now. But do me a favor, will you? Can you just be sure I make it out of the building all right? Keep your door open a crack and I'll call out to you when I reach the foyer."

"Sure," she said distractedly, her mind obviously trying to get a handle on things. "But what's going on? Do you think this has something to do with Jamie's death?"

"I don't know," I said, shaking my head. I took one step back toward the door and stopped. Something had just occurred to me.

"Alicia, when I buzzed you tonight, did you release the lock more than once?"

She pursed her lips, trying to remember. "Yes. I heard you buzz a second time and I figured you hadn't gotten the door. Why?"

"I *did* get it the first time, but after I started up the stairs I heard it go off again, and then I think someone came in behind me. I just assumed it was someone visiting another tenant in the building. But now I'm thinking that person may have been following me."

I could tell by the wigged-out expression on her face that the only thing she wanted to do at the moment was phone her boyfriend and demand that he get out of work early. But she did as she promised and kept the door ajar as I raced down the stairs. As soon as I was in the foyer, I called out to her. I heard a muffled "Good-bye" and the sound of her door slamming.

I stepped outside with my heart in my throat. The street

was crowded with people, some obviously hurrying home from work and anxious to let their weekends unfurl, others coming in and out of shops or gazing into store windows. There didn't appear to be any suspicious men lurking about. I hurried down the steps and up the street, staying close to the road. There was a cab on Houston with its off-duty light on. I ran toward it, flailing my arms.

"Which way?" the driver asked after he'd rolled down the window.

"The Village," I said. "*Please*. Someone may be following me."

He nodded for me to get in.

Back in my apartment I turned on the lights, gave a quick scan of the rooms, including the door to my terrace, and then flung myself onto the couch without even bothering to take off my coat. My heart was still beating hard.

Once I'd calmed down a hair, I mulled over who could have followed me into Jamie's apartment tonight—and why. On the cab ride home it had occurred to me that some squatter might have been living in the apartment and returned home while I was snooping around in there. But the apartment had been empty of *anything*. Besides, my assailant's coat had seemed, at least to the touch, expensive, possibly even cashmere.

I was pretty sure that what I'd suggested to Alicia was the real story: The person who attacked me must have followed me into the building by buzzing a few apartments and having Alicia respond, thinking it was me. Once he'd seen me go into Alicia's apartment, he'd probably waited one flight below or above. Alicia and I had spoken in the hall before I went into Jamie's, and he must have picked up the gist of what was going on. Once he knew I was in Jamie's apartment, he found the door conveniently unlocked and came in after me.

The bigger question, of course, was *why*? There was the chance it was a total stranger, a predator, someone who had observed me getting out of the cab and walking the half block to the building. In fact, at the moment he shoved me down, the first thing that flashed through my mind was that he wanted to rape me. But the time between when I'd jumped out of the cab and rung Alicia's bell was no more than three minutes, and it was hard to imagine that someone could have gotten a bead on me that quickly. No, that seemed as unlikely as the squatter theory.

I thought back to when I'd first headed downtown. I emerged from my apartment building and chatted with the doorman for a moment. Then I walked to the corner of Broadway and 9th and spent five minutes praying for an empty cab to drive by. Someone could have been waiting outside my building and then tailed me downtown. There'd been several other available taxis right behind the one I hailed. I only wished I'd gotten a better look at my attacker. It was so dark inside Jamie's apartment and I'd been so discombobulated that I'd observed almost nothing—other than the fact that the figure had seemed big enough to be a man—and he had a nice coat.

There was one thing I was sure of. For the last few days I'd been looking under rocks, and finally a nasty thing had crawled out. My fears ever since Ashley's death no longer seemed so foolish. Someone was after *me* now. But none of the clues added up. Was the man who attacked me someone who knew Peyton or Jamie, or was he simply hired muscle in some grand conspiracy against Peyton's business? What, if anything, did it have to do with Peyton's wedding? Had my attacker been trying to kill me off like the other bridesmaids or just scare me— or prevent me from seeing Jamie's apartment? I had a ton of questions, and not a single answer was in sight.

I realized suddenly that I needed to call Maverick and warn her. I found her business card in my purse, which was lying alongside the couch. Using the phone on the end table, I reached her at the home number she'd scribbled on the bottom. I relayed the story of what had happened and urged her to be careful.

"This is like a nightmare," she exclaimed. She sounded ready to cry.

"Were you able to reach Prudence?" I asked.

"No, not yet. I kept getting this annoying little recorded voice saying she wasn't there. I finally called her husband's work number and was told they were on a ski holiday in Switzerland. They're due back on Sunday night."

"Try her then, will you? I doubt anyone is planning to hop on Virgin Atlantic and go after her, but I still want to make sure she's in the loop. In fact, give me the number, will you, just so I have it?"

She read it off to me and I scribbled it down. We signed off warning each other to take care.

Still in my coat, I looked at my watch. Almost nine. Jack would be arriving shortly. I forced myself up from the couch, threw my coat in the closet, and went to the kitchen in search of a beer.

I'd originally planned to pick up some decent takeout food on my way back from the East Village, figuring Jack probably wouldn't have had a chance to eat and might want something. But I'd been so desperate to get home, I'd forgotten. My refrigerator held out little hope. The only thing approaching a meal was leftover pasta from my dinner with Landon: a hard, ugly ball of cold fettuccine that looked as appetizing as a human brain. I decided to order a deep-dish pizza and serve it with the leftover salad greens from last night. I didn't have much of an appetite anyway.

Jack called at ten, en route from LaGuardia. If traffic proved to be anything less than a nightmare, he'd be at my place before eleven, he said. I used the time to take a hot, sudsy bath, hoping it would take the edge off my nerves. But all it did was make me think of Jamie. It gave me the creeps to be lying there amid the lavender-scented suds.

As I was toweling off, I noticed that my face was drawn and that I had a tiny twitch thing happening above my right eye, as if a beetle had gotten under my skin and were wiggling around in there. *Gloss* was always running articles with titles like "Are You a Stress Mess?" Right now I could definitely answer in the affirmative.

Something had also gone haywire with my sex drive. Usually by Friday night I'm ravenous for Jack and the sex happens before anything else—sometimes on the living room floor, sometimes with half our clothes still on. But tonight my libido seemed to be missing in action. I had about as much interest in sex at the moment as I had in hand-washing my panty hose.

By the time Jack rang up, I was dressed in pink sweatpants and a T-shirt, and I greeted him at the door with all the energy and levity I could muster, which was next to none. He looked, as always, awesome. He's about six two, slim, with sandy brown hair and a face that has a "whole is greater than the sum of the parts" quality to it—nice blue eyes, a full mouth, a straight nose, but no

one drop-dead feature. Yet somehow they all come together to create something very handsome.

He was all buttoned up in a camel-hair coat and
Burberry scarf, and he didn't look at all like a guy who'd
been trying to get to New York most of the night. But then
Jack was one of those guys who never looked disheveled.

"I hope you don't mind that I brought all my stuff
here," he said, setting down his overnight bag. "I figured
if I took the time to drop it off at my place, it would be
midnight before I got over here."

"No problem," I said, smiling and trying to sound
normal.

"Hmm, pink," Jack said, gazing at my outfit. "Not a
color I usually see you in, but I like it."

He stepped forward and embraced me, kissing me tenderly on the lips at first with that lovely soft mouth of his
and then harder and more urgently. I kissed him back, but
I knew that, Jack being Jack, he would pick up on the dis-
combobulation I was experiencing.

"You still feeling pretty stressed over all of this?"

"Yeah. Plus there was a little incident tonight."

"Tell me."

I started the story with the two of us still standing there
in my foyer. Jack listened attentively, though at one point
he peeled off his coat and the sports jacket beneath and laid
them over an antique chest that my mother had given me.

When I finished, Jack had plenty of questions. But before I began answering, I led him to the kitchen, where I
poured us each a glass of red wine and nuked the pizza
I'd had delivered. We took our food and wine to the dining table and resumed our discussion. He pushed me with
his questions, trying to get me to recall details about the

second buzzing of the intercom and whether I'd noticed anyone behind me on the street before I'd gone into the building.

"Maybe someone in the neighborhood just happened to see you and decided you were an easy target," he hypothesized. "Then he followed you into the building."

"I know, I thought of that, too. But I really wasn't in the street long enough for some sexual predator to have spotted me and targeted me as his next victim. For the past four days I've been talking about bizarre coincidences, but I refuse to buy that tonight was a coincidence—that some unknown assailant just happened to show up when I entered Jamie's building. No, someone was stalking me tonight, from the moment I left my apartment, and it's obvious it has to do with the other three deaths. I think all three girls were murdered."

"Are you going to call the Greenwich police about this?"

"No, I'm sure it wouldn't do any good. It's totally out of their jurisdiction, and they'd probably say it's the kind of thing that happens all the time in New York. What I need is some evidence that shows that just one of the deaths was not an accident."

"Like what?"

"That's just it—on the surface there doesn't seem to be *anything* suspicious about the cases. Apparently the police found no sign of forced entry in Jamie's apartment, and it's hard to imagine her taking a bath with someone there. Robin had a reputation as a food junkie, so it's totally plausible that she might have gone off her diet. And Ashley—well, she'd gone over to the barn to check on the work being done, so it's within the realm of possibility that she fell off a stepladder. Whoever is doing this is maddeningly clever. Though I guess I should be grateful that I finally know for sure that something sinister is going on—that I'm not dealing with some aberration of the laws of probability or the Peyton Cross Curse."

"Why do you think he was so obvious in your case? There was certainly nothing accidental looking about what happened to you tonight."

"That's a good question. Maybe . . . maybe the murderer has killed the people who matter—the ones with incriminating information, for instance—and just wants to scare me off. Or maybe he's unraveling and isn't going to bother making anything else look like an accident."

As I was talking, I heard my voice grow more and more frantic. I took a deep breath and let the air out slowly.

"Here," Jack said, pulling me out of my chair and onto his lap. "Let me take care of you tonight. You need some TLC."

"Would you mind if that's all I let you provide?" I asked as I shifted slightly on his lap. "My butt's sore from falling on it, and I feel so stressed out I could scream."

"Not a problem. In fact, why don't I pour you another glass of wine and give you a back rub?"

"Sounds wonderful," I said, feeling a rush of tenderness. We cleared the table, poured fresh glasses of wine, and retreated to my bedroom, where I lit a few candles and peeled off my sweatpants.

Though we'd been dating steadily for several months and Jack had rubbed my shoulders and neck on occasion, he'd never given me an actual back rub, and he turned out to be quite fantastic at it. I shouldn't have been surprised, because as an athlete he had strong hands, and as a shrink, he was excellent at tuning in to someone else's needs. Using some lotion by my bed, he straddled me and worked from the tops of my shoulders down to my waist. Unlike most guys, whose idea of a massage is to run their hands up and down your back like a snowplow a couple of times and then expect you to be grateful, Jack took his time, using slow, deep strokes. I felt my muscles relax and my tension start to ease a little.

"Now where's that sore spot on your butt?" he asked quietly. Outside my window the wind had begun to howl, but I felt as if I were in a wonderful cocoon.

"Right side," I muttered, my face in the pillow.

"I promise to be gentle," he said.

His hands moved lower and began to knead. It felt amazingly soothing but also erotic, and suddenly, unexpectedly, I felt something in me begin to stir. I moaned without meaning to.

"No, no. I promised I'd behave," he said.

"Jack," I said, turning my face to him, "I want you, I really do. Besides, it will probably be the best cure of all."

"Tell you what," he said. "I'll agree if you let me do all the work."

I started to protest, but hey, I'm only human, and the invitation just seemed so unbelievably delicious. As I lay on the bed practically quivering, he took off everything but his boxers. Then he slowly stripped off my underpants. Pinning my arms back along my head, he kissed me tenderly at first and then harder, more intensely, his tongue thrusting in my mouth. With my hands still pinned, he worked his way down my body, taking my breasts in his mouth and letting me feel just the edge of his teeth.

I squirmed, almost unable to bear it. I suddenly felt rabid with desire, so different from how I'd felt only mo-

ments before. When I didn't think I could bear it anymore, he kept moving, working his way down my body,
using both his mouth and his fingers. The wind rattled the
windows of my bedroom as I felt Jack's tongue explor-
ing, finding, driving me crazy. I climaxed so intensely, I
felt as if I might go airborne. A second later Jack entered
me and climaxed himself within seconds.

Unfortunately, the state of bliss I found myself in
didn't last long. Though I wasn't plagued by insomnia
that night, I woke on and off, troubled by dark, undefined
dreams, and by the time I showered the next morning I
was feeling wired again.

Jack and I had bagels and coffee and decided that after
he had taken his stuff over to his sublet, we'd spend part
of the day browsing galleries in Chelsea. It didn't seem as
if I'd be in much danger in daylight or with Jack along
with me. As soon as he left, I called Peyton, and this time,
finally, I reached her.

"So what's going on there?" I asked. "Are there any
new developments?"

"I take it you saw the item in the *Post*?"

"Yes. Has it caused any damage?"

"Damage? That fucking piece was like the iceberg that
rammed the *Titanic*. I'm being besieged by the press. Two
people who booked us for parties have called to check on
what the cancellation policy is. And the candidate I had
for Robin's job pulled out—without any explanation."

"What does your PR agency suggest?"

"They want me out and about, acting totally bullet-
proof. David had a dinner with clients last night, so I
went to an event in town on my own. People were *gawk-
ing* at me—I felt like I'd been indicted for something."

I told her about my experience the night before.

"What?" she asked. I could tell I had frightened her. "I don't understand this. Why would someone do that to you?"

"I'd say it's because I'm next on the list. And Peyton, you've got to be careful. You may be on that list, too."

"But why?" she nearly wailed. "Why is someone doing this?"

"I don't know yet. There's a good chance that it's connected to *you.* Your wedding, for instance—like we talked about. Or your business. Someone may be trying to sabotage you."

In the shower that morning I'd decided that since I'd produced nothing to indicate that the deaths weren't accidental, I was going to come at the situation from a different direction. My next step was to search for *motives.* I wanted to return to Greenwich on Monday and begin snooping around. I asked Peyton if I could bunk down at her place again.

"You're always welcome, of course. But what's the reason, if you don't mind my asking?"

"I'd like to do a little research, including talking to a few people at Ivy Hill."

"Of course," she said. "I know the circumstances aren't so great, but I've enjoyed seeing more of you lately."

The Peyton curveball once again.

I signed off, telling her I'd see her at the farm around midday. I made myself another cup of coffee and took it into the living room along with my composition book. After reading over everything I'd written so far, I jotted down the details I could remember about my conversation with Alicia, my inspection of Jamie's apartment, and the attack by the person in the long wool coat.

Jack returned shortly afterward. We visited several galleries, ate lunch at a café in Chelsea, and then caught a movie. At one point I sneaked out of the theater to use the restroom. While I was in the stall I heard someone quietly enter the bathroom. Fear shot through me, until I peeked out and saw that the person was just a fellow moviegoer, a woman in her sixties dressed in a North Face parka. That night I suggested to Jack that we have dinner at my place. I made chicken with two vinegars and forced Jack to watch *Breakfast at Tiffany's* because I knew I could count on it to distract me.

The next morning, after a late breakfast, Jack headed off on an errand. His Village sublet was coming to an end, but the landlord had told him he had an even better place in the building that he could switch over to—and he was going to check it out today. We agreed to meet up at my place around two.

My appointment with Carol Blender was at noon, which would allow me plenty of time to go up and back before Jack returned. I hadn't told him I was going, fearful that he'd be worried about me being out alone. I was still anxious myself, but I didn't think anyone would harm me in the light of day. I glanced around as I stepped out of my building, but no one seemed to be skulking about. I hailed a cab on Broadway, going the wrong way, and gave the driver directions. As he made the turn on 8th Street to head over to Third Avenue, I looked behind me. No one appeared to be tailing us. By the time we were on the northbound FDR Drive, we practically had the road to ourselves.

The place Carol Blender suggested was way up on the

Upper East Side, on the corner of East 86th and York. I might as well have gone to Scarsdale. It was more of a coffee shop than a restaurant, and it was already packed with people. A woman with a red coat was standing right inside the entrance, waiting.

"Carol?" I asked.

"Yes, that's me," she said without smiling. She was younger than she'd sounded on the phone, about thirty-eight or forty, with shaggy black hair and dark eyes. She looked like the kind of person who didn't bother with perfunctory politeness, who made you work hard to get even a smile. She hardly seemed like a therapist, and I wondered suddenly if she might simply have been a friend of Robin's, someone Ashley hadn't been familiar with.

I let her take charge, since it appeared that we were in her neck of the woods. She told the hostess we preferred a booth, and I followed the two of them to one of the last empty two-seaters at the back of the restaurant. All around us people were wolfing down bacon and eggs, sharing their booths with bunched-up parkas and scarves.

"So how do you know Robin?" she asked as soon as we'd taken our seats.

"We were bridesmaids in a wedding together. Were the two of you friends?"

"No, she was a client of mine."

"You were her therapist?" I asked. So my original hunch had been right after all.

"No," she said. "Her nutritionist."

"*Nutritionist?*" I said.

"I'm sure she could have found someone good in Greenwich, but I worked with a friend of her mother's in the city, and I think she preferred to go with someone she felt she could trust."

The waiter interrupted us for our order. Based on her revelation, I expected Carol would go for something disgustingly healthful, and she didn't disappoint: an egg-white omelet, whole-wheat toast, and hot water. I ordered an egg-salad sandwich and coffee, without apologies.

"Did her working with you have something to do with the antidepressants she was taking?" I asked after the waiter had left. The restaurant was filled with the sounds of clattering plates and conversation, and I practically had to shout to be heard above the din.

"So you know about that. Yes, she was on this restricted diet, and she felt she needed some guidance. Needless to say, I'm horrified about her death. We talked just before New Year's and she seemed to be doing fine."

"The going theory is that she cheated on her diet. That she loved to eat and one day just couldn't say no to something on the off-limits list." I let the remark hang there in the air.

Carol shook her head. "No way," she said. "There is no way in the world Robin intentionally ate a food with tyramine. I know for sure that someone did this to her."

CHAPTER 8

OMIGOD, DID SHE have some kind of proof? I wondered. Was I about to be handed the smoking gun I so desperately needed?

"How do you know? Tell me," I urged.

"Robin was a total zealot about the diet," Carol declared. "There's no way she would have eaten something that was supposed to be off-limits for her."

"But you said you knew for sure. What did you mean by that?"

"I just *know*," she said emphatically. "Yes, Robin did love food, but she also loved what the drug was doing for her. It was the first time since high school that she felt really good about life, that she wasn't battling depression. I work with a lot of people on restricted diets—mainly because of heart problems—and most of them resent the hell out of it. But Robin didn't feel that way. She felt *saved*. That said, she didn't want to spend the rest of her life feeling deprived. That's why she came to me. She wanted me to create an eating plan that she could enjoy."

There was no smoking gun after all. The only thing Carol Blender had was her conviction.

"Was that really possible to do?" I asked. I felt deflated, annoyed that she had gotten my hopes up for nothing. But I was still curious to know more about the subject. "It seems as if so many foods were a no-no."

"Yes, the diet's restrictive," she said. "But there *is* some room to play. For instance, people think you can't have any cheese, but as long as it's not aged, you're fine. I told Robin to treat herself to tomatoes and mozzarella. If she felt the urge for cheese and crackers, she could have Boursin or flavored cream cheeses.

"And I'm a hundred percent sure Robin never cut any corners," she continued. "In fact, the reason she called me before New Year's was that she'd been at a benefit of some kind and had taken several sips of a cup of coffee that she realized after the fact had been flavored with chocolate. Chocolate's not a total no-no, but they suggest you really try to limit your consumption. Robin paged me, nearly out of her mind. I told her everything was fine, that the chocolate in the flavoring amounted to practically nothing. Someone who gets hysterical about that isn't going to turn around and fix herself a salami sandwich."

The waiter arrived with our plates and slid them onto the table. I took a bite of my sandwich as Carol sawed off a section of her all-white omelet, which looked about as appetizing as a braised washcloth.

"Okay, let's talk for a minute about how someone could do it," I said. "Any ideas?"

She frowned, thinking.

"It's possible, of course, they could do it unintentionally, not knowing about Robin's situation—like what happened with the chocolate. But Robin was generally good about asking what was in everything she consumed. So if that's not what happened, someone sneaked it into her food. Which wouldn't be all that hard. You could put cheese in a sauce, for instance."

"Wouldn't she smell it, or at least taste it?"

"I guess cheese isn't the best example. Another possibility is wheat germ. That's loaded with tyramine."

"And is the flavor pretty mild?"

"I'm a nutritionist, not a chef, so I'm not all that familiar with disguising tastes. But I know it *can* be done."

According to Ashley, Robin had left for Vermont in the morning. Had someone paid her a visit beforehand, bearing food? Or had she stopped someplace on her way out of town? That's something I'd have to ask about when I returned to Greenwich.

I'd elicited everything I could from the nutritionist, and I was anxious to bolt. I took the last two bites of my sandwich but had to wait until she'd finished her omelet, which she did at a maddeningly slow pace, setting down her fork after each bite. It was as if she were waiting for some all-clear signal from her stomach before she could resume. As I paid the check, she begged me to keep her posted, and I promised I would.

Since I was almost positive no one had followed me uptown, I ended up taking the subway home after walking four blocks west to the station on Lexington Avenue. My train car was half-empty and I wrote as I rode, scribbling down a few notes from my meeting. I hadn't learned much, but what she'd shared had at least bolstered my belief that Robin hadn't played Russian roulette with a wedge of Roquefort.

As I approached my building from the station, I slowed my pace and surveyed the area. A few people were hurrying down the street, braced against the biting wind that had kicked up in the past few hours. But no one was just standing around, looking as if they were casing the place.

I had a half hour before Jack was due back, and I decided to use it to draw up my to-do list for Greenwich. After making coffee, I took my mug and my composition book to the pine dining table that's at the far end of my living room. After thumbing through to a clean page, I jotted Phillipa's name at the top. When I stopped by the farm tomorrow, she'd be one of the first people I would talk to. She'd apparently been mad as a bull about being excluded from the wedding day lineup. I knew it was a long shot, though. Being banned from the bridal party hardly seemed motive enough for killing three women. Even if being rejected had fueled a murderous rage in her, wouldn't she have directed that rage at *Peyton* rather than us—a group of women whose only sin had been wearing butt-ugly dresses not of our own choosing and so much hair spray that you could have bounced a basketball off our heads? Still, I wasn't going to ignore any possibilities.

While I was on-site, I planned to chat with the salesclerk again to see if she'd recalled anything useful, and also Mary, Peyton's executive director. As Maverick believed, there was a chance someone was doing this to cast a pall over both Peyton's business and her burgeoning ca-

reer as a media star. Mary would know if there was a former employee who hated Peyton's guts—or a competitor
who was also vying for first place in the "I'm the Next
Martha Stewart and You're Not" contest. Of course, I
could also ask Peyton about it, but she seemed to be
mildly paranoid about everything having to do with her
business, and Mary might have a more objective view.

I also wanted to find a way to meet David's ex-wife.
Though David had insisted that it was far-fetched to consider her a suspect, Peyton had seemed very suspicious of
her. I wanted to chat with her and see exactly how much
she resented being the *former* Mrs. Slavin.

I'd stop at the Greenwich Library, too, at some point.
The newspaper in most towns that size featured a "police
blotter," a listing of all recent arrests, and I'd go back to
the last April and see if I could locate information on the
accident that had delayed us the night of the rehearsal
dinner.

Another place I wanted to visit was Wellington House,
the historic mansion where Peyton was married. Maybe
visiting it again might jog loose a memory of something
significant. If I could only figure out what strange thing
Robin had been referring to, I might be able to see a clear
motive on someone's part. So far I'd come up empty-
handed.

After refilling my coffee cup, I grabbed my purse and
dug out the pack of photos I'd taken from Robin's
drawer. I spread them out on the table in front of me.
Jamie had apparently given these photos to Robin for
safekeeping, so it stood to reason that the "something
strange" was captured or hinted at in these pictures. But
nothing at all seemed amiss. Beyond the two solo shots of

Peyton and the one of her and David kissing under the trellis, the pictures were mostly of the bridesmaids or guests—mingling, talking, dancing. There was a shot of Trip speaking to a man by the bar, a business associate of his and David's, perhaps. The only photo that wasn't of guests was a view of the ballroom just before dinner had been served. The tables sparkled with silver and candlelight. Mary was in the edge of the frame, speaking to a waiter. Just as Megan Bliss had said, Mary had been stuck playing two roles that day.

Suddenly a thought occurred to me, and I kicked myself: Maybe one of the pictures was missing. I counted them and compared them to the negatives. Twenty-six. They were all there.

I picked up my pencil and composition book again. As much as the whole wedding angle intrigued me, I didn't want to lose sight of the fact that the murders might have nothing at all to do with the wedding—or even the fact that the three women were bridesmaids. As I'd already considered, Jamie might have been involved in something that led to her death, then Robin and Ashley were killed because the murderer suspected they knew too much. If that was the case, I was clearly under suspicion now—either of knowing too much, too, or of butting in.

I also needed to keep in mind that my attacker Friday night had seemed like a *man*. I wasn't a hundred percent certain—it could have been a woman, someone big and wearing an overcoat—but that was my sense. At this moment, there were no men smack in the middle of the radar screen—though David's fight with Trip intrigued me. Of course, even if my attacker *had* been a man, that didn't mean the murderer was. The murderer could be a woman who had hired someone to try to scare me off.

The phone rang just as I felt ready to blow a fuse in my brain.

"Sorry to be so late calling." It was Jack. "I ran into a few complications."

"Everything okay?" I asked.

"Could be better," he said, clearly irritated. "The landlord doesn't think the apartment's going to be available after all. So my sublet is about up and I've got no place to live. I was tempted to strangle him on the spot, but since there's a small chance it *could* work out, I had to restrain myself."

"Oh, Jack, that's too bad. Do you want me to get out the real estate section of the *Times* ? We could even look at a few places today."

"Nah, that's a lousy way to spend a Sunday. I'll call some agents this week from Washington and see if I can get them on the case. You're not looking for someone to split *your* rent, are you? I'd even go sixty-forty."

It took me a few seconds to comprehend the full meaning of what he'd just said, and when I did it almost knocked the breath out of me. I couldn't be sure from his tone, however, whether or not he was merely jesting.

"Are you just kidding?" I asked.

"Yes. No. Maybe not. Look, this is hardly the moment to discuss it. I'll see you in about half an hour, okay?"

"Uh, sure," I said. His comment had left me pretty much tongue-tied.

As soon as I hung up the phone, my heart began to do this odd little skipping thing. Up, down, up down. I couldn't tell exactly what was happening, but there was one thing I knew for certain: It wasn't jumping with joy.

I circled the apartment aimlessly a few times, like one of those demented wildebeests on the Discovery Channel whose brain is playing host to a parasite. I finally ended up in the kitchen, where I poured myself a glass of Chardonnay from a near empty bottle I used for cooking. It was early in the day for wine, but I felt edgy, because of both Jack's comment and all the coffee I'd consumed. The wine tasted woody, like a cardboard box. I poured it down the drain and opted for a glass of Saratoga water instead.

Just sim, I told myself. Maybe Jack had merely spoken off the cuff and had never actually given a moment's thought to living with me. But when I'd asked if he was kidding, he'd said, "Maybe not." Did this mean that he had been toying lately with the idea of taking our relationship to some new level? My heart felt as if it were careening around my chest like a squash ball, hopelessly confused.

But *why*, I asked myself, was I feeling so weird? And why, for that matter, should his words even surprise me? We'd known each other since last May, and though we'd gotten off to a bit of a rocky start, we'd been seeing each other exclusively since October. And not just on weekends. Since my schedule was the more flexible one, I'd made a few trips during the week to Washington. And we'd also spent five days right after Christmas at Lake Louise in Canada for a travel piece I wrote. Jack would be moving to New York for good this summer, and I'd already given some thought—as I'm sure he must have—

to how our relationship was going to intensify when we were in the same city 24/7.

But summer was still a long way off, and up until fifteen minutes ago I'd told myself that I still had plenty of time to get used to the idea of seeing Jack more often and really figuring out my feelings for him. I felt as if I'd gradually been falling in love with Jack—but I wasn't totally there yet.

I decided the best thing to do right now was just to ignore the phone conversation. Jack's sublet situation might work out in the long run anyway, and there was a good chance the subject wouldn't come up again.

In the time I had before he arrived, I worked 411. I got the phone numbers I needed, including one for Mandy Slavin and her address. Then I called both the Greenwich Library and Wellington House for directions. There must have been an event going on at Wellington House because I could barely hear the person over the music and clinking of glasses. As I set down the phone, I thought suddenly of the bartender I'd talked to at the wedding reception. He'd stood in one spot for hours, not only serving everyone, but also surely surveying the scene—and probably swapping comments about it later with the other help. Maybe he knew something.

His name had been Chris something, and he'd been by far the best-looking guy in the room—about six feet tall, blue eyes, sun-kissed brown hair, a struggling actor, he'd said, who supplemented his income by modeling and taking on the occasional bartending gig. At first I'd assessed him as a jerk. That's because when he'd handed me a glass of red wine, he'd suggested that next time I should try a drink called a buttery nipple.

I'd shot him the most withering look I could summon. But before I'd had a chance to turn away, he'd flashed me a killer smile and said he'd only suggested it because he'd overheard my name was Bailey and the drink was made with butterscotch schnapps and Baileys Irish Cream. I'd smirked and strutted off. "If you prick us, do we not bleed?" he'd called out after me. Shakespeare delivered by a guy that hot was hard to resist. I'd refilled my glass often that night and flirted with him each time. He'd asked for my number toward the end of the reception, and I'd said I'd take his instead. But in the end I never got around to calling him. I'd just started dating an investment banker who made me weak in the knees (until, that is, I discovered he believed in diversification in matters of the heart and flesh), and then before long Jack arrived on the scene. Besides, during one of my exchanges with Chris I'd realized he was only twenty-five. I was practically old enough to have baby-sat for him when he was a kid.

But now the idea of talking to him made sense. I still probably had his cell phone number, I realized. I scrolled through my Palm and found it—and his last name: Wickersham.

As the phone rang, I realized there was a good chance it wasn't even his number anymore. But it was. An easygoing voice announced, "This is Chris. Leave a message."

I reminded him who I was and how we had met and said I needed to ask him a quick question. Mine was the kind of message that didn't stand a huge chance of being returned, but I wasn't sure how else to play it. If I tried to be coy, he might find it obnoxious, considering I'd never called him last April. If I sounded serious and claimed it was important, he might be worried that I'd given him an STD—until, that is, he remembered he hadn't bedded me.

The buzzer rang just as I was hanging up, and knowing it was Jack, I felt a weird twinge of guilt. I reminded myself that I was calling Chris solely for research purposes and had no intention of getting into any talk involving buttery nipples—or nipples of *any* kind.

Jack seemed perfectly normal when I opened the door, and I realized that I was the only one who'd been disconcerted by our exchange on the phone. He gave me one of his big Jack smiles, his cheeks red from the cold and the wind, and then leaned down to kiss me. As our lips met, we both felt the prick of an electric shock and jerked back from each other.

"Sorry about that," he said, touching his lip with a gloved finger.

"It must be really dry in here," I said.

My voice sounded weird to me, an octave higher, as if my vocal cords had been mysteriously tightened. I told myself to relax, to forget about the remark made earlier and just be myself. Another clumsy moment followed when I reached for his coat and nearly jabbed him in the eye. I felt as awkward as I had the one time I was on a first date with someone my mother had set me up with.

After I found Jack a beer and refilled my seltzer glass, we sat in the living room at either side of the couch, facing each other.

"Knowing you, you probably worked today," Jack said, stretching his arms. "How's your piece coming, anyway? You think the husband definitely did it?"

"Yeah. Yeah, most definitely," I said.

I launched into a long, detailed description of the guy—his upbringing, his complicated relationship with his parents, his failed career as a restaurateur, his checkered history with women. In fact, I offered enough information to fill an A&E *Biography* special on him. I knew it was the kind of stuff that interested Jack, but I also knew that I was doing my best to keep the conversation away from the sublet. By the time I finally wound down, Jack was watching me intently. He had a PhD in psychology, and he knew the early stages of panic when he saw it.

"So is he a borderline personality?" I asked finally. "Or—"

"Bailey, what's the matter?"

"What do you mean?" I asked disingenuously.

"What's going on? And I'm not talking about this guy who probably bludgeoned his wife to death."

"Oh, you mean why do I seem a little tense? It's just this whole situation I'm in right now—it's nerve-wracking."

"Has something else happened since I saw you?"

I kicked off the pair of white, beaded moccasins I was wearing and tucked my feet under me. I knew my fidgeting was only making me look even more like a psycho chick, but I couldn't stop myself. What I needed was one of those tranquilizer darts they use to subdue wild animals.

"No," I said. "I did pick up a little more information today. And I made plans to go back to Greenwich tomorrow—to see if I can learn anything else."

"Just promise me you'll be as careful as possible. No going into empty apartments and things like that."

"Don't worry. I'm not going to be cavalier about this."

"And I want you to call me—during the day. I want to know where you are."

"Sure, sure," I said, and took the last sip of my seltzer. "Of course." I was having a hard time looking him in the eye.

"It's because of what I said on the phone, isn't it."

I tried to make my eyes pop out in surprise. "What do you mean?" I asked, again disingenuously.

"When I asked about the possibility of my moving in here. It made you uncomfortable."

"N-not really *uncomfortable*," I sputtered. "Just surprised. I—I wasn't expecting it." I sensed my cheeks redden, and my whole body started to feel warm, like a chicken beginning its revolution on a rotisserie.

"Surprised?" he said, his blue eyes taking me in.

"Well, yeah. We'd never discussed living together."

"Well, I didn't know I was suddenly going to lose my apartment. I'm sorry that I caught you off guard."

"Not a problem."

"Really? I know it may be a little early for you and me to be talking about sharing space, but things seem awfully good between us, and I've certainly thought about the possibility of us living together one day. I almost get the feeling that we're not on the same page. Or is this just Bailey being Bailey?"

"Bailey being Bailey? What's *that* supposed to mean?" I asked, irritated.

"Gun-shy. Like last summer. You were nervous about jumping into a relationship with both feet."

"Oh please, Jack," I said, shaking my head. "We've been over that ground. I *was* a little gun-shy last summer, but I hadn't been divorced all that long. Being gun-shy after a breakup is perfectly normal—and prudent. I'm sure most *shrinks* would agree." I used the word *shrink*, Jack's pet peeve, which was a cheap shot—but my anger was on the rise.

"If it was an isolated incident, they might say that," Jack said, a slight edge to his voice. "But not when it's clearly a pattern."

"A *pattern*?" I said, totally annoyed now. "Aren't you forgetting that I used to be married? *That's* hardly being gun-shy. In fact, it's a bigger commitment than *you've* ever made to someone."

He started to open his mouth, then bit his tongue. I rarely saw Jack riled, but he was close to being there now.

"What were you going to say?"

"Nothing."

"Oh yes, you were. Something about my marriage. Probably some psychobabble about me going for the wrong type and knowing deep down it would never work out."

"You said it, not me."

I rose from the couch, livid. "That takes a lot of nerve."

"I'm sorry I've upset you, Bailey," he said, his voice softening. "Please sit down. I really care for you. And I know that because of everything that's happened in your life, commitment's not the easiest thing for you. I just don't want to get shut out."

I caught my breath. "What do you mean by 'every-thing that's happened' in my life?" I asked, almost in a whisper. All I could do was pray that he wasn't taking this where I thought he was.

"You know what I mean. Your father. His not being around much because of his job. Then dying when you were so young."

I felt tears prick my eyes, and if I hadn't been so furious, I might have started to cry.

"You have no right to drag that into our discussion," I said, my fists balled at my side. "And besides that, I'm not your freakin' patient. Is that what you've been doing the whole time we've been together, Jack—analyzing me?"

"Of course not," he said, rising from the couch. "Bailey, try to calm down." He moved toward me, his arms outstretched, palms up. I took a step backward, away from him.

"I don't want to talk anymore," I said.

"We don't have to. Why don't we go out and get an espresso?"

"I want to be alone," I said, shocking even myself by my declaration. "I think you should go, Jack."

He started to protest, then bit his tongue again. As the expression on his face altered from dismayed surprise to annoyance, he turned on his heels, strode across the room, and yanked his coat from my front hall closet. In two more seconds he was out the door.

Good, I thought. Then, momentarily, I was filled with the urge to run after him. But I didn't.

For the next two hours I just stewed in my apartment. After pouring myself a hot bath with a blob of bath gel the size of a jellyfish, I did one of those soak-and-sob marathons I hadn't engaged in since the weeks following my divorce. I couldn't tell for sure what was making me more miserable. That Jack wasn't here tonight? That the thought of living with him didn't entice me as it should have? That he'd infuriated me by using my father' s death to explain my reluctance to embrace the idea of cohabitation?

Was Jack right? Was my father's death dogging me even to this day? Did the idea of commitment scare the hell out of me? Had I picked my first husband because I knew it would never last? Yes, my ex *had* turned out to be a terrible excuse for a husband, but it's not as though he'd announced on the first date, "God, you have gorgeous blue eyes, and by the way, I'm a pathological liar and compulsive gambler." Regardless of whether or not I was a closet commitment-phobe, I resented Jack's turning the evening into an episode of *Dr. Phil*.

After drying off, I put on clean clothes just to make myself feel better and decided to eat dinner in the coffee shop in the building. It was already dark outside, but the entrance was only a few feet from where my doorman stood and I knew I'd be safe.

It was utterly freezing out, and the coffee shop was more empty than usual for a Sunday night. Clearly no one wanted to venture out on such a miserable evening. I ordered a glass of Cabernet, an English muffin, and a salad of tomatoes and onions—hardly the world's most exciting dinner, but the thought of a hamburger dripping with grease nearly made me gag. For the first few minutes I actually felt okay. I was still flushed with self-righteous indignation, and I kept myself busy sipping my wine and flipping through a few sections of the Sunday *Times*.

But by the time I'd finished, I'd begun to feel that

weird, ragged lethargy you experience about thirty minutes after you've sucked down a jumbo bag of M&M's and are in rapid descent from the sugar high. I'd bitten off my nose to spite my face. I'd tossed Jack out of my apartment just to make myself feel better but now I was on my own for the evening, with no opportunity to patch things up with him. And there would be no chance to make amends tomorrow—he'd be back in Washington. Plus, I'd hardly been very fair to him. *Gloss* had a column called "Marriage Secrets Your Mother Never Taught You," which always advised readers to conduct fights by using phrases like "I feel . . ." rather than "You asshole" and to take the time to sort everything out. But I'd made digs at Jack and then blown him off. I suddenly felt overwhelmed by the urge to call him.

After only a few sips of coffee, I paid the bill and hurried home. Anxious to get to my phone, I dashed through the vestibule, offering the doorman a quick hello.

"Hold on, Bailey," he called out to me. "Someone left something for you." He ducked into the tiny room off the vestibule and returned, holding out a manila envelope.

"Was it Jack, the guy I go out with?" I asked, feeling a wave of relief.

"Not sure who left it. I found it on the bench after I'd helped someone with their packages."

"Oh well, thanks," I said.

I walked into the lobby and tore open the envelope.

Inside was a piece of white paper, 8½ by 11 in size, with a single word printed in black marker. The word was *DON'T.*

CHAPTER 9

Wʜᴇɴ I ᴅʀᴏᴠᴇ into Greenwich on Monday morning, bundled up in my long black down coat and an itchy black cloche, there was still a ton of snow piled on lawns and in banks along the sides of the road. It was even colder than it had been the week before. Yesterday the temperature had begun what was predicted to be a descent into the teens, and if you were outside for more than ten seconds, it felt as if someone were ripping a large Band-Aid off your face.

I planned to stop at the library before heading for the farm, and I found it easily enough. The building was huge, obviously new, and I assumed it owed its existence in part to the fortune of some mogul who'd been in need of a big charitable gift-tax deduction. I pulled my Jeep into the parking lot in the rear of the building and headed up the large set of stairs at the back.

Before opening one of the glass doors, I turned and

scanned the steps and the parking lot behind me. The only people heading in my direction were senior citizens and mothers with toddlers who were practically immobilized in their fat little snowsuits. But that did little to assuage my fears. Ever since I'd stepped out of my apartment building that morning, my body had been humming so loudly with anxiety that I could almost hear it, like the steady, annoying whine of a tabletop fan. The *DON'T* note had freaked me. It meant that my attacker from Friday night had dared to walk right into my apartment building. What I didn't understand, however, was why I was being given a warning. Had Friday been just a warning, too? Did that mean that if I took my nose out of things, I wouldn't be shoved in front of a midtown bus one day? Had the others been warned in some way first? Surely Ashley would have told me if she'd received a threat.

As soon as I'd digested the note, I returned to the vestibule. The doorman had said that he hadn't seen who'd left the note, but I pressed him, asking if there was anything at all that he could tell me. What he did do was lead me outside to where one of the building porters was chopping at a patch of ice on the sidewalk with a shovel. The doorman explained the situation and asked the porter if he'd seen anything. No, nothing, he said. But as we turned to go, he called out to us.

"A man," he said. "He come out of the building a little while ago. I never see him before. Maybe it was him. Maybe not."

"What did he look like?" I asked urgently.

"I don't know. Tall, I think. Long coat."

A man. A long coat. Was he really the one who'd left

the note? If he had, it was surely the same guy who had assaulted me Friday night. As I let myself back into my apartment and turned on the lights in both the living room and the bedroom, my thoughts took a side step. Was it possible that *Jack* had left the note? He'd been wearing a long coat tonight, and the porter might never have seen him before. Did the note mean "Don't do this, Bailey. Don't be such a jerk"? No, that was ludicrous. No matter how angry Jack might have been, I knew for certain that he'd never do something threatening like that, especially at a time when I was concerned about my own safety.

I tried Jack's number right after that. I wanted to apologize for acting immaturely, for not allowing us an opportunity to sort out the problem. I also knew how comforting it would be to hear his voice. But all I got was his voice mail. I tried two more times, once as late as eleven, and still no answer. He might have been screening his calls, not wanting to talk to me. I never left a message.

At about ten after eleven the phone rang and I figured it had to be Jack. I let it ring twice, just so I wouldn't seem desperate. But it wasn't Jack. It was a guy's voice I didn't recognize asking, "Is this Bailey Weggins?" An alarm sounded in my head.

"Yes," I said cautiously. "Who's this?"

"It's Chris," he said. "You called me earlier."

"Oh, uh, sorry," I stammered. "Thanks so much for returning my call. I wasn't sure you'd even remember me."

"Sure, I remember. I've been hanging by my phone ever since you took my number, wasting away. I weigh about fourteen pounds now."

I laughed. "Sorry about not calling before. My work

got pretty crazy. I'm a writer, and I end up having to travel a fair amount."

"Understood. I've been on the road a lot lately myself."

"Acting?"

"Here and there. Mostly modeling right now. I'd like to pack that part of it in, but it pays the bills, so I'm stuck with it for the time being. I've spent the last month in Miami—that's where most of the work is in the winter."

"Is that where you're calling from—Miami?"

"Yeah. It sounded as if you had something pretty important on your mind."

"Important. And pretty weird."

I took him through an abbreviated version of the saga—the three deaths and Robin's question to Ashley. After I'd given him a second to express his astonishment at the whole thing, I asked if he recalled anything seeming strange to him that day.

"Gosh, it was so long ago," he said. "Lemme think . . . I mean, there was the bride. I don't think I'd ever met anyone as strange as her."

"What do you mean?"

"She's obviously a friend of yours, so I should watch what I say, but she was an awesome bitch that day. Fortunately I don't have too much downtime in my work, so I haven't done a huge amount of weddings, but of the ones I've done, I've never seen a bride so involved. Usually it's the mother shrieking at the staff or one of those wedding helper babes. But this chick was all over everybody."

"Yeah, well, she's developed into a major control freak since I knew her in college. But what about something more serious? A quarrel between two of the guests? Someone making a threat? Doing something dishonest?"

"Nah, not off the top of my head. I'll think about it, though. And you know what? There's a guy down here, another model, who worked that gig, too. I'll ask him if he remembers anything."

"That's great. I'd really appreciate it."

"I'm probably gonna be down here for a lot of the winter. But maybe when I get back we can grab that drink."

"Sure," I said. The chances of him calling in three months were next to nil, so there was no reason to go into a long song and dance about my being involved. "And look—I really appreciate your calling."

That turned out to be the high point of the evening. The rest of the night was pure hell. My insomnia, which I'd kept mostly at bay since I'd met Jack, returned with a vengeance, like some swamp monster that had been waiting in the ooze, with all the patience of an immortal, for just the right opportunity. I flailed around in bed, alternating between feeling fearful for my life and miserable about Jack. What if he was so mad he'd decided he was never coming back?

As I'd driven along I-95 to Greenwich today, I'd decided that the only consolation about having to spend the day in Preppyville, investigating three deaths, was that it would keep my mind off my spat with Jack.

Once in the library I headed toward a large room with the word *Periodicals* over the entrance. The person manning the desk in there was a dapper guy in his late sixties or seventies, dressed in a blue-and-white-striped dress shirt and tie, possibly a retiree who was just volunteering. I explained that I wanted to look something up in the police blotter in the *Greenwich Times* from last April and asked if they had papers that far back—or would I have to resort to microfilm.

"May I make a suggestion?" he asked. "If it's the police blotter you're looking for, I'd use the *Greenwich Post*. We've got a year's worth down that aisle over there, and they've got an even bigger police blotter than the *Times*. If someone so much as spits on the sidewalk, they cover it."

He turned out to be absolutely right. The *Post* was a small community paper, tabloid style in format, and as I opened the edition for the Saturday of the wedding, I saw that they had more than two full pages' worth of assaults, larcenies, fender benders, DUIs, and other assorted infractions under the heading "Police Watch." It appeared that nothing had been denied inclusion. There was an item about a dog biting a FedEx deliveryman, one about a guy arrested for sneaking into his tenants' homes and using their cable and computer services, and another about two girls who had gotten into a catfight in a bar and attempted to yank each other's hair out.

It took me only a few seconds to find what I'd come for—under the subhead "DUI." "Greenwich resident Andrew Flanigan, 22, of Davidson Street, Greenwich, was arrested Friday evening after the car he was driving ran a stop sign and collided with another car at the corner of Spruce and Horton damaging both vehicles. A Breathalyzer test administered by police at the scene showed that he was intoxicated. It was his third arrest for DUI in two years. He is being held in lieu of a $2,000 cash bond to appear in State Superior Court. The driver of the other vehicle, Sam Dirney, 47, of Cos Cob, sustained minor injuries. He was treated at Greenwich Hospital and then released."

So the driver who'd caused the accident had been drunk. That certainly upped the ante. It meant he'd be in more trouble than he would have been simply for running a stop sign. I would try to track him down sometime over the next two days.

As I pushed open the front door of the library, the wind shoved it back at me, forcing me to give the door all my weight just to get through. Stepping outside, I watched a woman coming up the stairs lurch backward as the wind whipped off the blue felt hat that was covering her head.

The first person on my Greenwich hit list was David's ex-wife, Mandy Slavin, and I'd decided that the best strategy was to drop by unannounced. Phoning in advance seemed like a poor idea because I was sure she'd tell me not to even bother. I had her address, and I'd gotten what seemed like decent directions from a gas station attendant on the way into town. I was just hoping that because of the weather she'd decided to hole up at home today instead of running around town shopping for shoes or whatever rich divorced chicks did.

I'd be lying if I claimed not to be slightly anxious about heading toward her house all alone. What if she really *was* the killer? But I was betting on the fact that owing to her divorce settlement, she probably had household help and wouldn't pull anything if other people were around. I decided that if I arrived at her home and it was empty or I felt the slightest bit uncomfortable, I'd hightail it out of there faster than you could say "community property."

It took me forever to find the damn place. Not that the

directions were bad, but her home was on a winding wooded road, and with the snow so high, it was tough to see the numbers on the gates. By the time I finally pulled into her driveway, it was noon.

It was an ultramodern white house with tons and tons of glass. Two vehicles were parked outside the garage: a beat-up blue Ford and a van that said "Bud's Landscaping." I was definitely going to have protection—if I managed to get into the house.

I rang the doorbell, expecting a maid to answer. To my surprise, it was opened by a woman I assumed was Mandy herself, a tall, stylish blonde, probably in her early forties. She was wearing tan pants, a tan turtleneck with an Hermès scarf knotted at the front of her neck, and diamond studs as big as hubcaps, which sparkled in the cold winter sun.

"Yes?" she said, curious but not unfriendly.

"Ms. Slavin? My name is Bailey Weggins. I know this is going to sound strange, but I need your help. I was a bridesmaid in Peyton and David's wedding. Three of the other bridesmaids are now dead. I'm desperately trying to figure out what happened, and I was hoping I could get some background information from you."

She gazed at me for a moment, not speaking, her pale blue eyes watering slightly as the wind whipped through the doorway.

"Why don't you at least come in from the cold?" she said, cocking her head in the direction behind her and swinging the door open wider. "And please, call me Mandy."

As soon as I stepped inside, I was enveloped in the warmth of the house.

"You said Bailey Weggins?" Mandy asked. "The writer Bailey Weggins?"

"Yes—yes, that's me," I said, taken aback.

"I've read some of your articles—in *Gloss*. They're quite compelling."

"That's nice of you to say," I replied. She'd caught me totally off guard by the compliment. Was she really a fan, or had she been busy researching me in recent weeks?

"I've learned the hard way, though, not to read them right before I turn the lights out at night," she said, smiling. "Why don't we go into the living room?"

I didn't feel any reservations about accompanying her into the house. For the moment, at least, she seemed hellbent on charming the pants off me rather than murdering me. Plus, as I trailed her down a long, wide hallway, I spotted a guy in a beige uniform and green apron, obviously from Bud's Landscaping, fussing with a huge vase of apple green flowers.

Midway down the hallway, Mandy turned left and I followed her into a stunning two-story living room. The colors were mostly neutral—white walls and curtains and two facing sofas covered in pale beige suede. But splashes of royal blue around the room brought it all gloriously to life: pillows and side chairs in blue-and-white batik, matching Chinese ginger jars, and ovals of blue on a large tapestry above the arched doors that led to the dining room. At the bottom-right-hand side of the tapestry was a big signature: Calder. A painting on the wall above the fireplace looked as if it might be a Picasso. If Mandy had any motive for trying to wreck David and Peyton's life, it certainly wasn't that she'd been stiffed in the divorce settlement.

"Your place is beautiful," I said, meaning it.

"It's a bit California for Greenwich," she said. "But I'm an L.A. girl, born and raised, and after my divorce I decided that since I couldn't move back there, I'd just bring it here."

"What prevented you from going back?"

"My daughter is only eleven—it's a very delicate age, so it's important that she not feel distanced from her father. I was about to have some coffee. Would you like some?"

"That'd be great," I said. I figured that since she hadn't been expecting me, there was little chance it was laced with cyanide.

We sat across from each other on the two facing sofas, and I slid off my coat. I was glad I'd opted for something a little on the dressier side—black slacks, a cobalt blue button-down shirt, and my black leather jacket. Nothing from Hermès, but I wasn't embarrassing myself, either.

As Mandy gracefully poured the coffee from some fancy-looking silver pot, I studied her. She was attractive and youthful looking, her blond hair fringed in a hip style around her face. Yet there was something oddly embryonic about that face—it appeared almost seamless and not quite formed in places, perhaps from work she'd had done to it. *Gloss* had recently run an article about the pluses and pitfalls of Botox and brow lifts and collagen injections that could super size your lips until they were as thick as fire hoses, but I had no skill at telling whether someone had actually indulged in one of these procedures.

"Here you go," she said, passing a cup to me. "So tell me. What type of information are you looking for?"

"Have you heard about the deaths?" I asked, taking a sip but keeping my eyes on her.

"I heard about Ashley's death the night it happened— a friend phoned me. Ashley had decorated her house a couple of years ago. But it wasn't until someone showed me the item in the *Post* the next day that I knew about all *three* deaths. Peyton and David must be totally grief-stricken."

"Uh, yes—of course," I said, caught off guard again. Could she tell from my stammering, I wondered, that Peyton and David were stricken by the experience, but not so much with grief as with concern as to what the fallout on them would be?

"I really don't see how I can help, however."

"I just feel that if I talk to enough people, I might stumble on something that could help me figure out what's going on."

"What's 'going on'? You don't really think there's some curse, do you—like the paper suggested? Of course, people do say that Peyton is from the Dark Side."

She offered the last remark with an impish smile.

"Is Peyton the reason your marriage broke up?" I asked.

She opened her mouth slightly, took half a breath, then cocked her head.

"Are you married?" she asked.

"No," I said, surprised to find the word catching in my throat. "But I *was* married—for a brief time."

"Then I assume you know that they're absolutely right when they say it takes two to tango. David *did* leave me for Peyton. But I hadn't been doing a very good job of minding the store. Men as rich and successful as David need constant vigilance. Trust me, I know. I stole him from his first wife."

"He was married *before* ?"

"Yes, for fifteen years. He was nearly forty when we met."

"Was that in California?"

"Sort of," she said. "I was a flight attendant, and we met on the red-eye. David strolled into the galley in his perfect white shirt with the sleeves rolled up and struck up a conversation. A year later we were married."

"You said you weren't as vigilant as you should have been. Any particular reason you let the ball drop?"

"To be honest, my heart wasn't in it anymore. Unfortunately, we didn't have what you'd call an *inspired* marriage. In fact, I'd been giving serious consideration to leaving myself. I'd signed a prenup, but it was a generous one. It guaranteed me a very nice sum if the marriage broke up *after* five years, as long as I wasn't unfaithful. That was the funny thing about David. He didn't have a problem cheating on *me*, but he couldn't bear the idea of being cuckolded himself. Anyway, there was no major financial incentive for me to hang in there. There was my daughter, Lilly, to think of, but . . . frankly, David does some things very well, but being an attentive father isn't one of them. I hope your friend Peyton isn't planning to have a family with him."

As soon as she uttered the last sentence, my mind flew back to my impression of Peyton last Wednesday: with her fuller-looking figure and slightly puffy face, I'd thought that she might be pregnant.

"I don't really know their plans in that regard," I said.

But I knew from her expression that she'd seen something register on my face.

"That must be Lilly, there," I said, pointing to a young blond girl in a silver-framed photo on a table.

"Yes, though she's about two years older now than she is in the picture."

"Oh wait, she was at the wedding. I knew she looked familiar."

"That's right," Mandy answered coolly. It was the first time *she'd* seemed disconcerted today. "Speaking of the wedding, you were going to tell me what your concerns were—about the bridesmaids."

"That's right," I said. Instinctively I glanced toward the doorway and out into the long hallway. The Bud's Landscaping guy was still there, fussing now with a potted tree. "I don't think there's any curse—and I don't think the deaths were accidents, either."

Her eyes widened, and she gazed at me for a moment without speaking.

"So you think the women were *murdered*?" she said.

"Yes—I do."

"What reason could someone possibly have for killing them?"

"I don't know. That's what I'm trying to find out. You're pretty removed from all this, but I thought you might be able to shed some light on it. Perhaps you're aware of someone who might have threatened David in the past."

She knew, of course, that she'd be on my list of potential suspects but that I would never come right out and say it. She stared at me, her eyes raised up and to the right, as if she were thinking. She was going to play along with me.

"Nothing comes to mind," she said, letting out a big sigh. "David's made a lot of money for clients, but he's lost money, too. People get very testy about that sort of thing."

"What about his partner?" I asked. "Did you know him very well?"

"Trip? What makes you ask about him?"

"Just curious."

"To be honest, I was surprised to hear that David had asked him to be his best man—they're more business partners than friends. But on the other hand, I can't think of anyone else he *could* have asked. David hasn't had much time for keeping up friendships over the past years."

"How do the two of them get along, do you think?"

"Well enough. Trip runs the hedge fund part of the business, and he's apparently a genius at it. David is more of a rainmaker, the one who brings *in* the business. So the two of them balance each other out."

She slid up the edge of her sweater sleeve and glanced at a gold Cartier Panther watch.

"You know, I'd love to chat longer, but I have people coming for lunch," she announced. "You're staying with Peyton, I presume. Why don't I call you there if I think of anything?"

"Uh, sure," I said. "I appreciate your seeing me considering I just showed up unannounced."

After she closed the front door behind me and I made my way to the Jeep, I considered giving myself a swift kick in the ass. The charming and disarming former Mrs.

Slavin had flattered me, then presented herself as someone eager to hear me out and even help, but she'd ended up cleverly eliciting information from *me*. She'd caught me off guard with her comments, and I'd managed to give away way too much: first, that I didn't think Peyton and David were prostrate with grief; and second, that Peyton might be pregnant. She'd also managed to learn that I was staying with Peyton. Probably the only reason she'd even invited me in was to find out what she could—and she'd managed it brilliantly. I felt like a little kid whose playmate has just tricked her into swapping her best Barbie for a single Pez.

But as far as motives for murder went, Mandy didn't appear to have one. She'd been awarded a nice chunk of David's fortune. And she hadn't been brokenhearted about his departure—or at least that's what she said.

Though I figured that Mandy's house was probably not far from Ivy Hill Farm, I didn't know the backcountry area well enough to find my way there, so I decided to retrace the route I'd taken from downtown Greenwich. As I sat in a snarl of traffic, I realized that I must not be far from David's office, and I made a quick decision to pop in there. I had no idea what I'd say when I got there—maybe just something about my concerns—but it would give me the chance to see Trip again and get a feel for him.

I checked the address in my Palm, asked directions from a man jumping into his car, and after enduring ten more minutes of bumper-to-bumper Beemers and Range Rovers, I pulled up to a seven-story contemporary building on Railroad Avenue. According to the lobby directory, the office was on the fifth floor. But when I rapped on the door, no one answered. Granted it was lunchtime, yet it seemed odd that no one was manning the phones.

I returned to my original plan and headed out to the farm. When I was still half a mile away, I spotted the top of the silo in the distance, and the sight of it once again made my stomach turn. In my mind's eye I saw Ashley lying on the hard stone floor, the halo of blood around her head. I glanced quickly in my rearview mirror. All I saw was the road and old stone fences covered with snow.

The parking lot of the farm was packed with cars. As I stepped inside the big red barn a few minutes later, I was greeted by an intoxicating lemony, garlicky smell and the sight of a dozen Junior League types in yellow aprons standing in a circle around Peyton. It was a cook- ing class—though apparently in its final stages. The butcher block center island was piled with steaming dishes, and from just a few words I could tell that Peyton was now dispensing her philosophy on the art of enter- taining. She paused briefly, caught my eye, and returned to her lecture.

"It's a good idea to constantly change the dishes you use so that you surprise your guests—and yourself," she announced. "My dinner plates are all in neutral colors: white, cream, and black. But I use them with interesting salad and dessert plates that I collect—Fiestaware, for instance, Chinese lacquer, and lots of eclectic antique pieces. One night lately, David and I had a small group over, and I served chowder by the fire in Bunnykin bowls I'd found at a flea market."

Oh please, was all I could think. The closest she'd been to any kind of bunny lately was the lining of her gloves.

Though I did need to talk to Peyton at some point, I was even more eager to connect with Phillipa. Thinking that she might be in the smaller kitchen, I slipped back out of the building and walked to an entrance at the far end of the barn, which, as it turned out, opened onto the hallway I'd been in last week. It was eerily quiet inside. I thought it was empty at first, but when I poked my head into the small kitchen, there was Phillipa. She was sitting all by herself on a stool at a small butcher block island, dressed in a blue oversize man-style shirt, though the effect was softened by a pretty necklace of crystal stones. In front of her was a plate of some kind of fritters, dusted with powdered sugar. She stared at it as if she were waiting for it to *do* something. When she glanced up at me in surprise, I noticed that she had powdered sugar on her lips.

"Hi there," I said. "Catering a party tonight?"

"No," she said bluntly. "Why?"

"Just wondering." I took a few steps closer to the island. "Are things back to normal here?"

"I'm not sure what you mean by *normal*," she said, pushing the plate into the center of the island with her perfectly manicured fingers. "Normal isn't a word I'd ever use to describe this place."

"I was just curious how everyone was doing . . . after last week."

"You'll have to ask them."

Gee, this was turning out to be as much fun as stripping old wallpaper. I pulled out a stool from the side of the island directly across from her and plopped down. She wasn't looking very good today. Her chubby cheeks were red from some kind of rash, and her blond hair was

styled in tight ringlets, like that ribbon you curl with scis-
sors on Christmas presents. I also realized that one of the
things that kept her face from being pretty was her eyebrows. She'd overplucked them and wrecked the shape in
the process, so that they resembled two pale commas
above her eyes.

"How about *you*?" I asked. "You must be feeling
pretty relieved you weren't in the wedding party."

"I was *always* relieved I wasn't in the wedding party,"
she said in annoyance. "I don't know how the rumor got
started that I was upset about it."

"You're Peyton's cousin. It would seem like you
should have been in it."

She blew her lips like a horse. "I wouldn't have been
caught dead in that yellow thing. It was proof that there
really is such a thing as a dress that doesn't flatter anyone. Someone *was* super pissed-off about not being included, but it wasn't me."

"Who?" I asked, startled.

"David's daughter, Lilly," she declared. "She wanted
to be a junior bridesmaid, and Peyton wouldn't let her.
She was livid, and so was her mommy."

CHAPTER 10

WAIT," I SAID, "let me get this straight. Mandy Slavin wanted Lilly to be in the wedding?"

"Well, I doubt she *wanted* her to be in it," Phillipa said. "But she's apparently obsessed with that little daughter of hers and doesn't deny her anything. I heard the kid has a Juicy Couture sweat suit in every color they make."

"And Lilly was okay with being in her father's wedding to another woman?"

Phillipa snickered. "I'm sure she wouldn't have cared if it was his *funeral* as long as she got the chance to dress up like a fairy-tale princess. She was the one who came up with the idea of being a junior bridesmaid, and Daddy consented. But when he ran it by Peyton, she ixnayed it immediately. And I got dragged into the middle of the whole thing."

"How do you mean?"

"The day of the wedding? I somehow managed to get stuck keeping an eye on Lilly. David doesn't have much family left, and the relatives he *does* have apparently had no interest in coming to see him pledge his undying love for the third time. And of course, all *my* relatives figured that because I'm fat and single, I wouldn't be having any fun anyway. Lilly couldn't have been more of a brat that day. I mean, her mommy had bought her an *alternate* little princess dress—which, honestly, looked better than the one you all wore—but that didn't cut it for her. Finally, about a quarter of the way through the reception, she starts bawling her eyes out and says she wants to leave."

That explained why I had so little memory of Lilly that day.

"Did you take her home?" I asked.

"No. She called her mother on her—get this—cell phone, and then I waited with her in the parking lot for thirty minutes until her mother drove over and picked her up."

"Mandy was *there* that day?" I asked, feeling the goose bumps spring up along my arms.

"Well, she didn't exactly help herself to the raw bar. But yes, she was in the parking lot. She gave me this incensed look through the car window, as if I were somehow to blame for her daughter's troubles."

"And then?"

"What do you mean, 'and then'?" she asked, seeming suddenly annoyed.

"Did she drive off?"

"How the hell should I know? I figured once Mommy arrived, my baby-sitting responsibilities were over. So no, I didn't see her drive off. I turned around and went back inside while she was sitting in the front seat, trying to talk little Lilly off the ledge."

No wonder Mandy had seemed momentarily disconcerted when I'd mentioned Lilly and the wedding. Boy, she'd done a bigger snow job on me than I'd realized. But what did it all add up to? Was Mandy knocking off bridesmaids out of revenge for the slight against Lilly? No matter how much she doted on Lilly, it hardly seemed like a motive for murder. Maybe, however, she resented the divorce and David's lack of attention to Lilly far more than she let on—and the junior bridesmaid slight was the last straw.

Another thought: Now that I knew that Mandy was onsite the day of the wedding, did that play into the "something strange" comment? Did Jamie witness Mandy and David having an altercation? Or Mandy doing something spiteful? I couldn't imagine what it could be, though. She didn't seem like the type to slash the tires of the honeymoon car.

I turned my attention back to Phillipa. The rash on her face—eczema, perhaps, or some kind of reaction to a toxic level of snarkiness in her system—appeared to have worsened in the few minutes since I'd arrived. I couldn't help but feel sorry for her. Her bitterness clearly ran deep, springing from experiences and injustices long ago. Had *she* been a little girl who'd yearned to be a princess and then been mocked or denied? Despite Phillipa's protestations, being banned from the wedding party *must* have bothered her. Maybe it really had troubled her enough to exact a horrible revenge. And she'd been missing in action for about half an hour the afternoon Ashley died.

"It must have been a drag having to deal with all that on the wedding day," I said.

"Is that something they teach you in journalism school?" she asked, letting the sarcasm work its way around the edges of each word. "Get people to warm up to you by acknowledging their *feelings*?"

"I don't know—I didn't go to journalism school. Look, you seem kind of annoyed with me, and really all I'm trying to do is find some answers. Something bad is happening here, and I don't want anyone else to get hurt."

"You mean, like yourself?"

"Sure. But others, too. What can you tell me about Robin and Ashley? Did you know either of them very well?"

"Well, we weren't bosom buddies, if that's what you mean. But I knew them. Ashley was in and out, but Robin ran the shop, so I saw her almost every day."

"What's *your* job here?"

"I'm part of the catering crew—also known as the kitchen slaves. I get to do fun things like stuff crème fraîche in four hundred red potatoes and add a dollop of caviar to each one."

"You don't sound as if you like it too much."

"Would *you*? I wanted to design jewelry, but it's impossible to get a job doing that. I had to let my mother beg Peyton to give me a job here."

"In the past couple of months, have there been any problems with the business? Problems, for instance, with competitors or clients?"

"There are barely any competitors left. Peyton's driven most of them out of business."

"Anyone especially angry?"

"I wouldn't know. Since you're interested, there is *one* freaky thing that happened. Late last year we had some near disasters with a few parties. The dates were down wrong on the calendar, and though we ended up pulling the parties together, we were short on food and it was all a huge mess. Mary thought the new office secretary had screwed up, and Peyton had her canned."

"Do you think that's really what happened?"

"I haven't a clue. I'm in the kitchen most of the time. But I can tell you this—it was almost worth it to see Peyton and Mary scrambling around in a total tizzy. For one party we were so desperate for food that we came within an inch of offering that dip you make with sour cream and dried onion soup mix."

She glanced up at a large black clock on the wall and slid awkwardly off her stool. Glimpsing her outfit, I realized how much her very appearance must antagonize Peyton. Her blue man-style shirt nearly reached her knees, and she had paired it with black capri-length leggings. On her feet were thick, lumpy white socks and filthy athletic shoes.

"I imagine Peyton isn't the easiest person to work for," I said, knowing I was running out of time with her.

"Didn't you live with her in college?" she asked. "Surely you must know all about coexisting with her." She crossed the room as she was talking and slid open a large wooden door, revealing shelves and shelves of canned and packaged food. She pulled down four or five items and gathered them in her arms.

"The other day when I was here," I said, ignoring her comment, "Peyton said something that upset you and you left the kitchen. Did you come in here to get away?"

"Actually," she said, her voice thickening with sarcasm, "I believe I went to the bathroom to take a chill pill." She made no eye contact when she said it, and I thought she might be covering up something. The question, though, was what.

"Speaking of Peyton," she continued. "I really need to get these over to the main kitchen. We're planning to test some recipes once the cooking class is over."

Off she went, without a good-bye. I felt sorry for her, yes, but she disturbed me, too. She was bitter and mean—and she seemed to like me about as much as she liked kids who wore Juicy Couture.

I wanted to catch up with Peyton, and Mary, too. But since I had the room to myself, I decided to use a few minutes to gather my thoughts. I pulled my composition book out of my bag and jotted down notes from my conversations with Mandy and Phillipa. Then I checked my various voice mails. At my work number was a call from a source finally getting back to me on my dead wife story, as well as another message from that reporter for the *New York Post*. On my home phone there was a message from Landon, checking in after the weekend. And last but not least, on my cell phone was a message from Jack.

"Bailey, let's talk, okay?" was all he said. I felt relief wash over me.

I couldn't wait to talk to him, but I didn't want to do it in the back kitchen of Ivy Hill Farm, where anyone could burst in on me at any moment. I tucked my composition book back into my handbag and found my way to the big kitchen. The cooking class had disbanded, and the work space had been taken over by Phillipa and two other helpers. Mary and Peyton were sitting at the table near the fireplace, which once again hosted a roaring fire. As I strode in their direction, they both rose in greeting from the table. Peyton even gave me a hug.

"I tried to signal for you to join the class," she said, "but you turned away too quickly. Where did you go?"

"I was just down the hall in the smaller kitchen. What's happening? Obviously the cooking school is up and running."

"Barely," Peyton said bitterly. "There are four fewer people than when we started. And we've had two dinner party cancellations."

"Those really might be legit, Peyton," Mary said. "The weather's been awful, and people all over town are sick. I think we need to wait and see what happens."

"It must be nice to have so much fucking patience," Peyton told her, rolling her eyes. Then she turned to me. "Have you figured anything out yet? About Ashley?"

"No, not yet," I said. I didn't feel comfortable going into details in front of Mary. "But then I'm just getting started."

"Well, I've got work to do. Are you okay finding your way back to my house later?"

"Yeah, I think so."

"Well, just show up whenever you want. Dinner's at eight. I hope you don't mind, but Trip is joining us."

Perfect. That would save me another visit to David's office.

"Not at all," I said.

"See you later, then. Mary, make absolutely sure no one disturbs me."

She strode to the back of the barn and flung open a door, revealing an enclosed wooden staircase. We could hear her stomping all the way to the second level of the barn.

I turned back to Mary, who offered me one of those smiles that involves only the mouth, not the eyes, so you can tell it's phony.

"Do you have a few minutes to chat?" I asked. "I'd love to get your take on things."

"Sure," she said, glancing over to inspect what was happening in the kitchen area. "But why don't we go over to my office in the farmhouse. We'll have more privacy there."

I bundled up in my coat and followed Mary outside and up the path to the farmhouse. The late afternoon sun was shining brightly enough to make me squint but giving off as much heat as a refrigerator light. The ground floor of the little farmhouse had been divided into a reception area and several offices. As Mary led me down a narrow corridor toward her office, I noticed a big office to the right. The girl who I assumed last week was Peyton's assistant was fussing with papers on the desk in there.

"Is this Peyton's office?" I asked. "Where was she going in the barn?"

"This is her main office, but she keeps a small writing office in the barn. As you might imagine, she's interrupted constantly during the day, so that's a place she can go without being disturbed. She's got a book to finish now."

"A book? I thought her book was coming out this year sometime."

"It is. This is the *next* one."

Later in the year, a small publishing company was bringing out a collection of my true crime pieces, hoping to turn me into the next Anne Rule. Just watch I thought—Peyton's books would end up best-sellers and I'd end up on the remainder table.

"Is that why Peyton hired you?" I asked. "To keep everything sorted out?"

She smiled in that automatic way of hers.

"There are actually two aspects to the growing Peyton Cross empire," she said matter-of-factly. "One is the personal celebrity aspect—press, public appearances. She's got an assistant who's helping her deal with all that, as well as a new PR firm. Then there's the business here—the store, the catering, the cooking school. That's what I'm in charge of. David made a big investment in all of this, and Peyton wants to be sure it's a success, that it's not seen as some glorified hobby for her."

We had entered Mary's office, a small room fairly cluttered with books and papers but decorated charmingly in muted greens. On the wall was a series of framed photographs of what appeared to be Provence—you could tell by all the lavender fields and big sunflowers.

"And how is it all going?"

"It's been a huge success. At least so far."

She took a seat behind a wooden table that served as a desk and indicated with a hand that I should sit across from her. As I slipped out of my coat and sat back in the chair, my eye caught sight of a bowl of perfect Granny Smith apples on the table.

"May I?" I asked. "I realize I've forgotten all about lunch."

"Of course. We should have offered you something when you were in the barn. Here, let me find you something to snack on."

From a shelf behind her she selected a box of crackers and placed them in front of me. Then she reached into a small refrigerator and pulled out a jar of something a light shade of purple.

"Do you like tapenade?" she asked.

"Love it," I said. "But it looks different from other types I've had—lighter in color."

"I mix it with some emulsified olive oil, which keeps it light—and a little egg."

She opened the jar and, using a plastic knife, spread some on several crackers for me. I took a bite of one, savoring the olivey taste and velvety smooth texture of the tapenade.

"This is amazingly delicious," I said. "And you came up with the recipe yourself?"

"Yes," she said, seeming almost embarrassed. "I help Peyton develop recipes for the parties we cater. It's one of the things I like best about my job."

"Speaking of catering, do you really believe the cancellations are due to the weather—and not to what's been happening?" I asked.

"It's hard to say. The next few weeks will be very telling. I'm just trying to keep from alarming Peyton any more than necessary. Ever since Ashley died, she's been a wreck. Maybe it's the cumulative effect, but she's actually been taking Ashley's death far harder than Robin's."

"How about you—how are you doing through all of this?"

"It hasn't been easy. Robin was a lovely girl, and we'd worked together for several years here. I practically had no dealings with Ashley, but still, her death was a shock, and having it happen so close was just terrifying."

The phone rang, and after excusing the interruption, she picked it up. She listened intently, her brow furrowed slightly.

"Sixteen," she said. "And the salmon's to be poached, not grilled. I'll be back over in a bit and I'll go over everything with you then."

Mary was clearly competent and sure of what she was doing, and from what I could tell, she used none of her boss's banshee tactics.

"What do you think about the three deaths—or at least the deaths of the two women who worked here?" I asked as she set down the phone.

"I know how odd it looks, and Peyton seems convinced Ashley was pushed, but I can't imagine anyone wanting to harm them."

"One possibility is that someone might be trying to destroy Peyton's business. Are you aware of anyone who could be out to get her? A competitor, for instance?"

She blew out a big gust of air. "To be honest, there have been a few *clients* who were less than thrilled lately. We did a couple of parties this winter that got mixed reviews, but they were only cocktail parties, and I don't think anyone's nursing a grudge. The bigger problem was a wedding we did a month or so ago at someone's home. It was a second marriage for both, and they wanted a small, elegant affair. They had a lot of money but weren't what Peyton would call A-list clients, and her heart just wasn't in it. She was supposed to supervise that day, but she got tied up at a photo shoot someone was doing on her and she spent very little time there. The couple claimed the food was lackluster and the service lousy. They complained terribly."

"Hard to imagine them *killing* anyone over it, though. What about any other problems? Phillipa mentioned that there had been a few screwups with the calendar."

Her lips parted ever so slightly in surprise. Had Phillipa shared private business she wasn't supposed to?

"Oh, that," Mary said. "We had a new secretary, and she unfortunately turned out to be an airhead. There was a terrible mix-up about a party."

"Phillipa said there was more than one incident."

"There might have been," she said, seeming suddenly distracted. "I don't remember off the top of my head."

"What do you do in a situation like that?"

"You scramble like crazy."

She seemed anxious to get off the topic. And after a glance at my watch, I realized that if I wanted to make a stop at Wellington House, I needed to get moving.

I thanked Mary for her help and for the tapenade and asked her to give me a call if she thought of anything that might be illuminating. As I left the office, the phone rang and I overheard her sorting out another problem, this one about a missing box of Bibb lettuce.

My Jeep was freezing inside, and I sat for a moment with the motor running, letting it heat up. Off to my right, through the passenger window, I could see the silo, casting a huge blue gray shadow in the snow. I wondered if anyone who worked at Ivy Hill Farm would ever be able to glance at it again without thinking of Ashley's death.

Before pulling out, I studied the directions to Wellington House. I got lost twice anyway. Finally on Old Hollow Road, I spotted the three-story gabled mansion in the distance.

Getting in was going to be tricky. I had decided to pose as a bride-to-be, fearful that being more direct would cause them to batten down the hatches. But when I'd called on my way from New York and asked if I could stop by today, I was told that the first available appointment was not for three weeks. I would just have to pop in unannounced and hope that with enough begging, they'd allow me to look around and even ask a few questions. I wasn't expecting to come away with a ton of info. But just being there, I hoped, might jog a memory of some kind.

Though the snow seemed even higher out here than it was in town, the driveway and parking lot had been plowed down to the gravel. Obviously events went on here all year long. After pulling in near a pack of four or five cars, I walked around the front. Everything seemed so different today from the last time I'd been here. I remembered that on the day of Peyton's wedding the dozens of forsythia bushes that rimmed the house were in full bloom, making me wonder if Peyton had made us wear those hideous yellow dresses so we'd match the scenery.

I reached the front of the building and walked up the steps onto the large wraparound porch. I knocked twice on the door and tried the handle. It was unlocked, so I pushed it open and walked into the foyer.

A dark-haired woman in a black-trimmed pink Chanel-style suit was standing by a desk, reading a sheet of paper. She glanced up in surprise as I entered. She let her eyes run from the tip of my head to my toes, and I could tell by the way her nose wrinkled that she wasn't fond of my getup. Maybe she'd never seen the cloches Ali MacGraw wore in *Love Story*.

"Hello, I'm Bailey Weggins," I announced as pleasantly as humanly possible. "I don't have an appointment, but I happened to be out this way and I was hoping I could talk to someone about the possibility of having my wedding here."

"I'm afraid you really *do* need an appointment," she said, clearly pleased to relay that piece of news. She reminded me of one of those doctor receptionists who seem totally invigorated when they get to announce that the doctor is unavailable to take your call.

"Would it be all right if I just looked around for a minute?"

"Unfortunately, we can't allow people to just wander around the premises unaccompanied."

"That's such a shame. I'm very interested in having my wedding here, but with my work schedule, it's hard to get out this way for an appointment."

She sighed deeply. "Why don't I see if Mr. Hadley has a minute to spare," she said. "He could at least provide you with one of our kits."

She walked off toward the rear of the house, looking back once in my direction—possibly to make sure I wasn't going to begin the tour on my own or dismantle the chandelier and abscond with it. While I waited I glanced around the huge foyer/reception area. The style was old-fashioned, but not depressingly so — walls decorated in pale gold striped wallpaper and covered with oil paintings, all in lovely carved wood frames.

Mr. Hadley emerged in less than a minute, swishing slightly as he walked. He appeared to be in his fifties, silver hair thinning on top, a wide, soft face, and an even softer-looking body, but he was dressed dapperly in a navy jacket, crisp white shirt, and yellow tie.

"Bradford Hadley," he said, offering his hand. "How may I help you?" His tone was effeminate, slightly snooty, but at least he seemed warmer to me than the Jackie Kennedy wannabe.

I offered an improved version of my spiel, one that I hoped would be more likely to secure a short tour. "I'd love to have my wedding here," I said, "but my mother has her heart set on a sit-down dinner for five hundred. I just wanted to make sure you could handle that number comfortably."

"Five hundred is *not* a problem," he declared. "When were you thinking of? We're completely booked for most of this year."

"Oh, I realize that. My boyfriend and I just got engaged, and we're thinking spring of next year."

I saw his eye fall toward my left hand, checking for the rock.

"In fact, I don't even have my ring yet," I explained. "It's being sized." It felt weird to pretend I was engaged.

"Why don't you follow me?" Hadley said. "I have just a few minutes before my next appointment, but I could at least show you the ballroom."

He led me through a large parlor, decorated in blues and creams and sporting a Steinway baby grand, and then down a long hallway toward the back of the house. On our left we passed a glass-enclosed porch with trees dotted with small oranges and the wood-paneled study where Chris had tended bar. Wedding day memories began to filter through my mind in little wisps and fragments. I'd been cornered in the study by a drunk and blustering friend of Peyton's father, who'd insisted that the best martinis were made with vodka, not gin, and then asked if I'd ever tried a threesome. Chris, observing my plight, had slipped from behind the bar and announced to the bore that there was a call for him from Hong Kong in the reception area. He'd stumbled off, never to be seen again.

"The house is quite fabulous—*and* enormous," Hadley said, pulling me away from my memories. "What's especially lovely is that people can spread out over many rooms, all of them exquisitely decorated. Guests wander in and out, sometimes getting wonderfully lost. We keep thinking we're going to find someone in a tux someday who's been here since 1982.

"Cocktails are generally served in the smaller rooms—or, weather permitting, outside—and then dinner and dancing follow in the ballroom. For a larger party like yours, we would need to set up tables in some of the adjoining rooms. Here we are—the ballroom. As you can see, it is *not* a small room."

It looked even bigger than I remembered, though that might have been because today it was almost totally bare of furniture, except for several long rows of gold-colored dining chairs stacked along the far wall.

"No, it certainly isn't," I said.

"I assume you've attended events here," he said.

"The Cross-Slavin wedding," I said. "Last April."

"Of course. A stunning event."

"Were you here that day? I don't recall seeing you."

"If I'm doing my job right, you're not *supposed* to notice me," he said. "I stay in the background, making certain everything is running smoothly."

"There was some incident that day, though, wasn't there? Something with one of the guests?" I was taking a wild stab, hoping that if something *had* occurred that day, he'd give it away.

"Not that I know of," he said, straightening. He looked truly taken aback, as if I'd suggested that all the toilets had gotten clogged and overflowed. "Well, I wish I had time to show you more, but, as I said, I'm expecting someone."

He led me back to the front of the house, flicking on lights in several rooms because dusk was rapidly setting in. I swung my head back and forth, as if I were at a tennis match, looking in rooms and hoping to conjure up a memory of something incongruous or strange, but nothing came to me.

A few minutes later, with Mr. Hadley's card and a promotional kit in hand, I hurried down the front steps. The temperature had dropped precipitously, and my breath came out in long white puffs through the inky blue twilight. Instead of climbing into my Jeep, I struck out onto a shoveled path that ran along the side of the house, just for a quick look at the outdoor property. To my right, beneath a foot and a half of snow, was a wide expanse of lawn where cocktails had been served the day of the wedding—leave it to Peyton to end up with a sunny April day in the seventies. Down the path, past a cluster of thick fir trees, I could see the carriage house, closed up tight for the season, and just before it an arbor with a snow-covered trellis—the one, I figured, where David and Peyton had embraced so passionately the day of the wedding. It looked completely different today, layered with snow. There was a sound behind me, something hushed, and I spun around. But nothing was there. It must have been the fall of snow from a tree onto the ground.

Back in my Jeep I fired up the engine, desperate for the warmth of the heater. Night was falling quickly, and as I drove away from Wellington House, its ground-floor rooms blazing with light, the terrain ahead seemed as bleak as an arctic tundra. The road was fairly deserted. Only a handful of cars passed me, and I caught sight of just one in my rearview mirror, far back, driving slowly. I found myself looking forward to being at Peyton's house, in front of one of the forty or fifty fireplaces and eating gourmet food.

Once back in downtown Greenwich, I found my bearings and headed out the other side of town toward Peyton's. I'd been driving for just a few minutes when car headlights once again appeared in my rearview mirror. One second they were small and pale, then they quickly exploded in size until they were a wall of blinding white light. Not only did the driver have his high beams on, but he was tailgating me. I didn't want to speed up—the roads were slick with ice in places—so I tapped on my brakes a couple of times, in what my brother Cameron once described as the universal "get off my ass" signal. But the driver didn't back off. Instead he accelerated, coming even closer. In the flash of a second, I realized the driver was after me.

CHAPTER 11

I HAD NO clue what to do. I was still a good two miles from Peyton's house. My cell phone was in my purse on the passenger seat just inches away, yet I didn't dare take my hand off the wheel to fish for it. For a split second I considered pulling into a stranger's driveway for help. But the homes were all set so far back off the road that I couldn't even see which houses had lights on. If I drove down one of those long driveways, I could find myself at the end of it with no one but the maniacal driver of the other car.

Out of desperation I leaned on my horn, letting it pierce the night. There was no one on the road to send an alarm to, but I thought the noise might make the other driver back off. It didn't. The car behind me accelerated, the sound of its engine roaring in my ears. It seemed only inches away from my bumper.

We were at the base of a hill now, and instinctively I

pressed down on the gas pedal, trying frantically to put distance between us. My Jeep hit a patch of ice and started to fishtail. With my heart thumping so hard it hurt, I tapped the brakes lightly just to get control again. The next thing I knew, my chest was hitting the steering wheel—the other car had rammed into the rear of the Jeep. I hit the brakes, harder than I should have, and before I knew it I was sliding into the left lane and headed right for a snowbank. I forced my foot down on the brake pedal, but there wasn't enough time to stop. The Jeep slammed smack into the snowbank. My body flew forward and then right back against the seat.

In relief I heard the other car roar by me. I sat there for a second, watching the taillights and trying to get my wind back. My chest felt bruised from hitting the steering wheel, but other than that I seemed okay. With one eye on the receding taillights of the other car, I turned the key in the engine. It had died when I hit the snowbank, yet miraculously it started right up again. I put the car in reverse and tapped the gas lightly. The Jeep made a loud groaning noise and refused to budge.

I tried putting the Jeep in drive this time and then reverse, hoping to dislodge it. But it was wedged firmly into the snowbank. Anxiously I glanced back up the road. The taillights had disappeared, but a car was now backing out from a driveway at the top of the hill on the right. I knew instantly what had happened. The person who'd rammed me had pulled into a driveway and was headed back.

I grabbed my purse. The smartest thing, I thought desperately, would be to stay in the car and call 911. Yet what if the driver had a weapon—a gun or even a crow-

bar that he could smash my window with before the police arrived? I needed to take another course of action.
After releasing the locks on the doors, I ducked down and
opened the driver-side door. It went only halfway,
blocked by the snowbank. I shimmied through the space.
Looking around frantically, I saw that there was a driveway about thirty feet below me—though the area was so
wooded, I couldn't see where the house was. As I scrambled over the snowbank my Jeep was protruding from, I
could hear the car slowly making its way down the hill.
The temperature was below freezing, but I was sweating
so much that I could barely feel the cold.

Once I was in the wooded area on the other side of the
snowbank, I headed toward the driveway. Running, it
turned out, was nearly impossible. Not only was the
ground thick with snow, but the surface had iced over,
and with every step, my boot would plunge through the
hard crust into the powder below and I'd have to ardu-
ously drag it out again before I could go farther. I wanted
to call 911, but I was afraid to stop for even a second. Finally I spotted the driveway through the woods, winding
like a dark ribbon. Rather than run along it, I decided to
stay in the woods, moving parallel to the driveway in
case the car turned in. I sped up, anxious to reach the
house. As I did, my right foot caught on the rim of the
hole it had just torn in the snow and I went flying. I hit
hard, with my legs and arms splayed on the icy surface.
My gloveless hands felt as if they'd landed on broken
glass.

I struggled up, near tears, grabbing my purse. As I
reached my feet, I heard the sound of a car engine
idling—the driver must have stopped out on the road. I

started to move again, my heart pounding in my ears, my right side burning. This time I tried to be more careful. Finally I spotted the house, a sprawling Tudor. The top floors were dark, but several lights were blazing on the ground level. After checking once to my left, I shot out of the woods, across the driveway, and up the snow-covered lawn to the house. When I reached the front door, I pounded as hard as I could. What if they didn't answer? People in Greenwich surely knew enough not to open their doors at night to strangers. As I stood there panting, terrified, I heard noises behind the door, and it was opened by a man of sixty or so.

"Please help me," I said, nearly breathless. "Someone ran me off the road."

He glanced past my shoulder, then back to me, trying to decide in an instant if I was telling the truth or part of some Manson family–like cult, out to rob and murder him.

"Yes, come in," he said, urging me along with an anxious wave of his hand. Maybe it was my stupid cloche that won him over.

"I'm Richard Crawford," he said after he'd shut and bolted the door. "Tell me what happened."

In his pin-striped suit pants and shirtsleeves, he looked as if he had just made it home from Manhattan and were about to imbibe his first cocktail of the night. After giving him the Cliff Notes version of the incident, I dug my cell phone out of my purse. I asked him for his address, then hit 911 and told the operator what had happened. Richard kept a furtive watch at the window. Next I phoned Peyton. Clara informed me that she was upstairs soaking in her Jacuzzi, but when I described my situation, she took the phone in to her. Peyton started to shriek when I told her what had happened. She calmed down long enough to explain that David had just gotten home and she thought Trip had arrived as well. Either, she said, could come and get me. I told her that I needed to wait for the police and would call back later with an update.

While I was talking, an older woman, Mrs. Crawford, I assumed, dressed in gray slacks and a matching sweater, hurried into the hallway, looking completely perplexed. I overheard Richard filling her in, and her hand flew to her mouth in shock.

When I got off the phone, she introduced herself as Evelyn Crawford and immediately went into kindly-mother-in-law mode, leading me to a couch in the living room.

"Let me get you some tea," she said. "This all must be perfectly dreadful for you, dear."

My mother had always discouraged us from accepting offers of food and drink in the homes of people we didn't know well, but I felt so ragged, I said yes. While I waited I made idle chitchat with Richard. He was a tax attorney, he said, who practiced in the city and had lived in Greenwich for twenty-five years. Above the mantel was a nearly life-size portrait of three towheaded children, who Richard explained were now all in their twenties. I figured they all probably appeared in Ralph Lauren ads as a sideline. Just as Mrs. Crawford returned with the tea, a black-and-white police car pulled up in front of the house, its lights flashing.

There were two officers, a male and a female. I described in detail what happened, including my suspicion that the vehicle that had run me off the road might have been an SUV—the lights had seemed high. I also told them that I'd been interviewed by Detective Pichowski on another case and that I thought the incident tonight was connected to it. After taking a few notes, the cops turned on their heels and headed outside. From the hall window we saw them set off down the driveway, letting their flashlights bounce around the wooded area I'd traveled through, and then we lost sight of them.

They returned about ten minutes later with news. Based on tire marks and footprints they'd observed with their flashlights, they could tell that not only had a vehicle pulled up alongside my car, but the driver had apparently followed me into the woods, stopping only a few feet in before returning to his car. My heart started to race again, imagining the person on my tail. If the lights hadn't been on in the Crawfords' house, he might have stayed in pursuit—and caught up with me.

The cops also said they had radioed the station and learned that Pichowski was not on duty tonight. They'd arranged for crime scene technicians to inspect the area first thing tomorrow morning.

That meant that getting my Jeep towed tonight was out of the question. They also didn't want me going into the Jeep to retrieve my overnight bag because I might muck up some of the footprints in the snow. The female patrol cop offered to drive me where I needed to go while her partner stayed behind and protected the scene. The Crawfords gave me their home number, and we agreed to talk in the morning. Despite the cold, they followed me outside and shook hands with me, wishing me luck.

The drive to Peyton's took only a few minutes—as it turned out, I'd been a bit closer to her place than I realized. The cop waited in the patrol car while I rang the bell. I could hear a flurry of footsteps, and then David flung open the front door, still dressed in his suit pants, dress shirt, and tie. Peyton and Trip stood right behind him.

"Peyton's been worried sick about you," David said. "We all have been."

I gave a quick wave to the cop and stepped inside.

"It was awful," I said. "But the police came right away, and they're going to document the footprints in the morning."

"Footprints?" Peyton exclaimed. "I thought this all happened in your *car*." She had changed since I'd seen her last, into black slacks and a soft white blouse. Her hair, in its trademark French twist, was damp around the edges, obviously from her Jacuzzi soak.

"After he rammed me, he drove up the road, turned around, and came back," I said. "I'd gotten out of my car by then and taken off, but he apparently started to follow me."

"This is fucking horrifying," Peyton proclaimed in something near a screech.

I had slipped off my coat as I was talking, and now I stooped to unzip my boots. For the first time I realized that my socks were soaked. Snow must have been forced down inside my boots as I scrambled through the woods.

"When exactly did this happen—and where?" David asked.

"About an hour ago on Rolling Ridge Road," I said. "I was on my way here."

David glanced at Trip, who was just standing there, taking everything in.

"God, Trip, you must have just missed it. You came that way, didn't you?"

"Actually I came the back route tonight," he said. "I wasn't coming from home. By the way, nice to see you again, Bailey. Sorry it has to be under such circumstances."

He offered his hand for me to shake; his grip was so tight that it pinched a little. How obnoxious, I thought. It didn't matter that someone had driven me off the road and I was still totally rattled by it. The guy had a power handshake, and goddamn it, he was going to use it.

"Look, if you'll excuse me, I want to freshen up," I announced. "I feel like a wreck."

"Of course," said Peyton. "Where's your bag?"

"In the back of my Jeep. I'm not going to be able to get it until tomorrow. Do you think you can loan me a dry pair of socks—and some Advil?"

"Of course, whatever you need. And then why don't we eat? You must be famished."

Peyton accompanied me upstairs, and while I found my way to the guest room, she headed off to her room for the socks. In the reflection of the bathroom mirror, I saw that I looked as horrible as I felt. My face was deadly white, and there was a scrape on my temple—probably the result of hitting a tree root or rock when I belly-flopped on the snow. And I had the worst case of hat hair I'd ever seen—it was matted to my head like the fur of a yak. I splashed water onto my face and, without drying my hands, used my fingers to fluff up my hair. From my purse I pulled out blush and lip gloss and used a little of each. The impact was next to zero.

"Here you go," Peyton said, coming into the bedroom.

She handed me two tablets and a pair of camel-colored socks. I could tell at first touch that they were made of cashmere, and my toes nearly whimpered in relief as I slipped them on.

"Just what the doctor ordered," I said, trying to sound chipper.

"What the fuck do you think is going on?" she asked, plunking down on the edge of the guest bed. She looked wild-eyed with worry. I knew that part of her concern must be for me but that she must also be anxious about the eventual ramifications of all of this on her business.

"I don't know, but I'm positive that the person who ran me off the road must be the same person who attacked me in New York—and that it's all connected to the deaths."

"Is there *any* chance it was just an accident tonight?" she asked. "I mean, could it have been some obnoxious driver tailgating you?"

"No way," I declared, shaking my head. "He got right up on my bumper with his high beams on. I'm not sure, though, if he'd actually planned to ram into me. That was partly my fault because I swerved and hit my brakes. But he was definitely being superaggressive. And then he turned around and came back after me."

"You keep saying *he*. Are you sure it was a man?"

"No—I couldn't see. I guess it could just as easily have been a woman, but my gut says it isn't."

"Do you think this same person killed Ashley?"

"Yes. Or he's in cahoots with someone who did. What I just don't have a clue about is *why*. The good news about tonight is that maybe the police will finally start taking this whole thing seriously."

She let out a long sigh, staring at the floor. For a moment she looked lost in thought, her eyes a deep loden green in the soft light of the room.

"Are you okay, Peyton?" I asked, resting a hand on her shoulder. Suddenly a memory flashed in my mind of the two of us in almost the exact same positions in our college dorm room—she on her twin bed, me with my hand on her shoulder. She'd just been ditched by a guy for the first time in her life, and I was trying to comfort her. She had seemed seriously distraught at the time but also ferociously determined, promising that one day he'd regret his mistake and beg to have her back. In recent years he'd probably kicked himself as he'd watched her on TV, flawlessly flambéing food in her perfect French twist.

"Yes, I'm fine," she replied, rising quickly and practically shaking my hand off her shoulder in the process. "We better go downstairs. The lamb will be like luggage if we don't hurry up and eat it."

I wanted to give Jack a call, but I didn't want to muck up the dinner plans any more than I already had. I followed Peyton downstairs, deciding that I would call Jack from my cell phone as soon as dinner was over and I was back in my room.

We ate in what Peyton referred to as the "informal dining room," apparently because the table only sat eight instead of a cast of thousands. The room was done mostly in reds, and there was a large bowl of pomegranates on the table, along with a row of burning votive candles from one end to the other. Clara didn't seem to be on duty at the moment, but there were two people serving: the young girl I'd seen washing the windows last week and a woman in a white jacket who I assumed was the cook. That had to be tough, making food to Peyton's liking.

"Are you feeling better?" David asked as he poured a 1983 Bordeaux for all of us in crystal wine goblets that twinkled in the candlelight. "You must tell us if there's anything we can do for you."

"I'm feeling much better," I said without meaning it. "And I'd love it if we could just enjoy the meal and talk about something else. I feel like I've already put such a damper on the evening."

"Don't be silly," he said. "This concerns us all. But I think it will make us all feel better if we try to focus on the food—and the wine."

The meal was pretty darn amazing. There was an endive salad with pears, walnuts, and Stilton cheese, which I'd learned to love on a trip to London. The main course was rack of lamb, just the right degree of pink on the inside and in no danger whatsoever of ending up in the Samsonite section of Macy's. It was coated, according to Peyton, in a mixture that included pistachio nuts, a crust she said she'd perfected for her cookbook. I assumed that her chef mainly followed her directions so that meals at her house were basically like Peyton cooking by proxy. Along with the lamb we ate yellow wax beans and roasted red potatoes tossed in mint, olive oil, and garlic. It should have taken my mind off all my troubles, yet I found myself struggling to enjoy it. My appetite was like a car engine that wouldn't turn over.

Peyton remained subdued through much of the meal, letting David play host. He was clearly practiced at dinner table chitchat. He brought up the stock market, politics, and how much he'd prefer to be on a golf course in the Caribbean right now.

"That probably sounds like a bore to you, Trip, doesn't

it?" he asked. "You're not happy unless you're bonefishing or dove hunting or doing something adventurous."

"Golf just doesn't do it for me," he said. "I can't move that slowly and still be happy."

"You're like Peyton. She doesn't have the patience for it, either. Do you, darling?"

"What? Oh, golf? Well, I enjoy it if I'm playing with you, David."

I didn't say much through any of it, just moved my food around my plate and observed the other diners. Having overheard the angry words David and Peyton had flung at each other last week—and considered the wedding coordinator's comments about them—I was intrigued by the dynamics between them. For starters, they just *looked* good together. They were both attractive and smart and poised, the perfect power couple. I could only imagine the dinner parties they held in the massive formal dining room, Peyton on her best behavior wowing the guests, David uncorking bottle after bottle of good Bordeaux and never ringing up the price in his head. As for their relationship, tonight things seemed *okay*—at least on the surface. The impression they presented was of two people in sync, in tune with each other's concerns and needs: For instance, David had mentioned earlier that Peyton had been worried sick about me; Peyton swore she liked golf as long as she was playing with David. Yet the odd thing was they rarely interacted. I wondered if they were still smarting from their tiff. Or, even worse, was the marriage not working as well as they had hoped? Maybe the age gap had turned out to be a bigger hurdle than they'd realized initially.

I also did my best to keep my eye on Trip. Unlike

David, he wasn't dressed in a conservative suit and tie. His was sleeker, maybe Armani, the kind you never wore a tie with. I knew he was considered a catch by some women, and he could certainly be categorized as attractive by most standards: the thick dark hair slicked back on the sides, the hooded dark-blue eyes, the strong but imperfect nose that suggested risks taken on rugby fields and mountainsides. But he was just too slick and wired for my liking. Tonight he seemed especially hyped-up, occasionally shooting his hands out from the cuffs of his jacket as if the sleeves were driving him insane. I couldn't help but feel that if I touched his arm it would be like accidentally brushing against a live telephone wire. And though he attempted to appear engaged, you could see by how tightly the skin crinkled around his eyes that his smiles were forced. What I couldn't determine was whether his disingenuousness was simply his way of coping with an awkward evening or due to something else entirely.

"And what about you, Bailey?" Trip said, yanking me back into the conversation. "I remember Peyton saying once that you were quite the traveler."

"I write a few travel pieces every year, mostly on Europe and South America. Nothing especially glamorous, though."

Dessert appeared to be the world's most perfect apple tart, but I might as well have been served a wedge of the sofa—I just couldn't summon any culinary enthusiasm. I took two bites and put my fork down. I felt positively fried, and thoughts about the accident kept creeping back into my brain. When Peyton suggested that we all have coffee in the library, I begged off, explaining that I needed to go upstairs and make several calls. I must have looked like a basket case because no one made any attempt to talk me out of it.

As soon as I was in my room, I tried Jack's number and felt a huge sense of relief when he answered on the second ring. I'd already decided that I was going to wait a day or two to tell him about what had happened on the road. If I shared it tonight, the conversation would be all about me—my situation, my safety—when it really needed to be about *us*.

"Hey, it's good to hear your voice," he said.

"Same here."

"Are you home? I just tried you there five minutes ago."

"No, I'm spending the night in Greenwich—at Peyton's. We just had lamb that was probably airfreighted from New Zealand earlier in the day."

"What's happening—any developments?"

"Not much. I spent some time at the library doing research—and I've been talking to people."

"You're being careful, right?"

"Of course, of course. How about you—what's going on?"

"I had a girl faint in class today. I'm not sure if I made her swoon with my dashing good looks or I bored her to tears with my lecture."

"I'd say it would have to be the former."

"Well, it's nice to see I can still have that effect on some women."

"Jack, you know you have that effect on me."

"Do I? I seemed to be having just the opposite effect

the other night. I'm sorry about what happened, by the way."

"Me too. I was totally wrong to tell you to leave my apartment. You'd never do something like that to me. I owed it to you to talk things out."

"We don't always think a hundred percent rationally during a fight. I was treading on some pretty sensitive ground with you, and I clearly didn't know when to back off. I'm surprised they haven't rescinded my license as a practicing psychologist."

"What do you mean, *sensitive* ground?" I asked, feeling suddenly annoyed. "My reaction the other night had nothing to do with you being on sensitive ground. I just don't think you have any right to psychoanalyze me."

"You're right. Look, let's move on, okay? I'm sorry— and I miss you. I'd love to see you this weekend."

"Of course. I'm looking forward to seeing you, too."

We talked for a few more minutes, just dumb stuff mostly. He signed off, reminding me one more time to be careful. I hung up, feeling relieved and yet with an unexpected sense of disquiet. Maybe because I hadn't disclosed the night's events and was now feeling a lump in my stomach because of it. Or maybe I was just bugged by the fact that Jack refused to stop *analyzing* me.

Once again without any jammies, I stripped off my pants and shirt but left on my underwear and my silk camisole. While washing up in the bathroom, I discovered a fresh, waffled bathrobe on the back of the door that I must not have noticed the last time I was here. The only thing that kept the guest room from being like a hotel was the fact that there was no breakfast order card to hang on the outer doorknob.

Wrapped up tight in the bathrobe, I turned the bed pillows on their sides and crawled onto the bed with my composition book. Then I just started scribbling. With some time finally to myself, questions emerged. How had the driver found me? I had told no one I was going to Wellington House, so he must have followed me from the farm and waited along the road until I was done at the house. I recalled seeing headlights far behind me as I drove toward downtown Greenwich. Unless the driver had just coincidentally spotted me on Greenwich Avenue, he had clearly been tailing me for all or part of the day.

All of which brought me back to the question I had scrawled last week in large letters in my composition book: *Why?* What possible reason would someone have for methodically knocking off bridesmaids? I considered all the possibilities again. There seemed to be three general areas for me to focus on.

Number one, someone was doing the killing in order to hurt Peyton and her business. It wasn't the most direct form of attack, but as Maverick had pointed out, the "ether" approach could be particularly effective. And, in fact, Peyton's catering business had already taken a few hits. I was curious about the scheduling mix-ups that had occurred several months ago. They'd been blamed on a careless secretary, yet I wanted to learn more about them. If someone's goal was to see Peyton's business tank, they might have started with mucking up her schedule and then, when that didn't have the desired effect, escalated things.

Second, the deaths might have something to do with the wedding. Jamie, and perhaps Robin—maybe even all the bridesmaids—might have witnessed something that day.

Or the wedding might have seriously irked someone—
Mandy, for instance, or Phillipa.

Last, the deaths might have *nothing* to do with either
Peyton or the wedding. Perhaps Jamie was killed by
someone she knew personally or through some shady
dealings she was involved in—drugs, for instance. After
several months of snooping around or thinking about it,
Robin put two and two together and confronted the killer
or let the info slip somehow. That meant she had to die.
And Ashley was killed shortly afterward because the
killer suspected that, as Robin's roommate, she also knew
more than she should have.

Whoever the killer was, he or she was obviously extremely clever. Each death was so different, yet all three
managed to look totally accidental. Which raised the
same question about the incident tonight that I'd had
about the attack in New York. Why suddenly be so obvious? Was the killer unraveling?

My head felt ready to explode in pure frustration, and
my chest was starting to really ache, despite the Advil I'd
swallowed. I tossed the composition book back into my
purse, shucked off the robe, and crawled between the
covers of the bed. I'd lain there only a few minutes when
I knew, despite how exhausted I felt, that sleep would be
elusive, like trying to catch up with someone in a dream.
After a few minutes of lying in the darkness, I heard footsteps, someone moving about at the far end of the hall. I
figured it must be David and Peyton coming to bed. I
gave it a few minutes and then switched the light back on.
Dressed in the robe, I opened the door and crept down the
stairs again. There was brandy in the library, and I was

hoping a few swigs would both ease my pain and calm me down.

I was halfway down the stairs when I heard voices— David's and Trip's—and the crack of billiard balls. They were playing pool toward the back of the house in the pub-style room that I'd glimpsed on my tour. Peyton, I realized, must have been the one who'd retired for the night. I tiptoed down the rest of the stairs and slipped into the library, where the embers of a fire still glowed like lava in the hearth. I found a bottle of Courvoisier on the bar, as well as a brandy snifter, and poured myself a decent-size helping.

"That must have been quite a fright you had tonight."

I jerked around so fast, the brandy bottle almost slid out of my grasp. Trip was behind me, jacket off, sleeves rolled. He looked at me intensely with his hooded eyes. Clearly the Bordeaux had taken some of the jangle out of his nerves because he seemed less jittery.

"I guess you could say that," I replied, trying not to act as flustered as I now felt. He was standing too deep into my space.

"May I?"

"Excuse me?" I asked.

"The brandy. I'd like another hit myself."

"Sure," I said, offering him the bottle. He smiled smarmily, like a carnie. As he took the bottle from me, our fingers touched for a split second, creeping me out.

"We ought to grab a drink together sometime," he said. "I get to the city fairly often."

"Thanks for the offer," I said, meeting his gaze, "but I'm seeing someone steadily these days."

"Too bad. Well, things have been known to change. Let me know if you're on the market again."

Eeeww, was all I could think as he slipped out of the room. I hurried back upstairs and nursed my brandy, sitting up in bed with the lights off. What had he meant by that comment that things change? Had I sounded hesitant or ambivalent when I'd stated my romantic situation? Did he really think he had a chance with me?

I took one last sip of brandy and closed my eyes. Thirty seconds later my cell phone rang next to my head. Jack, I thought, just checking to see if I was okay.

"Bailey, sorry to call so late, but I thought you'd want to know this."

"Who is this?" I asked. The voice was friendly and vaguely familiar, but I couldn't place it.

"It's Chris. Remember?"

"Oh, sorry," I exclaimed. I'd done the exact same thing to him the other night.

"I know it's late, but like I said, I thought you'd want to know. I bumped into that other bartender, Kyle—you know, the one I mentioned? I started asking him questions, and—well, he says something strange *did* happen at that wedding."

CHAPTER 12

WITH THE CELL phone squeezed between my shoulder and ear, I hoisted myself onto my elbows and fumbled for the light switch.

"What was it?" I exclaimed as the bedside lamp illuminated half of the room.

"I have no idea. He was very cagey with me. But I could tell he wasn't bullshitting. As soon as I asked him, he got this look in his eyes, and I could see something register with him. I tried to get him to cough it up, but he kept insisting he needed to tell you personally."

"Can you stand over him and force him to call me? I hate to make you go to any trouble, but it's really a life-and-death matter. Things have intensified since I last talked to you."

"How do you mean?"

"Someone followed me tonight. And they ended up running me off the road."

"Hey, that's pretty serious. But I'm afraid when Kyle says he wants to tell you personally, he means *in person*. Is there any chance you could come down here?"

"To *Miami*?"

"Yeah. Look, this dude Kyle is a jerk. I mean, he once told me he likes to fly under the IRS radar, so that gives you an idea what you're dealing with. But I'm almost positive he's telling the truth when he says he knows something. And he was adamant that he needed to tell you directly."

"But even if I came down there, what guarantee would I have that he'd still be around?"

"Oh, he'll be here. The only reason to go to New York would be for some major ad campaign—and that ain't gonna happen for him."

"Gosh, let me think about it," I said, my mind racing. "Can I give you a call tomorrow?"

"Sure. I'm shooting part of the day, but just leave a message on my cell and I'll get back to you."

I thanked him for calling me with the info and said good night. Then I just lay in bed for a while with the light on, contemplating what I'd learned. Though I had no clue whether it had led to three deaths, I finally had confirmation that *something* had happened at the wedding. Unfortunately, I was going to learn what it was only if I flew to Miami and talked to some male model, who from the sound of it had an IQ in the double digits. And booking a flight at the last minute wouldn't be cheap.

A thought gurgled up to the top of my brain. There was a woman in Ft. Lauderdale I was planning to interview for my next *Gloss* article—on identity theft. I'd spoken to her briefly as I was putting the proposal together, and we'd agreed that I'd fly down there in early February when I started my research. Maybe I could move up the interview and kill two birds with one stone. And that way *Gloss* would pick up the tab. Of course, if the police finally kicked into action today, I might not have to go at all—I could just give them the lead.

The rest of the night was awful. I thrashed around in bed for what seemed like hours, unable to get my mind off my accident and Chris's revelation. My chest hurt like hell, and my neck was sore, too, from being jerked when I hit the snowbank. I also just plain felt scared. I knew that the Slavin residence probably had a top-of-the-line security system, but beyond the gates there was someone who wanted to harm me, and he might very well be waiting for me in the morning. When I finally did drift off, I had one of those four-alarm nightmares you get only every couple of years. I was wading in a lake and looked up to see someone sinister watching me from the shore. I started running, but I was running in water and each step was like lifting my leg through molasses. The sheer terror of it finally woke me. I sat up in bed, nearly shaking, my bruised chest damp with sweat.

It took forever to fall back to sleep, and I awoke just after six. Though I'd barely touched the wine and had had only a few sips of brandy, I felt hung over from fatigue, as if I'd downed three jumbo-size frozen margaritas without realizing it. Part of me, a little part, yearned to wriggle down into the covers and just stay there, hibernating. But the other part, the bigger part, was anxious to be up and moving. Since Pichowski obviously worked the day shift, I wanted to hook up with him as soon as possible.

I took a shower and put on the same clothes from yesterday. A fire was already burning in the hall fireplace when I descended the stairs. Clara was standing just to the left of the fireplace, talking on the phone. She pointed toward the kitchen, which I took to mean that food or people or both were waiting there.

This time Peyton and David were sitting at the table. He was hiding behind *The Wall Street Journal*, and Peyton, dressed in a blue wrap dress, was frowning at her plate in disapproval.

"What is it about the word *firm* that's so hard to grasp?" she asked, though David did nothing to acknowledge the question. "Every day I say firm, and every day I get runny."

I suspected she thought I was Clara or one of the other servants and the statement was being made for that person's benefit, because when she turned her head and saw me, she seemed surprised.

"Oh, you're up," she said. "We weren't sure if we should wake you or not."

"That's okay. Good morning, David."

"Good morning, Bailey. I hope you're feeling better today."

"Do you want eggs?" Peyton asked before I had time to answer. "I can't guarantee they'll be to your satisfaction because that seems to be a very big hurdle for us here, but we can put in an order and see what happens."

"No, just a bagel or something," I said, noticing the same overflowing muffin basket that had been there last week. I pulled out a chair, and just as I did, David dropped the paper and rose from the table.

"If you'll excuse me, I've got to make a call before I leave today," he announced. "How are you getting out of here, Bailey? Will you be able to retrieve your car this morning?"

"I hope so," I said, pouring myself coffee from an in-sulated silver pitcher on the table. "I'm going to call the police as soon as I've had breakfast. Hopefully I can pick up my car sometime this morning."

"Why don't we have our caretaker drop you off there? He's an able-bodied guy, and he can make sure no one tries to pull anything this time."

"I'd appreciate that," I said.

As he left the room, he leaned down and kissed Peyton on the top of her head. She followed his retreating backside with admiration in her eyes.

"Nice, huh?" she asked as the door swung back and forth. She said it in a slightly lascivious way, as if Brad Pitt had just left the room wrapped in nothing but a towel.

"Definitely," I said, hoping she couldn't tell from my expression that for me David held about as much sex appeal as a gas pump. "You guys happy and everything?"

"How could we not be? Of course, these days it's hard to concentrate on my marriage when my life is going to hell. Mary called this morning to say we lost a very big party. They're *claiming* they have to postpone it for personal reasons, but I'm sure they're freaked out about this whole Peyton Cross Curse business. What the fuck do they think is going to happen? That their guests will drop dead from eating my crab dip?"

"Oh, Peyton, I'm so sorry. But I think the tide is finally going to turn. After what happened to me last night, the police are going to realize that someone is behind all of this. They're bound to open an investigation."

"Are you going to stay on the case as well?"

"I'm going to play it by ear after I see what the police have planned. There are a couple of things I want to

check out before I head back to New York today. I also
wanted to ask you a few questions about your business."

"My *business*?" she said. "What about it?" While she
spoke, she nudged at her eggs with her fork, like someone goading a cornered animal with a stick.

"As we discussed, one possible motive for the murders
is that someone wants to spoil things for you. I heard that
you had a few mix-ups with parties late last year. I'm
wondering if it could be connected to all of this—someone trying different ways to discredit you. How much do
you know about this secretary you had to fire?"

"Practically nothing. She'd only been there since the
summer."

"What did she do to screw things up?" I asked, picking a croissant out of the basket. "Mary was slightly
vague about it."

Peyton rolled her eyes. "I know it makes Mary uncomfortable because she seemed to feel sorry for the
girl—despite the fact that she was a total disaster."

"But what exactly did she *do*?"

"One of her jobs was to keep track of the master calendar—it's on a big board on the wall and also in the computer. Once we sign a contract for a party, the secretary
fills in all the information on the calendar. But she messed
up three times—once in October and then twice around
the holidays. The first two times, the dates of the parties
on the master calendar were later in the month than the
dates on the contract. I told Mary to boot her stupid fanny
out of there as fast as she could. After the second incident,
we checked all the parties and weddings listed on the
board against their individual contracts to make sure she
hadn't made any other mistakes. The reason we didn't

catch the third fuck-up is that she hadn't even filled it in on the calendar. We were stupid not to have dragged out every contract and double-checked them all."

"But aren't there conversations with clients during the days right before the party—in which you'd all of a sudden realize you had your signals crossed?"

"In some cases, yes. I mean, that certainly happens with a new client. You book the party, and then, as you get closer to the date, you start to review the plans together. Some of the women in this town have to go over every detail ad infinitum. What would you expect, considering they have nothing better to do with their days than eat lunches of nothing but lettuce leaves with their girlfriends and have their hair blown out? But with clients who've used us a million times, they might just call, book a date, and then leave it all to us. They get the contract and confirmation letter and we might not hear from them again. The week before the party, we call to touch base with them, but neither the client nor the person from my office might ever say 'this Thursday'—or 'next Friday.' In slower months I might actually even remember when a party is, but around the holidays, no way. This year we had at least two parties booked for every night."

"So in each of the three cases, it was an established client you'd done parties for in the past?"

"That's right," she said, weighing what I'd just asked. "Which means in each case we'd have had very little reason to talk to them prior to the event. So do you think that little brat did it on purpose?"

"Well, three times just seems like a lot. Unless she was incredibly sloppy or lazy or suffered from dyslexia. You knew the girl. What did she seem like?"

"Kind of naive. Do you think someone *paid* her to sabotage me?"

"That's an interesting question. Do you know where she is now?"

"I haven't a clue. Maybe Mary knows."

"There's just one more thing I'm curious about," I said. "What time did you leave the farm last night?"

"About six. Why?"

"Was Phillipa around?"

"No, she left earlier. She said she had a doctor's appointment. I've never met anyone who sees the doctor as much as she does."

She began ranting about Phillipa's hypochondria, about how she once had to be on crutches for two weeks because of a plantar wart, but I was only half listening. If Phillipa was the one who was after me, she could have slipped out when she saw me leaving the farm and followed me to Wellington House, parking along the road someplace until I came out.

I took two more swigs of coffee, excused myself, and ran back upstairs. Using the landline on the bedside table, I phoned the police. Needless to say, the cops I'd dealt with weren't still on duty, and it took me forever to hook up with someone who knew my situation. Finally someone came back on to report that investigators had already been out to the Crawfords' this morning. I was free to retrieve my car.

"Wow, that was fast," I said.

"They wanted to take a look at things before the sun had a chance to alter the conditions."

I asked to be transferred to Detective Pichowski's line. A woman informed me that he was expected in about half an hour. I asked for directions and left a message saying that I'd be stopping in later. Next I called the Crawfords. Evelyn answered and explained that though Richard had left for work, she would be there all morning. And she had good news. The police had shoveled out the area around the front of my bumper and moved the Jeep into the driveway. There was no need for a tow truck after all. And no need to do serious damage to my MasterCard.

As I hurried downstairs, my feet making no sound on the thick carpet, I discovered David thrusting his arms into his overcoat.

"Is the caretaker on-site?" I asked. "Believe it or not, my Jeep is ready to be picked up."

"Why don't I drop you, then?" he said. "I'm headed that way now."

Without waiting for household servant assistance, I found my coat and hat in the front hall closet, as well as my boots, which someone must have administered to last night because the insides were now bone-dry. While David retrieved some papers from the library, I ducked into the kitchen to say good-bye to Peyton, who was in the midst of lecturing a young woman on the distinction between firm and runny. She stopped long enough for me to say good-bye. She said she'd be heading over to the farm in a few hours, and we agreed to talk soon.

Inside David's Jaguar it was toasty warm, so someone obviously had started the engine earlier in the morning. If I wasn't careful, I was going to get used to all the little privileges of the very rich.

We drove slowly through the front gate, and as we came to a halt at the end of the driveway, I looked up and down the road in both directions. A bright red sports car shot by, but that was the only vehicle on the road. David asked for the Crawfords' number on Rolling Ridge, and we turned in that direction. Twice within the first minute out of the driveway, I saw him check his rearview mirror.

"You must be feeling very anxious," he said. Still wearing his buttery brown leather gloves, he handled the steering wheel agilely.

"Yeah, I am. But I think I'll feel better when I speak to the police. They apparently examined the scene early this morning."

"Do you really believe they'll find any evidence?"

"Not much, perhaps," I said. "But because of what happened last night, I think they'll finally start taking this seriously. Speaking of which, there's something I wanted to ask you. I spoke to Phillipa yesterday and she shared something that I hadn't heard before. She said that Mandy was very upset that Lilly couldn't be in the wedding."

He snorted, as if he'd heard it one too many times.

"I'm aware of that, of course. But we smoothed out everything over nine months ago. Lilly got to wear a dress that cost about a thousand dollars more than the bridesmaid dresses, and she was perfectly happy."

"She left the reception early—she had Mandy pick her up."

"It was all a bit overwhelming for her—which was to be expected. What are you suggesting, anyway?"

"Are you sure there's no chance Mandy could be responsible for all of this?"

We'd just hit a bend in the road, and as soon as he'd maneuvered the car around it, he turned his head toward me, brows furrowed.

"That sounds like a theory *Peyton* might be floating."

"Actually—I think that's the Crawfords' driveway up on the right—it interests me, too."

"Like I told you the other night, I just can't imagine Mandy murdering someone over this. She wasn't happy about the divorce, but she got over it. The last I heard, she was dating some guy ten years younger than her. What do they call that at that magazine you work for— a stud muffin?"

"I guess. I write the crime stories. I don't run into many studs in my line of work, and if I do they're often psychopaths."

As Evelyn had reported, my Jeep was no longer in the road, but as we approached the Crawford driveway I could see the impression of the front fender in the snow-bank, as well as the pockmarks from where I—and someone else—had climbed over it. David pulled the Jaguar into the driveway, and as he did I turned around just to make doubly sure no one was following us.

"You're okay with me just leaving you here?" he asked, coming to a stop. "I mean, do you trust these people?"

"Yes, they were very good to me. The worst that could happen is that they'd try to convince me to become a Republican."

As I reached for the car door, he laid his hand on my arm.

"Peyton has always said you're quite the girl," he remarked, his voice warm but at the same time full of authority. "And I know you want to get to the bottom of all of this. But don't be foolish, Bailey. You had a close call last night, and you need to stop the amateur investigator stuff."

"I *will* stay out of it if the police finally decide to get

involved. But what was I supposed to do up until now—
be a sitting duck? Like Ashley?"

He considered my words, silent for a moment, then
reached under his coat and slid a wallet from his pants
pocket. He opened it and withdrew a business card.

"Why don't you call and let me know how it goes with
the police today?" he said, handing it to me.

He waited until Mrs. Crawford had let me inside. I
stayed only long enough to fight off an offer for tea and
to thank her again for all her help. Once I was alone outside, I quickly checked both ends of the Jeep. It was
dinged up in the front and slightly worse in the back, but
nothing I couldn't live with for now.

The minute I turned out onto the road, I began to feel
scared out of my wits again. I checked the rearview mirror
every other second, and even though my Jeep had yet to
warm up, my hands were sweating on the steering wheel.

As soon as I reached town, my anxiety began to re-
cede. It was broad daylight, traffic was brisk, and I'd
soon be at police headquarters.

The station was in an old limestone building on a side
street not far from Greenwich Avenue. I waited in an un-
furnished vestibule as a desk cop behind a thick glass
window listened to a haughty middle-aged man complain
about kids on snowmobiles in the woods behind his
house. When I was finally able to ask for Pichowski, I
was told he was actually in another building just around
the corner. I walked down a short street called Police
Alley to a nondescript two-story building, where the detective squad occupied the second floor.

I gave my name to a receptionist behind a window and
waited in the corridor for ten minutes. A secretary came

out and told me it would be a few more minutes. Ten minutes later she finally returned and asked me to follow her. I was overdue for a cup of coffee, and I felt my energy flagging.

Pichowski sat in the middle of the room at the last metal desk in a row of six, which butted up to six identical ones, face-to-face. About half were occupied with other detectives, making phone calls or skimming reports, the remains of their breakfasts still in paper wrapping on their desks. Pichowksi rose and greeted me. He was wearing the same suit jacket he'd had on last week and a wide orange-and-green tie that suggested he'd given in to a bad-tie urge. Several crumbs nestled in his brown mustache—as if he'd hurriedly finished a doughnut when he'd heard I was waiting outside.

"Good morning, Ms. Weggins," he said, rising to shake hands with me. "Here, please sit down."

He pointed to a gray folding chair next to his desk. As he settled back in his own seat, one of those big ergonomically correct chairs, I did as he said, slipping off my coat and letting it fall behind me. The room was overheated, and though someone had cracked a window, it was having about as much impact as trying to let a breeze into hell.

"When we met last week, I thought you said you were just out here for the day," he said. "Do you spend quite a bit of time here?" He had one of those fake curious looks on his face, the kind people have when they ask a question they already know the answer to.

"No, not generally," I said. "But after Ashley's death I was very concerned. I came back out again to talk to some people—and to spend time with Peyton Cross."

"To talk to people?"

"Yes. To be honest, I was very alarmed by everything that had happened. I wanted to see if I could find some answers."

He tossed that around for a second in his mind, started to say one thing, then appeared to switch gears.

"So tell me about last night," he said. "The patrol cops filled me in, of course, and we had some people out there this morning to look at the scene. But I'd like to hear it all from you."

I let out a sigh without meaning to. I just felt so relieved to finally have the chance to talk to someone who could *do* something about it. I went through the whole story, sharing my suspicion that I was probably followed from the time I left the farm. All around us detectives and a few support staff types bustled about, looking busy, though I suspected a few might be eavesdropping. When I finally finished my story, I leaned back in my chair and looked at Pichowski expectantly. He pursed his lips together, obviously mulling over my tale.

"I have no idea why someone is doing this," I said after he failed to comment. "I mean, I have a few theories, but they're in the infancy stage at this point. But as you can see, someone is clearly out to get me. And I think it sheds a whole different light on the other deaths, don't you?"

"Miss Weggins," he said at last, "I realize you had a scare last night when your car hit the snowbank. But I must tell you—we have no evidence whatsoever that anyone was after you."

CHAPTER 13

It FELT AS if my heart were being squeezed in someone's fist. Could I possibly have *misunderstood* him?

"Excuse me?" I said, trying to keep my voice steady.

"What I said is that there's no real evidence anyone intended to harm you last night."

The fist squeezed harder. He couldn't *possibly* believe this was all just another coincidence. Two officers on the scene last night had announced that they'd found evidence.

"I'm not following," I said. "Uh—what about the footprints? The officers who came to the scene told me that they could tell someone had gotten out of their car and followed me into the woods."

"Yes, that's true. Someone did stop and follow you. But it was a gentleman who lived just up the road, on the opposite side. He spotted your vehicle in the snowbank as he was coming down the hill, and he pulled over to see what had happened. He says he could see you running in the woods and he started to go after you, thinking you might be hurt. But then he decided that the best course of action was to call the police."

"But what—?"

"We have a record of his call to the police, and we followed up with him this morning. Plus, we examined the footprints and determined that there was only one set other than yours, and they matched the boots this man was wearing."

I closed my eyes, struggling to sort through the confusion in my mind. I'd seen the taillights disappear last night and then moments later a car coming out of a driveway. I'd assumed the car had turned around. But that didn't seem to be the case.

"Okay," I said calmly. "I see now what happened. I thought the driver who struck me had turned around. But it was clearly this—this Mr. What's-his-name pulling out of his driveway. But that doesn't alter the fact that the other car ran me into a snowbank."

Pichowski pursed his lips together again, raising his cheeks and mustache on his face. He was beginning to remind me of a big, blubbery walrus.

"I'm not questioning that, Miss Weggins," he said, his tone suddenly patronizing. "But if I've read the report correctly, you admit that you hit your brakes. I'm thinking that you may have inadvertently caused the other car to ram into you."

I couldn't believe what I was hearing. He was treating me as if I'd come in to report that I'd located Amelia Earhart. I knew cops needed to be skeptical, but I couldn't believe he was being so dismissive.

"But this guy was on top of me," I protested. "He was incredibly hostile. At the very least, he left the scene of an accident."

"I'm not suggesting he wasn't hostile. We have some obnoxious drivers out here, and they get *particularly* obnoxious on these back roads, regardless of weather conditions. I'm thinking what happened is that someone got on your tail and was being very aggressive. When you went into a skid and tapped your brakes, he accidentally hit you. Now, you have every right to be upset. It was a hit-and-run, and we're going to be looking out for the vehicle. But my point is that the driver was most likely a stranger and was probably as surprised as you were by what ended up happening."

I hadn't wanted to share the tale of me being attacked in Manhattan for fear of being viewed as a buttinski, but I felt I had no choice now. I spilled the story, waiting for the look of recognition in his eyes. Instead he shook his head and flipped his palms up.

"I don't want to make light of the situation, but it sounds like your typical New York story. That's the city, isn't it?"

"Yeah, right," I said, resigned. I could see now that nothing I said was going to convince him. I could hardly blame him, could I? I just didn't have the evidence to support my claims. Plus, by mistakenly claiming that the driver had turned around and come back for me, I'd undermined my credibility. I wondered even if he viewed me as an opportunist, a crime writer who was conjuring up sinister stalkings so I could hype the story and turn the whole thing into an even juicier article.

All around us was the hum of conversation—detectives droning on the phone or to one another—but I could tell by the way they stood and the cock of their heads that each of them was definitely tuned in to Pichowski's exchange with me. They were probably getting a real charge from hearing him talk some sense into the girl from the city with the overactive imagination.

"Actually, I thought you'd be *happy* with the news," Pichowski said. "You were concerned someone was after you—and I assume you thought it might be connected to these other deaths. But as I said, we don't think that's the case. You can relax now."

I slid my arms quickly into my coat and picked up my bag from the floor. It was time to get out of there before I said something I'd regret.

"Well, thank you for taking the time to investigate the situation," I said, forcing a smile. "Have a good day." Without waiting for him to say good-bye, I rose from the chair and strode across the gray linoleum floor. As I opened the glass door into the hallway, I could feel about twelve pairs of eyes on me.

I practically bolted down the stairs and over to the parking lot. As I sat there in my Jeep, letting the heater warm the interior before I took off again, I felt my anger begin to morph into despondency. I'd been so sure that the police were finally going to get involved, to come to my rescue. But that wasn't going to happen. There was a killer on the loose, someone who apparently wanted me out of the way as well, and no one was trying to stop him or her.

My overwhelming instinct at the moment was to point my Jeep toward I-95 and just limp back to New York. But what good would that do? As I'd discovered, New York wasn't safe for me, either. I couldn't allow myself to fall into a slump; if the police weren't going to look for the killer, *I* would have to continue to do it. I needed to stick with my plan and make a few more stops in Greenwich today. And sometime this week I was definitely going to get on a plane bound for Miami. Hopefully a piece of information that could change everything was waiting there for me.

I wondered suddenly if I should have mentioned the latest development, the male model in Miami who was holding a potentially important piece of information. I'd been so distracted in there that I'd forgotten all about it. On second thought, mentioning the bartender probably wouldn't have helped much. I laughed ruefully to myself as I imagined the expression on Pichowski's face if I'd told him that the case might be blown open by a guy who waxed his chest.

I'd parked in a small lot across the street from the police station, and I glanced around in all directions before I pulled out. The most dangerous thing on the road at the moment seemed to be the rich blond mommies in monster-size SUVs.

The one big thing I had left to do in Greenwich today was to drive by the home of Andrew Flanigan, the guy who had been arrested for drunk driving the night of the rehearsal dinner. But first I wanted to pay another visit to the salesclerk at Ivy Hill Farm, something I'd planned to do yesterday before I'd run out of time. When I'd pressed her for information about Robin last week, she'd admitted that she'd been too flustered to think, and I wanted to take another stab at it. In the past twenty-four hours, I'd been following leads related to Peyton and her wedding, but I wasn't going to overlook the fact that the deaths might be related to something else entirely in Robin's and Jamie's lives.

Fortunately, the same girl was on duty when I arrived. I spotted her through the window, listlessly wiping the countertop with a cloth. As I entered she stopped chomping on her gum midchew and lodged it with her tongue somewhere between her gum and her cheek—clearly Peyton had decreed a "no gum chewing in front of a customer" rule.

"Sorry to catch you off guard, but I just wanted to check back in," I told her.

"Okay, but I can't talk too long right now," she explained. Her brow wrinkled in worry, and she stuck her hands in the pockets of the big yellow apron that covered her clothes. "Ms. Cross likes to check the store as soon as she gets to the farm, and if everything isn't just right, she gets really, really annoyed."

"It won't take long. The other day we were talking about how Robin had seemed kind of worried in the weeks before she died. You haven't recalled her saying anything unusual, have you?"

She shook her head glumly. "No, nothing," she said. "But she probably wouldn't have confided anything to me anyway—on account of her being my boss."

"That's understandable."

"You know what's sad? After you and I talked last week, I was thinking that Robin actually looked pretty happy the day she died. She was looking forward to going skiing. She loved to ski so much."

"Wait. You saw her that Friday—the day she died?" I asked, my mind racing.

"Yeah—she came by here in the morning for a little while. She needed to take care of a few things before she took off for the weekend."

That was a major detail, one that Ashley must not have known about. It meant that the "bad" food Robin ate could have been from the farm.

"Did she grab something to eat here? And do you remember who was around—I mean, was it the usual group who works here?"

"I don't remember anything like that—it was a few weeks ago, and I didn't have any reason to pay attention."

"One more question. Robin's husband. Do you know anything about him?"

"You mean her *ex*-husband?"

"Uh-huh. I heard he works on Wall Street. But he lives around here, right?"

"I think he moved into the city. He still stays in their old house sometimes, Robin told me, but once they split up, he also got an apartment in New York. He works for Merrill Lynch, or maybe it's Smith Barney. He used to call here after they first got divorced, but Robin would never take the calls. He finally stopped a month or two ago."

"A month or two ago? Are you sure it was that recent?"

"Uh-huh. Because he asked her to his company Christmas party. I overheard her discussing it with him."

"Really? Okay, thanks. I— Wait, she wasn't seeing anyone else before she died, was she?"

"No, I don't think so. Like I said, she really didn't discuss her love life with me, but I got the feeling that she had no interest in dating right now. She always used to say she was focusing on getting strong. There was that one guy who seemed interested in her—you know, that guy who works with Mr. Slavin, but she looked like she could have cared less."

"What guy who works with Mr. Slavin?" I asked, trying not to sound as though I were pouncing. "Trip?"

"Uh, maybe I shouldn't say anything."

"No, it's fine. Peyton wants me to look into this."

"Yeah, Trip. Sometimes he and Mr. Slavin come by the farm, and a few times lately that guy stopped by the shop. I think Robin had had a drink with him—just to be friendly—but I got the feeling he thought it was more than that. She seemed totally uninterested when he came by."

Was that just Trip on the prowl as usual? Or was there something more significant to it?

She looked anxiously over my shoulder at the window, and I spun around, my heart skipping. No one was there. I realized that she was probably just watching for Peyton.

"She really keeps you on your toes, doesn't she," I said.

"*Ms. Cross?* Yeah, I mean, I know she believes in perfection, but it can be hard. Sometimes even if you're doing a great job, it doesn't count."

Something stirred in my mind.

"The girl who got fired here recently—the office secretary. Did you know her?"

"Yes," she said, her voice catching. "She and I were friends even before she started working here. It upsets me to even talk about that whole thing."

"Why? Tell me. Maybe I can help."

"She got blamed for things she didn't do. And now

she's stuck without a reference. She went out to San Francisco a few weeks ago to see if she could find a job there."

"I was told that she filled in dates wrong on the master calendar. Are you saying she didn't do that?"

"There's no way she could have done that. Melanie is so amazingly reliable. And even if it did happen once— maybe she goofed like people do sometimes—there's no way it could have happened *three* times. And you know how she's sure she didn't do it? One party, she says, was on her birthday, and she clearly remembers writing it in on the calendar that day. But later it was on another day."

"So she thinks someone changed it?" I asked.

"Someone *must* have changed it. What other explanation is there?"

"I know this girl was your friend, but I need to ask this: Is it possible she messed up the dates on purpose?"

"But why would she have done that?" she asked, almost in a wail.

I hesitated, choosing my words.

"Maybe she'd been treated poorly here—yelled at by Peyton—and she was looking for some way to express her anger."

Again, she shook her head sadly. "No. Melanie wanted to be like Peyton Cross. She even made excuses for her when she'd blow a gasket."

She glanced up over my shoulder again. It was clear she was nervous about being caught chatting, and I decided I should get out of there before she developed some full-blown fear of flogging. I asked for Melanie's number, which she gave me after consulting a pink leather address book from her purse.

I hurried toward my Jeep, trying to digest all the tidbits I'd just learned. Unlocking the Jeep, I also realized that my stomach was rumbling. I hadn't had more than a passing interest in the croissant this morning, but my appetite had returned now with a vengeance, and so had my yearning for caffeine. There were a few little tea shops along Greenwich Avenue, and I decided to drop by one before I found Andrew Flanigan's house. Before firing up the Jeep, I glanced around the parking lot. There was no sign of anyone or anything suspicious, but I did spot Peyton's Range Rover. She must have just arrived.

Downtown Greenwich was bustling, and just when it appeared as if my hunt for a parking place would be in vain, a white BMW abandoned a spot right in front of me. I walked half a block and discovered a small café under a blue-and-white awning. The two window tables were filled with several sleek Lycra'd women in their thirties who'd obviously dropped by for lattes and a chat after spinning class, but there was a table in the back all by its lonesome. That's where I set up shop.

Since it wasn't eleven yet, breakfast was still being served. I ordered a mushroom omelet, and by the time it arrived I'd drunk a cup and a half of coffee. I'd also pulled out my composition book and jotted down the details of my disgusting encounter with Detective Pichowski and started on the fascinating pieces of info that the salesclerk had shared.

For starters, the Trip thing. From what I'd been able to determine so far, the guy would come on to a hand broom if it would only tell him how hot he was, so his flirting with Robin might be nothing more than Trip being Trip. But then again, it might not be. Maybe his conversation with David at the church had revealed more than it should have, and Jamie had realized that. Had he been trying to ingratiate himself with Robin to see what she knew? It still seemed far-fetched, though. If there had been something so explosive in Trip and David's argument at the rehearsal, wouldn't I have remembered it? And why take so long to silence all the bridesmaids? No, I couldn't put Trip at the top of my suspects list just because I disliked the guy.

Then there was Brace, the ex-husband. I hadn't thought much about him until now, but I didn't like the fact that he'd been hounding Robin this fall. Ashley, of course, had mentioned that he'd pestered Robin, but she'd never mentioned the time frame quite the way the salesclerk had. Over the years I'd done more than one article on women who'd been murdered by former partners. The guy would at first make every effort to win her back, often in the most sane way he could manage—flowers, love letters, sappy poetry, even skywriting. When she didn't take the bait, he might lie low for a few weeks, waiting for her to miss him and realize the error of her ways. When he finally saw that his case was hopeless, he'd kill her. Brace lived in both Greenwich and New York, giving him access to all three women. And he could have easily followed Ashley and me to the farm the day she died. But why would he kill Ashley or Jamie—or, for that matter, come after me? That idea seemed to lead to a dead end, too.

I was also very intrigued by the shopgirl's conviction that the secretary Melanie could not have written in the wrong dates for the parties. Which meant one of two things: Either she didn't realize how careless—or possibly evil-minded—her friend was, or Melanie *hadn't* messed up the dates. Someone might have purposely changed them around in order to wreak havoc in the world of Peyton Cross. And that someone would have to be a person who worked at the farm and who knew that changing the party dates for established clients was likely to go unnoticed.

And last but hardly least was the news that Robin had stopped by the farm on her way to Vermont. She was a known grazer, and she could easily have grabbed something to eat there that day—or been given something to eat by someone. Something with too much tyramine in it.

It didn't take long for Phillipa to pop up on my mental screen. She was most likely working the Friday Robin died. She also could have sneaked into the office at some point and mucked up the party dates. And she was missing in action at the very time Ashley was killed. God, could being banned from the bridal party have really turned her into a serial killer? Or could some older, nastier grudge Phillipa held against her cousin cause her to try to destroy Peyton's business, even going so far as to kill her bridesmaids?

It was all so bewildering. And of course, none of these scenarios—involving Trip, Brace, or Phillipa—seemed to have anything to do with a strange occurrence at the wedding, which I hopefully would soon be learning about in Miami.

I always despised people yakking on cell phones in restaurants—in voices so loud that the whole room had to hear. But my table was pretty secluded, and I decided to make a few quick calls. After finding her number on my Palm, I phoned the woman I hoped to interview in Ft.

Lauderdale. She seemed taken aback when I announced that I was hoping to talk to her *this* week—anytime on Thursday or, if that was out of the question, Wednesday afternoon after I arrived from New York. After running me through a list of everything she needed to accomplish this week, including having her dog checked for diabetes, she agreed to shift her plans around to accommodate me before work on Thursday morning. With that in my pocket, I called the travel agency *Gloss* uses and asked them to get me a flight to Miami on Wednesday morning with a return on Thursday midday, as well as book a room at the Delano, a hotel I'd stayed at once before. I tried Chris's cell phone after that and left a message on his voice mail saying that I was coming to Miami tomorrow and to please call me back.

Next, I got the main numbers for Merrill Lynch and Smith Barney from 411 and after several calls found that Robin's ex-husband worked at the Wall Street offices of Merrill Lynch. I left a message on his voice mail, giving my name and saying simply that I needed to speak to him and would call back. He wasn't exactly at the top of my suspect list, but I figured it would be worth speaking to him to see what he knew about Robin. If she'd been in touch with him in the fall, she might have mentioned her concerns to him—and perhaps with more specifics than she'd shared with Ashley.

At this point the waiter shot me an annoyed look, as if he didn't appreciate the fact that I was using the café as a home office. I lowered my voice even more as I called the fact checker at *Gloss*, switching an appointment I had with him tomorrow to late this afternoon.

I also quickly checked my messages at home and at

work. Landon had called, wondering if I was okay, and so had my mother, who was in Boston between jaunts abroad and fortunately didn't get the New York papers. There were also several calls from friends, including Cat. I promised myself that I would return calls later and also drop in on Cat when I swung by *Gloss*.

Hearing all the messages, thinking about my trip to Miami—it made me eager to be back in New York. I briefly deliberated bagging the trip to Andrew Flanigan's house. But I just as quickly talked myself back into it. I didn't want to leave any unfinished business in Greenwich before heading off to Miami. I'd already decided not to pay Andrew an unexpected visit. If for some reason he *was* the one after me, I'd be putting myself in too much danger by doing that. But I hoped to pick up a vibe by looking at his place and maybe, if he wasn't at work, to see what kind of car he drove.

I paid the bill, leaving a generous tip. It took me twenty-five minutes to find the Flanigan place, stopping three times to ask for directions. Davidson Street turned out to be on the wrong side of the tracks in Greenwich, though up until this point I hadn't realized there even *was* a wrong side. The house was a small two-story clapboard, painted a robin's-egg blue that looked ugly as sin with the chocolate-cherry-hued shutters. There were a couple of banged-up aluminum-and-mesh folding chairs on the porch, as if no one had gotten around to bringing them indoors when the seasons changed.

I drove by the house and ended up circling the block because there was no easy place to turn around. Back on the street, I pulled into an open spot catty-corner from the house. I noticed two things as soon as I killed the engine.

There didn't appear to be a single light on in the house, suggesting that no one was home. And at the end of the driveway was a one-car garage with the door raised about two feet. I could see the wheels of a vehicle.

So someone might be home after all. *Or*, this was a second car. Was it a black SUV?

I watched the house for about ten minutes. No sign of movement anywhere. I had come in hopes of getting a vibe, but I wasn't feeling anything one way or the other. I decided that the least I could do before leaving was determine if the vehicle was an SUV.

I climbed out of the Jeep and checked the street in both directions as I crossed to the other side. Not a human in sight. The driveway was slick with ice and frozen snow, and I almost landed on my ass a couple of times as I made my way along the length of it, keeping my eye on the house for activity. There was a small porch attached to the side of the house with a couple of steps leading down to the driveway, and an old brown rag rug lay over the railing. Through the door I could suddenly hear a dog begin to yap. Shit, I thought. I needed to move fast.

I reached the garage and peered underneath. I was staring at the rump of a Honda Civic. I straightened up and started back down the driveway. I hadn't taken five steps when I heard the crack of a door opening. A woman in her early forties with fried blond hair stepped out into the cold, a scowl on her face.

"Can I help you?" she asked, sounding not at all as though she wanted to. She was wearing only a black turtleneck and stretchy brown pants. She folded her arms against the cold.

"Uh, sorry," I stammered. "I was just looking for someone."

"*Who?*" she demanded. She was too old to be Andrew's wife or girlfriend—could it be his *mother*? Maybe he didn't even live here anymore.

"Uh, Andrew," I said. By using his name I would find out once and for all if he lived there. If she said he was home, I would just take off.

"Is that right?" she said, her voice hardening even more. "Well, you're out of luck."

Good, I thought, this was my chance to elicit some info.

"I was just passing through, and I thought I'd look him up. It's been ages since we've seen each other. How's he doing, anyway?"

She stared at me suspiciously for a moment, doing some kind of mental calculation.

"Not good," she said finally. "He hung himself last summer."

CHAPTER 14

I—I'M SORRY," I said. I was too thunderstruck by the news to think of anything else to say.

"I'm Andrew's mother, by the way. Sue. You better come inside. I don't want to be talkin' about it out here."

"Sure, thanks," I said, crossing the short distance to the house. I felt a pang of guilt, but I needed to know what had happened. As I climbed the steps to the small porch, I saw that up close she looked much older. Her skin was lined with age and grief. She opened the door and the dog, a Pomeranian, I thought, immediately started yapping again, trying to jump on me.

"Shut up, Nugget," she said, shooing her gently with a foot. "If you pet her, she'll stop."

I obliged by bending down and patting Nugget's head a few times. She licked my hand with a tongue that felt like wet sandpaper.

The room was a mess of dirty dishes, dusty

tchotchkes, and houseplants that looked as if they were watered every four or five weeks. One ivy plant was growing out of a ceramic floor pot in the shape of a lower torso, waist to knees—with no clear sex.

"Here, have a seat," Sue said, pointing to the kitchen table. It was littered with bunched-up sections of the newspaper and a plate hardened with egg, like something from the last days of Pompeii. I sat down gingerly, pushing away a cup and saucer with the tip of my finger.

"I'm sorry to have to tell you like that," she said, flopping into a seat across from me. In one hop Nugget was nestled in her lap. "But there's no easy way."

"When did he—when did it happen?" I asked.

"Last summer. August. You can't imagine the hell I've been through since then." She picked up a pack of nicotine gum from the table, rapped it two or three times against her other hand until a piece popped out, and then stuck it in her mouth.

"Was he depressed?" I asked. "I—I know he drank sometimes."

"Yeah, he was depressed all right," she replied, the words almost strangled by her despair. "Did you know about his DUIs? He got his third one last spring. Blew over a three on the Breathalyzer, and that was it. He convinced himself for a while that the lawyer was going to pull some miracle out of his ass. But it didn't happen. Andy finally realized at the end of the summer that he'd be going to prison. He couldn't take it. He was afraid of what would happen there. You hear those horror stories—of guys raping other guys."

Oh God, I thought. The accident on the night of the rehearsal dinner had sealed his fate in a horrible way.

"What stinks is that he was just a few blocks from here. If he'd just made it those last few blocks, it would all be different. Mike always said Andy had shitty karma."

"Is that Andy's brother?" I asked. I was wondering now about avenging angels.

"Yeah, he moved to San Diego after all of this. I don't think he's ever coming back."

"What about your husband?" I asked.

"He's been gone forever."

It was hard to know if she meant he was dead, too, or had, like the father in *The Glass Menagerie*, fallen in love with long distances. All I knew for sure was that Sue Flanigan hadn't been busy murdering bridesmaids—and that I needed to get out of her kitchen.

"I'm so sorry for your loss," I said. "I shouldn't take up any more of your time, though."

"You can't go until you tell me about Andy," she said, laying a hand on my arm. "How did you know him?"

"He was just—just a great guy. Look, I'm so sorry, but I'm suddenly not feeling so well. This has been such a shock for me."

I pulled my arm out from under her hand and started to turn toward the door. She rose as well, practically dumping Nugget on the floor. The dog eyed me suspiciously, and I wondered if she was going to grab my pants leg in her tiny teeth and try to prevent me from leaving. Instead she just followed me as I made my way toward the door.

"What's your name?" Sue asked, right behind me, the wariness back in her voice.

"Bailey. Bailey Weggins."

I reached out to shake her hand, which she extended without any enthusiasm. Her blue eyes, which moments ago had been damp with tears, were now dark and hard as river stones.

I hurried down the stairs and made my way cautiously across the frozen driveway. I sensed her standing on the side porch watching me, but I didn't turn around to check. I unlocked the Jeep, slipped in, and pulled out of the parking spot.

Ten minutes later I was merging onto I-95, a sick feeling in my stomach. How different the ripple effect of that accident had been for Andrew than for the rest of us. We'd been inconvenienced, sure, and we'd been verbally bullwhipped by Peyton for being late. But it had doomed Andrew. As disgusted as I was about drunk drivers, I couldn't help but feel distraught that he had taken his own life, that his addiction had ruined him. I hadn't had the nerve to ask where he'd hung himself, but I suspected it was there in the house, perhaps in the basement below where I'd sat. Despite the fact that I felt justified, I felt guilty about lying to his mother.

I stuck in my CD of Maria Callas's arias. There was something about it that always managed to soothe me, and I needed it now. I felt so distressed by everything that had happened during my stay in Greenwich. What stupid idiot had once declared that the suburbs were a haven?

Thanks to heavy traffic, I didn't hit the city until close to two-thirty. I was mildly concerned that I hadn't heard back from Chris yet. I'd left my cell phone on the whole way back, expecting him to get in touch, but it never rang. I was totally dependent on him for my trip to Miami, and if I didn't connect with him today, there'd be no point in going. I reassured myself with the fact that he'd been reliable so far, and I figured that when he had a break from his shoot, he'd be in touch.

Back in my apartment I finally changed into fresh clothes. Then I began to dig some summer duds out of the back of the closet. According to the *Times*, the temperature in Miami was going to be in the eighties this week, so I picked out two pairs of capris, a sleeveless cotton dress, and a few cotton tops. What I didn't bother with was a bathing suit. Besides the fact that I probably wouldn't have time for a dip, my body hadn't seen the sun since early September, and I was disgustingly white. I'd look like a giant latex glove lying on the beach.

After I'd thrown my things into my black rolling bag, I tried Brace again. This time he picked up. I introduced myself and mentioned that I'd called earlier.

"Yeah, I got the message. What can I do for you?" His tone was abrupt but neutral. It didn't give away whether the name Bailey Weggins meant anything to him.

"I'm very sorry about Robin's death," I told him. "I met her at Peyton Cross's wedding. I was hoping you might have a few minutes to talk to me about her."

"Talk? About what?" Now his voice had the slightest edge.

"Her roommate, Ashley, came to see me early last week and expressed concerns that Robin's death wasn't an accident. I promised Ashley I would look into it, and now with Ashley's death, I feel even more of a reason to. To be honest, I don't even know what I'm looking for. But I'd really appreciate just a few minutes of your time to talk about Robin."

Superlong pause. I could hear his co-workers in the background barking to one another or into their phones.

"Yeah, okay," he said finally. "You in the city?"

I said that I was, and he suggested Friday. I asked about the possibility of tonight after work.

"I could squeeze it in," he said. "But I've only got fifteen minutes or so."

"That should be fine."

"Six-thirty, then. Why don't you meet me at Ravick's on Hanover Square. I'll be at the bar."

"Okay, great," I said.

"So how'm I supposed to know you?" he asked.

"I'm five six, blue eyes, blondish brown hair around chin length."

"All right. Six-thirty." He broke the connection without a good-bye.

I was relieved he'd be able to see me tonight, but it meant that the rest of my afternoon was going to be crazed. Before I met up with Brace downtown, I was going to have to head uptown for my meeting with the fact checker at *Gloss*. There was no way I could put it off. My most recently completed article was shipping next week, and there were some details I needed to review with him.

I managed to make it to *Gloss* by three-thirty, and though it was earlier than we'd planned to meet, the fact checker had time for me. We were done by four. Rather than bother going back to my apartment before meeting Brace, I decided I'd try to get an hour's worth of work done at my office, despite the fact that I felt ready to crawl out of my skin. I opened my computer to my *Gloss* article on the dead New Jersey wife. It had been several days since I'd even glanced at my draft, and it felt as if I were reading something in a language I knew only four words of. I tweaked a few lines here and there and then changed them back. It became clear that I was going to have to take my laptop to Miami and try to work on the plane. If Chris ever called, that is. I still hadn't heard from him, and I certainly wasn't flying a thousand miles without doing so.

As I sat staring into space, someone tapped on my partly closed door. I pulled it open, and to my surprise Cat Jones was standing in the hall. The mod look was gone, and she was now all motorcycle mama: black leather skirt with big silver studs up the sides, a tight black knit cardigan over a white lace-fringed camisole, and sky high black leather stilettos. She looked as if she might be itching to hog-tie someone to a bed.

"Are you lost?" I asked.

"No, I had to have a little *chat* with the fashion department, and I saw your light. I left you a message and haven't heard back, which is unlike you. Is everything okay?"

"Not really," I said, keeping my voice low. "I was going to stop by later. I'm pretty sure now that all three women were murdered."

She stepped into my tiny office, pushed the door closed, and pulled over a straight-backed chair I kept against the wall. I noticed that her legs were totally bare. Cat's MO, like that of all the *Gloss* fashion editors, was to forgo hose not only in the summer, but during as much of the rest of the year as she could get away with. But it wasn't even twenty degrees today. It seemed as ridiculous as setting off across the Atlantic in an inner tube.

"That's horrible," she said, easing into the chair. I updated her on the incident on the Lower East Side, the warning note, and my experience last night in Greenwich.

"Do the police have any suspects?" she asked, frowning.

"No, they still refuse to see the whole thing as anything but a bunch of accidents. I've been digging around myself, but I don't have anything substantial yet."

"You mean not enough proof?"

"No, not enough *motive*. There are a few pissed-off players on the scene, but I'm not sure if any of them have a big enough reason to have done it."

She pressed her hands together to form a steeple and rested her chin on the point of it.

"*Cherchez la femme,*" she said quietly.

"Huh?"

"It's a French expression," she said. "When a husband starts acting funny or decides he wants out of a marriage, he might say he needs his space or some bullshit like that, but more likely than not there's a woman somewhere. What I'm saying is that people don't take big actions for little reasons. You need to find a major motivator in the situation."

"Yeah, but so far I'm not having any luck."

"And you're really certain these two attacks on you were both by the killer?"

"*Yes*, I'm sure," I said, feeling defensiveness beginning to swell in me. "I mean, *I* was in both places, so why couldn't *he* manage it, too?"

"Look, I'm not doubting the story," Cat said. "I just—"

At that moment her assistant stuck her head in the door.

"Your conference call is ready."

"I'll be right there," she told her. Then, turning back to me, she said, "Look, why don't you call me later at home? I want to talk more about this. And be careful, okay?"

"Sure," I said, trying not to sound sullen.

In frustration I lowered my head in my hands. Why did I always end up sounding like the chick who cried wolf these days?

After a minute of stewing about my predicament, I decided to just get the hell out of there and head for the bar. I might end up being a few minutes early, but it would give me a chance to get the lay of the land and feel more control on Brace's turf. I made one quick call to the travel agency, making certain everything had worked out with my arrangements, and then hurriedly packed up.

On my way out through the pit, I spotted the photo editor standing at his desk in his cube.

"Hey, Adam," I said, striding toward his partitioned-off work area. "Do you have a second?"

"Yeah, if you make it kind of quick," he said. "What's up?"

"I want to talk about male models."

"You dating one?" he asked as he shoved four or five black portfolios to one side of his canvas-colored love seat. He was wearing white wool pants and a very loosely knit white sweater over a white silky thermal top. It looked as though he'd gotten tangled in a hammock.

"No, no, nothing like that," I said, taking a seat. "I've got to interview one in Miami tomorrow night, and I need some advice. This guy has some info I need, but he's playing hard to get. How can I make sure he opens up to me?"

"Truth serum."

"You mean give him some sort of party drug?"

"Uh-uh," he said, shaking his head so that his long blond curls whipped back and forth. "Alcohol. Supply him with lots of vodka."

"These guys all like to drink?"

"Oh yeah—except . . ." He stopped and stroked his chin, deliberating.

"What?"

"If he's got a shoot the next day, he won't want to drink—it'll give him carb face. Then let's go to plan B."

"Which is?"

"Get him to talk about himself. Just ask lots of questions about him, him, him, and before long he'll be telling you *anything* you want to know."

"Are they all like that? Total egomaniacs?"

He cocked his head, considering. "No, not all. The ones who just stumbled into it—you know, guys who got discovered on the street by a scout—they're not like that. It's just the other ninety-nine percent."

Ten minutes later I was headed south on the number 4 train, which I'd picked up after taking the R to 57th and Lexington. As I was climbing the stairs of the Wall Street station, my cell went off and Chris was finally on the line.

"Sorry not to call you right back. They wouldn't let us take a break, and they yelled at anybody who whipped out a cell phone."

"Not a problem. Look, I'm all set to fly down there tomorrow morning. Do you still think we can hook up with this guy?"

"Yeah, I already took care of it. It turned out he was on this shoot with me today, and after I got your message I told him that you were coming down. He agreed to meet up with us tomorrow night at nine—at a place called the Sky Bar. Where are you staying, anyway?"

"At the Delano."

"The Sky Bar's at the Shore Club, just a short ways from the Delano."

I hesitated for a split second before I asked the next question.

"Can I buy you dinner first—for the trouble you've gone to?"

"Sure. Why don't we eat by the pool at the Shore Club. I'd feel better if we didn't have to worry about getting there on time. Like I said, Kyle's a bit of a flake."

We agreed that I'd leave a message for him tomorrow, confirming that I'd arrived. He said he'd make a seven o'clock dinner reservation for us.

By the time I hung up, I'd reached Ravick's. It was an old-style publike bar and restaurant in the basement of an 1800s building on Hanover Square, a tiny park that seemed left over from another era. I found the place packed primarily with guys in suits, obviously traders, brokers, and bankers fortifying themselves after a grueling day of winning or losing millions. The only Wall Street type I'd ever dated was an investment banker who went by the initials *K.C.* When he wasn't shagging other women, he couldn't have been more charming.

It took me five minutes of endlessly cocking my head up to catch the bartender's eye. I ordered an Amstel Light

that arrived icy cold. And then I waited. I'm pretty good
with faces, but I wasn't a hundred percent sure I'd recognize Brace.

He came in about ten minutes late, and I *did* recognize
him as he stamped his feet by the door. I started to raise
my hand to grab his attention, but before I had a chance I
saw him scan the bar and pick me out easily with his
eyes. I stiffened—those were cold, determined eyes.
Could they have been trained on me in Jamie's apartment
and on the icy Greenwich road?

"Sorry to make you wait," he said as he reached me.
Up close I saw that his hair was more strawberry color
than blond, kind of like Peyton's, and it was receding
slightly at the top. His skin was pale and freckly, and his
eyes were the color of old pennies. Extremely creepy. Not
my type, but two women near us at the bar swiveled their
heads as if George Clooney had just wandered in.

"I guess I described myself pretty well," I said.

"I saw you with Ashley," he said, his face expressionless. "The day she died."

He sloughed off his coat, letting it fall around the
stool. He was wearing a navy suit, a white shirt, and an
expensive-looking blue and green tie. He caught the bartender's eye in a millisecond and ordered a "J.D. and
water." I also saw him catch the eye of one of the two
women near us at the bar and hold it just long enough.

"What were you doing there that day?" I asked.

"Like I'm sure she told you," he answered, smirking,
"I was looking for some jewelry I'd given Robin. I
wanted it—for sentimental reasons. But she claimed
Robin's brother had already hauled everything away."

"You're probably wondering why I wanted to see you," I said, switching gears.

"I sure as hell wouldn't be here if I *wasn't* wondering that."

"Then I'll get right to the point. I don't think Robin's death was an accident."

He smirked. "Oh, so you're buying into this whole Curse of the Mummy thing?"

"No, I think she was murdered."

"Murdered?" he said. The two girls shot their heads back in our direction.

"Yes," I said, my voice lowered. "And I think Jamie and Ashley were murdered, too."

His drink arrived and I offered to pay, but he shook his head and tossed a twenty on the bar. He removed the red straw from the glass, flicking it fast a couple of times against the rim. Then he took a long sip, staring out into the sea of suits.

"You get your rocks off playing Nancy Drew or something?" he asked finally, looking back at me and licking his lips.

"I'm not interested in getting my rocks off. I'm interested in finding out the truth. I was in the wedding party myself, and I have no intention of being killed in some so-called freak accident this month."

"Well, I don't know shit about that whole wedding situation. I'd already been given the boot by that point."

"But I heard you and Robin were considering a reconciliation."

"I'm not gonna pretend differently—I was willing to try to make a go of it again. Robin and I had drinks a couple of times last summer and talked about it. At first she seemed open to the idea. Then she goes and pulls the plug. I made another stab at it back in October or November. But she'd moved on. I decided it was time for me to do the same thing."

"During the times you had drinks together, did she ever say anything about being worried about anything or concerned for her safety?"

"Nope. But like I said, if your theory has anything to do with the wedding, I was out of the picture—"

"Forget the wedding for a second. All three women were bridesmaids, but maybe there's some other kind of connection. Robin and Jamie were friends, and Robin was very upset about her death. Maybe someone killed Jamie, and Robin had some clue about it—so that the person had to murder her, too. Then the killer thinks Ashley might know information, too. It becomes this whole chain reaction thing, starting with Jamie."

"It always comes back to Jamie, doesn't it." As he spoke, he had the look on his face that you get when you've just sniffed a carton of spoiled milk.

"What do you mean?" I asked.

"Robin got in *so* thick with her. It was Jamie this and Jamie that. Listening to her talk that way used to really chap my ass."

Yuck—I was going to have to work hard to drive that nasty image from my mind.

"Why do you think they became such quick friends?" I asked.

"Who knows why chicks do anything?"

"Hazard a guess for me, would you?"

"Okay. Robin had a real needy streak in her," he said, staring into his drink as he spoke. "It's what caused most of the problems in our marriage. She wanted me to be there 24/7, but I couldn't always do that. I have a job that calls for wining and dining clients when I'm not on the Street. And of course, it didn't help that she worked for the world's fattest ego. We split, and then along comes this Jamie, who apparently was always flattering her, making her feel good. Robin ate that kind of shit up. But from what I could tell, Jamie was a user—and she was using Robin big-time."

"How so?"

"She planned to open this gourmet food store downtown, kind of like the one Robin ran for Peyton, and it sounded to me like she was pumping Robin for any info she could. I bet once the store was open, she would have dropped Robin in a nanosecond."

"It doesn't sound, though, like the store was ever going to get off the ground. I don't think she had any investors."

"Oh, she had investors all right," he said, staring into his drink before taking another long sip. "She'd even picked out the space—someplace on the Lower East Side."

"You're kidding—how do you know that?"

"Robin asked me to eyeball the business plan. Jamie had gotten a lease, and she had the money lined up."

Now that *was* interesting. Both Peyton and Jamie's neighbor Alicia **ha**d been under the impression that Jamie had still been struggling to pull it all together.

"So was it a decent plan?" I asked.

"I told her I had no interest in taking a look or in getting involved in Jamie's little business."

"It sounds like Jamie rubbed you the wrong way."

He tore his gaze away from his drink and stared into

my eyes. "I didn't say that," he said in irritation. "I said I had no interest in wasting my time on her business. And I said she was a user. But she wasn't using *me*. I didn't even know the chick."

He glanced at his watch and took one big gulp of his drink, finishing it off.

"Gotta go," he said, practically slamming the empty glass back down on the bar. He grabbed his coat the way a lion would grab a cub by the scruff of its neck and hurried to the door. Once again he hadn't bothered with good-bye.

I sat there alone for a few minutes, finishing my beer, rolling what he'd told me over in my mind. Something kept nudging at my brain, the way our family dog used to paw at my leg when he saw me eating a doughnut, but I didn't know what it was.

One thing I did know, though: I didn't like Brace. Maybe it was my bias against Wall Street broker types. Or maybe it was those weird copper-colored eyes that seemed as out of place in nature as green dirt. I could understand why Robin had felt he wasn't there for her in the marriage—he didn't seem like the kind of guy who had much time for anyone. And boy, had he disliked Jamie. He had practically bristled when he'd talked about her.

The thing that had been nudging finally pushed through. It was something Ashley had said to me when she'd first told me about Robin and Jamie's friendship: "They bonded over bad men."

According to Brace, Robin had been susceptible to Jamie's flattery and guidance. What if Jamie had discouraged Robin from getting back with her ex? Yesterday I'd dismissed the idea of Brace as a killer, because why

would he have murdered Jamie? But perhaps he had
killed because he believed she was all that stood in the
way of his getting back together with Robin. And when
he was finally sure Robin would never reconcile with
him, he had killed her, too. And Ashley? Maybe he'd
killed her because he suspected that she knew—or was
about to uncover—the truth.

CHAPTER 15

Since I had no plans for the evening, I figured I'd spend it alone, ricocheting between feeling fretful about my stalker and glum over Jack; but Landon rescued me in the end—along with the best BLT I'd ever eaten. I'd finished my beer at Ravick's and then bundled up for the trip home. The street traffic had thinned out by the time I emerged— the Wall Street crowd either headed back to the 'burbs or out for expensive dinners farther north. I lingered on the sidewalk in front of the pub just long enough to make sure that Copper Eyes wasn't hiding in the shadows someplace, waiting to follow me. Then I grabbed the first cab I saw. I swiveled around so many times, checking out who was behind us, that the driver started eyeing me suspiciously in his rearview mirror.

I felt too jittery to roam the neighborhood for groceries, so I had the driver let me off right in front of my building, and I prayed there might be something in my kitchen worth consuming. But all I found in the fridge was an expired container of cottage cheese and some limp, ragged red-leaf lettuce that at first glance looked like the head of Medusa. It had been a while since I'd taken any Advil, and the bruise on my chest was starting to throb again. I was just about to throw myself down on the couch in despair when I spotted the message light on my phone. It was Landon, fifteen minutes earlier. "Are you *alive*?" he asked. "If you get home early, tap three times on the wall. Or stop by for a sandwich."

Sandwich turned out to be an understatement. It was toasted Tuscan bread layered with crispy bacon, baby spinach, and actual red tomatoes he'd secured someplace. Each bite evoked summers spent on Cape Cod with my mother and brothers. Landon served them with red potatoes tossed in vinaigrette and a big bowl of Niçoise olives.

"I know it's all wrong for mid-January," he said, sitting across from me at his antique walnut dining table. He was dressed in jeans and a turtleneck fisherman knit sweater that almost engulfed his chin. "But these were the only ingredients I had in the larder."

"It's just great," I said, wiping mayo off my mouth with my napkin. "It's perfect comfort food."

"Are you in need of comfort food, dearest?" he asked, reaching across the table to touch my arm. "You do appear a little green around the gills."

"Yes, I'm in desperate need of comfort. As *you* would say, my life has gone to hell in a handbasket."

"Oh, no, do tell. Does it have something to do with Ms. Peyton Cross to Bear?"

I spilled everything, starting from the attack last Friday night right through to my drinks tonight with Brace.

"How dreadful," Landon exclaimed as I wrapped up my saga. "What in the world do you think is going on?"

"I still haven't a clue. Since there's not a shred of evidence the deaths were anything but accidental, I've been busy trying to focus on finding a motive."

"And?"

"There are several people who have reasons to be pissed off about Peyton or the wedding, but nothing seems big enough to kill someone over. For instance, David dumped Mandy for Peyton, but that was two years ago, and if she was going to take revenge, why direct it at the *bridesmaids*? Peyton humiliated Phillipa, but again, why take it out on us? And though Trip seems to have unsuccessfully put the moves on a few of us, a bruised ego surely isn't enough reason to turn into a serial killer."

"What about this Wall Streeter you met with tonight?"

"Yeah, he's worth taking a closer look at. He was clearly bummed about splitting with Robin. At first I dismissed him because I couldn't understand why he'd *start* by killing Jamie, but now I'm wondering if he thought she was trying to make sure he and Robin didn't get back together. The hitch is I can't figure out why he'd also have to kill Ashley. He may have thought she suspected him, but she *didn't*—or she would have told me so. What *she* kept harping on was some occurrence at the wedding. And I can't ignore that, either."

"It's all enough to make one's head spin," he said, clearing the plates. He returned from the kitchen with a plate of chocolate biscotti.

"Did you ever hear the expression *Cherchez la femme*?" I asked.

"Of course. I used to say it to my sister when her husband started taking their bulldog for hour-long walks at night. And it turned out I was totally right. Of course, what I should have said was *Cherchez la femme avec le chien*."

"What do you mean?"

"He was having an affair with one of my sister's closest friends. She had a dog, too. The two dogs had the pleasure of watching them schtup each other in a hotel room."

"Well, Cat used that phrase with me this afternoon. I hadn't heard it before but I realize what she means. I need to find a clear, straightforward motive on someone's part."

"You mean like greed?"

"Yes. Or rage. Or revenge for some significant wrongdoing. I'm just hoping that the answer is waiting for me in Miami—that this bartender-model guy really saw something. It's supposedly hot down there, and I can't wait to be in the sun. I don't think I've ever been so cold in my damn life."

"Well, when that boyfriend of yours finally moves to New York, maybe you won't be so cold."

"Hmm. That's a whole other story. We had a bit of a blowup the other night."

"Oh, don't be mad at Jack. He's too yummy."

"Do I strike you as someone who has a commitment problem?"

"Is that what he said?"

"More or less. He started to do this psychological profile of me—implying that I had a history of being skittish in matters of the heart. He made it sound as if getting me to commit was about as easy as teaching a cat to swim. Do you think that's true?"

He picked out a biscotti and broke it in two. A few chocolate crumbs spilled onto the table.

"You're avoiding my eyes," I observed.

"I'm just thinking," he said. "Of course, I've only gotten to know you since your divorce, so I have no idea what you were like *before* then. I'd have to say you *do* seem a bit skittish about getting involved. But isn't that to be expected? I have a friend who told me she was three years into her second marriage before she'd recovered from the first. And the wonderful thing about you, Bailey, is that you're your own girl. You're not Liz Taylor. You don't have some driving need to hook up with the first man who admires your tits."

"I wish I could needlepoint," I said. "That would look great on a pillow."

It was close to eleven when I let myself back into my apartment, too late, I realized, to call Jack. Since he'd been the one to break the ice with me, I'd planned to ring him tonight, to say hello, to continue our efforts to get back on an even keel. But he had an early class on Wednesdays, and there was a good chance I'd wake him up if I phoned now. Instead I went on-line and checked the forecast for Miami one more time. It was still supposed to be in the eighties all week long. I added a halter top to the stuff I was taking with me in my carry-on bag.

As I was slipping into flannel pajamas, imagining how tomorrow I'd be sleeping butt naked against satiny hotel sheets, the phone rang. Please, don't let it be Chris with some problem, was all I could think. But it was Jack.

"There you are," he said.

"Did you call before?" I asked. "There wasn't a message."

"Just once, but when I didn't get you, I tried your cell phone and left a message on that."

"I was over at Landon's," I revealed. "I was going to call you when I got back, and then I saw how late it was. How are you? Any more girls swoon in your presence today?"

"No, and I found out that the one who did yesterday has been diagnosed with chronic fatigue syndrome. So it apparently had nothing to do with me. How about you? Any new developments with the case?"

"I talked to a few people today, and I've dug up some interesting stuff. But it's not adding up to anything yet. My big news is that I have a promising lead in Miami, and I'm going to run down there tomorrow for a day and a half."

"*Miami?* What in God's name for?"

"Do you remember me mentioning that Robin asked Ashley if she'd noticed anything strange about the wedding? Well, I keep coming back to that. And it turns out that one of the bartenders who worked the reception apparently did notice something odd. But he's reluctant to talk about it on the phone. So I'm going down to Miami where he's working as a model. To interview him. I've got something to do for *Gloss* down there anyway. I mean, I'd have to go down there anyway this month."

I realized that I was talking too fast and too long, like a kid careening down a hill on an oversize bike.

"I can't believe you have to go all the way down there. You, the infamous Bailey Weggins, couldn't charm him into telling you on the phone?"

"Well, I didn't actually talk to *him*. I talked to a friend of his. He's the one setting up the meeting."

"Jeez, Bailey, this is sounding like the proverbial wild-goose chase."

"Jack, why don't you let me be the judge of that, okay?"

There was a long silence, the kind that was unpleasant and almost palpable, like a sopping wet dishrag.

"Well, look," Jack said finally. "I was just calling to say good night. There's a chance I may be coming in early on Friday—I don't have any appointments. Are you going to be back by then?"

"Yes. Like I said, I'm only going down for a day and a half. I'll be back by late Thursday afternoon. Once you know what flight you're taking, just let me know."

"I'll leave a message on your cell phone. Good night, then."

"Good night, Jack. I—well, look—have a nice day tomorrow. I'll call you from Miami."

I'd barely put down the phone when I felt a lump begin to grow in my stomach. There had been the most dejected, almost defeated sound to Jack's "good night," as if he'd given up on something. On what, though? Trying to talk some sense into me about the Miami trip? Or on *us*? Sure, we'd had a blowup, but there was no reason to think that one fight should put us on the road to relationship ruin. Yet things had gotten so *clunky* between us since Sunday, and I *was* acting bizarrely. I'd sounded defensive and prickly talking about my trip to Miami, and that kind of approach was hardly going to help things get back to normal between us. Yet at the same time I couldn't help feeling bugged by him lately—the "I know what's best for you" attitude he'd whipped out tonight, topped only by the "I know you better than you know yourself" attitude he'd displayed on Sunday. What had happened to us? This was a guy who only a week ago could make me feel positively loco in lust.

I told myself that things would surely return to normal when I saw Jack in person, that it was impossible to normalize things over the telephone.

My flight for Miami was at nine-twelve, and I was up by six, relieved to see that though it was as cold as a meat locker outside, the skies were clear. I took a ten-second shower, ate a bagel with coffee, and made one phone call, which turned out to be surprisingly fruitful: I rang Prudence in London. It was just before twelve UK time.

Until now, I hadn't been very focused on Peyton's maid of honor, as she was pretty far from the action in London. But in searching for motive I was desperate for info, and maybe she'd remember something the rest of us hadn't.

Her clipped, haughty tone reminded me a little of Ashley's, though Prudence had a light version of a British accent, sort of like Madonna's. As soon as I identified myself, she informed me that she'd heard from Maverick, then peppered me with frantic questions.

"I wish I knew what was going on, but I don't," I said. "I have a question for you, though. Was there anything at all about the weekend that seemed *off* to you—or weird?"

"Weird?" she asked, as if the word were almost foreign

to her. She was, from what I recalled, the richest and most buttoned-up of Peyton's friends. Weird to her was probably people who laundered their own clothes.

"What I mean," I said, clarifying, "is someone acting inappropriately—or suspiciously."

"Not that I recall *now*. I actually didn't get to mingle much that day. Unfortunately, I was stuck sitting next to David's best man, Trip. He seemed ready to crawl out of his skin."

Hearing Trip's name triggered another question. I asked her if she recalled anything specific about the blow-up between David and Trip at the church the night before.

"Oh, that nasty little tiff. David was pretty upset— which is unusual. You practically never see him at a full boil. I think Trip must have really screwed something up. David asked him where the profits were from—from this company called Phoenix, I think. Yes, that's right—I remember it because it was the name of my yoga studio."

"Say that again."

"He yelled, 'Where are the profits from Phoenix?' I guess Trip had blown something."

"Hmm, I don't know anything about that world. My brother does, though, so maybe I'll ask him about it."

"Do you think *my* life could be in danger?" Prudence asked fretfully. "Should I be taking precautions?"

I told her that she should be careful, but at the same time it didn't appear that for now anyone was going to head across the Atlantic after her. I nudged her off the phone then, promising to give her an update when I had more time.

The rest of the morning went like clockwork, as if just

for this day I'd been given a pass to avoid all of life's hassles. The car service that was taking me to the airport arrived on time, there was no line at security, and the flight was smooth. And when I stepped out of Miami International Airport to hail a cab, the feel of the sun on my face was pure bliss. My stress slipped away from me like a shawl tossed onto a chair. I realized that part of my pleasure derived from finally feeling safe. The killer clearly wasn't opposed to travel—he'd killed Jamie in New York, Ashley in Greenwich, and Robin possibly in Vermont. But I'd told only Jack about my Miami plans, and I was banking on the fact that I had nothing to fear.

It got even better when I arrived at my hotel. I'd stayed at the Delano once before, but I'd forgotten just how magical it was and how much it plays with your mind. You step into a lobby that's minimally furnished—mismatched leather chairs and tables on a wide planked wood floor. The ceilings are high, about eighteen feet, and there are big white columns and row after row of gauzy white curtains. Being there makes you feel as if you're in a dream sequence in a movie, one loaded with Freudian symbolism.

Though I'd booked my room last minute and in the high season, I'd somehow managed to score an ocean view. The water was blue in some spots and gray in others, and it looked cold. My room, however, was seductively warm and enchanting. It was all white, like a sanctuary—white bed, desk, chair, blinds, and a potted white orchid sitting on a plant stand. Even the wooden floor was white, painted and then glazed, so that you could practically see your reflection in it.

I'd taken off my faux fur–lined jeans jacket at the airport and bunched it under my arm, and now I stripped off my pants and sweater and underwear. After peeling back the white cotton duvet, I flopped on the bed naked, allowing the Miami heat to seep into my pores. A smile formed on my lips as I lay there, listening to the distant pounding of the surf. Then, to my surprise, I started to cry. I realized that what I was feeling was pure and utter relief.

I let myself bawl for a few minutes, long enough to soothe my frayed edges but not so long that my eyelids would swell up to the size of Idaho potatoes. I took a quick shower and put on a pair of black capris, black sandals, and this cute little white halter top with black buttons up the front. It was high enough to hide the black-and-blue mark on my chest.

It was now two o'clock, and that meant I had five hours to kill before I met up with Chris. I decided I would use the time to simply relax on the beach, walk, and think a little. I was tempted to take my composition notebook with me, but I felt it might be better to allow my brain to idle for a while and generate some revelation on its own. The only thing I stuffed in my tote bag was the novel I was reading. Before I left my room, I left a message for Chris on his cell, confirming my arrival—as promised. I also left a message for my brother Cameron, asking if I could pick his brain.

First stop would have to be lunch, though. Other than a bag of plane pretzels, which had tasted like compressed sawdust, I'd had nothing to eat since six that morning. I found a table out on the terrace of the hotel, where a scattering of late diners still lolled about. I ordered a lobster Caesar with a glass of white wine so deliciously icy that my lips nearly jumped back in surprise. Maybe I could just move here for a few months, I thought. And leave all my troubles up north.

As I drank a cappuccino, I could feel the beach beckoning just a stone's throw away. I paid the bill and headed down there. Sandals in hand, I began to walk, letting the warm sand run through my toes. The sight of the ocean and the sound of the waves hitting the beach and then pulling back brought to mind those trips I'd taken, some as a kid with my family to Cape Cod and others, as a travel writer, to more far-flung places—Costa Rica, the Côte d'Azur, the Amalfi coast. After twenty minutes in one direction, I turned around and came back. I found a lounge chair near the hotel, dragged it under a palm tree, and read. It was only a few minutes before I drifted off into a deep sleep.

By the time I woke up to the sound of the breeze swishing in the top of palm trees, it was five. I was sticky with sweat and slightly dizzy from sleeping in the heat.

Back in my room, I showered and drank half a bottle of water, then took time getting ready. I'd brought a sundress with me, but the evening was turning cool, so I opted instead for white slacks, a white, peasanty top that fell off my shoulders, and a pair of brown sandals. As I was swiping on lip gloss, I realized that some of the Zen state I'd been feeling had started to evaporate. I was getting nervous about having dinner with someone I barely knew, about whether this Kyle dude would show up, and about whether he'd tell me something that would make the whole trip worthwhile. By the time I left the hotel for the Shore Club, I was practically buzzing with trepidation.

Sometimes you meet a person and then see him or her again and you're startled by how your brain took such a lousy picture. That wasn't the case with Chris. He was sitting at a table waiting for me and looked exactly as I remembered him. That gorgeous face with the full lips and cleft in his chin. His light brown hair was cut short on the sides but spiked up and tousled a little in front like summer grass, and his eyebrows were one shade darker, adding to the charm of his face. He was wearing a pale green polo shirt that matched his eyes. It also accentuated something I hadn't noticed when he'd been in his waiter's tux the day of the wedding. He had two Chinese characters tattooed on his arm.

"Hey," he said, standing to greet me. He kissed me on the cheek, and as he did I rested my hands on his upper arms. They felt as hard as the side of a steer. "You're letting your hair grow."

"Yeah," I acknowledged. "Though it's in that kind of awkward stage now—not quite long enough to put up. Thanks for ordering the nice weather, by the way."

"I hear it's been a bitch up north. I found out this afternoon that I have to fly up there for an audition next week, and I'm not looking forward to it."

"For something good?" I asked as we both sat down, me in the chair next to him since the spot across from him hadn't been set.

"Could be," he said, and smiled, a sort of half smile he did by pulling over the left side of his mouth. "It's a soap. I've already done some under-fives for them, and now they're considering me for a bigger role. It would be great to finally get out of this modeling thing. It's been such a catch-22. It bores me to tears, but it pays pretty well, and I'd rather be doing this than waiting tables or tending bar."

"Has acting been your goal all along?"

"Definitely. I majored in theater and came straight to New York. I'd never once thought about modeling, but a guy I did a showcase with suggested it as a roundabout way of getting into television commercials. It's nearly impossible to get an agent for that stuff, and you just have to try everything you can think of. In the last couple of months, I actually managed to back into a few commercials that way—you know, I did the print ad and then next thing you know they're considering me for the TV campaign. And now it looks like I might finally have an agent. In fact, I'm thinking that after my audition, I may not even come back down again."

"Where do you stay when you're down here?" I asked. As soon as I'd said it, I worried that it sounded as if I wanted to get a handle on what his digs were like, in case I might want to head back there later.

"I bunk down in an apartment with a bunch of other guys," he said. "It's just a crash pad, really, in a building with a zillion other models. They're nice enough, but I swear I've never seen a group of people so obsessed with their looks. These guys actually bring weights to photo shoots and then pump up right before they go on set. Sometimes I think it's a miracle I get cast in anything."

He took his eyes off me in search of a waiter and flagged one down with just a lift of his chin. There was something mature and sophisticated about him that seemed incongruous with his barely-off-campus looks. When the waiter arrived I ordered a glass of rosé, which seemed fitting for the place and the night. Chris, I noticed, had already ordered a drink that looked like vodka on the rocks. Apparently he wasn't worried about carb face.

"So tell me more about your situation," he said after I'd ordered my wine. "It sounds like a real nightmare."

"It is—and it's gotten even more complicated since I spoke to you." I fleshed out what I'd shared with him earlier and described some of the facts I'd learned in the last day. I also told him about my dispiriting last encounter with the Greenwich police.

"It sounds like you're in some kind of Hitchcock movie," he said, shaking his head.

"I know. I keep circling around the truth but never know what it is. That's why I was desperate to talk to this guy Kyle. You got the feeling he really did see something?"

"Let's put it this way—I don't know if he *saw* something, but he definitely *knows* something. I could tell just by looking at him. Speaking of Kyle, why don't we order and then I'll swing by the bar, which is his usual haunt. We agreed on nine, but he's the type who'd come an hour early, not find us there, and then just split."

The waiter arrived with my wine, and we ordered dinner. Then Chris excused himself and stood up. I saw for the first time that he was in light khaki pants and sandals. I watched him go, a confident but easy stride, the mark of someone who'd always known he was hunky but hadn't really cared all that much. If Landon were sitting right next to me, I knew just what he'd say: "That might be the greatest ass I've ever seen."

The night had grown slightly cooler, and I draped the pashmina I'd brought around my shoulders. While I waited I sipped my wine and listened to the sound of the ocean crashing against the beach. Jack drifted into my thoughts. We had talked about heading somewhere warm like this in March or April—maybe to the Yucatán. A sense of foreboding came over me out of the blue, but I had no idea why.

The waiter appeared at my right elbow, with our plates lined up on the inside of his forearm. He looked at me with a quizzical expression, silently querying me if it was okay to set them down.

"He'll be right back," I said.

Chris had been gone longer than I realized, and I glanced back at the hotel, scanning the area. There was no sign of him. I felt a tiny swell of panic. Was this just one more part of the Hitchcockian movie? I suddenly wondered. Was Chris not coming back? Would the next scene be me frantically searching the Sky Bar for Chris and for Kyle? I lowered my head into my hand and tried to slow my breath.

"Sorry."

It was Chris appearing out of nowhere behind me. He slid into his seat and dropped his napkin back in his lap.

"It's pretty spread out in there, and after I took a sweep around, some guy tells me he thought he saw Kyle earlier. So I did another sweep. I see this guy again, and then he tells me he remembers that he saw Kyle someplace else instead. The good news is that Kyle told this bozo that he's headed over here later."

"Terrific," I said, and took another sip of wine. I couldn't believe how rattled I'd been.

Chris ordered a glass of wine, and I had another. Over the next half hour we ate and talked. His father, he told me, was an engineer, and he had spent some of his early life in the Middle East and Asia. Maybe all the moving around and the subsequent sense of displacement were what had prevented his ego from becoming inflated. I realized as we spoke that our dinner was seeming dangerously close to a date. Chris was easy to talk to and even easier to look at. I knew I should bring up Jack, but there was no right minute to do it without it seeming as if I'd dropped a sixteen-pound ham on the table.

I was relieved when he suggested we skip coffee and head for the bar. He fought me for the check, but I insisted, saying that he was the one helping me in a bind.

The Sky Bar was nearly packed when we arrived, and the feeling was electric. People talking and shouting amid the exotic decor—sheer white curtains, climbing plants, Moroccan hanging lanterns.

I ordered a sparkling water, and so did Chris. We stood against the bar and talked some more—about his days studying theater, my writing career. All the while, Chris let his eyes roam the room. At one point we glanced simultaneously at our watches, and I saw to my shock that it was nine-twenty. I felt a wave of panic again. Chris told me to hang by the bar while he took another sweep around the room. I stared into the crowd. The place was loaded with lots of guys who all could have been models, some white, some black, some Latin. Chris returned five minutes later, shaking his head.

"Look, don't worry yet," he said. "Just as he could have been an hour early, he could be an hour late."

We waited a few more minutes, Chris's eyes always on the crowd and me foolishly scanning, too, though I had utterly no idea what Kyle looked like.

"I don't believe it," Chris said out of the blue.

"What?"

"He's lying ten feet away from us—on that daybed."

There was a bunch of daybeds in the bar, places to enjoy your buzz or ram your tongue down the throat of someone you'd met ten minutes earlier. I followed Chris's eyes to one directly ahead of us, where a guy and two girls lounged against half a dozen large pillows in bright, exotic fabrics. Though I must have laid eyes on Kyle at some point at the reception, he was totally unfamiliar to me.

Taking my hand, Chris led me over there. Kyle didn't spot him until we were right in front. He smiled without bothering to get up.

"Hey, man," Kyle said, grasping Chris's arm in one of those full-forearm shakes. His sandy-colored hair was longish, parted in the middle, and looped up from a slight widow's peak to fall in waves on either side of his face. He had narrow eyes, and his upper lip curled up toward his nose in the hint of a scowl. I realized after a second that he wasn't forming an expression—his features were naturally set that way. Kyle had come out of the womb looking like a bad boy.

"This is Bailey," Chris said. "The girl I said was coming down here."

He looked momentarily stupefied and then nodded. "Oh yeah. How ya doin'?"

"Great. It's so nice to meet you," I said. "Have you got a second to talk?"

He sighed and shrugged his shoulders. The two girls, whose boobs were spilling out of their tops, just lay there sullenly, not saying a word.

"Can I buy you a drink?" I asked, remembering Adam's advice.

"I'm cool," he said, eyeing me up and down. He was probably thinking I was too ancient to speak to. "So, Chris, I got that big catalog job. The Italian one. I'm so stoked, dude."

"That's cool. Listen, Bailey's come all the way down here to talk to you. We can't go into all the details, but this is a pretty urgent matter."

"This doesn't involve the cops, does it? I mean, I'm not gonna have that CSI Miami guy knocking at my door, am I?"

"No, nothing like that," I said. "I just need to know what happened at the wedding that day. Chris said you saw something freaky."

"It's not that I saw something freaky. But something freaky happened to me. It was with one of those bridal chicks—not the bride, but the ones in the ugly dresses."

I looked at him expectantly.

"I scored with one of them that day," he continued. "Upstairs in some sort of dressing room. That's why I didn't want to get into it over the phone."

"Which girl?" Chris asked.

"I don't remember her name. She had short black hair, though."

"Jamie?" I asked.

"If she's the only one with short black hair, yeah. Like I said, I haven't a clue what her name was."

"And that's *it*?" I asked, unable to disguise my frustration.

"Hold your horses. No, it's not *it*. The girl went ballistic on me."

"Why?" I asked. "Did she think you took advantage of her?"

"Hardly. I bet that chick has a fuck buddy in every state. No, I tried to take her picture. She had this little camera with her, and I thought she'd like a shot of herself in the postfuck afterglow. And she goes bananas. Tells me not to touch it, and then she starts punching at me."

"And that's what you consider to be something freaky happening at the reception?" Chris asked in annoyance.

"Hey, man, the chick hit me in the mouth with her fuckin' hand. That's pretty freaky, if you ask me."

Chris touched my elbow and led me away.

"God, what a moron," he said. "Look, I'm really sorry about this. I dragged you all the way down here for nothing."

"No, it's okay. What he said is huge."

"What do you mean?"

I held out my hands in excitement. "He tried to use her camera and she went nuts. I knew she took a bunch of pictures that day, and I bet she was just trying to make sure nothing whatsoever happened to the film in the camera. I think what I'm looking for is in those pictures."

CHAPTER 16

CAN YOU GET your hands on the pictures?" he asked. He had to practically yell over the din of the bar.

"I've *got* them," I said, raising my own voice. "I've always suspected that they were important somehow, but this seems to confirm it." I let my gaze absently roam the room as I began flipping through the photos in my mind, trying to recall each one of them.

"Where are—here, why don't we find someplace better to talk," Chris shouted. He reached for my hand and began to pull me through the crowd. The room was jampacked now, and eighty percent of the people looked as if they were models, movie stars, or international drug dealers. Chris's hand felt smooth and strong, and holding it made my heart skip nervously.

"So where *are* these pictures?" he asked as we stepped into the lobby, which seemed as serene as a Zen garden compared to the Sky Bar.

They were in my room at the Delano, tucked safely away in my tote bag. Yet I didn't want to say that. I was afraid that in Chris's mind it might amount to some kind of invitation.

"They're back in New York," I lied. "I've stared at them over and over, and I just don't see anything in them. But there *must* be something there."

"I just can't believe I made you come all this way for so little payoff."

"But it's not a little payoff. It's really helping me focus on what matters. Up until now I've been chasing all sorts of angles—things like whether someone might be trying to sabotage Peyton's business, even whether David's ex-wife is staging the revenge of the forsaken flight attendant. But I realize now that I've got to concentrate on the wedding weekend. That's what Robin was always worried about."

I glanced at my watch. It was after ten, and I needed to be up at the crack of dawn the next day. And I was dying to see the photos again. Now that I had better reason to believe in their significance, something might finally jump out at me. Before I could announce my need to return to the Delano, Chris offered to make sure I got back safely.

"Why don't we go by the beach, though," he said. "It's a much nicer walk."

The beach was nearly deserted, except for a few couples out for romantic strolls. I slipped off my sandals and carried them in the hand next to Chris, just to be sure he didn't reach out for me again.

I didn't want to do anything to encourage the notion of us on a date. The ocean was as black as the sky, except for the faint white foam of the waves and the pinpoints of light from a cruise ship far off on the horizon. I'd taken one cruise in my life and had been bored to tears, yet whenever I see a ship at night, strung with lights like a carnival and looking like a dazzling jeweled brooch on the horizon, I feel an overwhelming yearning to be on board.

We walked in silence. I watched the black waves and thought about the pictures. Chris, hands stuffed in his pockets, seemed lost in thought. At one point two men passed us, arm in arm, and one of them ran his eyes over Chris. I couldn't blame him. He was so drop-dead good-looking that it could make someone blubber.

Finally the Delano appeared ahead, white as a cruise ship itself.

"I'll walk you to the lobby," Chris said. "I'm gonna catch a cab home from there."

"Are you working tomorrow?" I asked. We'd reached the pool and were walking along the rim of it toward the hotel area. There were still people scattered at some of the tables, drinking or eating late night suppers.

"No, I'm just gonna hang out, read, maybe do some body surfing."

"I can't tell you how much I appreciate what you did—talking to Kyle for me, convincing him to show tonight. I'm sure it wasn't easy. Now that I've met him, I can see that getting him to do anything must be like trying to lasso an eel."

He threw back his head and laughed. "Well put. But look, Bailey, on a more serious note, will you do me a favor and just let me know what happens? This is scary stuff, and I'm going to be wondering about you."

"Sure," I told him. "I'll give you a call and let you know."

"I have to say I admire you for not being intimidated by this whole thing. I bet you were one heck of a Girl Scout."

"I appreciate that," I said, smiling. We were in the lobby now. The sheer white curtains blew in the breeze, as if someone had zigzagged through them only seconds before and then disappeared. I realized with relief, just from Chris's tone, that there would be no campaign to get in my pants.

"And again, thanks for everything," I said.

"I was happy to help. Let me know if there's anything else I can do. And thanks for dinner, too."

I reached out to shake his hand. He took my fingers instead, leaned forward, and kissed me. It wasn't much more than a brush of his lips, but it was long enough for me to feel their softness and to taste a hint of wine. Long enough, too, for me to feel a jolt of desire.

"That's for good luck," he said, smiling.

Okay, it's not so terrible, I assured myself as I opened the door to my hotel room. He'd caught me off guard with the kiss, which, I reassured myself, I'd done nothing to encourage. Yes, I'd responded physically, but who wouldn't have? The guy was a professional hottie, someone whose photographs alone were supposed to make women weak in the knees. Plus, I had other things to worry about now.

I dug the pictures out of my tote bag, but I didn't look at them right away. I wanted to be sure I could give them my full attention with absolutely no distractions. After washing off my makeup, I stripped to my underwear and slipped on a cotton camisole. The chambermaid had switched the air conditioner on low, but I turned it off and instead opened the window a crack. Instantly a breeze wiggled its way through the opening and the pounding sound of the ocean filled the room. I turned back the bed-covers and, pictures in hand, plopped down, my back against the pillows. One by one I went through them: Peyton in her glory, Peyton and David kissing, Trip talk-ing to a male guest by the bar, Mary surveying the ball-room, half a dozen shots of all the bridesmaids but Jamie, and assorted guests. I knew practically none of the lat-ter—most were family members of the bride and groom or friends of theirs from Greenwich. I realized it would be helpful to have someone more familiar with all the players examine the pictures with me.

Peyton. She was the perfect candidate. In fact, I should have solicited her help earlier.

Despite my nap on the beach, my eyes felt heavy with fatigue. But I didn't want to go to bed until I'd called Jack. I had promised to ring him from Miami, and I knew that if I didn't, especially in light of how our last conver-sation had ended, it would only accentuate the clunkiness between us. I used my cell rather than the hotel phone to dial his number. All I got was his answering machine. As I listened to his deep, melodic voice, I glanced at the clock at the bedside table. Close to eleven. It was odd for him to be out this late on a school night. I left a message saying that my trip had proven fruitful and that I was looking forward to seeing him this weekend. My voice sounded odd to me, as it had last Sunday in my apart-ment—an octave higher and kind of staccato. Was I feel-ing guilty about the kiss from Chris? Or was it simply because of the awkwardness that had formed between us lately? I wondered what Jack's assessment would be as he listened to my message.

Despite my churning emotions, I slept through the night, the first time I'd accomplished such a feat in a few days. When I woke, the sun had just come up and the sky was bleached of color. There was a lump in my stomach as I threw my summer clothes into my bag. Though I was eager to show the wedding photos to Peyton for her insight, I was nervous about being back home, easily in the sights of a killer.

Since I'm bad with directions, I'd arranged for an inexpensive car service to take me to my appointment in Ft. Lauderdale rather than rent a car. The drive took about thirty-five minutes, less than I'd expected, but then we were doing a reverse commute. The woman's house, in a lower-middle-class neighborhood, was a small white bungalow with louvered Caribbean-style shutters and a yard overgrown with junglelike plants whose fronds bobbed gently in the morning breeze. But inside there was none of that Graham Greene feeling. The walls were painted an ugly mustard yellow, and the only pieces of furniture in the living room were a dingy white couch and two black director's chairs.

With so much on my mind, I'd been afraid that I'd have a hard time concentrating on the interview, but I'd worried for nothing. The woman's case was riveting. In applying for a car loan she'd discovered that someone had stolen her identity and she'd spent the next five years trying to get it back. The stress had given her colitis and wrecked her marriage. "I used to be a fun person," she said to me desperately.

On the way to the airport I packed my tape recorder and jotted down a few impressions in my composition book. As we reached the exit to the airport my phone went off. It was my brother Cameron.

"What's up?" he asked. "You sounded anxious to connect."

I had no intention of telling him about the murders. I adore my brother, but he's a bit of a scaredy-cat—when we were growing up his idea of an adventure was playing Marco Polo in a swimming pool—and he's always suggesting my work is "too close to the edge." If I spilled anything to him about my current situation there was an excellent chance he'd not only go into anaphylactic shock but also blab to my mother. Instead I made it seem as if I were working on some kind of human interest story. Without naming names, I described David and Trip's business and the words Prudence had overheard.

"He said, 'Why didn't you book a profit on Phoenix'?" Cameron asked.

"I think so. Could there be some significance to that company, do you think?"

"Never heard of it. Sounds like it might be Asian. But the other part of the phrase interests me. That could mean something."

"Like what?"

"Well, you know how a hedge fund works, right?"

"I know it has nothing to do with garden hedges, but that's about it."

"Hedge funds buy and sell securities. They're kind of like stocks. A hedge fund manager is always managing the profits and losses and trying to come out ahead. Some of these securities are on exchanges, so it's easy to keep track of how they're doing, but others are less visible. You have to depend on the expertise and integrity of the manager to mark them accurately—as far as their profits and losses go."

I was glad he couldn't see me because my eyes had started to glaze over. I tried harder to concentrate, knowing that what he was saying might prove important.

"You still there?" he asked.

"Yeah, yeah."

"So as you can see, there's room for some game playing. When I hear that this guy David yelled at his manager and wanted to know why he hadn't taken the profits on something, it makes me wonder if he was moving profits around somehow."

"And you're not supposed to do that?"

"Hell, no. Let's say he has a trade that doesn't work out and he decides to mismark it—so instead of it being down forty percent, he marks it down ten percent. Then maybe he uses some of the profits from another trade to hide the loss—and mismarks that one, too. But there are all sorts of ramifications. Investors who should have profited from the good trade lose out. Plus the IRS gets screwed, too."

I didn't speak for a minute, trying to digest what he'd shared. If what he'd suggested about Trip was true, it was major. It meant that the spat the bridesmaids overheard in the church that day wasn't just some minor scuffle between business associates—it was David probing about whether Trip had engaged in something unethical. Had he ever been able to prove it? And if he had, why would David continue to work with Trip? Perhaps because, as people always said, he was brilliant at making money.

"You still there?" Cameron asked again.

"Yeah, I'm just thinking. So could he go to jail for what he did?"

"Oh sure. So is this really for a story you're working on?" he asked suspiciously.

"Uh-huh."

The car had pulled up in front of the terminal and the driver hopped out to open my door. I said a rushed goodbye to my brother, promising to call him and explain when I had more time to talk—which I had no intention of doing.

I waited until I'd caught my breath and the plane was in the air before I withdrew the photos from my purse once again and spread them on the tray table. David and Trip's argument might be at the root of everything, but how could that tie in with the photos that Jamie had seemed so desperate to protect? I stared at the one of Trip and the mystery man and began to play out a scenario: What if for some reason Jamie understood the significance of the words exchanged between Trip and David in the church. Perhaps the next day she overheard a discussion between Trip and this mystery man at the reception that shed even greater light on what she'd heard in the church. She took a photo in order to capture the moment. Later she approached Trip about what she'd overheard, perhaps threatening to blackmail him. She needed money for her business—*and* hadn't she finally gotten it? Eventually Trip decided he was left with no choice but to eliminate Jamie. Maybe Trip was even the new man in Jamie's life, the visitor in her apartment the night she died. The next thing you know, Robin started asking questions. And sure enough, Trip started hanging around with her, ingratiating himself, trying to find out what she knew. Clearly he saw her as a threat, because she ended up dead, too. And eventually so did Ashley.

But why start coming after me? I flashed back on a moment in the kitchen with David the day after Ashley's death. David had encouraged me to put the deaths behind me, but I'd vowed to learn what was really happening. I'd tipped him off that day that I was going to snoop—and perhaps he'd shared our conversation with Trip.

Of course—and here was a thought that made my blood turn icy—David could have as much to lose as Trip. If he'd realized what Trip had done and let him off with a warning, he was culpable. Frantically I searched my memory. Peyton said that David was in New Haven the afternoon that Ashley died, though she'd had trouble reaching him. But Trip had been missing in action.

I thought of the moment Monday night in Peyton's library when Trip had appeared silently at my side. He'd suggested we have a drink sometime. It made my stomach turn to think of how he'd let his hand linger on mine when he'd reached for the bottle of brandy.

Yet I didn't want to get ahead of myself. I hadn't a shred of evidence that Trip had done anything—including anything improper in his hedge fund business. It all fit together, but my theory was just a hunch and nothing more. When Peyton examined the photos, something totally different might emerge.

"I just love big weddings."

I nearly jumped. It was the woman next to me in the middle seat, who had already fruitlessly tried to engage the man by the window in conversation. She was about sixty, her hair styled in one of those poodle perms and wearing a turquoise-and-pink rayon tracksuit. My stress had totally bitchified me, and I had to fight the temptation to tell her, "Just shut up," or threaten to put her hair on a leash. Instead I simply ignored her and slid the photos back into the envelope.

Sipping a tomato juice, I tried to calm down by working on my dead-wife article, but it didn't help. The only thing I could focus on was Jack—and at this point, conjuring up thoughts of my supposed boyfriend was anything but reassuring. Why hadn't he called? What would it take to normalize things between us again? Did the fact that I'd been stirred by Chris's kiss suggest some bigger problem?

By the time I was in a car service headed toward Manhattan, I was so wired that I could barely stand it. I knew I had to return to Greenwich as soon as possible—not only to review the photos with Peyton, but also to talk to David about Trip. I decided I would leave first thing in the morning.

There'd been no messages on my cell phone when I'd disembarked from the plane, but there were a ton of them on my answering machine at home: Landon wondering how I was; Maverick checking in; my brother Cameron mistakenly returning my earlier call at home; a friend from Brown announcing she was coming in from San Francisco next week; a writer pal asking for advice about a seemingly insane editor.

My wired, bitchy mood seemed to energize me, and as I was making myself a cup of coffee, it occurred to me that there was no reason not to drive out to Greenwich tonight. It was about four, and though it would mean I'd hit rush-hour traffic, I'd be there by early evening and could meet up with Peyton at her place. Waiting until to-morrow, in fact, would be torturous, particularly now that I sensed I was closing in on the truth.

The housekeeper answered when I called Peyton's and made an announcement that I should have been prepared for. Mrs. Slavin had a party tonight, in Darien.

"She said she won't be staying for the whole thing, though," she said after I'd sighed in frustration. "I'm ex-pecting her back at around eight."

"Oh, great," I said, relieved. "I don't want to disturb her when she's on-site somewhere, but if she calls, will you tell her I'm coming up tonight? I'd appreciate being able to stay the night one more time."

I spent the next few minutes pacing my apartment, coffee mug in hand, making a game plan. My priority was to have separate conversations with Peyton and David. I was hoping that information I gathered would help me determine if I should clearly be focusing on Trip.

As I was packing a new bag for the night, Jack finally called.

"You get back okay?" he asked. It was clear from the background noises that he was outdoors someplace.

"Yeah, about an hour ago. Are you just leaving work?"

"Actually, I'm two blocks away, walking down Uni-versity Place."

"You're kidding me," I exclaimed. The news, for some reason, weirded me out, as if he'd just announced he was leaving for a year's sabbatical in Tokyo.

"Since I didn't have any appointments tomorrow, I ended up hopping on a shuttle after my last class today. Have you got a minute? I thought I might stop by."

"Um, of course," I said.

"If this isn't a good time . . ."

"No, no, it's fine—I'm so glad you're here. You just caught me off guard for a second. Come on by."

As I set the phone down, my mind was a blur of conflicting thoughts and emotions. Jack's early arrival in New York would put the kibosh on a trip to Greenwich, and frankly that irritated me. I was desperate to be there, to show the photos to Peyton, but there was just no way I could bail on Jack tonight. It would seriously piss him off, considering everything that had happened. Beyond that, I really did need to talk to him in person and help nudge us back into our old groove. There was something else I was feeling, too—an inexplicable unease. It spilled through me like a wave rushing into the nooks and crannies of a sand castle.

I used the few minutes before Jack arrived to change from the jeans I'd worn on the plane to a short brown-and-camel tweed skirt, a cashmere camel sweater, and high brown boots. A little spiffy, but I wanted to look nice. I also made more coffee and cracked open a couple of windows; the cold snap had broken while I was away, and the temperature had to be near forty. From my window I could see that the snow had shrunk to mere slivers on the rooftops to the west. With nothing else to do, I sat on the couch and just waited. I felt jittery, as if I'd just been signaled over for speeding and was waiting for a trooper to emerge from his car in the night.

It took Jack longer than it should have to walk the few blocks to my building, and I started to wonder what in the world was going on. When he finally arrived with a Starbucks bag, I realized he'd stopped to get us coffee. He was wearing jeans, a white shirt, and his brown leather jacket, one of Jack's few nods to bad boyism. He kissed me, but it was a quick, distracted kiss—the kind he might offer if we'd been apart for a few hours running errands. While I hung his jacket, he pulled two cappuccinos from the bag and set them on the coffee table.

"It's so nice you came up a day early," I said. My voice sounded stilted, like someone making small talk in a high school play.

"I'll be honest—I was anxious to talk to you after what happened on Sunday. It's really been eating away at me."

"Me too," I said, taking a seat beside him on the couch. I popped the lid from my cappuccino and took a sip, but it was hot and burned the inside of my lip. "Like I said on the phone, I should never have made you leave like that. It wasn't fighting fair."

"Well, you're generally a pretty fair fighter, so I clearly made you very angry." He smiled wanly then, though there was something very sad in his blue eyes. My heart picked up speed.

"Let's just put it behind us, Jack," I said softly.

He took a deep breath, and I saw his chest rise beneath his crisp white shirt.

"That's what I wanted to come by and talk to you about, Bailey. I don't think it's possible. I think that argument Sunday revealed something about our situation. And what I've come to realize over the past few days is that I don't feel it's going to work between us."

His last few words had been barely audible to me, as if he were speaking underwater. The whole moment seemed totally surreal.

"Are—are you saying you want to break things off with me?" I asked, incredulous.

"No, the last thing I want is for us to break things off. But I'm afraid there may be no choice."

"I'm not following," I said. I felt confused, disconcerted. Tears fought to break out from behind my eyes.

"The other night you said that by getting married, you'd made a bigger commitment than I ever had. I—"

"I was angry—I didn't mean anything disparaging by that."

He lifted the lid off his own cappuccino and took a long sip. I could see him forming words in his mind.

"I know you didn't. But you're right. Up until this point in my life, I haven't had any desire to make a major commitment to someone. But I've realized in the past weeks that I've been feeling closer and closer to you, and when that apartment situation came up, I suddenly saw that I finally *do* feel ready—and I want to make that commitment to *you*. But that doesn't seem to be in the cards. I apologize for sounding like I was analyzing you the other night, but the bottom line is that making a commitment to me isn't something you feel comfortable doing. And it would be too tough for me to hang around, hoping you'd change your mind."

"Tell me exactly what you mean by commitment, Jack," I urged. "You mean our *living* together?"

"Yes, but not just because my sublet fell through or as some open-ended arrangement. I'd see it leading to something. I'm in love with you, Bailey, and I can picture myself married to you."

I had a hard time swallowing. I felt a surge of tenderness, thinking of how Jack felt about me, but at the same time, I could sense panic circling me, ready to pounce. I stood up from the couch and walked back and forth the length of the room, combing my hands through my hair. It was growing dark outside, and the cityscape outside my window had begun to take on the look it always had at night of a backdrop for a play—inky black sky, buildings dabbed randomly with lights. I could feel myself pulling words from someplace. I realized that they'd been forming all week, but I'd never spoken them to myself.

"Jack, I care so much for you," I said, turning my gaze back to him. "And I think I may be in love with you, too. The last few months have been so wonderful. But what you say is true. I don't think I *can* make that kind of commitment to you."

"I know you—"

"But I just want to clarify something. I think what bothered me the other night so much was being characterized as someone who *can't* make a commitment—either because of my past or because I'm still being rocked by my stink bomb of a marriage. I admit my divorce really did knock me off my feet. And not just the breaking-up part. Finding out that the person I was married to had this secret life was horrible. But it's not like I've got this big bruise that's preventing me from falling in love again. Like I said, I think I might very well be in love with *you*—but I just feel I'm not yet ready to make a commitment. It's too soon for me."

He stared at me with his deep blue eyes, and I felt the most enormous wave of sadness. It was going to be over with Jack and me. Right now. Right this very second. On some deep level, I'd known it all week.

"There's no way, right, that we could just go back to dating the way we had been?" I asked plaintively.

He used both hands to push himself up from the couch.

"As much as it pains me to say it, no," he said. "Based on how I feel about you, it wouldn't be a happy situation for me. And you wouldn't like it, either. You'd feel constantly pressured."

A sob began to form, making my chest heave.

"Jack, I just can't believe this," I choked. "It's just all happening so fast. I can hardly bear it."

He came toward me, resting a hand on my shoulder. "I know. Like I said, I don't think I knew the extent of how I felt until last weekend."

He walked into the foyer and yanked his leather jacket from the hanger in the closet.

"But you don't have to leave right now, do you?" I asked anxiously. "Don't you at least want to have dinner or go out for a drink?"

"What would the point be? This is going to be really hard for me, and I'd rather just rip the Band-Aid right off than slowly tug at it. But listen, Bailey, promise me you'll be careful until this case is solved. I'm going to call you in a few days and see how everything is going, okay?"

Before I could say another word, he leaned toward me and kissed me softly on the mouth, just a hint longer than he had before. Then he opened the door and was gone.

CHAPTER 17

I WAS ON the road to Greenwich by six o'clock, with a headache that throbbed so much I could actually feel the skin on my forehead pulse. And my stomach was churning like the ocean before a storm. I opened my window a crack in order to get some air. According to the road signs, littering was punishable by a three-hundred-dollar fine. I wondered how big a fine they would slap on me for engaging in projectile vomiting.

I stuck in my Callas CD, but this time it was like the proverbial fingernails on a chalkboard, and I immediately turned it off. After using one hand to scrounge around for my earpiece, I called Landon, figuring he'd just be getting in. He answered on the fourth ring, breathless.

"Where are you?" he asked. "I just rapped on your door thirty seconds ago."

"I'm in my car, heading back to the land of the rich

and superrich. Have you got five minutes to talk? I know you just walked in the door."

"Of course. What's up?"

"Jack broke up with me."

"What?"

"Well, to put his spin on it, I forced him to break up with me."

"Was it because of the swimming cat thing?"

"Huh?"

"You said he thought it was as easy for you to make a commitment as it was for a cat to learn to swim."

"Oh, right. Yes, that's the alleged reason. He admitted last night that he had really fallen for me lately—I mean, he even used the L-word. And a minute later he used the *M*-word. But then he told me that he sensed I wasn't going to make the leap and that he couldn't bear to wait and wonder. The next thing you know, he's out like trout."

"What a crybaby," he said loyally. "If he doesn't think you're worth waiting for, he's definitely not worth being with."

"Yeah, I guess. But I see it from his point of view, too. Ever since he mentioned the notion of living together, I've felt completely skittish, and things would never have been good between us with him at such a different place from me."

"Are you bummed?"

"Completely. I can see now that I'm simply not ready for a big commitment, but at the same time I liked what I had with Jack. I feel miserable—you know, that totally limp feeling you get when you can barely summon the energy to look sideways."

"I wish I could think of something to say to make you feel better," Landon said. "Usually when people break up I try to console them with the fact that they'll lose weight, but you don't need to."

"Just tell me you're around this weekend. I can't bear the thought of being alone."

"The most exciting thing I'd planned to do was marinate a pork tenderloin, so, darling, I'm all yours."

We agreed to talk tomorrow, after I determined just how long I needed to be in Greenwich. I was relieved to have someone to hang with, but it did little to ease my misery. Part of the problem was that the split had more or less come out of the blue. Our conversation on Sunday had thrown me a curveball, but I hadn't seen then that it was the beginning of the end.

With my marriage there had been plenty of warning— more, in fact, than anyone in their right mind could ever want. With the benefit of hindsight, I could remember the exact moment it had all begun to unravel, though at the time it had been such a simple thing, like a tiny hole in the sleeve of a sweater. He'd seemed jumpy one night, preoccupied, and I'd assumed it must be work.

"You okay?" I asked. "Are you worried about a case?"

"Yeah, but I'll figure it out," he answered. When I looked at him across the room, however, I saw that his eyes were wide in alarm, as if someone had just told him that the devil really *did* exist. I pressed a little, but he shook his head and went to bed. I decided to take him at his word.

It got worse then, over the next weeks—the jumpiness, that is. He paced rooms, rarely sat still, never wanted sex, and ran us around to all those restaurants downtown. I started to think it might be drugs, maybe even crack, because he didn't seem to be enjoying himself enough to be screwing someone else. I started the desperate searching of pockets but turned up nothing. His secretary began to call, looking for him during the day. Then some of my jewelry disappeared, and soon after I learned it was gambling— thanks to a tip, so to speak, from a buddy of his. Only after we separated did I realize how much of a disaster it was. A good deal of our money was gone. The only reason he didn't get the apartment was that it was in my name, purchased with the help of a small trust fund from my father.

By the time it was finally over, I'd pretty much gotten used to being without him—physically and emotionally. That's not to say it wasn't awful, especially learning that for so many months my life wasn't what I'd thought it was. But I never missed him after he was gone.

I'd had no such time to even envision life without Jack. I would never again lie beside him watching an old movie as the city slowly fell to sleep. Never walk through the Village on a Sunday morning with him, never anything. If a little voice had told me on Saturday night that I was having sex with Jack for the last time, I would have been incredulous.

It was in my power, of course, to change everything. But I just couldn't. I simply didn't feel ready to live with someone again.

I called Peyton's house as I was nearing Greenwich, and Clara informed me that Peyton had checked in just a short while ago. She'd said it was fine for me to stay again and that I should come anytime, but it now looked as if she wouldn't be returning until nine or ten. That was only a few hours away, yet it seemed interminable. At a red light I considered my options. I could go out to the house and hope to talk to David privately before Peyton returned. Though he might still be at the office. With one eye on the light, I called his number. A secretary answered, despite how late it was.

"Mr. Slavin is out at the moment," she said after I'd explained I was a friend of both his and Peyton's. "But he's actually coming back to the office later. You might try again in a little while."

Another possibility jumped to mind: Mandy Slavin. She was familiar with David's business, and she might easily be able to identify the mystery man in the photo with Trip. I decided to pay her another surprise visit.

When I arrived in Greenwich, I pulled my car over and double-parked along a side street, just making certain no one was behind me. The only way someone could have been following me was if they'd just happened to see me roar into town, and that was highly unlikely—but I wasn't taking any chances.

Coast clear, I headed toward Mandy's. At one point, I thought I was lost, and just being out on the back roads again began to scare me. I was about to turn around when I realized that I hadn't yet entered her neighborhood.

A few minutes later I spotted her white house from the road, and it glowed glacierlike, ablaze with lights. As I pulled into the driveway, I was greeted by the sight of a dozen or so cars—Beemers, Jags, Mercedes, a few Lexus sedans, all gleaming from the reflected light of the house. A guy in a tux answered the door, and behind him I could hear the sounds of a cocktail party in full swing. He ushered me in, clearly assuming I was an invited guest.

From the shadow behind the door, a woman in black stepped forward and asked for my coat. After surveying the crowd that had spilled from the living room into the hallway and not seeing Mandy, I headed in search of my hostess. Last week she had seemed mildly entertained by my visit, but she hadn't had thirty people in her home, and I doubted she'd view my drop-in today with the same equanimity. Yet I couldn't turn back. I was too anxious for answers.

Waiters slid silently among guests with trays of hors d'oeuvres, and I helped myself to some kind of fancy cheese tart that was nestled in a mound of what appeared to be shaved Parmesan. As I popped it in my mouth, I saw several people stare at me. Did I look that much like an outsider?

I zigzagged through the crowd, and after determining Mandy was in neither the living room nor the dining room across from it, I made my way in the direction of a cluster of people at the end of the hallway. They were standing at the entrance of a study or library, which like the rest of the house was ultramodern in design. The far wall was mostly window, and it looked out at a row of fir trees that had been lit from below, creating a startling mural. Mandy stood with two men right in front of it, tossing her head back in laughter. She was dressed in a low-cut emerald green cocktail dress that hugged every curve. The hair around the crown of her head was pulled back taut, giving her cat's eyes and showing off her hubcap earrings, which sparkled from the light of the fireplace.

A waiter passed her, and after snagging him with her hand, she whispered in his ear. He bowed his head slightly, as if he'd been given an order by the queen. As she returned her attention to her fan club, she caught sight of me. The expression on her face transformed instantly into the kind of welcoming countenance she'd probably offer a Jehovah's Witness who'd decided to pop in and pass out some flyers. I crossed the room to her anyway.

"Well, what a surprise," she exclaimed. She introduced me to the two men, and before I could get a word out, she quickly announced, "Gentlemen, will you please excuse us for a moment?" They shot a glance at each other, murmured quick farewells, and slunk off.

"Mandy, please excuse me for—"

"What exactly are you doing here tonight?" she demanded. It was said with a smile for the benefit of the guests nearby, but her eyes were as friendly as a fox's.

"I apologize for barging in on you like this, but things have been heating up, and I need your help on just one small matter."

"Please make it quick, then. As you can see, I'm entertaining a houseful of people." Clearly she wasn't going to bestow any of the "I'm an L.A. girl born and bred" charm I'd been given a taste of last week. I pulled the photo of Trip out of my purse and slipped it discreetly into her hand.

"I need to know about the man Trip is talking to. Do you recognize him?"

Her lips curled, somewhere between amused and sardonic. I felt goose bumps along my arm as I realized that the photo had touched a nerve.

"What is it?" I pressed.

"His name is Scott something. He knows David from

the Belle Haven Club. I'm sure Trip met him through David."

"Would they have any business dealings together?"

"I have no idea. Like I said, I think he and David were mostly sailing buddies."

"Why did you smile?"

"Because he made a ridiculous pass at me once. He told me he could make me squeal with pleasure."

She flicked the photo back toward my hand. "Is that it, then?" she asked as I tucked the picture back into my purse.

"Just one more thing," I said, summoning my nerve. "When we talked the other day about the wedding, you never mentioned that Lilly had been excluded and how upset she was. That must have been hard on both of you."

She locked eyes with me, her face expressionless. I became conscious that a few of the guests nearby were glancing at us curiously. Maybe they thought I was accusing her of trying to hook up with my man.

"It certainly wasn't a pleasant experience. But how lucky for us in the end—I mean what with the way Peyton's bridesmaids are dropping like flies."

With a swish of silk she turned away from me and strode off. A good Greenwich hostess would never leave a guest standing solo, so it was clear to anyone watching that I had offended her in some way. I tried to look nonchalant and momentarily studied the view from the window. There was still snow on the ground, but it looked wet and sloshy, and the treetops were partially hidden by fog. The January thaw had clearly begun.

Though people were still eyeing me, I made my way through the room. Once in the hallway, I felt anonymous again. As I headed toward the door, I saw that a lacquered table against the wall was laid with platters of food: cheeses and olives, rolls of prosciutto, and a bowl of tapenade. It looked light and creamy, like Mary's. Famished, I furtively picked out a cracker and dipped it into the tapenade. It tasted like hers, too.

"Who is the caterer?" I asked the waiter to my right.

"Bon Appetite," he said. I would have to let Mary know that the competition was on to her dip.

It was practically steamy outside. Water dripped from the tree branches, making large plopping sounds when it hit the ground. I slid into my Jeep and turned on the ignition, then my defogger. I felt majorly frustrated. On the plane I'd gotten my hopes up that the picture of Trip and the stranger held all the answers. In the brief moment in which Mandy's lips had curled into that knowing smile, I'd been convinced that she was going to reveal something that would pull everything together for me. But she hadn't. That didn't mean Trip *wasn't* the bad guy. It meant, however, that the photo Jamie had taken of him didn't hold the key to the murders after all. Then what photo *did*? What was the photo that Jamie had wanted desperately to guard? As I sat there, a car pulled into the driveway and a woman stepped out while the driver found a parking place. She was in a white fur coat that looked as if it were made of polar bear.

A thought occurred to me. Ashley had mentioned that Robin's brother had hustled over to the town house shortly after his sister's death and carted away her possessions, including a box of photos. I had counted the photos in the envelope, and I knew they were all there, but what if there was another roll or two of Jamie's photos among Robin's possessions? Maybe I couldn't find a clue in the pictures because I was looking at the wrong roll. I searched my memory for the name Ashley had mentioned to me. It was Tom, perhaps—or Ted. I called 411 and asked for any Lolly in Greenwich. There was a Tom on Three Oak Road.

A woman answered in a high, singsongy voice. I identified myself as one of Peyton's bridesmaids and asked for Tom.

"Tom's not here," she said. "He's in Dallas on business. But I don't know if he'd want to talk anyway. He's still very, very upset, and this whole thing about the curse on the bridesmaids is very disturbing to him."

"I realize it must be. But I'm just trying to figure out what's really going on. Could I please just ask you a couple of questions?"

"How do I know you're not a reporter?"

"You can call Peyton. She'll vouch for me."

"All right, all right. I don't want to disturb Peyton—she's been good to us. What exactly is it that you want?"

"Just tell me this. I know you picked up some of Robin's possessions. Were there any photos of the wedding and reception in there?"

"Just one. It was of the wedding party—in a frame." I realized it must have been identical to the one Peyton had given me as a remembrance.

"And you're sure there's not an envelope someplace—you know, of photos?"

A child wailed in the background, and I knew I was going to lose her soon.

"Well, we haven't gone through everything yet," she said. "We were anxious to get her stuff out of there."

"What do you mean?" I asked.

She was silent, and the kid wailed again. It sounded as if he also might be kicking the wall.

"I really have to go," she announced.

"Please," I said desperately. "I think my life is in danger, and I need to know what's going on."

"We had reason to believe that Ashley might be picking over some of Robin's things."

" 'Picking over'?"

"I'll put it another way—helping herself to some of Robin's things."

"But—who told you that? I can't imagine Ashley doing that."

"I'm not at liberty to say."

"But Ashley was very concerned about the nature of Robin's death. She was probably just looking for clues."

"No, it was more than that. I shouldn't say anything else. And I really do have to go."

She dropped the phone without a good-bye.

I quickly dug my composition book out of my bag and jotted down what she'd said so I'd remember the exact words. It made no sense to me. Ashley had been truly distraught about Robin's death, and it was hard to imagine her rummaging through Robin's belongings and slipping a necklace or two into her pocket. Robin's ex-husband flashed through my mind. Had he been making trouble for some reason? It was just one more frustrating question in this case.

I glanced out the window of my Jeep, making certain no one was hanging around where they shouldn't be. Before I backed out, I saw that I had a message on my cell phone. Part of me hoped it was Jack. I didn't know what

I would have wanted him to say, because I knew there was no hope of going back to where we'd been only a week ago.

But it wasn't from Jack. To my utter surprise, there was a message from Phillipa, asking me to call on her cell phone.

"It's Bailey," I said when I reached her. "What's up?" In the background I could hear voices and the whirring noise of a motorized appliance.

"Would you mind holding for a second?"

She must have walked into another room because the background noises gradually receded and then disappeared abruptly, as if she had shut a door.

"I heard Peyton say that you were in Greenwich tonight."

"That's right. Are you working the party with her this evening?"

"No, I'm out at the farm. I'm prepping for another party tomorrow night. But I need to talk to you." She sounded less grumpy and irritated than when I'd spoken to her on Monday—in fact, there was something almost needy in her voice.

"What is it? Is everything okay?"

"Not really, no." Now her voice sounded almost strangled with emotion.

"Phillipa, what is it?" I urged.

"It's about Ashley. I think I know what happened to her."

CHAPTER 18

I CAUGHT MY breath and instinctively swung my head in either direction, making sure no one was near the car.

"You know who *did* it?" I asked, barely able to get the words out.

There was a long pause, and for a moment I thought she'd hung up on me.

"Philli—"

"Yes, I know," she said almost in a whisper. "I mean, I'm pretty sure I do." She sounded as if she were about to cry.

"Who?"

A voice suddenly burst through the quiet of the background on her end, and I heard the intake of Phillipa's breath. I wondered if she might be in danger.

"Phillipa?" I said. "Are you all right?"

"Yes, yes. I have to go—they need me back in the

kitchen. Could you come out here? We'll be done in about an hour and we could talk then."

"Can't you tell me anything now?"

"No, no. I can't—right now. But I have to talk to you. It's urgent."

"All right," I said. "I'll be out there in an hour. You'll wait for me, right?"

"Of course, of course. I have to go now."

I turned off my phone and leaned my head back against the car seat. Was this it, then? I wondered. Was this the night I finally found out the truth? Maybe Phillipa had seen someone go into the silo last Wednesday afternoon when she'd fled the kitchen and had been afraid to reveal it until now. Was it Trip? Or maybe she hadn't seen anything but instead had finally realized the significance of certain information that she'd dismissed earlier. Sometimes someone's offhanded comment can suddenly make a formerly unimportant fact stunningly relevant. Could that be what happened to Phillipa?

On the other hand, was it possible that Phillipa was trying to trick me? Maybe *she* was the killer and was attempting to lure me out to the farm after everyone was gone. Yet she had sounded so distraught and desperate— and Phillipa didn't strike me as a master of the Stanislavsky method of acting.

Though I was inclined to give her the benefit of the doubt, I wasn't going to take any chances. The best bet, I decided, was to arrive earlier than we'd discussed, while there were still people around. I glanced at my watch. David might be back in his office by now. I had time to swing by there, see if I could connect with him, and then head out to the farm.

When I pulled into the parking lot of his building fifteen minutes later, a bank of lights was on on the fifth floor—David's floor—though the rest of the building looked deserted. Watching my back, I entered the building and took the elevator to five. There wasn't a soul around, not even a cleaning crew. I hurried to the door of his office suite, knocked once, and then tried to open it. It was locked. I heard a sound behind me and spun around. It was only the *whoosh* of the elevator, beckoned to another floor. I rapped on the door four or five times and was just about to bolt when a young guy in blue shirtsleeves, no more than five years out of Dartmouth or Williams, swung it open.

"Can I help you?" he asked, appearing not particularly eager to do so. I could tell he assumed I'd gotten lost on my way to the periodontist in the building.

"David Slavin. Is he back yet from his meeting?"

He eyed me curiously. "I think he might be," he said. "Whom should I say is calling?"

I gave my name and he motioned for me to come into the reception area, a room with walls the color of raw silk and a deep blue-and-yellow Oriental rug that looked as if it had never been stepped on.

"Why don't you wait here and I'll check," he said. As I stood in the middle of the carpet, he strode off down a hallway, glancing back at me once over his shoulder. What was it about me that made people in Greenwich think I was about to abscond with the furniture?

A few seconds later David appeared, also in shirtsleeves. He had a pair of tortoiseshell reading glasses perched on his nose and an expression of alarm on his face.

"What is it?" he asked. "Has something happened?"

"No, no, I'm sorry if I worried you. There was just something I needed to talk to you about. Do you have a few minutes?"

"Peyton told me you're staying at the house tonight. Maybe we could speak more comfortably there?"

"I hope you don't mind, but I'm on the verge of something important, and I—"

"All right," he interrupted, putting a hand on my shoulder, "why don't you come in?"

There was no sign of Trip as we walked along the corridor. David's office turned out to be spacious but impersonal. It had an Oriental rug even thicker than the one in reception and a desk the size of a houseboat, but the only personal touches were a photo of David and Peyton on the desk and an oil painting, above the couch, of a sailboat cutting through a wave. Maybe David was one of those powerful types who had no interest in making their offices homey—or maybe he'd been too busy making zillions to play decorator.

He closed the door and, gesturing for me to take a seat on the couch, leaned back against the mahogany desk, one butt cheek on and one off. It was the kind of position that said, "I don't need to get too comfortable because you won't be staying long."

"So what's going on?" he asked impatiently.

"I don't know if you've talked to your contacts at the police department this week, but they think my accident Monday night was just an isolated incident—that I was run off the road by somebody who was just in too much of a hurry or had flunked his anger management class."

He regarded me pensively, not giving away whether he'd heard from the police or not.

"I take it you don't buy their theory," he said.

"No, I don't," I said. "The driver was way too hostile for that. Plus, I was attacked in New York as well. It's very clear that someone's after me, and I'm convinced it has something to do with the deaths of Peyton's other bridesmaids."

"You don't think they're accidents?"

"No."

He lifted his hands, palm side up, then let his arms fall, so that they smacked the front of his thighs.

"I don't know what to tell you, Bailey," he said. "You're a smart girl, and you seem convinced. But where's the proof that someone killed these women? And for God's sake, what's the motive?"

"That's what I wanted to talk to you about," I said, sitting up taller on the couch—though it did little to correct the discrepancy in our sitting positions. "It seems Robin may have suspected that Jamie's death was related to something that happened the weekend of your wedding. And the more I investigate, the more I think that may be true."

He stared at me above his glasses. "Go ahead," he said.

"Do you remember the night of the rehearsal dinner? You and Trip were having a discussion with each other about work."

He scrunched up his mouth in irritation. "How could I possibly remember something I was talking about at dinner nine months ago? It's like asking me what kind of aftershave I was wearing that night."

"Just let me finish. It wasn't at the dinner. It was in the church, during the rehearsal. And it was a very heated discussion. You and Trip were behind some screens, and you didn't realize all the bridesmaids were on the other side."

Using his index finger as a hook, he pulled off his reading glasses and, rotating his position, tossed them behind him on the desk. I wondered if he did that so I couldn't see the expression registering on his face.

"Okay, it's sounding vaguely familiar," he said, facing me again. "But so what? Trip and I have plenty of heated discussions. It's the nature of our business."

I managed a smile, trying to demonstrate that I wasn't being combative.

"I can imagine," I said. "But there was something you said that night that interests me. You wanted to know why Trip hadn't taken profits on one of the deals he was working on. I'm wondering if Trip could have been doing something unethical with the business—like hiding certain losses—and Jamie realized it after hearing your discussion. She might have tried to blackmail him about it."

David rose from the desk. I could tell he'd taken a large breath because I could see his chest swell beneath his gleaming white shirt. With a hand on each side of his waist, he took a few steps toward the window and then turned back again.

"So where is all this leading?" he asked. "You're not suggesting that Trip killed those women, are you?"

"I'm sorry, but I think it's a possibility. Jamie had a chip on her shoulder from what I can tell, and she was trying to fund a project of hers. If she thought Trip was up to no good, she may have asked him for money in return for keeping her mouth shut. As a matter of fact, it seems she suddenly got the money she needed shortly before she died."

"And what about Robin and Ashley? Why would he want to harm them?"

"Before we get into that, *was* Trip doing something he shouldn't have?"

He screwed up his face in concern—though it seemed forced to me.

"Quite honestly, I'd be *very* surprised to find Trip was up to something he shouldn't have been. He's extremely good at what he does, and we've had a terrific run. There'd be no reason for him to hide losses. I know I was barking at him that night, but I was probably feeling more stress than usual because of the wedding, and I did have some concerns about a few transactions. Not that I suspected anything unethical. They just didn't make sense to me."

"And . . . ?"

He shrugged. "Trip reassured me. After Peyton and I returned from Greece, I took a look myself. Everything seemed perfectly fine."

I wasn't sure I could believe him. If Trip had done something dishonest, it could all come crashing down on David in the end, so he may have been lying to protect himself and his business.

"So my theory makes absolutely no sense to you?"

"As I said before, you're a smart girl, Bailey, and I'd be stupid to out-and-out dismiss what you have to say. I'm going to take a look at things again, even more closely this time. How would that be?"

"That would be good. I think it's important to be sure there's nothing he might have been trying to cover up."

"Great. In fact, I'll look back at those records before I come home tonight. Like I said, I didn't spot any red flags when I examined them before, but perhaps I over-looked something. Why don't we discuss it later? Though for now, I'd prefer to leave Peyton out of this."

"Sure," I said. I could tell from his body language that I was being dismissed now—he'd edged his way down the room, closer to the door, and was rocking on his toes, signaling that he was eager for me to be on my way.

"Where's Trip tonight?" I asked, rising from the couch. The last thing I wanted to do was bump into him.

"He left at least an hour ago. I know you're feeling very tense over this whole thing, but I honestly don't be-lieve you have any reason to worry about Trip. Are you going straight back to our house?"

"I'm headed out to the farm for a brief stop. I should be at your place within an hour."

"Fine. I'll call and make sure the housekeeper makes up a plate for you."

He did that thing again of kissing me on both cheeks, as if he were the ambassador from France, and then of-fered me a politician-style handshake. Something was definitely odd. As I rode the elevator to the lobby, I con-sidered whether I could simply have hit a nerve with him. He'd obviously been worried last spring about Trip's transactions, and he may have done exactly as he told me—talked to Trip, taken a quick look at the records, and then dismissed his doubts. Now here I was giving him a reason to face them again. But it might be more than that. What if he'd actually looked at the records and found out that Trip was guilty? Earlier I'd assumed that if he'd caught Trip in illegal shenanigans, he would have dismissed him. But David valued Trip highly, and perhaps he'd let him off with a warning because he hadn't wanted to jeopardize his money machine. A scary thought scooted across my mind: What if David was in with Trip on everything? Could David have helped Trip kill the bridesmaids? Or had he even done it alone?

By the time I slid back into my Jeep, my head was pounding, the same headache that had been ambushing me on and off for the last few days. It was due, I was sure, to both stress and mental exhaustion. I felt at times as if my brain were going to burst from the endless questions racing through it. Yet tonight, finally, I had the feeling I was closing in on something. It was time now to head out to the farm to see Phillipa and learn exactly what she knew.

I was extra cautious when I left the parking lot. David had said Trip was long gone, but I wasn't going to take his word for it. I kept my eye on my rearview mirror the entire drive out to Ivy Hill, but no one was on my tail.

The closer I got to the farm, the more adrenaline I felt pumping through my body. I couldn't wait to hear Phillipa's revelation. As I turned the bend on the last stretch of road toward the farm, I gasped. A light was burning in one of the uppermost windows of the silo.

Who could be in there at this hour? Or was this part of some weird plan of Phillipa's to spook me? I didn't trust her, and I returned to the idea that she might be laying some kind of trap for me. I counted three cars in the parking lot, but I didn't get out of the Jeep until I spotted activity through the window of the larger barn.

It was clear as I stepped into the kitchen that things were winding down for the night. One girl, whom I recognized from my first day at the farm last week, was swabbing the counter with her coat on, and the other two, in coats as well, were lingering nearby, clearly waiting for the third to finish. They looked up in unison when I stepped into the room.

"Oh, hi," said the girl at the counter, recognizing me. I remembered that Peyton had called her Ginger. "We thought you were Phillipa."

"Phillipa?" I asked. "Isn't she here? I was supposed to meet with her."

"She's on her way to the party," Ginger said. "Peyton called here a little while ago and told her to hightail it over there. When we heard your car we thought she'd forgotten something."

"I can't believe it," I exclaimed. "Did she say when she's coming back?"

"Oh, she won't be back tonight. We're locking up now."

"Did she leave a *message* for me?" I asked. I could hardly blame Phillipa for being dragged away by Peyton, but that didn't stop me from being miffed.

The three women exchanged looks and shook their heads.

"Give me a second, will you?" I asked, pulling my cell phone out of my purse. I'd shut it off earlier when I'd gone into David's office, and as I checked it now I saw that I had a voice mail. It was Phillipa, about fifteen minutes earlier, explaining that Peyton had demanded her presence in Darien and that she hoped we could speak tomorrow. Again, she said it was urgent.

"We really need to lock up," one of the girls said a tad petulantly.

"I'm sorry," I told her, shoving my phone back in my bag. "Where's Mary, by the way?"

"She's sick today," Ginger said. "That's why everything is such a mess." She flipped a light switch near one of the refrigerators that darkened the half of the barn she was standing in. It made me think of the light burning in the silo.

"Why is there a light on in the silo? Is someone over there?"

Ginger walked toward the cluster of us by the door and glanced out the window with her neck twisted so she could see upward.

"Shit, one of the workmen must have left it on," she muttered. "They started working in there again. Peyton will kill us if we don't turn it off."

"Let her," said one of the other girls. "There's no way I'm going in there."

"Look, why don't I turn it off," I volunteered.

"You don't mind?" Ginger asked, surprised. "It would give me the freaking creeps to go in there."

I shook my head. I wasn't exactly relishing the idea, but this would finally be my chance to see the spot that Ashley had fallen from.

"I'll tell you what. When I get inside I'll flick the light to show I'm okay. Just give me the key and then I'll give it to Peyton later. I'm spending the night at her house."

"Well, there's no lock on there yet. You just have to shove to get the door open. It sticks like crazy."

She hit a code in the security box by the door and then flipped off the last of the lights. In the darkness I became conscious for the first time of the kitchen's night sounds: the hum of the refrigerators, the *whoosh*ing of the dishwasher. The four of us filed silently outdoors.

Each girl had her own car, and they called out goodbyes to one another before climbing in. Ginger glanced back at me as she unlocked her door. From the expression on her face, it was clear that she thought I was out of my mind for hanging around.

"Do you want us to wait?" she called out.

"No, that's all right," I said. "Oh, by the way, someone is ripping off your tapenade recipe. I had it at a party here in town tonight."

"We don't do tapenade," she said.

I pondered her remark as she climbed into her car. She started the engine and waited. From the trees behind the farm came the call of an owl, two short hoots followed by a long one. I glanced toward the silo, where the one light from the second level cast a glow onto the wet, melting snow below. Time to hustle. I wanted to see the top floors of the silo and then get the hell out of there.

My boots weren't waterproof, and the path to the silo was puddled with melted snow. By the time I reached the silo, my feet were soaked and squishy. As predicted, the door to the silo was unlocked, but I struggled with it just as Peyton had done last week. It made a loud groaning noise as I pushed it open. There were no lights on in the lower chamber, but some of the light from the upper level filtered down, and I could see the outline of the circular staircase. Before entering, I took one quick look behind me. Toward the south I could see a glow along the horizon, the lights of Greenwich, but right here on the farm, it was empty and silent.

Remembering where Peyton had reached for the lights, I found them after a few seconds of fumbling. The lower level burst into full view, lit with a surreal brightness. I flicked the light off and then on again. As I heard the caravan of cars start off, I did a quick scan of the room. There were still some boxes piled against the wall, though the paint cans had been taken away. And on the stone floor, in the place where Ashley had lain, was the stain from her blood. You could tell someone had scrubbed and scrubbed at it because it was now a faint shade of pink. The only way to get rid of the rest would be to dig up the stone and replace it.

I shut the door and started up the staircase. On the second level I stopped for just a second to switch on the lights and glance around. Though I knew on a rational level that each floor of the silo had to look about the same as the lower level, I'd imagined something bigger up here. But the space was really nothing more than a circular balcony, about twelve feet wide around. Ashley had said that the silo was being turned into a gallery, so obviously an array of pictures would eventually be hung on the walls for viewing. I continued climbing to the third level, the one where Ashley had supposedly fallen from—and the one where the lights had been left on tonight. My heart was beating double time, and I almost jumped when I spotted the stepladder set against the wall. It had to be the one Ashley had stood on that day. I stared at it for a few seconds, thinking. Then I put down my purse and dragged the ladder over to a spot underneath a canister light in the ceiling. As I did so, I glanced over the wrought-iron railing. The ground floor of the silo seemed terrifyingly far away. I've never been afraid of heights but the long cylinder of empty space made my breath quicken in anxiety.

I looked back at the stepladder and tried to picture the scenario the police had described: Ashley putting in the light bulb so she could see, losing her balance, tumbling over the railing. Even if the other deaths hadn't occurred, I would have had a hard time with that theory now that I actually saw the setup firsthand. With the stepladder right under the light, it was still a few feet away from the railing, and it was hard to imagine how just by losing her footing she could have been projected such a distance. If she'd lost her balance, wouldn't she have simply fallen backward?

If someone had shaken the ladder, however, they could have easily propelled her over the railing. But how would someone have sneaked up on her here? Ashley would have heard them coming up the stairs. It had to have been someone she trusted, someone she felt comfortable talking to while she was at work fixing the light. Another thought was that she'd never been on the ladder at all, that the killer had simply pushed her over the edge and later set up the stepladder. But the railing was fairly high, and it wouldn't have been easy to toss someone over the edge—still, it could be accomplished if you were strong and determined enough.

The thought had barely formed in my mind when I heard the groan of the door, echoing up through the silo. I froze, terrified. For a few seconds it was silent again, and I wondered if the wind had simply blown open the door. Then there were footsteps—quiet, cautious ones. With my heart beating wildly, I edged as quietly as possible to one of the windows. There was another car in the parking lot, not far from mine—even through the mist I could see that it was a dark boxy vehicle—a van or an SUV. Was it the SUV that had run me off the road? I stepped back toward my purse and fished frantically for my cell phone. I took a breath and pressed 911. Maybe it was simply a night watchman, wondering about the light and my car. Maybe it was just one of the workers. Maybe it was even Peyton. But I wasn't going to wait to find out.

Whispering hoarsely, I told the female operator the location and said that there'd been a break-in. I begged her to send help ASAP. She asked me twice to try to speak louder, but I was afraid that if I did, the person below would hear. She promised to stay on the line until help arrived, and I gripped the phone tightly in my hand.

I had no idea what to do. It was silent now down on the ground floor, but I could sense the person there, listening. Then I heard the clang of one foot on the staircase. Glancing upward, I could see that the fourth floor was just like the third. Though going higher would offer no safety, it would buy me a minute or two of time, something I needed until the police arrived. But I couldn't bear the thought of being trapped up there, cowering until whoever was below finally ascended to the top.

I glanced around desperately for anything I might use as a weapon. A few feet away was a box with tools, a bright steel hammer resting on top. With my free hand I grabbed the hammer and then whispered into the phone again.

"Are they *coming*?" I asked frantically.

"Yes, the police are on their way. Please stay on the line."

Slipping the phone into one pocket of my coat and the

hammer into the other, I forced myself toward the stairs and began to descend them. Please let it be a watchman, I pleaded to myself. But as I rounded the curve of the stairs, I saw my pleading was useless. Trip was standing on the second floor, watching the stairs.

"What are you doing here?" I asked. It came out as a little frog croak.

"Well, I might ask the same of you," he said sarcastically. "But then you seem to have given yourself license to go anywhere you damn well please in Greenwich."

"If you're looking for Peyton or David, they're not here. In fact, I was just leaving for their place." It was such a dumb thing to say, but I had this wild, crazy idea that if I didn't act alarmed, I could just ease my way out of there.

He snickered at the absurdity of my comment.

"Noooo," he said, stretching out the word mockingly. "I'm not looking for Peyton or David. I'm looking for *you.*"

I nearly wet my pants as he said it. I saw that beneath his heavy wool coat, he wore jeans and a pair of brown leather boots. He'd clearly gone home from the office and then come out again. David must have called him and told him I was headed to the farm. Did this mean David was in on the whole thing?

"How can I help you?" I asked. Another absurd comment, but all I could think was that I needed to make everything go in slow motion until the police arrived. Trip didn't answer, just shook his head hard from left to right, as if I'd said something totally insane. He was standing in the center of the floor, a few feet away from the staircase, and out of the corner of my eye, I tried to calculate whether he'd catch me if I tried to bolt for the first floor.

"If you're thinking of making a run for it, I wouldn't," he said.

"Well, I'm sorry, but I really have to go," I said, gripping the hammer in the pocket of my coat.

"No, you and I need to have a little chat."

From the pocket of his long black coat, he pulled out a gun.

CHAPTER 19

I WAS SCARED, really scared. I was also experiencing this ridiculous urge to laugh from contemplating the hammer in my pocket. It would be a big help now, wouldn't it? What was I supposed to do—hurl it at him like a boomerang and knock him out cold before he had the chance to shoot?

Somehow this one, still rational square inch of my brain took control. It commanded me to stay calm, to do nothing to make Trip agitated.

"Trip," I said quietly, "why are you doing this? Why would you point a gun at me?" I hoped the 911 operator had picked up enough of what I'd said to realize that there was now a gun in the picture.

Trip laughed, though it came out more as a bark. His eyes looked wild, as if he'd helped himself to some laudanum before dropping by.

"Why am I doing this? No, the question is why are *you* doing this? You're the one trying to hurt me."

"What do you mean?"

"Oh, please," he said, turning his head slightly and looking to the side, as if there were people offstage he hoped to enlist in support of his displeasure. "You know exactly what I'm talking about. You wouldn't let sleeping dogs lie, would you? You went to see David tonight, and now he's going to start digging around, looking for stuff, and everything is going to be a big fat mess."

"I just wanted to be a good friend to Peyton and David. They—"

"If you were such a good friend, you would have just stayed the hell out of it. Yeah, I moved a little money around, and the feds don't like that sort of thing, but none of our clients got hurt in the end. Now David'll figure it out, and it's all gonna blow up in our faces."

"That wasn't my intention, Trip. I didn't even know when I—"

"I tried to warn you, you know? Back when you first got started. David told me how you were foaming at the mouth about the deaths and about wanting to uncover the truth and outsmart the police and all that shit. I could tell his wheels were spinning and you might start him looking into things all over again. I thought if I gave you a warning, you'd be smart enough to back off. But you just don't like to take a hint, do you?"

"So that was you in New York, then? In Jamie's apartment?"

"Bingo."

"Does that mean you left the note? And ran me off the road?"

He swung his head to the side again in exasperation. "See, there were two other warnings. I tried to play fair, give you a chance to butt out."

Despite how agitated he was, he seemed eager to talk, and I had to keep him at it, looking as though my curiosity could not be contained. I kept my eyes on *him*, not the gun or the railing to his left. It would be so easy for him to send me over the edge.

"How did it all start, Trip? Did Jamie come to you?"

"That Jamie was quite the opportunist, you know? She didn't know what she'd heard between me and David, but she knew it had to mean something. She called me, started fishing around, trying to figure out if she was on to something. Yeah, Jamie was a real bottom feeder."

"Is that why you killed her?"

He froze, holding my gaze like someone gripping the edge of a bridge. Then he threw back his head and began to cackle, as if I'd said something so hilarious that he could barely stand it.

"You just don't get it, do you," he said as the laughter wore down.

A big wind blew out of nowhere, whistling through the shingles of the silo, and when it finally died down, we could hear the crunch of cars on gravel. With the gun still pointed at me, Trip backed toward one of the windows.

"You called the police?" he exclaimed as he gazed below. "You little bitch."

I had a sudden picture of him grabbing me and taking me hostage.

"No, I swear I didn't. Maybe some kind of alarm got tripped because we're in here after hours."

He froze in position—that is, every part of him except

his eyes. They darted back and forth as he tried to determine what course of action to take. Two seconds later he made his move. He bolted down the stairs, the clanging sound of his footfalls reverberating up the center of the silo.

I rushed to the window myself and gazed below. A police car was bumping along the driveway to the farm, almost at the parking lot. Dropping the hammer to the floor, I headed for the stairs. Just as I reached the second-level landing I heard the groan of the front door swinging open, followed quickly by the word "Halt!" I stepped over toward the window and peered out again. Two cops had spilled out of the police car and had their guns trained on the door of the silo, where Trip was obviously standing. He must have quickly put down his own gun because one of the cops approached the silo, and then I saw him lead Trip toward the car. I bolted down the last flight of stairs. As I reached the bottom, the second cop, a dark-haired guy no more than twenty-five, stepped through the open door of the silo. He still had his gun drawn, and I instinctively put my hands in the air.

"Are you okay?" he called out, lowering his gun.

"Yes, he never touched me. But he scared the hell out of me."

"What's going on here, anyway? Do you work here?"

"No, but I'm a friend of the owner, Peyton Cross, and I have her permission to be here. It's a long story, but this man attacked me on several occasions and came after me tonight with a gun. I believe he's a murderer and was responsible for a death here last week, as well as two others. I've had several conversations with Detective

Pichowski about all of this, and it's important that he be contacted."

He eyed me cautiously, his monobrow furrowed. "I need you to come down to the station. But you can't ride in the back of the patrol car with a suspect. Do you have your own car?"

"Yes, it's the Jeep out there."

As we stepped outside into the night, I saw Trip being guided into the back of the patrol car by a woman officer, his hands cuffed behind him. When he caught sight of me out of the corner of his eye, he jerked his head back and screamed in our direction.

"That woman is insane! She's just making trouble."

The cop who had escorted me out of the silo gazed at me, almost warily this time.

"I want you to follow right behind us, okay? I want to see you in my rearview mirror."

"Of course. But just please tell Detective Pichowski I'm coming."

I was counting on the fact that once I was with Pichowski and could explain the whole thing to him, everything would finally be okay.

I took off in my Jeep, following the patrol car. My heart was no longer beating like a madwoman's, but I was bone tired, as if all the fear I'd felt had somehow calcified in my body. As soon as I had maneuvered onto one of the main roads, I called Peyton's house. According to Clara she wasn't yet home, but David was and I poured out the story to him.

"Can you get hold of Peyton and let her know what's happened?" I asked.

The next hour was grueling. I was told that Pichowski

had gone home for the night but would now be returning. He didn't show until thirty minutes after I did, so I was left to sit by his desk in the nearly empty detective room and stare at greasy Subway wrappers and stacks of crime reports. He was pleasant enough when he arrived, though it was clear right from the get-go that he wasn't going to fall on his knees and beg my forgiveness for having dismissed my concerns. I could tell that all his skepticism about me wasn't going to be washed away until he'd thoroughly investigated my story about tonight and could prove it was true.

I went through everything, starting with my memory of the argument between David and Trip and working my way up to the visit to David. I made a point of emphasizing what Trip had stated about David tonight—that he was worried David would start digging into things. I knew the situation might end up being pretty bad for David professionally, and I wanted to be sure the police understood that he didn't appear to be directly involved.

"Has Trip confessed to anything?" I asked Pichowski.

He pursed his lips in that ugly way of his. I was tempted to advise him that it was an expression he should never make again.

"I'm not able to say just at this moment," he announced as his eyes glanced over the notes he'd taken. "Let me just be clear on several points. Mr. Furland indicated to you that he had run you off the road and attacked you in New York?"

"Yes," I said. "He said those had been warnings."

"What about the deaths of the three women? What exactly did he say about those?"

"I started to ask him about them, but then he heard

the police car and ran down the steps. He mentioned Jamie to me. He admitted that she had called him, suspicious about the argument he and David Slavin had. He said she was a real bottom feeder."

"But he didn't admit to murdering her?"

"No, but it makes sense, doesn't it?" I said. A younger-looking detective who'd been on the phone hung up and handed Pichowski something to read. I couldn't tell if it was about this case or something totally unrelated. While Pichowski studied it, my mind replayed the evening, and I suddenly thought of Phillipa. She had said she had evidence. Possibly she'd seen Trip the day of Ashley's death. I wanted to raise her name with Pichowski, but I didn't feel it was fair to do that until I had talked to her myself and heard exactly what she had to say.

After Pichowski finished reading, he asked what my plans were for the evening. It had occurred to me as I was driving to the police station that I would love to head straight back to New York tonight. But I was exhausted.

"I'm going to be staying at Peyton's home tonight," I said.

He told me that the case was still coming together, and he wanted me to be available tomorrow for another discussion.

"About what time—do you know?" I asked. "I need to arrange my schedule."

"Unfortunately, I can't say. It depends on a variety of factors. Why don't you just plan to be around the whole day."

It was after ten when I finally showed up at Peyton's. I wanted to call her en route, but I was too fatigued even to take out my cell phone. David answered the door, dressed in black slacks and a blue cashmere cardigan, kind of like Mr. Roberts, Lotto winner. A second later Peyton came charging into the hall, wearing minty green sweats. David took my coat and suggested we retreat to the library, where a few small orange embers still glowed in the hearth. I was dying for a cup of tea, but the help had apparently been discharged for the night and Peyton wasn't volunteering. Instead, I poured myself a glass of sparkling water from the tray on the bar and drank the entire glassful down in two seconds.

"You've got to fill us in," David said as I wiped my mouth with the tips of my fingers. "What exactly happened?"

"Just let me sit down first," I said. "I don't think I've ever felt so exhausted."

After crashing onto the sofa, I described what had happened, just as I had for Pichowski. David wore a scowl through most of my recounting; Peyton listened intently with the tip of her thumb pressed hard against her teeth.

"This is perfectly dreadful," David said. "And it sounds as if I triggered the whole damn thing by calling him."

"You told him I'd driven out to the farm?"

"Yes, and I'm sorry about that—it was totally inadvertent. I called him after you left and asked him point-blank if there was any connection between the deaths and the conversation that he and I had the night before the wedding. I think I said something about the fact that you and I were going to talk again after you got back from the farm—never imagining him bounding out of bed and heading out there to find you."

"But why did he kill *Ashley*?" Peyton demanded, speaking up for the first time.

"Ashley?" David said with a look of impatience. "Why, for god's sake, did he kill *all* of them?"

I revealed my theory about the blackmail.

"I think that's how Jamie got the money for her business. She threatened to go to the SEC or the IRS. Granted, she didn't have any proof, but she had the name of the company, Phoenix, and Trip knew she could have directed the authorities that way. My guess is that Jamie said enough to Robin to make her, first, suspicious that Jamie's death wasn't an accident and then, later, suspicious of Trip. She possibly put it together and said something to him. He was apparently hanging around her this fall. Maybe he simply *suspected* she was getting closer to the truth. I'm not sure.

"As for Ashley," I said, turning toward Peyton, "she'd been digging into Robin's death, saying to people that she thought Robin and Jamie were murdered, not the victims of accidents. She was a clear danger to Trip. Just for the record, though, Trip never acknowledged anything to me about the murders."

Peyton pressed her thumb to her teeth again. She seemed oddly subdued tonight. Knowing Peyton, knowing how in her mind all roads always led back to her, I wondered if she was pondering how tonight's events would affect David's business and then her own life.

David sighed. "You've got to tell me, Bailey. What exactly do the police know about Trip, and what he was up to at Slavin Capital?" It was as if he had read my mind.

"I had to tell them what I knew, David. But Trip indicated that this was something he was into by himself, and I made that clear to the police."

"All right," he said, suddenly distracted. "I think it would do us all good to turn in right now."

"I'll be the judge of when I need to go to sleep," Peyton snapped.

"Actually, I think I *will* head up now," I announced. I could understand why things would be tense tonight between Peyton and David, but I had no interest in sticking around to watch matters deteriorate.

"Of course," Peyton said, turning back to me with a solicitous smile. "Feel better."

The first thing I did when I got upstairs was to pour myself a hot bath. Even though the night wasn't especially cold, I'd started to shiver, and I felt achy all over. I wasn't sure if it was the early stages of a flu virus or the aftershocks from all the stress I'd experienced tonight. I lay in the hot, sudsy water for half an hour, my mind churning. What, if anything, had Trip admitted to the police? Did they have any evidence whatsoever to tie him to the murders? Would they at least be able to charge him with running me off the road? And what had he meant when he'd yelled, "You just don't get it, do you"? What didn't I get? I needed to reach Phillipa first thing in the morning. She might have information or evidence that would help nail Trip.

I lifted myself with a groan from the tub and changed into cotton pajamas. This was my third night at Peyton's in two weeks and only the first time I actually had an overnight bag with me.

I switched off the lights and lay in the dark, working over even more questions. Would the police notify the

SEC? How big an impact would this have on David's business? For that matter, how big an impact would it have on his marriage?

I felt hopelessly tired but at the same time wide awake—and still a little frightened. I could only hope that David would never be stupid enough to let Trip into the house if he showed up tonight, his bail posted. I also found myself thinking of Jack. How nice it would have been to be able to call him right this minute for comfort. I wondered if there would ever be a point in the future when we would be friends, when I could phone him some night for some shrink advice for an article I was doing, not minding that there might be a half-naked chick sitting beside him on the couch. Right now the thought of Jack with another girl made me feel like puking.

I tossed and turned for what seemed like hours. As I finally started to drift off, a thought flashed in my mind: Jamie's photographs. Now that I knew Trip was the killer, how did the photographs fit into everything? Was the shot of Trip talking to that man significant after all?

Once I finally fell asleep, I was out cold. When I awoke to gentle knocking on my door, the bedroom was filled with a soft gray light that signaled it was way past my usual wake-up time. I yelled out, "Yes?" at the same moment I squinted at my watch. To my dismay, it was ten forty-five. As I pushed myself up in bed, Clara opened the door and stuck her head in.

"Good morning, Miss Weggins," she said. "Sorry to wake you, but I thought you might want to be called now."

"Gosh, I can't believe I slept so long. Has Peyton gone to work?"

"I'm not sure, but she left a note for you." She pulled from her pocket a folded piece of stationery in a pale shade of yellow and handed it to me. Peyton had written to explain that she was conferring with her PR team for a few hours this morning but would return to the house after lunch. She suggested that since I was stuck in Greenwich for the day, we might take a walk together in the afternoon.

"Okay, thank you, Clara," I said, refolding the note. "Is it possible for me to get some coffee?"

"There's breakfast laid out for you in the kitchen. And by the way, Ms. Cross's cousin Phillipa called for you. Twice."

I thanked her and told her I would take care of it. After staggering out of bed, I phoned the farm on my cell and asked for Phillipa. She was off buying supplies and wasn't expected back until midday. Over the next two hours I showered, ate an omelet prepared by Clara, roamed the house and waited anxiously for calls from Pichowski and Phillipa. Finally, close to one, Phillipa phoned.

"I have to talk to you," she said as soon as I picked up. "It's more urgent than ever."

"Did you hear about Trip?"

"Yes, yes. Everybody's talking about it. And that's why I *have* to see you as soon as possible."

"Did you see Trip that day—the day Ashley was killed?"

"I can't do this on the phone," she said, "I have to meet with you in person."

"All right." I sighed, frustrated by her continual dangling of this carrot in front of me. "I probably shouldn't leave the house, since the police said they might need to talk to me again. Could you get away for a while and come over here?"

She hesitated. "Yes, I guess so. Peyton's gone off somewhere."

I figured it wouldn't take her long to drive to Peyton's since she was probably familiar with the back roads, and I was right. She arrived in less than fifteen minutes as I stood in the giant hallway finishing a cup of coffee. I'd grown so used to *sour* Phillipa that I was shocked to see how drawn and panic-stricken she looked today. The expression on her face seemed to say she suspected that nearly everyone she knew had been body-snatched and replaced by alien imposters grown in giant seedpods.

Since Clara was at work in the kitchen, I suggested we go down to the library to talk. But a maid was buffing away with something lemony, so Phillipa, still wearing a long tan raincoat that made her seem even shorter, led me to a room she knew of toward the back of the house. Decorated in shades of purple and lavender, it was a small sitting room that I'd never noticed before—the kind of undesignated room you could find only in a house as huge as this one.

"Tell me what's the matter," I said as soon as I'd closed the door behind us.

"Trip didn't do it. I'm almost positive."

I felt my mouth fall open stupidly. "Then who *did* do it? Do you know?"

Tears welled up in her eyes and were quickly nudged down her cheeks by others. She caught one with her tongue and brushed at the rest with the back of a manicured hand.

"I—I'm responsible for Ashley's death," she said. "At least partly."

I caught my breath, and involuntarily my eyes shot toward the door as I calculated how easily I could get by her and out of the room in case I was in danger. Phillipa realized in an instant what I'd just done.

"I didn't *murder* her, if that's what you think," she wailed. "It was an accident." She began to cry really hard, her shoulders bobbing up and down.

For a second I did nothing but stand there in total confusion. Then I stepped toward her.

"Here, Phillipa, why don't you sit down," I said, guiding her to a plump purple armchair. "Tell me everything."

She cried some more, and as she swiped away the tears, she smeared her iridescent pink lipstick. I noticed a box of tissues in a rattan box on an end table and pulled one out for her.

"When you left the barn that day, did you go over to the silo?" I asked, trying to urge her along.

"Yes. Peyton said something so nasty to me that I thought I was going to cry. I sometimes hide out in the back kitchen, but I knew someone was in there putting groceries away. So I went over to the silo. I forgot all about the fact that Ashley was there."

"And something happened with her?"

"No, I never even saw Ashley."

"What do you mean? I—"

"I tried to get the door open, but it sticks. I was pushing on it and shoving on it with my hip, and when I threw my whole body into it, it finally gave way. At the same time, I heard this huge crash. I thought that I must have jarred something and made it fall—so I took off without even entering the room. I went to my car and sat there with the motor running. Later I slipped back into the barn through the back entrance."

I stared at her incredulously, trying to make sense of what she had told me.

"So are you saying that the crash was Ashley falling?" I asked slowly.

"Yes, it must have been," she said, her lip trembling. "I may have startled her when I kept shoving at the door. I swear I didn't realize it at that time. Like I said, I thought I'd just knocked something over or made something fall off a wall. I thought Peyton would be furious and start yelling that it was because I was overweight."

"How do I know for certain that you didn't actually go in the silo and push Ashley over the railing?"

"What?" she asked, aghast. "Why would I do that? Besides, I'm terrified of heights, and I would never go above the ground floor."

I kept thinking, trying to get the whole thing straight in my mind.

"And while you were in your car, you never saw anyone enter or leave the silo?"

"No. And the way my car was facing, I would have seen someone coming or going."

"So when did you finally put two and two together?" I asked.

"Not until after the police came. All you'd said when you came in with Peyton was that Ashley was lying dead on the floor. But from what the police were saying, I finally figured out that she'd fallen over the balcony. And all of a sudden, I realized that when I shoved on the door

I must have startled her so much she fell off the stepladder."

"Why not 'fess up *then*?" I asked. On the one hand, I felt sorry for her, blubbering pathetically in front of me, but I also was totally annoyed by her. She'd withheld the truth while I'd been stumbling all over the eastern seaboard trying to find answers.

"I should have, I know. But I was terrified. I caused the accident and then I left. If I'd opened the door, she might have been alive and they could have saved her. Only, I just let her die. I figured they'd arrest me if I confessed. But then you were asking so many questions, and I couldn't keep it in any longer, knowing what I'd done. That's why I called you. And now with Trip arrested, it's even worse. Can you help me? *Please*."

She began to sob and wail again. I half expected Clara to charge into the room with a stun gun.

"Look, Phillipa," I said, resting my hand awkwardly on her shoulder. "I saw Ashley's body. I doubt there was any way she could have been saved. The important thing is that you've told the truth now. Trip threatened me with a gun last night, and he's been up to some bad things, but it sounds as if he wasn't responsible for Ashley's death. You have to call the police—okay? Even better, I think you should go there right away."

"They're going to think I'm horrible."

I reassured her they wouldn't and gave her Pichowski's name. She knew where the station was, she said, and promised to drop by there immediately. She also begged me not to say anything to Peyton or David until she had had time to speak to the police.

On the way to the front door, she stopped off in the

powder room to address her makeup meltdown. While I waited for her to emerge, I absorbed the full impact of what she had shared with me. Pichowski and company were right after all. Unless Trip had sneaked into the silo before Phillipa fled the barn, there was a good chance Ashley's death really was an accident. I remembered how jumpy Ashley had been that day. I could imagine her on the stepladder, fussing with the light bulb, when all of a sudden she hears an unexpected visitor trying to gain entry. She leans out, craning her neck in order to see down below, and with the final thrust that knocks open the door, she completely loses her balance. The next second later she's toppling over the railing to her death.

But what about the other deaths? Just because Trip hadn't murdered Ashley didn't mean he wasn't responsible for Jamie's and Robin's deaths. Trip admitted to me that Jamie had wanted to blackmail him. But what if he'd never taken the bait, figuring she didn't have enough to go on? After all, David had made a surface check of the numbers and found nothing improper at the time. Trip's words rang in my ears again: *You just don't get it, do you.*

That would mean, then, that he had attacked and threatened me not because I was snooping around about the murders, but because I was looking into the wedding weekend. He'd clearly heard from David that I had vowed to turn over every stone, and he was worried that I might recall the flap between him and David in the church and decide it was significant. It could force David into digging deeper than he had the first time.

If Trip had come after me simply to scare me off from opening a Pandora's box, had someone *else* killed Jamie and Robin? Or had their deaths really been accidental and

I'd been on a wild-goose chase for the last two weeks? Something Cat Jones said to me flashed across my mind. She'd told me that she didn't necessarily believe the girls had been murdered, but she thought the deaths were connected. Were they simply some kind of weird chain reaction—Jamie dies, and Robin, distraught, doesn't pay attention to what she eats and dies, too? Then Ashley, on pins and needles, is startled by a noise and falls. Knowing all that I currently knew, part of me felt like a fool for having thought there was a serial killer, yet in my gut I still believed Jamie and Robin had been murdered. Their two deaths just seemed so improbable. Who was the killer, though? I was all the way back to square one. Maybe finally showing the pictures to Peyton would offer a clue.

Phillipa emerged at last, and I walked her to the door. It was mild but overcast out, and there was still a light fog on the ground. As we said good-bye, I made her promise that she would drive directly to the police station. I also told her that I would call Detective Pichowski and let him know she was coming. I didn't trust her not to chicken out.

I'd no sooner closed the door than Clara entered the hall with a phone in her hand. It was Mrs. Slavin, she said, holding it out to me.

"What's going on?" Peyton asked after I'd said hello.

"Not much," I replied. I wished that I could share Phillipa's secret, but I'd assured her I wouldn't. "I'm just cooling my heels here, waiting to find out if the police need me anymore. Have you heard anything?"

"David spoke to Trip's lawyer. He says he had nothing

to do with any of the deaths—but then, what would you expect him to say."

"Are you out at the farm now?"

"Yes, but I'll be home in an hour or so. Mary is supposedly handling the party tonight. I was furious with her about last night—we had an important party and she never showed. She left me totally understaffed and unprepared. She claimed she had a personal emergency."

"Well, unless I'm at the police station, I'll see you in a little while."

"Why don't we take a walk? The property is beautiful and I'd love to show you."

"Great, I could use the fresh air. Oh, listen. There's something I'd like you to do for me. I have some photos of your wedding reception that Jamie apparently gave Robin for safekeeping. I'd like you to look at them for me."

"What on earth for?"

I was stymied by the fact that I couldn't tell her about Phillipa's confession, couldn't share with her that Trip might very well be innocent. "I think they might have some significance in all this—though I better wait till later to explain it all to you."

"All right," she said, as if her mind were no longer on our conversation. "I have to go now. I'll see you later."

After she rang off, I phoned the police. Pichowski was "unavailable," but I left a message saying Phillipa was coming down there with important information and that I would follow up later.

I returned the phone to Clara in the kitchen and asked for a cup of tea. She offered to bring it to the library when it was ready. There was no fire in there today, and the room felt drafty and unwelcoming. While I waited, I moved idly around, surveying the leather-bound books, the pieces of Asian sculpture that were probably centuries old, the photographs of Peyton and David on the mantel. I picked up their silver-framed wedding photo, studying it. And suddenly something hit me like a blow to my head.

I set the photo back down and tore out of the room, nearly colliding with the tray-toting Clara.

"Just leave it on the table, thanks," I yelled. I raced up the stairs to my room, grabbed my purse, and hurried back down to the library again.

Like a maniac I dug the envelope of wedding photos out of my purse and spilled them onto the coffee table, rifling through them until I'd found the one of Peyton kissing David. They were locked in an embrace, and you could see only the far left side of his face and body, but it was easy to assume it was David—he was dark haired, dressed in a tux, and kissing Peyton as if the future of the American Stock Exchange depended on it. Yet there was a discrepancy. In the photo on the mantel David was wearing a boutonniere. In this shot, he didn't have one on.

I took the photo with me to the mantel and held it up next to the other. David's hair looked shorter on the sides in the mantel photograph than in the picture Jamie had taken. I squinted, gazing down at the photo in my hand. He wasn't wearing a wedding band in this one.

The man Peyton Cross was kissing so passionately in the arbor wasn't her husband at all.

CHAPTER 20

THEN WHO *WAS* this guy? The embrace was far too passionate to have been given by a guest wishing Peyton well on her wedding day. Was this someone Peyton had a fling with up until her marriage, or was it a guy she was *still* hot and heavy with?

It almost didn't matter. Because regardless, the end result if David saw the photo would be disastrous. According to Mandy, David couldn't tolerate the idea of being cuckolded, and if he found out about the kiss—and the relationship—he'd have Peyton's head.

Jamie had not only witnessed the moment that gave new meaning to the phrase *You may now kiss the bride*, but she had also documented it. This was the reason she was hiding the photographs at Robin's. This was the reason she had guarded her camera with her life during her shag session with Kyle, he of so little brain mass.

And was this why she was dead? Had Peyton killed her? And then Robin?

I took a deep breath and urged myself to think calmly. The thought of Peyton as a murderer—a murderer of two of her closest friends, no less—was overwhelming, and I didn't want to just hysterically take off in that direction. I slipped the photos back in the envelope on the coffee table and roamed the room, cogitating.

As much as I tried to dismiss this new theory, it seemed to make sense. Jamie must have blackmailed Peyton—that would explain not only the falling-out between Peyton and Jamie last summer, but also the sudden funding for Jamie's gourmet shop. Jamie might have reasoned that Peyton was a fatter pigeon than Trip, and revenge on the woman she envied would certainly have been sweeter. Had she confided her nasty little plan to Robin? Probably not, because Robin didn't seem to have any grudge against Peyton. But she gave her the photos for safekeeping, and after Jamie's death, Robin suspected there was something sinister at play related to the wedding. I stopped in front of the mantel again and stared at the shot of Peyton and David one more time. Such a tiny detail, a boutonniere, yet I felt furious with myself that I'd missed it.

"*Here* you are!"

I whirled around like someone who'd just been tapped on the shoulder in a cemetery. Peyton was standing in the entrance of the library, still wearing her mink coat.

"Aren't you—I thought you were going to be at the farm for a while," I said, feeling fear gush through every limb.

"Mary's got it under control," Peyton said. "Plus, with

everything that's happened, I thought it would be nice to just hang with you." She smiled broadly at me, as if this were the happiest day of her life.

"Thanks. I—I was just having some tea. Clara made it for me." I felt completely at a loss for words. I saw her eyes fall to the coffee table.

"Oh, are those the photos?" she asked.

"Uh, yeah," I said, quickly stepping toward the table and scooping up the pictures in my hand. "There's no urgency, though. They may mean nothing at all, actually. Didn't you want to take a walk?" I now had as much interest in a hike around the property with her as I would in hanging on to the back of a Manhattan bus while riding a skateboard, but I needed to discourage her from reviewing the photos.

"It can wait a sec," she said, holding out her right hand emphatically. "Here, let me see them."

There seemed to be no choice but to relinquish the pictures. She would clearly be suspicious if I didn't.

"Thanks," I said, and handed them over with a weak smile. "I didn't see anything odd myself, but maybe you will." I wondered if she could pick up on my lie—and/or my anxiety.

She flicked through the pictures at a fast clip, the way someone would sort through a stack of mail after work when what they really wanted to do was rip off their panty hose and mix a cocktail. I saw her hesitate for a split second and her face darken. I knew she had spotted the one of her and the mystery man. But she composed herself again quickly.

"No, nothing," she said, her voice too loud. "But I'll take a longer look later. You ready for the walk? I asked

Clara to dig up a pair of my hiking boots for you. We're
the same size."

I searched frantically through my mind for some way
to get out of the walk but couldn't find one. I'd informed
her just a few minutes ago that I was game. I couldn't
very well change my mind without making her realize
that something was up.

"Um, sure," I said. "But let's not make it too long—
it's going to get dark in an hour or so."

"I'll be down in about two minutes," she said, beaming. "I'm just going to slip into some jeans."

I reached out my hand for the photographs.

"I'll keep these for now," she declared, stuffing them
into their envelope. "I want to look through them more
carefully after we get back."

I watched her leave, the envelope grasped in her hand.
Without the pictures, I had nothing. But short of tackling
her to the ground, there'd been no way to pry them loose
from her. My only hope was that rather than torching
them with a match in her bedroom, she really would hang
on to them long enough to go through them again—and
I could somehow extract them from her.

I didn't relish the idea of being out in the woods with
Peyton, yet it would be smart to keep her in my sights.
The only question: Was I in any danger? I didn't think so.
Up until ten minutes ago I hadn't a clue she was the killer,
and she'd clearly sensed my ignorance. I just prayed she
hadn't picked up any vibe from me just now. She'd
seemed wired, but that was probably from coming face-
to-face with the incriminating photo. I rifled through my
bag for my cell phone and wedged it into my jeans
pocket, just to be on the safe side.

She was back in less than five minutes and motioned for me to follow her. She led me through the kitchen into a large mud room. Two pairs of hiking boots stood at attention there, waiting for us. I stuck my feet in the pair she pointed to and laced them tightly, and she did the same with hers. Once we were finished she slipped into a weatherproof jacket and then pulled another one off the hook for me.

"What's the terrain like out there?" I asked, trying to sound chatty and normal.

"You'll see. It's a little woody, but there's a path. And it's so pretty. I find it always relaxes me."

I followed Peyton through the mud room door out into the backyard. The sky was overcast, and the ground was steaming with fog.

As we started across the yard, a man in a navy barn jacket emerged from behind the garage. He was about forty, with skin that was lined from the sun and wavy blond hair just long enough to tuck behind his ears. It wasn't until he spoke that I realized he was the Australian caretaker.

"Good afternoon, Mrs. Slavin," he said, offering a warm smile.

"Where are you off to, Brian?" Peyton asked impatiently.

"One of the workers said the snow took down a tree in the northwest corner," he said, falling into step beside us. "I wanted to check it out before dark."

"You can do that tomorrow. I need you to take a look at my car. The seat belt on the driver's side seems stuck."

He stopped in his tracks, a perplexed expression on his

face. For a second I thought he was going to protest, but he clearly thought better of it.

"Sure," was all he said, and turned to retrace his steps.

Peyton and I traversed the wide expanse of snow-covered lawn past a rectangular indentation that was obviously a swimming pool and patio. At the far end we entered a cluster of trees. The snow was still at least a foot high in places, but wet and beating a fast retreat. Every so often you could hear a clump of snow fall from the trees and plop onto the ground.

"How much of the land out here is yours?" I called out. Peyton was just ahead of me, and I had to shout at the back of her French twist.

"About fifteen acres," she said. "It's amazing to have this amount of land in Greenwich. The lots are big out here, but rarely this big."

I was sorry to hear this—I would have liked knowing neighbors were closer by.

We walked for about ten minutes, trudging along a snow-covered path that was already scarred with footprints—someone had obviously been along the path earlier in the day. We came to a small stream that must have recently thawed because it ran with the abandon of water that had just been freed. There was a large stone in the middle of it that Peyton placed one foot on and used to spring to the other side. I tried to do the same, but I slipped on the wet stone and one foot landed in six inches of water.

"Careful," Peyton called out, and reached for my hand. She grabbed it and pulled me across to the other side. Despite the fact that my jacket was unzipped, I could feel myself beginning to sweat.

"It's crazy, isn't it," she said, "how everything is melting all of a sudden?"

"The legendary January thaw," I said. I was finding it nearly impossible to make light conversation with her. Everything I said came out stilted.

We continued along the path, down a slope through a more wooded area, thick with fir trees and bare oaks and maples. There wasn't another house in sight, and when I glanced back over my shoulder, I couldn't see any portion of Peyton's massive home. It was far more secluded than I'd imagined. I was suddenly overwhelmed with the urge to get the heck out of there.

"Shouldn't we think of turning back?" I asked.

"Turn back? You've never been known for turning back, have you, Bailey?"

"Not when it makes sense to stay. But it's so wet—and it's getting dark."

"Just a bit farther. I want you to see the clearing."

At the bottom of the slope we emerged into a small clearing. Off to the right was an immense flat area ringed with trees. A meadow obviously lay beneath the snow there.

"Pretty, isn't it?" Peyton asked, halting on the trail.

"Hmm, sure. Look, I'd like to get back to the house. It's been a tough twenty-four hours for me."

"But don't you want to know why I did it?" she asked.

She was just ahead of me on the little trail, and she turned toward me with a smile as she spoke. I froze in place.

"What are you talking about?" I asked weakly.

"Oh, come now, Bailey. I know you know. I saw it in

your eyes when you were standing in the library. You must have just figured it all out."

I swallowed and glanced up at the sky. It looked as if it had been smudged with soot.

"I knew there were pictures, you know," she continued. "Jamie told me she had proof. But I couldn't find them at her place."

"Is that why you went to Jamie's that night—to find the pictures?" I asked. It seemed pointless to pretend.

"She actually *asked* me to her place. That bitch wanted to talk about her pathetic little store, the one where she was going to sell white bean dip to winos. She blackmailed me into giving her the money for it, but she honestly believed it was a shrewd business move for me. Plus, she loved seeing me sweat. Jamie just couldn't bear that I had everything. She left me with no choice but to kill her."

"Why are you telling me this?" I asked.

She laughed and zipped up her jacket a few more inches. The unseen sun had begun to drop, lowering the temperature.

"What harm does it do to tell you?" she asked, shrugging. "You have no proof. No one would believe a word you said. I mean, the Greenwich police already think you're insane. Every day you've got a different theory."

She was a sociopath—self-focused, incapable of seeing other people as real or worthy of respect, in love with risk, convinced she was not only smarter than anyone else, but invulnerable. The early warning signs had been there since college, but I'd never picked up on them.

"How did you do it?"

"*It?*"

"Kill Jamie."

"It was easy. She'd already had half a bottle of wine when I got there, and then she had more. When she was done talking to me, she suggested that I see myself to the door while she ran her bath—as if I were the fucking cleaning lady. I just stood in this little entranceway of hers, trying to make a plan. After I heard the water stop running, I went into the bathroom. And then I just dumped the CD player into the tub."

"And Robin?"

"I really didn't want to hurt Robin. But she wouldn't shut the fuck up about Jamie's death. She kept saying it might have to do with the wedding, and finally she let it slip that Jamie had given her some pictures. I asked to see them, but she kept putting it off. I think she was worried I might be involved somehow. It was clear that the pictures didn't mean anything to her—but I was afraid she'd eventually figure it out."

"How did you get the tyramine into her food?"

She laughed, as if I'd just amused her to death. "Give me a little credit, Bailey, will you? Despite what my enemies say, I *do* develop my own recipes. I heard Robin ask one of the kitchen workers to make her a smoothie for the trip to Vermont. I just added the Brewer's yeast when no one was looking. It's loaded with tyramine."

"And—and Ashley? You didn't have anything to do with her death?"

"I have no fucking clue what happened to her. Maybe it *was* Trip. Oh, she was starting to get on my nerves big-time, too. She had this whole conspiracy theory going, like something out of that movie *JFK*. I knew the pictures might still be around, so I had Robin's brother come and get everything."

"So it was you who told him that Ashley was picking over Robin's stuff?"

She laughed. "Yes. Ashley would have freaked if she knew that. She was so damn proper. But I didn't realize until we talked on the phone today that Robin's moron of a brother had left the pictures behind. So, see, you can't hold me responsible for Ashley. That's why I let you be the detective. I needed to know what had happened, if someone was somehow on to me and trying to damage my business or threaten me. Weren't you sweet to point the finger at Trip."

"Who was it?" I asked.

"Who?"

"The guy in the picture."

"I told you about him, didn't I? I was seeing him long before David. He is a superb piece of ass, but I couldn't marry him. His net worth is about equal to what I charge for seared tuna for six. I thought it would be fun to have him at the wedding. He actually screwed my brains out that day in the carriage house, which Jamie *didn't* see, but that kiss alone would have been enough to make a vein pop in David's head. According to the prenup, he could leave me and not have to give me a cent. I could never make Ivy Hill everything I want it to be. It's too damn expensive."

I didn't dare do anything that showed I was panicky— because I wasn't sure how Peyton might react—but I was desperate to get out of there. I glanced back over my shoulder at the trail leading back to the house. She caught the movement of my head, stopped, and turned toward me.

"You're not thinking of going back, are you?" she asked gaily. "I'm so enjoying this."

"Don't you think we should turn around? It's getting late."

She smiled and reached into the pocket of her jacket. I ducked as fast as I could.

"Bailey, please," she said, her eyes wide in mock surprise. "What do you think? That I'm going to threaten you with a gun like *Trip* did? You're my friend. Thanks to you, I have an ironclad alibi for Ashley's murder. Trip will take the rap for all three deaths, and if you try to claim differently, you'll only agitate the police, who aren't too fond of you as it is. Plus, like I said, you could never prove anything anyway."

I straightened up and held my breath as she withdrew her hand. She was holding the envelope of pictures.

"Of course, we wouldn't want these around anymore, would we?" she asked.

With a flick of her wrist she flung the pictures onto the wide expanse of white snow, as if she were throwing a Frisbee for a dog to catch. Then she brushed past me and began to stride in the direction of the house.

I watched her move off, her French twist beginning to unravel, then I glanced out to the spot where she'd tossed the pictures. The envelope had sunk into the wet snow, but I could see the gray patch where it had settled. I stepped over the rim of snow along the edge of the path and sprinted across the meadow.

But it wasn't a meadow. I don't remember what I noticed first—the slickness underneath or the sudden low groan. I was on ice. And it didn't appreciate my presence.

I stopped in my tracks, not sure what to do. I was at least twenty feet out onto the surface of what must be a snow-covered pond, a pond that was apparently starting to thaw. I had no idea how deep it was, but based on the circumference, I guessed it might be at least ten feet. I was afraid that as soon as I took a step, the ice, which had already protested my weight, would start to crack.

Up ahead of me to the right, I could see Peyton. She had turned around and was now making her way back to me. There was something dark in her hand that I couldn't make out. As she drew closer I saw it—a rock. In one deft movement she hurled it so that it landed two feet in front of me. The ice groaned again, and this time I felt it begin to buckle underneath. A crack appeared in the surface and then sped like the burning wick of a firecracker.

I felt desperate with panic. I was a decent swimmer, but the water was freezing and I was in a heavy coat and boots. I held my breath, thinking that if I didn't move a muscle, the ice wouldn't crack any more. But it felt as foolish as closing my eyes in the hope that no one could see me.

Water began to gush from the crack, and I felt the patch of ice I was standing on begin to slowly sink. Suddenly I remembered something I'd heard long ago, when I was covering a winter disaster north of Albany. The smartest strategy on melting ice is to lie down and spread your weight around.

I slowly lowered myself and eased onto my belly. The pictures were just inches from me, and I grabbed them and stuffed them in my pocket. I tried to reach into my jeans pocket for my cell phone, but just that little bit of wiggling made the ice give even more. There was another large groan and crack, and water rushed in all around me. In a matter of seconds my boots and pants were soaked with icy water. I gasped, the wind knocked out of me. I tried to scream for help, but it was a strangled little sound that barely penetrated the gloom of the fading day.

There was one more crack, and I was suddenly in the middle of the pond, holding on to a single piece of ice like a kickboard. My legs felt as if they were wrapped in steel, but I did my best to move them in a frog kick and maneuver toward the rim of the pond by the path.

As I got closer to the edge, I looked up and saw that Peyton had made her way there. She now held a large branch in her hand. Had she had a change of heart? I wondered desperately.

"Please help me, Peyton," I yelled. My legs, which only moments ago had stung from the cold, were now close to numb.

"Just grab the branch," she said, thrusting it out over the water toward me.

I kicked my legs and tried to thrust myself a few inches closer. As I reached for the branch, she pulled it back and then rammed it into the chunk of ice I was hanging to, as if trying to sink it.

"Peyton, stop, please!" I screamed.

She drew the branch back like a tennis racket, and this time she swung it, whacking me across the side of my face. I raised my left arm like a shield, anticipating another blow, and as I did, I slipped from my ice board. I was now in water up to my shoulders, and the shock took my breath away. For the first time I realized that I was in danger of drowning.

Suddenly, way off to the left, I heard a voice, and as I dog-paddled away from the shore, trying to avoid another blow from the branch, I saw a man in a dark coat come running down the path. As he drew closer, I realized in desperate relief that it was the caretaker, Brian.

"What's going on?" he called out to Peyton. She drew the branch back again and now she swung at him with it. He ducked, making her miss. She tried again, and this time he caught the branch with his hand and yanked it away from her. She took a step toward him with one arm raised, and he decked her, knocking her to the ground with one punch. Then he turned his attention to me.

"Here, take this," he called, holding out the branch to me. My arms were aching, and I could no longer feel my legs. I tried to make them move, but they just hung in the water like bags of sand.

"You can do it—come on," he urged.

With all the energy I could summon, I did a feeble breaststroke through the water, coming closer to the edge again. I grasped the branch, and the caretaker pulled me toward him. When I was within a few feet of the shore, he reached into the water, yanked my right arm, and hauled me onto the bank of the pond.

"Thank you," I gasped as I felt the ground beneath me. "She tried to drown me."

"I know. I saw. Look, you've got to get out of those wet clothes before you end up with hypothermia. Here, take my jacket, but get your coat and shirt off first."

He nearly tore off his jacket and then turned his back to me so I could undress. I was shivering uncontrollably, but I managed to strip off my jacket and shirt. I glanced over to Peyton. She was still down for the count, but beginning to writhe in the snow.

"Okay, that's better," the caretaker said as he turned back to me. "What the hell is going on here, anyway?"

"She killed two people, and I found out. It's a long story." My teeth chattered as I spoke.

"We've got to get you up to the house," he said. "You could die if you don't get warmed up."

"But what about Peyton?" I asked.

He glanced at her with a frown. "We can't leave her here alone. Do you think you can make it back on your own? I'll call Clara on my mobile and have her start down to meet you."

"Okay—I guess," I said. I honestly wasn't sure I could make it. I felt exhausted and breathless. The caretaker helped me as I struggled to my feet out of the snow.

"Just follow the path," he called out to me as I started off. "And let me know when you reach the house. Clara has my number."

I stumbled in the direction of the house, my teeth chattering so loudly that I could hear nothing else. It was growing dark out and colder. I took my eyes off the path just once—to look behind me and make certain that Peyton wasn't following me.

CHAPTER 21

Landon hadn't had time to marinate the pork tender-loin when he fed me late Friday night. So he served me some cheeses he had in his fridge, which I ate along with an entire French baguette. It felt as if I were carbo loading for the New York City marathon, but beggars can't be choosers. I had nothing in my own refrigerator except two clumps of aluminum foil that I was afraid to open. And I had no interest in being alone.

"Bailey?" Landon asked, pouring me another glass of Bordeaux.

"Hmm?"

"Do you feel any better now?"

"Yeah, thanks." To some degree I meant it. I felt totally warm in his apartment and also safe. But emotionally I was a basket case. Six hours ago I'd been close to drowning. Six hours ago I'd learned that Peyton was a murderer.

My run—or rather stumble—back to Peyton's house had been pure misery. Though my torso felt warmer with the caretaker's coat covering me, my feet were frozen stiff, and each step was painful. Clara and a woman I'd never seen before met me almost halfway and helped me back. The next hour was crazy and bewildering. I told Clara to call the police while I changed, but she seemed reluctant to do so—in denial, perhaps, or fearful of angering her employers. So I did it myself. Two police cars arrived, including one with Pichowski and Michaels, and shortly thereafter David showed up, having been alerted by Clara. He was all in a tizzy, uncharacteristic for him. Peyton was taken into custody, but I never saw her. At that point I was sequestered in the library. By the time Pichowski spoke to me, I knew he'd already taken a statement from the caretaker, and on this occasion there wasn't any skepticism in his eyes. He wanted me to stay over until the next day, but there was no way I was going to spend one more second in Greenwich. I told him I was going back to New York but would happily drive up to police headquarters the next day if they needed me.

"I'm terrified just hearing the story, Bailey," Landon said, pulling me away from my thoughts. "You must have been sure you were going to die."

"I really thought I was. Not at first. I got close to shore and I figured I was going to be okay. But when Peyton slammed the branch into me and I had to paddle back out, I suddenly realized, I'm *not* going to make it. If that caretaker hadn't come down . . . God, I can't even bear to think of it."

"Why do you think he showed up, after Peyton told him not to bother?"

"He told me later that after he went off on the bogus assignment of fixing her seat belt, he figured he still had time to check out the fallen tree. Besides, he considers David his boss, he said, not Peyton, and he didn't feel comfortable blowing off a job because she told him to."

Landon took a sip of his wine, both elbows on the table, his eyes lost briefly in contemplation.

"Did you *ever* suspect Peyton?" he asked, setting the glass back down again.

"No, not for a second," I said, smearing the last clump of some creamy blue cheese onto a piece of bread. "Because I got fixed on this idea of a serial killer, of one person being responsible for all three deaths. Peyton was with me the entire time Ashley was in the silo, so I never once considered her. I should have, though. I can't believe I didn't—her motives should have been so clear. Remember when I was talking to Cat about this and she used that phrase *Cherchez la femme*? It was about finding a motive as strong as a lust object. Peyton had that kind of motive—money—and the irony is that she was *la femme*."

"But at least you figured out the truth in the end. Which is more than the cops can claim credit for."

"I guess."

"Bailey, don't be so hard on yourself. She's a very clever lady. Didn't she single-handedly invent mango crème brûlée? There's no way you could have known."

I smiled ruefully at his joke and shook my head. "There was one giveaway, and I missed it. When I think back on it, Peyton seemed very freaked out after Ashley's death, but she hadn't seemed that distraught about Robin's. That's because she didn't know what the hell was going on with Ashley. All of a sudden a third bridesmaid is dead, but she didn't kill *this* one. I'm sure she wondered if someone was toying with her, trying to send her a message. That's why she didn't mind my snooping around. She wanted me to help figure out the Ashley part of the equation."

"But wasn't she afraid you might learn the truth about the other murders?"

"Apparently not. I think she really believed she'd done a brilliant job of making them appear to be accidents. The only evidence was the photo, and she thought she'd taken care of that by having Robin's brother and sister-in-law cart everything off."

"She's really quite awesome, isn't she?"

"Oh yeah. The thing about Peyton is that for someone so narcissistic, she's always paid attention to detail. That's what made her such a perfect domestic diva. And it's also what made her such a perfect murderer. Electrocuting Jamie was a spur-of-the-moment thing but also extremely clever—a great example of thinking on one's feet. She knew Robin took medication and had to watch what she ate. She obviously did a little research and found out all she needed to know to kill her. And wasn't what she did with me clever, too? At first I thought tossing the pictures was a spontaneous gesture, but later I realized it was planned out. There were tracks in the snow, and she'd probably gone down to that area recently and realized that the ice was melting."

"How could she have brought herself to kill her friends?"

"In her mind she had everything to lose if she didn't. David was footing the bill for the Peyton Cross empire. If he'd gotten so much as a hint that she was unfaithful, he would have cut everything off. There'd be no Ivy Hill Farm."

"But these attacks on you—in New York and on the road in Greenwich. They had nothing to do with Peyton, right?"

"Right. They were all Trip's doing—which just added to her paranoia. She must have been freaking out about who this other predator was."

"So no one was really after her business, were they?"

"What do you mean?"

"You told me earlier that someone might be trying to screw with her business. Weren't there party cancellations?"

"Someone *was* trying to screw with her business. But that turned out to be a whole separate thing."

It wasn't all that exciting, and I doubted Landon would want the details. But I'd put it together on the drive home. Something about the tapenade I'd sampled at Mandy's had bugged me. It was such a distinct recipe, and I wondered how the other caterer, Bon Appetite, could be doing it, too. Then Mary had been missing in action for the party Peyton's catering division had planned. On the drive back to the city tonight, I had called Mandy and asked her point-blank if Mary was the head of Bon Appetite. And she admitted she was. Mary, it turned out, was in the process of launching her own catering operation while still working for Peyton, and Mandy was thrilled to give her business a boost. Anything to get at Peyton for scarring poor little Lilly for life. My guess was that Mary was the one who'd messed up the party dates late last year. She'd wanted to undermine Peyton's business as much as she could, which would provide her with more leverage in Greenwich. She might have also been the one who tipped off the New York papers to all the bridesmaids' deaths. After all, she'd learned about ether damage from Maverick. Mary looked like the devoted employee, but she clearly had no loyalty to Peyton. Peyton probably did something to screw her over at some point—or maybe she just hated being treated like a house servant.

"So what do you think will happen to Peyton?" Landon asked. "Do you think they'll be able to get her for the murders?"

"I honestly don't know," I said, staring at the ruby glow of my wine. "She'll definitely be prosecuted for attempting to kill me. I just thank God the caretaker was there to witness it. As for the murders, I'll have to wait and see. There's the picture of her and her boy toy, whoever he is. I called the *Gloss* photo editor at home, and he said water is real bad for negatives but there's a chance they aren't completely destroyed. I'm sure the police will find a money trail from Peyton to Jamie. Now that we know she used wheat germ in Robin's shake, there may be some trail involving that as well. Oh, and Pichowski told me tonight that after he arrested Trip, he ordered the police report from New York and it turns out that on the night of Jamie's murder, someone reported seeing a woman in the building with strawberry blond hair worn up on her head. It wasn't viewed as significant at the time because everything pointed to the death as an accident. But it puts someone who looks like Peyton at the scene."

I poured one more splash of wine into my glass. I'd been hoping to get a buzz going, but it wasn't happening. Nothing seemed to make a dent.

"Do you want to crash on my couch tonight?" Landon asked. "Just so you're not alone."

"Oh, that's so sweet of you," I said, smiling warmly at him. "But I've got things to take care of at my place."

Back in my apartment, I took my second hot shower of the night. As I stepped out of the tub, I saw in the mirror that the bandage Clara had applied to my face now hung by a hair, so I peeled it the rest of the way. There was an ugly purple-and-red welt on my cheek and also an inch-long gash. In the back of my medicine chest I located an ancient tube of antibacterial ointment and applied it, followed by my last Band-Aid. Then I slipped into a pair of flannel jammies and crawled into bed.

My bedside lamp cast a warm amber glow, and out my window I could see my fabulous stage backdrop of a view. From the vantage point of my bedroom, the world seemed wonderful. And that only made it harder for me to accept that Peyton Cross—the girl I'd shared four tons of frozen yogurt with freshman year in college and who had once called a boy I was crazy about, pretending to be a poll taker so we could learn his weekend plans—had killed two of her friends and tried to do the same to me.

What I also couldn't escape as I lay scrunched under my down duvet was the fact that it was Friday night and Jack wasn't there. It was the first Friday night in three months that he hadn't slept beside me. Earlier I'd been tempted to call him and describe everything that had happened, but it didn't seem fair to play that card. I was going to have to learn how to get along without him.

Surprisingly, I felt okay about it. Because I realized that I was about to embark on some new stage in my life. Yes, I was once again divorced and dateless, but this time around I was going to experience it differently—as someone who wasn't feeling bruised and sorry for herself. There might be all sorts of interesting adventures waiting for me. Chris had left a message on my cell phone earlier wondering what was up with the case, and then I'd left a message for him, promising to fill him in. Maybe once all my bruises healed and I no longer looked as if I'd broken the pavement with my face, I'd see him again.

And I hoped that down the road I really would be ready for a commitment, to someone as nice as Jack. That old, tired expression popped into my head—"Always the bridesmaid, never the bride." Perhaps someday, a long time from now, I'd actually be a bride once more. But there was one thing I knew for sure: As long as I lived, I'd never be a bridesmaid again.

More
Kate White!

Please turn this page
for a preview of

OVER HER DEAD BODY

available wherever
books are sold.

CHAPTER 1

What you see isn't always what you get.

The trouble with clichés is that they're so downright tedious, you fail to pay any attention to the message they're meant to convey. And sometimes you really should. I know because during a particularly hot and muggy summer in New York City, that particular cliché jumped up more than once and took a large, hard bite out of my butt.

On the initial occasion, I was an idiot to have been blindsided. It was the last week in May, a Wednesday, and Cat Jones, my boss at *Gloss* magazine, had invited me out to dinner. Now, there was nothing inherently odd in Cat treating me to a meal—despite our work arrangement, we'd always been friends in a weird sort of way. But she'd suggested that we meet at six forty-five at a kind of out-of-the-way place in the Village, and that's

when the warning bells should have sounded. As a friend
of mine once pointed out, when a guy suggests dinner at
an untrendy restaurant before seven o'clock, you can be
damn sure that he's going to announce he's in love with
another chick and he's hoping for a fast escape before
you start to sob and lunge for his ankles. My mistake was
not realizing that the same warning applied to bosses, too.

I *did* suspect that the dinner was going to be more
work related than personal. For the past few years I've
been under contract with *Gloss* to write eight to ten crime
or human-interest stories a year. Cat had worked out the
arrangement herself when she'd first arrived at *Gloss* and
was in the process of turning it from a bland-as-boiled-
ham women's service magazine into a kind of *Cosmo* for
married chicks. I'd always pitched my own story ideas,
and they were green-lighted pretty quickly. But lately I'd
been batting zero, and I didn't know why. Perfect example: Two weeks ago I'd suggested a piece on a young
mother who'd disappeared without a trace while jogging.
The husband had become the main suspect, though interestingly it was she, not he, who'd been having an affair.
Cat had nixed the idea with the comment "Missing wives
just feel *sooo* tired to me." Tell that to the Laci Peterson
family, I'd been tempted to say—but hadn't. My hunch
was that Cat had suggested dinner together so she could
offer me insight into what kind of crime *didn't* put her to
sleep these days.

I arrived at the restaurant first, which is typical when
dealing with Cat, but at least it gave me a chance to catch
my breath. It was a small, French country–style restaurant on MacDougal Street in the Village, and I ordered a

glass of rosé in honor of the weather and the ambience. As each group of new diners strolled through the door, they brought a delicious late spring breeze with them.

Let this be a hint of how delicious the summer will be, I prayed. I was thirsty for a summer to end all summers. In January, I'd broken up with a guy I'd really cared about, and though I wasn't eager for another serious relationship right then, I was hoping for *some* kind of romantic adventure. I'd had a brief fling in late winter with a male model in his early twenties, ten years younger than me, but then he'd relocated to Los Angeles. After that it had been slim pickings unless you count four or five booty calls with an old beau from Brown who had become so stuffy that I practically had to ask him not to talk. I'm pretty in a kind of sporty way—five six, fairly slim, with brownish blond hair just below my chin—and generally I'd never had trouble wrestling up dates. I was banking on the fact that my dry spell might end now that we were in the season of nearly effortless seductions.

Cat sauntered in about ten minutes late, and heads swiveled in her direction. She's in her late thirties, gorgeous, with long, buttery blond hair, blue eyes, and full lips that never leave the house unless they're stained a brick red or dusky pink. She was wearing slim turquoise pants and an exotic gold-and-turquoise embroidered top that made her look as if she'd just come from the kasbah.

"Sorry I'm late," she said, slipping into her seat. "Minor crisis."

"Diverted, I hope."

"Unfortunately, no. I'm having a huge problem with the new beauty editor. Her copy is about as exciting as the instructions that come with a DVD recorder, and her judgment sucks."

"What did she do this time?"

"She signed up for a junket to Paris without clearing it with anyone."

"Really?" I said, feigning interest just to be polite. I felt about as much concern as I would have if Cat had announced she could feel a fever blister coming on. "What else is going on?"

Before she could answer, the waiter scurried over. Cat ordered a glass of Chardonnay and asked for the menus ASAP. Hmmm, I thought. She seemed in a hurry, almost on edge. I wondered if something might be the matter.

"So, where were we?" she asked as the waiter departed.

"I was asking what else was new."

"Oh, the usual," she said distractedly. "It's been kind of crazy lately."

"How's Tyler?" I inquired, referring to her little boy.

"Good, good. He managed to graduate from nursery school last week even though he bit two of his classmates during the last month. I thought the parents were going to ask that we have him checked for rabies. How about you? Are you going up to your mother's place on Cape Cod this summer?"

"I'll go up a couple of times, but just for weekends. Both my brothers will be around with their wives and I end up feeling like a fifth wheel with them—though they try their darnedest to be inclusive."

"So you're not madly in love with someone these days?"

"No, and that's okay. All I would love this summer is a fabulous fling with someone."

"Sounds good. You're still in your early thirties and you've got plenty of time to get into something more serious. Shall we look at the menus?"

Oh boy. Something was definitely up. She was moving things along so quickly that the next thing I knew she'd be asking the waiter to connect me to a feeding tube. As soon as we'd ordered, I decided to take the bull by the horns.

"Is everything okay, Cat?" I asked. "I have the feeling that something is on your mind."

Cat studied the tablecloth with her blue eyes, saying nothing. I could see now that she was nervous as hell.

"Cat, what's up?" I urged. "Are you in some kind of trouble?"

"No, not exactly. Bailey, I've got bad news, and it's so hard for me to say." As she raised her head, I saw a half tear form in the corner of her left eye.

"Are you having *marriage* problems again?" I asked.

"No, it doesn't involve me," she said. "It involves you."

"*Me?*" I said, thunderstruck. I couldn't imagine what she was talking about, though I felt a wave of irrational panic, the kind I always experienced when an airline clerk asked me if I'd packed my own bags. "Why? What's going on?"

"Let me start at the beginning," she said after taking a deep breath and straightening her already straight utensils. "You're aware, I'm sure, from some things I've said over the past year, that *Gloss* has been *challenged* on the newsstand. At first I blamed my entertainment editor for not being able to book me the right people. Then I began to see that it was something more fundamental than that. My whole vision for *Gloss* when I first arrived there was to make it fun and sexy and juicy, full of the most important news in a young married woman's life. I wanted the magazine to generate buzz. And it worked brilliantly — for a while."

She paused and took a long sip of her wine. I had a bad feeling about where this was headed.

"Well, I've been doing some research — focus groups, phone surveys. It's the most fucking draining experience in the world, but in the end it's been worth it. I feel I have some answers. And it's clear to me that the world is changing, women are changing, and I'm going to have to change directions with the magazine."

"How do you mean?" I asked. It came out in the form of a squeak, like the sound a teakettle makes after you've turned it off but it's filled with enough leftover steam for one last desperate peep. "I think that these days *Gloss* needs to be less about buzz and more about bliss."

"*Bliss?*" I said, almost choking on the word. "Are you talking about things like, uh, aromatherapy and savoring the sunrise?"

"Believe it or not, yes. Women are stressed, and they want relief from that stress. We need to create features in the magazine that help them deal with all of that. Look, Bailey, it's not my cup of tea. I think you know me well enough to know that my bullshit meter goes off the minute I hear words like 'feng shui.' But I'm fighting for my survival here."

"So where do I fit into all of this?" I could feel my dread ballooning like one of those pop-up sponges that has just been submerged in water.

"This is so hard for me to tell you, Bailey. You know how much I care about you—and you also know that I think you're an amazing writer. But I've come to realize that I need to seriously pull back on the crime stories for the magazine. I've rejected a bunch of your ideas lately, and it's not because there's anything wrong with them. I just look at each one and I can't picture it in the new mix I've got in mind. You can't have page after page on how to live a serene life and then jam in a story about a woman whose husband has smashed in her skull with a claw hammer and dumped her body in Lake Michigan."

I'd done some discreet snooping over the past year, and I was aware that circulation numbers at *Gloss* had become less than stellar, that Cat was probably under a ton of pressure. I'd even considered the idea that she might lose her job down the road and I'd be out of the best of my freelance arrangements. But I'd never entertained this particular permutation—or thought that anything would happen so soon.

"But what about my human-interest stories?" I asked, floundering.

"I wish I could include them," she said, looking at me almost plaintively. "And I've thought over and over about whether there's a way to fit them in. But they're just not on the same page with what we'll be doing. I need to make *Gloss* very *visual*. In some ways, pictures are the new words today. I'm not saying that we'll have only photos in *Gloss,* but the articles we run will be shorter—and *gentler."*

Her words stupefied me. It was as if she'd just announced that she had written an op-ed-page article for the *Times* in favor of creationism. I was too dumfounded even to offer a reply.

"But don't worry," she continued with a wan smile. "You have five articles left on your contract, and of course I'm going to pay you the entire amount."

"And then that's it?"

"Bailey, this is killing me to say it. Yes, that's it. *Gloss* is in trouble and I need to fix it—or they'll hire someone who will."

For a few seconds my anger found a foothold, but it didn't get very far. What was the point in being furious with Cat? I could tell she was being honest and that she believed her job was on the line. But that didn't make it any better for me. I felt hurt, disappointed, even, to my surprise, humiliated, as if I'd been handed a pink slip and told to clear out my desk within the hour.

The dinner came and we picked at our food. Cat tried to praise my writing some more, and I suggested we move on to other topics, which turned out to be as easy to find as the Lost City of Petra. Neither one of us bothered with coffee, and when she offered me a lift home, I lied and said I had to make a stop nearby.

"Here's a thought," she said, lingering on the sidewalk beside her black town car. "Would you be open to writing a different kind of piece for me?"

I smirked involuntarily. "You mean like 'How to Optimize Your Chi'? No, I don't think so. But thanks for asking."

"Bailey, I'm sorry, truly sorry," she said.

"I know," I told her. "And I'm sorry if I sounded sarcastic just then. It's just that you've really thrown me for a loop."

The driver, perhaps trained to run intervention at awkward moments, leapt out of the car and opened the door. Cat slid in and waved good-bye soberly. As the car moved soundlessly down MacDougal Street, I thought: Of course she doesn't want to jeopardize her job at *Gloss*. God forbid she should ever be forced to take a taxi instead of a Lincoln Town Car.

I slunk home on foot through the Village, like a little kid who had just been banished from the playground for having cooties. It took only fifteen minutes for me to make it to my apartment building on the corner of 9th Street and Broadway, but the short walk gave me a chance to assess my new lot in life.

Financially the situation was in no way a disaster. Ever since my ex-husband, the Gamblers Anonymous dropout, had run through much of our mutual savings and hawked some of my jewelry, money matters had made me extremely anxious. But I was really going to be okay. I wrote for other magazines besides *Gloss,* and my relationship with most of them was good. And luckily I also had a backup source of income. My father died when I was twelve, leaving me a small trust fund that provides a regular income each year. Nothing that puts me in the league with the Hilton sisters, but it helps pay for basic expenses, like the maintenance on my one-bedroom apartment in the Village and a garage for my Jeep.

What I was going to have to kiss good-bye, however, were all the extra niceties I'd been enjoying thanks to my generous *Gloss* contract—everything from cute shoes to *el grande* cappuccinos to the occasional Saturday afternoon massage. I'd gotten used to them, spoiled, like one of those women who can have an orgasm only with a Mr. Blue vibrator.

I'd also miss having an office to go to, someplace to mingle with other human beings. And there was something else, I suddenly realized to my horror. In the fall, a collection of my crime articles was being published by a small book company, and now I wouldn't have the *Gloss* affiliation to leverage. What would the jacket say? "Bailey Weggins is a freelancer who works out of her own home. When she isn't writing she enjoys going through her coat pockets looking for spare change." Cat had even promised to help with PR, since so many of the articles in my book had first appeared in *Gloss*. Now I'd have to rely on the book company's tiny, and reputedly weak, publicity department. I'd heard from another writer that the last time they'd gotten someone on the *Today* show was for a book on Margaret Thatcher's leadership style.

After letting myself into my apartment, I helped myself to the last cold beer in the fridge and checked the calendar on my Blackberry. I had a fairly busy week ahead, but I'd have to make time to talk to editors and see if there was the potential for another contributing editor gig someplace else. I'd forgotten that tomorrow night I was having drinks with Robby Hart, an old pal from *Get,* the magazine I'd worked at before *Gloss*—and where I'd first met Cat. Robby was a great networker and the perfect person for me to brainstorm with.

As it turned out, my drink with Robby was the only step I ever had to take in my job search.

The spot he'd chosen for us to meet on Thursday night was a wine bar on the Lower East Side. Robby was already at a table when I arrived, dressed as usual in a cotton plaid button-down shirt with a white undershirt peeking out from underneath. I guess you can take the boy out of Ohio, but you can't take Ohio out of the boy. As soon as he spotted me, he stood up to greet me and offer one of his big toothy Robby smiles. He'd never been Mr. Svelte, but I realized as we hugged each other that he'd put on some weight since I'd seen him last.

"Wow, it's so good to see you," he said. "It's been too long."

"I know. I've been so looking forward to this."

The waiter strolled by just as I was sitting down, and I asked for a glass of Cabernet.

"Nice 'do," Robby said, pointing with his chin toward my hair. "I almost didn't recognize you."

"Thanks, I decided to grow it out. But just watch—once it's finally long enough to make it into a sloppy bun, they'll be out of style."

"Well, at least you've got some to grow," he said. Robby was my age but totally bald.

"So tell me—how's the new gig?" I demanded. "I'm dying to hear."

Robby had stayed at *Get* until it folded, then gone in desperation to *Ladies' Home Journal,* where he'd assigned and written celebrity pieces for several years. Three months ago he'd bagged a job as a senior editor for *Buzz,* the very hot celebrity gossip magazine. Circulation at *Buzz* had languished until the top job was taken over about a year ago by Mona Hodges, the genius—and notorious—editor known for resuscitating ailing magazines. Sales had since skyrocketed, and in a recent profile, Mona had claimed that forty-nine percent of her readers would choose an evening reading *Buzz* over sex with their husbands.

"Well, I've got to admit, it's awesome to be at such a buzzy magazine," he said. "When people used to find out I worked at *LHJ,* all they'd do was ask if I had a recipe for chicken chili or knew how to get ink stains out of clothes. But when someone finds out I work at *Buzz,* their eyes bug out."

"That's fabulous, Robby," I said, but as soon as I said it I saw his eyes flicker with uncertainty. *"What?"*

He squeezed his lips together hard. "On the other hand, it's been a tough learning curve," he conceded. "They expect your writing to be very cute and snappy, and I'm not so experienced with that. The chick in the office next to me wrote this line about Hugh Grant the other day—she said he had the kind of blue eyes you could see from outer space—and all I could think was why can't I write something like that? Though I think I'm finally starting to get the hang of it."

"Do you work late most nights? I heard someone say that there were sweatshops in Cambodia that have better hours than *Buzz.*"

"Mondays are the worst because we close that

night," he admitted. "Sometimes I'm there till five a.m. Tuesdays are the one early night 'cause things are just gearing up again. The other nights—it all depends. They say it's going to get better now that Mona has finally settled in."

"And you're covering TV?" I said.

"Mainly *reality* TV. Behind-the-scenes stuff. Are the bitches really as bitchy as they seem? Who's bonking who? The head of the West Coast office says we should just change the name of the magazine to *Who You Fucking?* I guess it's pretty dumbed-down stuff from what I used to be doing, but what difference does it make?"

"What do you mean?"

"Well, we tried to make the celeb stuff at *LHJ* more *journalistic*, but it was wasted effort considering who we were dealing with. I suggested to a celebrity's publicist once that we could approach someone like Maya Angelou to do the interview, and you know what he said to me? He asked to see her clips."

I laughed out loud.

"So you see," he continued, "there's a watermark you can never get above, anyway."

"*Buzz* can get pretty nasty, though—right?"

"It's mainly this one gossip section that's down and dirty. It's called 'Juice Bar.' You don't want to get on their radar if you can help it. The rest of the magazine is cheeky but not nearly so bitchy."

"Well, are you happy you made the switch?" I asked skeptically as the waiter set our drinks down in front of us.

"Overall, yes. It's great experience and the pay is certainly better. I got a twenty-thousand-dollar bump in my salary—which I need right now. I wanted to tell you this in person—though it's still hush-hush: Brock and I are applying to adopt a kid."

"Oh, Robby, that's fabulous," I said, giving his hand a squeeze. "You'll be a fantastic parent." And I meant it. Robby was one of the kindest, most thoughtful guys I'd ever worked with, and I knew that he'd always felt frustrated that as a gay man he couldn't have a child.

"Thanks," he said, beaming. "I'm dying to be a dad. The problem is Brock's business has been hit or miss lately, and if our application is going to be accepted, I need to have a well-paying job. So I just need to grin and bear it and hope I can get on top of things."

"Wait—I thought you said you were on the other side of the learning curve."

"Sort of. I mean, I think I've started to get the hang of the *style,* but the weekly pace is still a problem for me. If I had more time, I could do a better job of polishing my copy, but I don't—and then later it gets tossed back to me for endless revisions."

"Is she really as tough to work for as people say?" I asked. I was referring to Mona Hodges. Though editor in chiefs could be tough, Mona's reputation made her unique in the pain-in-the-ass-to-work-for category. She was reportedly cold, demanding, arbitrary, and at times even abusive. Some people believed that Mona had been spurred to be this way so she could stand out from the pack by generating press about her antics—the all-publicity-even bad-publicity-is-good-publicity theory. She supposedly was insanely jealous of Bonnie Fuller, the editor of rival publications. Bonnie had a far more illustrative track record in getting ratings to skyrocket and improve the quality. Though Bonnie had the advantage of having a longer tenure in the business and so had more time to make her mark, it still galled Mona, who was impatient to get recognized. The "I be bad" strategy apparently was meant to get Mona recognition faster, even if *hers* was all negative.

He rolled his hazel eyes. "Well, she can come on strong if she doesn't like what she sees. I heard her verbally bitch-slap the poor mail guy the other day because he'd left a package in the wrong place. But she's a genius at what she does, and our sales are through the roof. There's a lot to learn from someone like her. I just wish I could get the hang of the copy."

"You feeling pretty stressed?"

"Yeah. And the worst part is I've been using Cheetos and chocolate as my stress reducers of choice. I'm so fat now that I have *man* tits. When Brock and I start telling the world we're becoming parents, people will think that *I'm* the one giving birth. But enough about me. How's your life, anyway?"

"Not so great." I told him the whole story and described how much of a curveball it had thrown me.

As I was speaking, Robby's eyes widened and his jaw went slack. With his elbows resting on the table, he stretched out both arms and flipped over his hands.

"Omigod, I just thought of something," he said. "I know the perfect job for you."

"*Where?*"

"*Buzz* magazine."

"Huh?"

"Wait till you hear this. They've decided to treat celebrity crime in a more journalistic way, rather than just write them up as gossip stories. And they're looking for some really great journalist types to do them—people they can offer contracts to. I never once thought of you because I knew your contract with *Gloss* ran through the end of the year."

"But is there really enough celebrity crime out there to make it worth their while?"

"Absolutely! I mean, every week some celebrity tries to leave Saks with a Fendi purse stuffed down her bra or shoots his wife with a Magnum. God, you'd be perfect for this. Needless to say, for selfish reasons it would be so great for me to have you there."

"But we just finished talking about how tough it is there."

"But it would be different for you," Robby declared, "Mona is secretly intimidated by anything truly journalistic. She wouldn't micromanage you because she doesn't see that as her strength. And it wouldn't be expected for your copy to be all cute and perky. You'd be in the power position. And from what I've heard, the crime stuff is going to be overseen by the number two guy, Nash Nolan. He looks like a bully, but he's perfectly decent. Please, let me set up the interview."

My mind was racing. I'd never once imagined myself at a magazine like *Buzz,* yet I had to admit I was intrigued. The magazine had become a must-read in the last year, and people would get to know my name—just in time for the launch of my book. That advantage could end up outweighing any negatives.

"But I don't really follow celebrities that much," I said, playing devil's advocate.

"You'll find out everything you need to know the first week on the job. There are only about thirty celebrities who matter anyway, and you don't even have to know their last names. Have you ever met Mona, by the way?"

"No. I've seen her picture in the *Post*, but I've never had the pleasure of a face-to-face."

"Look, there's no harm in just talking to her, is there?"

No, there didn't seem to be any harm in talking.

"Okay, I'd be open to an interview," I told him.

Robby beamed when he heard my reply. "She'll love you," he said. "And she'll turn on the charm in the interview—within limits, of course, because it's Mona we're talking about. There are two things you need to watch out for. When she's talking to you, she'll lean in and stare at you really intently. The first time I met her, I thought she was checking out my pores and I half expected her to prescribe an exfoliant before I left. And she's wall-eyed—in just one eye. Always look straight at her face. Don't make the mistake of following the bad eye—it drives her insane when people do that."

I let Robby go ahead and set up the appointment.

My appointment with Mona ended up being on the Wednesday after my drink with Robby. The *Buzz* office, to my surprise, was only a few blocks south from *Gloss*'s, at Broadway and 50th. It took up half of the sixteenth floor of the building; the other portion was occupied by *Track,* an upstart music magazine owned by the same company. Robby had once told me that *Buzz* staffers sometimes bumped into people like Justin Timberlake at the reception area.

There were plenty of people bustling around in the large open offices when I arrived. Their blasé expressions remained unchanged as I was led through by Mona's assistant, yet I could sense some of them following me with their eyes. Perhaps a few were wondering if I was a potential replacement for them.

The front wall of Mona's office was made entirely of glass, but the blinds were drawn today. Her assistant asked me to wait outside, and through the half-open door I could hear a woman and a man in conversation.

"Take a few days to review it, but then we need to get moving on it," said the man, his voice moving closer toward the door. "Try to give Stan a call as soon as you can."

A second later, a short, compact man about fifty, dressed in a dark suit, charged by me. I recognized him as Tom Dicker, the owner of the company. His picture appeared in the *New York Post* and *Daily News* almost as often as Mona's did. I barely had a chance to give him a thought when Mona herself stepped outside, dressed in too tight black pants and a sleeveless neon yellow top, and ushered me into her office.

Robby was right about the fact that she'd attempt to be charming. Mona smiled pleasantly as we shook hands, though her voice was oddly flat, with a slight midwestern accent. Robby was also right about the wall-eyed thing. As Mona's left eye drifted off, I had to fight the urge to follow it—or worse, turn my head, because that created the illusion that someone had snuck into the room and was standing just behind my shoulder.

I'd heard people make fun of her looks, but her face wasn't unattractive, especially for someone in her early forties. It's just that the wandering eye kept her from being pretty. And at around five five she was slightly pudgy, a fact made prominent by the pants she'd chosen. Her best feature was probably her hair. It was auburn colored and glossy as a movie stallion's—though she was wearing it in an unfortunate new shag cut with loads of layers heaped on her head. Her hair was just too thick for that kind of style, and it made her look as though she might be distantly related to a Wookie.

Without bothering to tell me to take a seat, Mona plunked down into the chair behind her desk, so I slipped into one facing her. She glanced at the package of material I'd sent over by messenger and then back up at me.

"So what's wrong with this deal you've got with *Gloss*" she asked bluntly.

"Nothing at all," I said. "But *Gloss* may be going in a slightly different direction, so I've been keeping my ears open for other opportunities."

"You read *Buzz*?"

"Not religiously," I confessed. Something told me it was smarter not to bullshit Mona. "But it's definitely a guilty pleasure I indulge in at times."

"I see you were in newspapers once. Why'd you switch to magazines?"

"I loved the pace of newspapers—and that wonderful sense of urgency that goes with it," I told her. "But you're limited stylewise. I decided what I'd do was get experience covering news, but then move into magazine journalism, where I had more freedom as a writer."

Well, aren't you special? I felt like screaming to myself as soon as the words were out of my mouth. I've always had a hard time finding that fine line between talking up myself the right amount and not sounding obnoxious.

Mona didn't seem to mind, however, and my comment led to a discussion of my background. Then she briskly described what the job would entail. She envisioned the person both writing stories and editing filed stories from other reporters. Through the whole discussion she leaned forward, staring at my face too intently— again, just as Robby had warned. She even stared when *she* was talking, as if she had never been informed of that unwritten rule dictating that when you're the one speaking during a conversation, you should glance away periodically so that you don't appear to be boring into the other person.

"Your stuff's pretty good," Mona said finally, leaning back in her chair. "And on one level you're the right type to do these stories for the magazine. But you've got absolutely no experience covering celebrities. Tell me why I should hire you."

"Actually, I think that my lack of experience with celebrities would be an advantage," I told her. "Cops and experts would take me far more seriously than someone who's usually covering the MTV Music Video Awards. I could also help you give stories the right context. For instance, let's say you have a situation like you did lately where a male star gets slugged by his wife because she caught him at a strip club and the wife ends up in jail. *Buzz* reported it in this wide-eyed way, as if no one had ever heard of a *wife* slugging her husband. But there's research these days suggesting that plenty of wives assault their husbands and that it's a much bigger problem than anyone ever realized. That info could make your story more interesting.

"Plus," I added, "if I needed contacts in the celebrity world, you've got a ton of people on staff who could help me."

Clearly thinking it over, she stared at me from behind her desk—or at least one eye did. I forced myself to look straight at her nose and not seem too eager. She stood up finally and told me she would let me know.

Two days later I got the call from Nash, introducing himself and asking for a meeting. At the end of it, he told me I had the gig. They would put me on a retainer and I would write the big New York–based crime stories and sometimes edit smaller ones filed by staff writers. If there was a major crime story on the West Coast, I could choose to go to L.A. myself or oversee the coverage using some of the West Coast staff. I would have a desk in the office and should plan on being on-site two or three days a week. After I made certain I would be dealing mostly with Nash, I said yes.

I won't deny that I took some satisfaction in phoning Cat and announcing my news to her.

"*Celebrity* crime?" she asked, feigning true curiosity. "You mean, like when they steal clothes from a photo shoot or have too much collagen injected into their lips?"

Sarcasm was something she rarely directed my way, but I didn't let it irk me. I knew she had conflicting feelings about my departure.

I showed up at *Buzz* the next Wednesday. It was an interesting setup. The offices were all glass fronted, and about half of them faced an open area of workstations that looked like the bullpen at a newspaper. The rest of the offices ran along several corridors in the back half of the floor. A big part of the open "newsroom" area belonged to the art and production departments; a smaller section closer to reception, which included about twelve workstations, was filled with mostly reporters and writers. For some reason it had been nicknamed "the pod."

Mona's office was near the very end of the open area, adjoining the art area and a section nicknamed Intern Village, where dazed-looking college students transcribed tapes and kept track of unfolding gossip on the Internet, on sites such as Gawker.com.

As a freelancer I didn't merit an office. The workstation I was shown to was a four-desk section of the pod, with a hodge podge of people. Directly next to me, separated by just a head-high gray partition, was a friendly-seeming writer named Jessie Pendergrass—about thirty, I guessed. Just behind us were another writer, Ryan Forster, and a photo editor named Leo something, who apparently spent his days screening paparazzi shots. As Jessie led me down one of the back corridors to show me where the kitchenette was, she explained that she'd recently switched out of "Juice Bar" to cover the music scene and general celebrity stuff and wouldn't get an office until she was promoted to editor. Leo, she said, should be in the art area but there wasn't enough room, and Ryan, like her, hadn't worked his way up to an office yet.

"Are they easy to sit near?" I asked, realizing that I'd have very little privacy.

"Leo's a good egg," she confided. "He used to be more hyper, but he started this nude gay yoga class and he seems much more mellow. Ryan's a loner. If you develop any insight into him, let me know."

The office decor was pretty bland—white walls, gray rugs, and gray partitions—though people had made an attempt to personalize their offices and workstations by sticking up pictures and tacky memorabilia. About sixty percent of the staff was female, and nearly ten percent of those seemed to have Johnny Depp photos staring soulfully at them from their cubicle partitions. What I couldn't believe was the amount of magazines lying around. Tossed on desks and chairs and strewn over the floor were endless copies not only of *Buzz,* but also of our main competition—*People* and *US Weekly,* as well as *Star,* the *National Enquirer,* and the *Globe.* People were constantly flipping through them for information.

The most amazing part, though, was the noise level. It was so much louder than at *Gloss*—in fact, you would have thought we were covering a war or a presidential election.

I spent the first hour of the day having Nash's assistant, Lee, show me the computer system. I was basically familiar with it—just needed a brief refresher course. Nash told me he'd meet with me after the eleven a.m. daily staff meeting, so I spent the next hour poring over a huge stack of back issues of *Buzz,* trying to soak up the style. I wasn't going to have to use words like glam, bling, or Splitsville in *my* copy, but neither did I want to be too heavy-handed. I also perused the daily "gossip pack," photo copies of everything from gossip columns to People.com to pages from the British tabs. By the time I finished, I knew far more than I'd cared to about Camilla Parker Bowles.

Every so often I'd glance up to see if Mona was in yet, but her office remained dark. Finally, I overheard someone say that she was making a television appearance and would be in around noon.

The daily meeting was over and done within fifteen minutes. It was run by a stern-sounding managing editor ("We call him the Kaiser," Jessie whispered) and focused on what stage every story was at. On the way back to the pod, Jessie informed me that Mona tried to hold idea meetings every week with a small group of writers and editors, but time didn't always allow for it. Cover story meetings happened only with the top-ranking people, and for secrecy reasons, very few people on staff knew what the cover story was until late in the game.

Mona finally arrived for the day moments later, stomping down the aisle along the pod with a frazzled expression, the kind you have on your face when you realize that your car has just been towed. Ten minutes later, she emerged from her office. She had several sheets of copy in her hands, and at first I thought she was headed in my direction. But she veered off into an office right near me.

"Why would you write a fucking lead like this?" she yelled from the doorway at the girl inside. I nearly rocketed out of my seat in surprise.

"I mean, it's fucking stupid," Mona continued. "Nobody cares about Maddox and his latest haircut. They want to know who Angelina is shacking up with."

Ouch. Robby had said she was tough. He hadn't used the term *she-devil*.

Even though I had my head lowered discreetly, I could see that after spinning around, Mona was barreling right toward me now. I wondered if I ought to hurl myself under my desk.

"Why did they put you here?" she asked as she reached my desk.

"I believe it's the only spot available, but it's fine," I told her. I noticed that all around me people's eyes went to their computer screens, as if she were a wolf or a police dog and they were afraid that making eye contact might trigger an attack.

"Suit yourself," she said, shrugging and walking off.

Midday a deputy editor e-mailed me to say that a reality TV star named Dotson Holfield had been arraigned that morning in Miami for indecent exposure. She asked that I work with Robby on the story. I had a few contacts in Miami that I offered him, and as I nibbled on a sandwich in his office, he reached one of them.

"What a loser," he said as he hung up the phone. "Holfield apparently wagged his penis at an undercover cop and told him to call it Brutus. I've got the perfect title for the story."

"Shoot."

"'Dotson Holfield Proves He Really *Is* a Dick Head.'"

"See?" I told him. "You *can* write cute."

"How you doin', by the way?" he asked.

"Good," I said, forcing a smile. "I realize I'm not in Kansas anymore, but hopefully I'll get used to it."

I had no more *direct* encounters with Mona that day, though I was almost always conscious of her whereabouts. Each time she left her office, it was like a hurricane making landfall. She'd charge over to the art department to demand changes in a layout, complain in Nash's doorway about some annoying celebrity handler, and stride right over to people's desks and toss their copy back to them. Around two, I caught sight of her gesturing in annoyance at one of her two assistants behind the glass wall that blocked off their desks from the art department. Jessie rolled her chair over to me.

"Can you guess what that's about?" she whispered.

"Somebody wrote an unfunny caption?"

"No, I suspect it's about the chicken salad. Mona has it for lunch every day at two. If the celery content is over thirty-five percent, someone's ass is on the line."

I was too speechless to reply. What have I gotten myself into? I wondered. But in truth I hadn't seen anything yet. At around six-thirty, Mona came trouncing out of her office packed like an Italian sausage in an orange Dolce & Gabbana evening gown and asked an editorial assistant two desks away from me to put concealer on the eczema patches on her back. I had to fight the urge to gag.

"God," I muttered to myself, "this is going to be murder."

Six weeks later, to my absolute horror, I turned out to be right.

BAILEY'S BACK
AND BETTER THAN EVER . . .

AND IF YOU MISSED IT BEFORE . . .

. . . PICK UP KATE WHITE'S FIRST NOVEL,
IF LOOKS COULD KILL

THIS IS THE NOVEL THAT INTRODUCED THE INDOMITABLE SLEUTH BAILEY WEGGINS. WHEN A POISONED BOX OF CHOCOLATES CLAIMS THE LIFE OF HER BOSS'S NANNY, BAILEY'S ON THE CASE, TRACKING DOWN CLUES ALL OVER THE NORTHEAST AND REALIZING THAT WORKING AT A FASHION MAGAZINE CAN BE KILLER . . .

AVAILABLE IN MASS MARKET
FROM WARNER BOOKS
ISBN: 0446-61257-X

1237a